The M

Clive Cussler is the author or co-author of over fifty international bestsellers, including the famous Dirk Pitt® adventures, such as *Crescent Dawn*; the NUMA® Files, most recently *Zero Hour*; the Oregon Files, such as *The Jungle*; the Isaac Bell adventures, which began with *The Chase*; and the highly successful Fargo adventures, such as *Lost Empire*. His non-fiction works include *The Sea Hunters* and *The Sea Hunters II*: these describe the true adventures of the real NUMA, which, led by Cussler, searches for lost ships of historic significance. With his crew of volunteers, Cussler has discovered more than sixty ships, including the long-lost Confederate submarine *Hunley*. He lives in Arizona.

Thomas Perry is the author of twenty novels, including the Edgar Award-winning *The Butcher's Boy* and the acclaimed Jane Whitfield series, most recently *Poison Flower*. He lives in southern California. You can visit him on the web at www.thomasperryauthor.com.

Find out more about the world of Clive Cussler by visiting
www.clivecussler.co.uk

The Mayan Secrets

CLIVE CUSSLER
and THOMAS PERRY

PENGUIN BOOKS

PENGUIN BOOKS

Published by the Penguin Group
Penguin Books Ltd, 80 Strand, London WC2R ORL, England
Penguin Group (USA) Inc., 375 Hudson Street, New York, New York 10014, USA
Penguin Group (Canada), 90 Eglinton Avenue East, Suite 700, Toronto, Ontario,
Canada M4P 2Y3 (a division of Pearson Penguin Canada Inc.)
Penguin Ireland, 25 St Stephen's Green, Dublin 2, Ireland (a division of Penguin Books Ltd)
Penguin Group (Australia), 707 Collins Street, Melbourne, Victoria 3008, Australia
(a division of Pearson Australia Group Pty Ltd)
Penguin Books India Pvt Ltd, 11 Community Centre, Panchsheel Park,
New Delhi – 110 017, India
Penguin Group (NZ), 67 Apollo Drive, Rosedale, Auckland 0632, New Zealand
(a division of Pearson New Zealand Ltd)
Penguin Books (South Africa) (Pty) Ltd, Block D, Rosebank Office Park,
181 Jan Smuts Avenue, Parktown North, Gauteng 2193, South Africa

Penguin Books Ltd, Registered Offices: 80 Strand, London WC2R ORL, England

www.penguin.com

First published in the United States by G. P. Putnam's Sons 2013
First published in the UK by Michael Joseph 2013
Published in Penguin Books 2014

001

Copyright © Sandecker RLLLP, 2013
All rights reserved

The moral right of the author has been asserted

Set in 11.38/13.42pt Garamond MT Std
Typeset by Jouve (UK), Milton Keynes
Printed in Great Britain by Clays Ltd, St Ives plc

Except in the United States of America, this book is sold subject
to the condition that it shall not, by way of trade or otherwise, be lent,
re-sold, hired out, or otherwise circulated without the publisher's
prior consent in any form of binding or cover other than that in
which it is published and without a similar condition including this
condition being imposed on the subsequent purchaser

ISBN: 978–1–405–91835–0

www.greenpenguin.co.uk

Penguin Books is committed to a sustainable
future for our business, our readers and our planet.
This book is made from Forest Stewardship
Council™ certified paper.

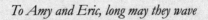

To Amy and Eric, long may they wave

I

Rabinal, Guatemala, 1537

Beyond midnight, Friar Bartolomé de Las Casas was still in his candlelit study in the Mayan mission at Rabinal. Before he went to bed, he had to write his daily installment of his report to Bishop Marroquin. Persuading the Church hierarchy of the success of the Dominican missions in Guatemala was going to be possible only if it was properly documented. He took off his black cloak and hung it on a peg by the door. He stood for a moment, listening to the night sounds – the gentle coo of birds, the insects chirping in the stillness.

He went to the wooden cabinet on the wall, opened it, and took out the precious book. Kukulcan, a man of royal lineage who was famous for his great learning, had brought this book and two others to Friar Bartolomé so he could examine them. Las Casas set the book on the table. He had been studying it for months, and tonight's work was going to be important. He placed a sheet of parchment on the table and then opened the marvelous book.

This page was divided into zones. There were pictures of six fantastic humanlike creatures he assumed were deities, all seated and looking to the left, and six vertical columns of complicated written symbols beneath them, which Kukulcan had told him was Mayan writing. The pages were a clean white, and the pictures were done in red, green and yellow, with an occasional blue. The writing was black. Friar Las Casas trimmed his pen to make it as fine as he could, divided his sheet into six vertical columns, and began to copy the symbols. It was hard, demanding labor, but he saw it as a part of his work. It was as much a part of his Dominican calling as his clothing – the white habit that signified purity and the black cloak over it that signified penance. He had no idea what the symbols meant or the names of the mythical deities, but he knew that the images contained deep knowledge that the Church would need to understand its new converts.

For Las Casas, managing the gentle, patient conversion of the Mayan Indians was a personal duty, a penance. Bartolomé de Las Casas had not come to the New World in peace. He had come with a sword. In 1502, he had sailed from Spain for Hispaniola with the governor, Nicolás de Ovando, and accepted an *encomienda*, a conquered land, and the right to enslave all the Indians he found on it. Even in 1513, after a decade of cruelty by the conquerors, and having been ordained as a priest, he joined in the conquest of the Indians of Cuba, while accepting another royal grant of land and Indians as his share of the plunder. As he thought about his early life now, he was sick with shame and regret.

When he'd finally admitted to himself that he had participated in a great sin, he'd begun his personal program of repentance and reformation. Las Casas would always remember the day in 1514 when he had stood up and denounced his past actions and returned his Indian slaves to the governor. Remembering that day was like touching the scar of an old burn. After that, he had sailed back to Spain to plead with the powerful for the protection of the Indians. That had been twenty-three years ago, and since then he had worked tirelessly, devoting his writings and his labor to making up for the wrongs he had done and countenanced.

He worked for several hours at his copying until he had finished the page. He placed his parchment copy in the bottom of a box of sermons with all of the other pages he had copied. As he moved about the small room, the candle flame flickered. He placed another clean sheet on the table, waited for the candle to be still and throw a steady yellow light again, and then started the next task. He dipped his pen in the ink pot and began with the date: 23 January 1537. Then his pen stopped, held above the paper.

He heard sounds that were familiar to him and made him instantly angry. He heard the feet of soldiers marching in a platoon, their boots hitting the damp earth, spurs jangling and sword hilts clanking as they swung against steel at the bottom of each soldier's cuirass.

'No,' he muttered. 'Not again, Lord. Not here.' It

was a violation, a betrayal. Governor Maldonado had broken his promise. If the Dominican friars succeeded in pacifying and converting the natives, there were to be no colonists arriving to claim *encomiendas* – and, above all, no soldiers. The soldiers who had not been able to conquer the Indians in these regions by fighting must not come in now and enslave them after the friars had befriended them.

Las Casas threw on his black robe, flung open his door, and ran down the long gallery, his leather sandals flapping on the brick pavement. He could see the troop of Spanish cavalry soldiers, all armed for battle with swords and lances, their Toledo-steel cuirasses and cabassets gleaming in the light of the bonfire they were building in the square across from the church.

Las Casas ran to them, waving his arms and shouting, 'What are you doing? How dare you light a fire in the middle of the mission square. The roofs of these buildings are nothing but straw!'

The soldiers saw and heard him, and two or three of them bowed to him politely, but these were professional fighters, conquistadors, and they knew arguing with the head of a Dominican mission was not going to make them richer or more powerful.

When he charged at them, they stepped aside or retreated a step but would not engage with him.

'Where is your commander?' he said. 'I am Father Bartolomé de Las Casas.' He seldom used his priestly title, but he was, after all, a priest, the first ever to be

4

ordained in the New World. 'I demand to see your commander.'

The nearest pair turned in the direction of a tall, dark-bearded man. Las Casas noticed that this man's armor was a bit more ornate than what the other men wore. His had filigree engraved on its surfaces, with gold inlay. As Las Casas approached, the man called, 'Fall in,' and his men lined up in four rows, facing him. Las Casas stepped between him and his soldiers.

'What are soldiers doing bursting into a Dominican mission in the middle of the night? What business do you have here?'

The man looked at him wearily. 'We have a job to do, Friar. Take up your complaints with the governor.'

'He promised me that soldiers would never come here.'

'Perhaps that was before he learned of the devil's books.'

'The devil doesn't have anything to do with books, you idiot. You have no right to be here.'

'Nonetheless, we are here. Pagan books have been seen here and reported to Fra Toribio de Benevente, who asked the governor for help.'

'Benevente? He has no authority over us. He's not even a Dominican. He's a Franciscan.'

'Those internal squabbles are your business. Mine is to find and destroy the evil books.'

'They're not evil. They contain the knowledge of these people and all the information that exists about them, their ancestors, their neighbors, their philosophy, language and cosmology. They've lived here for thousands of years, and their books are a gift to the future. They tell us things we could never find out in any other way.'

'You're misinformed, Friar. I've seen some of them myself. There are nothing but pictures and signs of the demons and fiends they worship.'

'These people are being converted, one at a time and voluntarily. Not the way the Franciscans do it, baptizing ten thousand people at a time. The old Mayan gods have been diminished to mere symbols. We've made great progress here in a short time. Don't waste all the work we've done by proving to them that we're savages.'

'Us? Savages?'

'Savages. You know – people who destroy art, burn books, kill people they don't understand, and make slaves of their children.'

The commander turned to his men. 'Get him away from me.'

Three soldiers took hold of Las Casas and, as gently as possible, pulled him away from the square. One of them said, 'Please, Father, I'm begging you. Stay away from the commander. He has orders and he'd rather die than disobey.' They backed away from him, turned, and ran back to the square.

Las Casas took a last look at the soldiers building their big bonfire. The soldiers running back and forth, breaking apart anything made of wood and throwing it into the bright flames that billowed above them into the sky, looked more like demons than any of the deities depicted in the Mayan books. He turned and moved along the back of the adobe mission buildings, staying in the dark, sheltered places. At the edge of the cleared land, he stepped on to a jungle trail. The foliage grew so thick around the trail that his progress was like moving through a cave. The trail led down toward the river.

When Las Casas reached the river, he saw that many of the Indians had come out of their huts in the village and that a fire had been lit. They had been aware of the arrival of the strange soldiers and had gathered in the center of their village to discuss what to do. He spoke to them in *K'iche'*, the language of the Mayans in this district. 'It's me, Brother Bartolomé,' he called out. 'Soldiers have come to the mission.'

He saw Kukulcan, who remained seated in the doorway of his hut. He had been an important chieftain in Cobán before he had decided to come to the mission, and now the others all looked to him for leadership. He said, 'We saw them. What do they want? Gold? Slaves?'

'They've come for books. They don't understand the books, and someone told them that Mayan books were all about evil and magic. They've come to find any books you have and destroy them.'

There were murmurs and expressions of consternation. The news seemed utterly incomprehensible to the crowd, as though someone had come to chop down the

7

trees, drain the rivers, or blot out the sun. This seemed to them an act of pure malice that could not gain the soldiers anything.

'What should we do?' Kukulcan asked. 'Fight?'

'All we can do is try to save some of the books. Pick out the most important ones and take them away from here.'

Kukulcan beckoned to his son, Tepeu, a man about thirty years old who had been a respected warrior. They spoke together in quick whispers. Tepeu nodded. Kukulcan said to Las Casas, 'There's no question. It has to be the one I brought to the mission to show you. That one is worth all the others.'

Las Casas turned and moved toward the jungle path. Tepeu was suddenly at his shoulder. 'We have to get up the trail before they find it,' Tepeu said. 'Try to keep up.' Then he began to run.

Tepeu ran up the path as though he could see in the dark, and being able to make out his silhouette ahead made Las Casas able to move faster too. They went up toward the mission at a full run. When they reached level ground, Las Casas could see a line of soldiers coming along the main road toward the Indian settlement.

Las Casas didn't need to watch the soldiers now. He had been part of the extermination of the Taino on Hispaniola, and he could picture exactly what they were doing. The first team of soldiers burst into a hut. A minute later, one of them came out carrying a Mayan book. He heard a man say in *Ch'olan*, 'I saved that from the city of Copán!' An arquebus shot shook the ground, and a flight of parrots rose from a tall tree in a flurry of flapping wings and screeches. The man lay dead in front of his hut.

As Las Casas and Tepeu slipped through the dimly lighted area behind the mission, Las Casas thought about Tepeu's family. Kukulcan had been a high priest, a scholar. His family was of the royal class. When disease had killed the last ruler, he had been chosen to lead. He and Tepeu had given up their elaborate feathered regalia when they'd left home, but Tepeu was wearing the dark green jade ear plugs, bracelets and bead necklace that only Mayan aristocrats were allowed to own.

They ran along the backs of the buildings toward the Dominican quarters, and they could see that the soldiers were returning from their search of the mission's collection of native objects. They carried armloads of books, ceremonial pieces and carvings to the bonfire.

Mayan books were long, folded strips made of the inner bark of the wild fig tree. The writing surface was painted with a thin white stucco, and the paints were made from native pigments. The books that the soldiers had found they tossed into the flames. The oldest ones were the driest and they ignited instantly – a flare of light – and then fifty or a hundred pages that had been saved for centuries were lost forever. Las Casas knew that in these books could be anything. Kukulcan

9

had told him some were mathematical treatises, astronomical observations, the locations of lost cities, forgotten languages, the acts of kings, going back a thousand years. In a second, the information, painstakingly written and drawn by hand, was reduced to sparks and smoke rising into the night sky.

Tepeu was quick and moved with great skill in the darkness. He opened the big wooden door of the church just enough to slip inside. Las Casas had the advantage of the black Dominican robe, which was shapeless and darker than a shadow. A few moments later, Las Casas caught up with him in the church.

He led Tepeu down the aisle of the church toward the altar, then to the right of it. There was a door that led into the sacristy. In the dim moonlight from the high windows, they passed by the alb and chasuble hanging on pegs set into the wall, the wooden chest where the rest of the vestments were stored, protected from the incessant humidity of the Guatemalan jungle. He led Tepeu out the small door on the other side of the room.

They left the church for the long, roofed-over gallery of the Dominicans' quarters. They padded along the brick walkway barefoot so their sandals would make no sound. At the end of the gallery, they entered Las Casas's study. Tepeu went to the simple worktable, where he saw the book. He picked it up carefully and looked at it with such intense devotion that he appeared to be greeting a living person, someone he had feared was lost.

Tepeu looked around the room. Las Casas had a native pot that was decorated with paintings of a Mayan king's daily activities. Las Casas had the side turned outward that showed the man's daily ablutions and not the side that showed him piercing his tongue to give a blood sacrifice. The pot held the friar's supply of fresh water and was tied with a kind of sling that the Indian acolyte used to carry it.

Tepeu poured the rest of the water into Las Casas's washbasin, then reached in and wiped the pot dry with a cloth. He put the precious book inside the pot.

Las Casas went to the cupboard on the wall that held several writing projects he was working on. He retrieved two more Mayan books and handed them to Tepeu. 'We should save as many as we can.'

Tepeu said, 'They will not fit. The first one is worth a hundred of these.'

'The rest will be gone forever.'

Tepeu said, 'I'll take the book far away to a place where the soldiers will never be able to find it.'

'Don't let them catch you. They think what you're carrying are messages from the devil.'

'I know that, Father,' Tepeu said. 'Give me your blessing.' He knelt.

Las Casas placed his hand on Tepeu's head, and said in Latin, 'Lord, let this man's righteousness be enough. He wants nothing for himself, only to be the preserver of his country's wisdom for future generations. Amen.' He turned and went to the cupboard, then returned with three gold pieces. He handed them to Tepeu.

'This is all I have. Use it to get what you need on your journey.'

'Thank you, Father.' Tepeu walked toward the door.

'Wait. Don't go out there yet. I hear them.' Las Casas went to the door and stepped outside. There was a strong smell of burning, and he could hear shouts coming from the village by the river. He stood with his back to the door while a platoon of soldiers pushed through three of his Dominican monks who were trying to keep them from entering the mission. Four soldiers broke into a storeroom down the gallery to search it.

Las Casas reached behind him, turned the knob, and opened the door of his study. He caught only a glimpse of Tepeu slipping out. He had the water pot on his back, with the strap around his waist and a tumpline over his forehead so much of the pot's weight rested there. He was across the clearing and into the trees at a run, but he was visible for only seconds, and utterly silent.

2

Off Isla Guadaloupe, Mexico: the present

Thousands of silvery fish swam past Sam and Remi Fargo, gleaming, turning this way and that in unison, as though they were all controlled by one mind. The water was clear and warm, and Sam and Remi could see far beyond the steel bars of their cage.

Sam held a three-foot aluminum shaft with a small, sharp barb on the end. It was a tool for the application of tags, and in the weeks since he and Remi had been on this voyage, he'd become adept at using it. He looked at her, and then ahead again, staring into the distance.

As they watched, a darker spot seemed to form itself at the limit of their sight, as though the tiny particles held in the water were coming together to form a solid shape. It was a shark. And as Sam and Remi had known he would, he turned toward them. He came at an angle, drawn, perhaps, by the dense schools of fish that had gathered near the steel shark cage and flitted in and out between the bars. But there was no question the shark was aware of Sam and Remi.

The Fargos were experienced divers, and they were both used to the idea that it was not possible to go into the ocean anywhere in the world without having a shark notice their presence. They had seen many sharks over the years, usually small blues that came close to investigate the wet-suited newcomers diving near the kelp beds not far from their home in San Diego, reject them as prey, and swim off. This shark embodied the other possibility – the nightmare predator, always swimming forward to keep the water moving through its gills, equipped with sight, smell, hearing, a network of nerves running along its body that felt even small vibrations in the water, and the ability to sense minute electrical discharges from the muscle contractions of its victims.

The shark's large tail gave a series of lazy undulations, and it moved toward them. As its outline became easier to see in the clear water, the shark seemed to grow. In the distance it had seemed large, but now, as it approached them, Sam realized that he had observed it much farther away. As it grew closer, it became immense. It was exactly what he and Remi had come to find – great whites that were over twenty feet long.

The shark swam through a school of fish that separated into two swirling swarms, then reunited into a school again, but the shark paid no attention to them. Its tail gave another undulation, and it glided ahead. The shark, its nose a flattish, pointed protuberance that seemed about four feet wide, moved through the water toward them, then turned again. Its body swung past the steel cage where Sam and Remi were hanging, so close that they could have reached out and touched it. The body was thick, and the pointed dorsal fin above it looked as tall as a man.

The shark didn't leave. It passed by them again. Sam and Remi remained motionless inside their cage. Even after many dives near the island, Sam found that during these long minutes he became conscious of the steel bars that had been welded into the cage. Were they solid? They had seemed to be when the cage had been lifted into the water by the crane. The welds, he now could see, looked short and hasty – maybe unreliable. The welder couldn't possibly have imagined the size and power of the creature just now passing by.

This animal was at Guadaloupe Island to find elephant seals and tuna, and Sam and Remi didn't look much like either. In their black wet suits, though, they looked a bit more like California sea lions, which could make them seem very tasty to a great white. Then, as abruptly as it had appeared, the shark gave a few twitches of its tail and glided away from the cage. For a few seconds, Sam felt intense disappointment. Considering their size and ferocity, great whites were sometimes surprisingly cautious. Had Sam missed his only chance to get this giant on record?

Then, without warning, the shark wheeled about, flicked its tail four or five times, and barreled into the broad side of the steel cage, its huge mouth gaping, revealing the rows of triangular teeth. Sam and Remi clung to the bars on the opposite side of the cage while the shark shook the forward part of its body, working to get its jaws around the cage but unable to accomplish it.

As the shark pushed the cage forward, the cage tilted, and Sam saw his chance. He jabbed the aluminum shaft into the skin at the base of the tall dorsal fin and immediately withdrew it, pulling it back inside the cage. The shark seemed not to have felt or noticed it. The barb was set, and the bright yellow shark tag, with its six-digit number, trailed from the base of the fin, looking tiny on the enormous fish.

The shark swam below the cage, and Sam and Remi waited. They half expected him to turn around, build up even greater speed, and ram the cage again, this time snapping the careless welds, breaking open the cage and spilling them out in front of his big, toothy mouth. But he continued about his business, farther and farther away, until he was gone. Sam reached up and tugged on the signal rope three times, then three more times. Somewhere in the other world above them there was the vibration of a motor, and the cage jerked, then began to rise.

They came up out of the water, lifted entirely up into the air in the bright sunlight, and swung on to the deck of the yacht. Remi took off her mask and mouthpiece, and said to Sam, 'So what do you think it was – that we didn't look appetizing enough for a second try?'

'Don't worry,' he said. 'You look scrumptious. I've been practising looking indigestible to prepare for this.'

'My hero.'

He pulled back the hood of his wetsuit, smiling. 'That was amazing.'

'Thanks to you, I'll never run out of subjects for nightmares.' She kissed his cheek as they stepped from the cage and walked toward their cabin to change out of their suits.

A few minutes later, Sam and Remi stood on the foredeck of the chartered seventy-eight-foot *Marlow Explorer*. It was a modern luxury yacht that could do twenty-four knots wide open, but, in the two weeks they'd been aboard, Captain Juan Sandoval never had the need to open up the twin Caterpillar C30 diesels. They were not in a hurry, crossing stretches of ocean to look for promising spots for finding great white sharks, occasionally putting into pleasant Mexican ports to refuel or buy provisions. The yacht was a bigger vessel than Sam and Remi needed. It had three full staterooms with their own baths, as well as separate quarters for the three-man crew. Captain Sandoval, mate Miguel Colera, and cook George Morales were all from Acapulco, which was the charter boat's home port. Sam and Remi had chartered the boat to take them to Isla Guadaloupe, about one hundred and sixty miles off the coast of Baja California, because it was a well-known spot to see large sharks.

They had volunteered to participate in a marine biology study run by the University of California at Santa Barbara to learn more about the movements and habits of great white sharks. The work of tagging them had been going on for years, but it had met with only limited success because most sharks that had been tagged were never seen again. Keeping track of individual great whites presented many difficulties. They were reputed to travel vast distances, they were very difficult to capture, and they were dangerous. But Isla Guadaloupe seemed to offer a special chance. It was a place where very large, mature great whites reliably appeared year after year. And if members of an expedition were willing to get in the water inside a shark cage, it might be possible to tag them without attempting a capture. Sam used his satellite phone to report the tag number and description of today's shark.

As the boat moved along easily on the open water toward Baja California, Remi let the wind blow through her long auburn hair to dry it. Sam leaned close to her. 'Still having fun?'

'Sure,' she said. 'We always have fun together.'

'That's not what you were thinking. Something's bothering you.'

'To tell you the truth, I was thinking about our house,' she said.

'Sorry,' he said. 'I thought spending some time away on a research project would help the time go faster. I figured you were getting tired of the repairs and remodeling.'

A few months ago, they had returned from the excavation of hoards of plunder hidden in crypts across Europe by the Huns during the fifth century. Three rival treasure seekers either believed that the Fargos had taken some of the valuable artifacts home with them, or they simply wanted to take revenge on the Fargos for beating them to the treasure. They had mounted an armed attack on the Fargos' four-story house on Goldfish Point in La Jolla and battered it to pieces. Since then, the Fargos had been overseeing the repairs and rebuilding.

'I was tired of it,' she said. 'Contractors were driving me nuts. First, you have to go with them to the plumbing showroom to pick out exactly the fixtures you want. Then you need a meeting to hear that they've stopped manufacturing that model and you have to pick out another one. Then –'

'I know,' he said, and threw up his hands.

'I hate the repairs, but I miss our dog.'

'Zoltán's fine. Selma is treating him like king of the pack.' He paused. 'When we started this trip over a month ago, they were hoping we'd be able to tag ten sharks. That big guy we just got is number fifteen. I guess it's time to hang up our tagger and head back.'

Remi pulled away a little so she could look into his eyes. 'Don't get me wrong. I love the ocean, and I love you. And who wouldn't like to travel around on a state-of-the-art yacht, going from one gorgeous spot to another?'

'But?'

'But we've been away for a long time.'

'Maybe you're right. We've accomplished more than we set out to do, and maybe it's time to go home, get our house finished, and start on a new project.'

Remi shook her head. 'I didn't mean right this minute. We're heading for Baja already, and we'll reach land at San Ignacio Lagoon. I've always wanted to see where the gray whales go to mate and calf.'

'Maybe after that we can keep going straight to Acapulco and get on a plane.'

'Maybe,' she said. 'Let's talk about it then.'

After another day, they anchored in San Ignacio Lagoon, then launched the plastic ocean kayaks. Remi and Sam climbed down into them, George Morales tossed their two-bladed paddles down, and they glided into the lagoon. It wasn't long before the first of the gray whales rose to the surface before them, spouted water and steamy spray from double blowholes, and then made a rolling dive downward, its tail working to leave a roiling, bubbly trail on the surface. They were silent for a few seconds – an animal the size of a city bus had risen in front of them and sunk again, leaving their little, orange plastic kayaks alone on the lagoon.

The Fargos spent the rest of that day and the following out in their kayaks. Whenever they met a gray whale, it would come close to them, apparently curious. Sam and Remi petted each whale on its head and back and then watched it go.

In the evening, the Fargos would sit at the table on the rear deck of the yacht with the crew and share a dinner of fresh-caught fish or Mexican delicacies brought from a restaurant in the small town of San Ignacio. They would stay out until long after dark, talking about the sea and its creatures, about their lives and their friends and families, as the night sky filled with brightening stars. After Sam and Remi retired to their cabin to sleep, they could sometimes still hear the sound of the whales spouting in the darkness.

Next, they moved south along the coast, making for Acapulco. On arrival, they called Selma Wondrash, their chief researcher. They had given her and the young couple who worked under her, Pete Jeffcoat and Wendy Corden, the month off, but Selma had insisted on staying in La Jolla and supervising the construction while they were away.

Selma answered, 'Hi, Remi. Zoltán is just fine.'

'It's both of us,' said Sam. 'Glad to hear that. And how's the construction going?'

'Just remember, the cathedral at Chartres took a few hundred years to build.'

'I hope you're joking,' said Remi.

'I am. There's not a single piece of woodwork left with a bullet hole in it. The lower two floors are pretty much finished, and everything works. There's still a bit of painting they're finishing up on the third floor, but your suite on the fourth floor still needs at least two weeks of work. You know what that means.'

'That there will finally be enough closet space for my shoes?' Remi said.

'Yes,' Sam said. 'And two weeks means four weeks in contractor language.'

'I love working for a pessimist. When anything goes right, you're so surprised. Where are you, by the way?'

Sam said, 'We're through tagging sharks. We're in Acapulco.'

'Is everything still okay?'

'It's lovely,' said Remi. 'Fresh fish, chicken mole, dancing under the stars, et cetera. It beats being shark bait. But we're thinking of coming home soon.'

'Just let me know. The jet and crew will be waiting to bring you home. I'll pick you up at the Orange County airport.'

'Thanks, Selma,' said Remi. 'We'll let you know. It's time to have some more fun. Our dinner reservation is in ten minutes. Call if you need us.'

'Of course I will. Good-bye.'

They were staying in one of the two towers at the hotel, and that night, just after they got into bed, they felt a brief tremor. The building seemed to rock for a few seconds, and they heard a faint rattling, but nothing more. Remi turned over and held on to Sam, then whispered, 'Another reason I love you is that you take me to hotels that have been remodeled to stand up to earthquakes.'

'It's not a trait women usually list for the guy of their dreams, but I'll take credit for it.'

The next day they checked out of the hotel and returned to the yacht. As soon as they reached the dock, they sensed something had changed. Captain Juan was up in the bridge listening to a Spanish-language radio station with the volume up so loud that they could hear it as soon as they were out of the taxi. George was standing at the rail watching them approach, his face a wide-eyed mask of worry. As soon as they stepped aboard, Sam heard the words *'sismo temblor'* and *'volcán.'*

'What is it?' asked Sam. 'Another earthquake?'

'It just came five or ten minutes ago. Juan might know more.'

Sam, Remi and George all climbed to the bridge and joined Captain Juan. When he saw them, he said, 'It hit down the coast in Tapachula, in Chiapas. Right near the border with Guatemala.'

'How bad?' asked Remi.

'Bad,' he said. 'They're saying eight-point-three, eight-point-five. Since then, there's smoke coming from Tacaná, the volcano north of the city. The roads are all closed by landslides for a long distance. People are hurt, maybe some killed, but they don't know how many.' He shook his head. 'I wish we could do something.'

Sam looked at Remi and she nodded. 'We've got to make a phone call. Start getting the boat ready to move. Anything you haven't done since we put in here, get it done now.'

Sam took out his satellite phone and went out to the foredeck. He dialed. 'Selma?'

'Hi, Sam,' she said. 'Coming home so soon?'

'No, there's trouble. There's been a major earthquake in Tapachula, down the coast from here. They need help and the roads to the city are blocked – maybe the whole area. I don't know what sort of airport they have in Tapachula, but I'd like you to call Doc Evans. Ask him to order a standard disaster medical package to be flown in to whatever hospital there is standing – whatever they'll need after a big quake. Tell him it's our treat. Get him a bank credit for a hundred thousand dollars. Can you do that?'

'Yes. If I can't reach him, I'll get my own doctor to authorize it. The airport is a different issue, but I'll find out if they can fly it in or if they have to drop it.'

'We're going to head south as soon as we can get loaded.'

'I'll stay in touch.' She hung up.

Sam hurried back to the bridge to talk to Captain Juan. He said, 'We seem to be in a position to do something more important than tagging fish.'

'What do you mean?'

'The roads to Tapachula are out, right?'

'That's what they say on the radio. They said it could take months to clear them.'

'Since we put in here, you've taken a lot of food and water on board already and filled the fuel tanks, right? I'd like to load up this boat with as much as we can carry and head down there. We can probably be there in a day or two.'

'Well, yes,' he said. 'A little more, maybe. But the company that owns the boat won't pay for a trip like that or for the supplies. They can't afford it.'

'We can,' said Remi. 'And we're here. So let's go buy the supplies.'

Sam, Remi, Captain Juan, George and Miguel went to work. Sam rented a large van, and they all went through Acapulco together, buying bottled water, canned food, blankets and sleeping bags, professional-level first aid kits, and basic medical supplies. They loaded their purchases on to the yacht and went out for more. They bought cans of gasoline, fifteen auxiliary generators, flashlights and batteries, radios, tents, clothing of all sizes. When they had put as much as they could into the living quarters, the hold, the forecastle, and even the bridge, they crammed the decks with large containers of water, gasoline and food and lashed them to the rails so they wouldn't shift in rough seas.

While they were finishing the loading, Remi set George and Miguel to calling Acapulco's hospitals to see if there were supplies and prescription medications that would be in demand in Tapachula. The hospitals sent packages of prescription painkillers and antibiotics, splints and braces for broken bones. One hospital had three emergency room doctors who wondered if they could get a ride to Tapachula on the Fargos' chartered yacht.

The doctors arrived in mid-afternoon with their own supply of medicines and equipment for the voyage.

Two of them, Dr Garza and Dr Talamantes, were young women who worked in the emergency room, and Dr Martinez was a surgeon in his sixties. They immediately stowed their kits and helped Sam, Remi and the crew bring the final vanload to the dock and on to the deck, then settled into the two unoccupied cabins belowdecks.

At four in the afternoon, Sam gave the order, and the yacht left the harbor to begin the five-hundred-and-ten-mile voyage by sea. Captain Juan worked the engines up to full speed and kept them there hour after hour, making for the disaster zone on a straight course that stayed well out in the deep water. The three crewmen and Sam and Remi each stood watches at the helm. When they weren't sleeping or helping with boat chores, they worked under the supervision of the doctors to divide some of the medical supplies into kits that could be delivered to small clinics, emergency rooms and individual doctors.

It was when they were moving back within sight of shore the next evening that they knew they were approaching the area of destruction. They were only a mile offshore from a populated area, but they could see no lights. Sam went to the helm and checked the charts. 'Where are we?'

'Salina Cruz,' said Miguel. 'It's a good-sized town, but I don't see any lights.'

'Can we go in a little so we can see better?'

'There are beaches, but there are also sandbars. We're heavily loaded, so we have to be careful.'

'All right,' said Sam. 'Go in as close as you can and drop anchor. We'll take a party onshore with the life-boat, see what we can do, and then come back.'

'All right.' Miguel moved in as close to shore as he dared and then dropped anchor. In a few minutes, as Sam, Remi and George were preparing the boat, Dr Talamantes came up on deck. She watched Sam and George lift one of the generators into the boat and then some gasoline to run it. She said, 'Be sure to save some space for me and my bag. The rest should be food and water.'

Sam said, 'We may need to make a few trips, but that's a good way to start.'

They lowered the boat off the stern, and Remi, Sam, Dr Talamantes and Miguel climbed aboard. Miguel started the outboard motor, and approached the beach at an angle. When they reached the surf line, he turned off the motor and cocked it up to get the propeller out of the water. The boat glided in, was given one final push by a wave, and struck the sand.

Sam and Remi jumped out of the bow and dragged the boat a few feet up on the beach. Dr Talamantes and Miguel then climbed out, and all four hauled the boat up farther. Miguel tossed the anchor out on to the beach in case the incoming tide reached it.

They began to unload the boat, and people ran down

to the beach to help them. Miguel and Dr Talamantes spoke to them in Spanish, and Remi translated for Sam.

'They've got some people with minor to moderate injuries,' said Dr Talamantes. 'They're in the school a couple of blocks up there. I'll go take a look at them and be back.' She took a flashlight and her medical kit and hurried up the road with two local women.

The others finished unloading the cases of bottled water, and Miguel spoke with a man for a minute, then said, 'This man works for the local medical clinic and he wonders what we're going to do with the generator.'

'That's as good a place as any to start,' said Sam. He looked around and saw that someone had brought a child's red wagon from the street above. They loaded the generator on to the wagon and hauled it three blocks to the clinic in the center of town. Sam made the connections and got it running within a few minutes. The lights in the clinic came on, dimly at first and then a bit stronger, as the generator chugged away outside.

As they were getting the clinic opened and taking patients, Dr Talamantes arrived. She said, 'I've already seen quite a few people at the school. All minor stuff, fortunately. I heard you were getting things up and running here.'

'Has anybody heard about what's going on nearer to the epicenter?'

'Tapachula is apparently a mess. A couple of boats have made it here, taking injured people out and looking for supplies they could take back.'

'Then we'd better get another load of supplies to shore and leave for Tapachula. Do you want to stay here while we go for another load?'

'Good idea,' she said. 'I can see a few patients while you're doing that.'

'Miguel, you stay with Dr Talamantes,' said Sam. 'George and Juan can help us reload the boat.'

Sam and Remi hurried down to the beach where the lifeboat was hauled up. As Sam lifted the anchor, Remi stood by him. 'Did you want a moonlight cruise for two or just want to show me what a good boatman you are?'

'A little of each,' he said. 'I also figured we could carry more supplies if we had fewer people.'

They pushed the boat into the water, and Remi got in and sat in the bow, facing Sam. Sam turned the boat around into the waves, pushed off, and sat in the center seat to row. He rowed the boat through the first wave, then the second, took another hard stroke, shipped the oars, stepped to the transom, started the motor, and shifted to forward. The boat knifed through the next wave, rose over the one after that, and then moved off-shore.

Sam could still see the yacht anchored in deeper water outside the surf, but, as he watched, he could see something had changed. There was the silhouette of another boat, a small cabin cruiser, pulled up close to their yacht and tied off to the side. He counted three men on the bridge and two more on the rear deck. As the lifeboat came closer to the yacht, he saw one of the strangers go to the steps and disappear belowdecks where the cabins were.

Sam cut the outboard motor, and, in the silence, Remi said, 'What's wrong?'

'Turn around and look at the yacht,' he said. 'We've got visitors. I'd rather approach quietly until I'm sure they're friendly. Watch them while I row.'

Sam moved to the center seat again while Remi sat in the bow and watched. They were still a few hundred feet from the yacht and its new companion. When Sam was a hundred and fifty feet away, he circled the yacht, came in behind it, and tied on to the starboard stern cleat, the side away from the small cruiser. He whispered, 'I guess we'd better make sure it's safe before we announce ourselves.'

Sam and Remi stood on the seats and listened. They could hear a lot of shouting in Spanish. The words were vague even to Remi, but the tone was angry. Sam pulled himself up on the ladder at the rear of the yacht so he could see. After a few seconds, he ducked back down. 'There are three men with Juan on the bridge. George is tied up and gagged on the floor. One of the men just punched Juan. I think they're trying to make him drive off with the yacht.'

'What do you want to do?'

'See what you can find in the lifeboat's safety kit. I'll look in the emergency locker on the yacht's rear deck.' He began to climb the ladder as Remi opened the kit in the bow.

She whispered to him, 'Look. A Very pistol.' She held it up. It was a vintage flare gun made of metal, not plastic. She brought out a plastic packet of flares, opened it, broke the gun apart, loaded one flare and put the others in her jacket pocket.

Sam whispered, 'A good start. Let's see what I can find up here.'

He silently stepped on to the rear deck, made his way to the sheltered spot below the steps to the bridge, opened the built-in steel chest, set aside a few life preservers, and found a second Very pistol. He loaded it, found a large folding knife inside the first aid kit, and pocketed it.

Remi appeared at his elbow and pointed up the steps to the bridge. 'Shall we?'

Sam nodded, and they climbed the steps. Remi crouched just below the level of the bridge on the right side and Sam crouched on the left. They listened, watching the shadows on the ceiling of the bridge caused by the instrument panel's lights. One of the men hit Captain Juan and he fell to the floor beside the bound George.

Sam stood and charged on to the bridge. He aimed his Very pistol at the apparent leader, who had just struck Juan. He said quietly, 'Drop your gun.'

The man smirked. 'That's a flare pistol.'

'So is this,' Remi said from behind the other two men. One of them began to turn, possibly to bring his gun around toward Remi.

Sam spun the man in the direction he had been turning and pushed him through the doorway and out over the deck, where he fell and lay stunned. Sam fired his flare gun into the torso of the man beside Remi and Remi fired into the torso of the leader beside Sam.

The cabin filled with a sulfurous, choking cloud of smoke, but they could still see the blinding magenta sparks cascading out of the flares, starting the men's clothes on fire and burning the skin beneath. The man Sam had shot dropped his pistol and used both hands to try to slap out the fire as he hurried down the steps, fell on the deck, got up, and jumped overboard into the water. The leader tried to go down without falling, but Sam planted a foot in the small of the man's back and propelled him out over the rear deck. The man landed on the deck beside his unconscious friend and then got up and hurled himself overboard into the water.

Sam handed Remi the folding knife from the emergency kit. 'Cut George loose.' He grasped both railings of the steps from the bridge and slid to the deck.

Sam glanced up and saw Remi kneeling at the entrance to the bridge, holding one of the pistols the burning men had abandoned. Sam knelt and picked up the pistol dropped by the unconscious man lying on the deck and stood beside the steps that led below to the cabins. He called down, 'Come up out of there. Come on. All hands on deck.' As he spoke, he was stepping out of his shoes. He moved barefoot to the upper side of the hatch behind the staircase. A man came up the steps, looking away from Sam. He had a pistol in one hand and Remi's computer in the other.

'Drop the gun but not the computer,' Sam said. 'Set it down gently.'

'Why should I do anything you say?'

'Because I have your friend's gun aimed at the back of your head.'

The man realized that the voice had been coming from behind him and slowly raised his hands to set the computer and the gun on the deck. Then he turned his head and saw one of his companions lying there.

Sam said, 'Your other friends went for a swim. What are you doing on this boat?'

The man shrugged. 'We knew any boat coming here would be carrying supplies and equipment because of the earthquake. Why else would anyone come now?'

'You were going to take food and medical supplies from people who need it?'

'We need it too,' said the man.

'What do you need it for?'

'To sell it and make some money. People will pay a lot for those things after an earthquake. Farther down the coast, they'll pay even more. Food and water are getting scarce. The roads are out, and the power is off, so things in the refrigerators are rotting.'

Sam said, 'Well, you're not going to get anything from us.'

The man shrugged, and said, 'Maybe you're right, but maybe I am.' He leaned back against the rail and folded his arms.

On the steps up from the cabins, there was new activity. The next person to appear was Dr Martinez. He held both hands above his head. After him came Dr Garza, with her hands held the same way. Then there was a young Mexican man with an expensive haircut, fitted, expensive jeans, and a pair of cowboy boots that seemed out of place on a boat. He had one hand on Dr Garza's shoulder and a pistol at the back of her head.

The young man said, 'If you'll put down your gun, I won't shoot her.'

'Be careful,' said Sam. 'Even hearing you say that makes my wife irritated.'

Remi was at the top of the steps on the bridge, aiming at the young man's head.

The man leaning against the rail glanced at her unimpressed, and said, 'Take his gun.'

The man lying on the deck got up and rushed toward Sam. Sam fired a round through the man's foot and the man fell to the deck and rocked from side to side, wincing and moaning and holding his foot.

As the young man in the expensive jeans moved his gun away from Dr Garza's head to aim at Sam, Remi called from above him, 'Last chance to drop it.'

Sam said, 'She's a pistol champion. Do you understand? She can put a bullet through the pupil of your eye if she wants to.'

The man looked up at Remi and saw her sighting down the barrel of the pistol she held with a steady two-handed grip. He considered for a moment, then set his pistol on the deck beside him, as Dr Garza hurried up on to the deck.

'Now, up with your friends,' Remi said. The man climbed to the deck and joined his two colleagues.

'All right,' Sam called out. 'Now, all of you, into the water.'

The man at the rail said, 'But –'

'Alive or dead, you're all going to get wet,' said Sam.

The man translated for his companions. The two uninjured men helped their colleague over the rail, then jumped in after him.

When Sam heard the final splash, he stepped to the stern of the yacht, picked up a can of gasoline, walked to the cleat where the small cruiser was tied, poured gasoline on its deck, then untied the boat and pushed it away from the anchored yacht. The five men swam toward it. When the boat had drifted thirty feet away from the yacht, Sam took out the Very pistol, fired a flare on to the cruiser's deck, and watched the bright orange flames roar to life. There was a smattering of applause from those left on the yacht.

He walked to the foot of the steps to the bridge. 'Juan!'

'Yes, Sam?'

'You and George feel healthy enough to work?'

'Yes.'

'Then start the engines, raise the anchor, and get us to that dock over there. Let's pick up Miguel and Dr Talamantes and get out of here.'

3

Salina Cruz, Mexico

Dr Talamantes and Miguel boarded at the dock a few minutes later. Both had run back to the beach when they'd heard the news that there was a boat burning off-shore and, when they'd spotted the *Marlow Explorer* heading for the municipal docks, they had gone to meet it. Within a few minutes, the whole crew were heading southeast along the coast again.

Three more times they stopped at darkened coastal towns to unload cases of clean water and canned food, flashlights, generators and gasoline. Each time, the three doctors came in the first boatload, equipped with their standard medical kits.

At each stop, after a few hours the doctors would announce that the emergency cases had all been treated and that there were local people who would take care of the minor complaints now that the medical supplies had been delivered. Sam would call everybody back to the beach, and Miguel would take them back in the life-boat. The last ones off the beach were always Sam and Remi. As soon as they were aboard the yacht again, the crew would raise the anchor, and the vessel would continue down the coast toward Tapachula.

At dawn on the fourth day, Sam and Remi were asleep in their cabin when Miguel knocked. Sam got up to open the door. 'What's up?'

'We can see Tapachula. Juan thinks you should come to the bridge.'

Sam and Remi dressed quickly and headed up on deck. When they climbed the steps to the bridge, they could see why Juan had wanted to wake them. Through the windshield they could make out the distant shape of Tacaná, the second highest peak in Mexico. It was a dark blue pyramid miles back from the coast, standing alone against the sky. This morning, it was emitting a line of gray smoke that trailed off to the east.

Juan said, 'It's technically active, but it hasn't had a big eruption since 1950.'

'Did they say on the radio that it was about to do anything?' asked Remi. 'Have they told people to evacuate?'

'They don't seem to know what's happening yet. They say maybe the earthquake shook something loose or opened up cracks. The roads are out, so I don't think the scientists have gotten there to measure anything yet.'

'How far is the volcano from the city?' asked Sam.

'Much farther than it looks,' Juan said. 'The mountain is four thousand meters, so it looks close. But we'll have plenty to do without the volcano. We'll be off Tapachula in twenty minutes.'

Remi went down the steps and then belowdecks to the cabins and knocked on doors. 'We're almost to Tapachula,' she called.

A few minutes later, the crew, the doctors and the Fargos were all up and having a simple breakfast of coffee, eggs and fruit on deck. It was difficult for any of them to keep from staring into the distance at the smoke from the volcano smeared across the sky. As they approached the city, they began to see the devastation – buildings that had half disintegrated in the shaking, leaving great piles of bricks beside walls that were, for the moment, still standing; long rows of telephone poles that had fallen, leaving electrical wires draped over parked cars or lying in the street. Here and there, in the panoramic view from the deck of the yacht, they could see small, steady fires that had probably begun when natural gas pipes had broken. One by one, they left the table to prepare to go ashore.

They had visited enough affected towns on their way down the coast to have improved their methods greatly. The three doctors, who had already replenished their medical kits, each packed two large backpacks with supplies they'd needed in the last towns. There were fires, so they brought burn medications and painkillers. There was fallen masonry, so they brought splints, sutures, and – for the worst cases – amputation kits. Sam, Remi and George lined up the cases of food and water, and loaded the first of the generators and gasoline cans. They knew from experience that their trip to shore would attract those eager to help as well as the desperate, so they included cases of flashlights, first aid kits, and tools for digging people out of collapsed buildings and for making temporary shelters.

At seven, while they were packing, they could already see people gathering on the beach to meet them. They loaded the heaviest items into the lifeboat before they lowered it to the water, then formed a line so they could hand the other boxes and packs from one person to the next down the ladder to the boat. When they were finished, the boat was a bit overloaded, so they had to carefully arrange themselves to keep it evenly balanced.

The trip to shore included the three doctors and Sam, Remi and Miguel, who would run the motor and bring the boat in safely. Miguel used the waves judiciously, positioning the boat at the proper angle so it would be propelled in rather than rolled over. Just as the boat was near the shore, he turned off the motor and tilted it up to protect the propeller. As the keel scraped at the bow, Sam and Remi jumped out and hauled the boat ashore.

The local people were overjoyed to see what they had brought. The three doctors were immediately surrounded by people eager to guide them to the local hospital and carry their medical supplies. Sam, Remi and Miguel unloaded the rest of the supplies on to the sand and pushed the boat back out to sea so Miguel could go back for the next load of food, water and a second generator.

Sam and Remi went with the doctors to get the first generator up and running at the hospital and then returned to the beach to get the second generator, when Miguel returned, and bring it to a medical clinic that was still standing across town.

The work went on all day and much of the night. As they distributed their cargo to various parts of town, they heard many stories. People were working with shovels and tractors and trucks to clear the roads to cities along the coast. Others with homes that had remained intact were taking in those whose homes were destroyed.

Through the next five days, there were aftershocks from the enormous quake. The first few were sharp and lasted uncomfortably long, but they seemed to get milder and less frequent as the days passed.

On the evening of the sixth day, Captain Juan was waiting on the rear deck of the yacht when Sam, Remi and the others returned in the lifeboat. His face was grave.

Remi nudged Sam. 'I think we're about to get some bad news.'

Remi, Sam, the three doctors, George and Miguel gathered while Juan fidgeted and cleared his throat. 'This afternoon I got a radio message from the charter company. They've been patient about things, but they want us to bring their yacht back to Acapulco.'

'Why?' asked Remi. 'We're still willing to rent it, and we haven't hurt the boat, have we?'

'It's nothing like that,' Juan said. 'They've been nervous because we've been using a luxury yacht to haul supplies, but they knew it was necessary and that we can fix anything that looks worn. But they've got a schedule to keep. In four days, another group will arrive in Acapulco, expecting the yacht to be waiting for them. There are contracts.' He shrugged and held out his empty hands to pantomime his helplessness.

'How much time do we have?' asked Sam.

'They want us to leave tonight. That will give them a day to have the decks cleaned and polished, the engines serviced, and new supplies loaded. I'm sorry.'

'All right,' said Sam. 'We've unloaded all the supplies we brought here days ago and now there's no need for the yacht. What do you think, Remi? Want to go back to Acapulco with the boat and fly home?'

'Not yet,' she said. 'I think we should stay a few more days. I've been hearing that the people who live near the volcano still need medical care and supplies.'

'Are you sure?' said Juan. 'That's not an easy trip. Don't get me wrong. I've seen you both working when I was ready to drop. I'm proud to know you.'

'We all are,' said George.

'It's been a pleasure for us too,' said Sam. 'But we'd like to try to help the people on the mountain. Right now, we'll go below and pack our things so you can get started for home.'

Dr Martinez said, 'I think I'd better go back with the

boat, if I may. I've been away from the hospital as long as I can be.'

Sam turned to the others. 'Dr Garza?'

'Dr Talamantes and I are staying for a few more days too,' she replied. 'And by the way, please call me Maria. We've been through so much together, I feel as though I've known you for years.'

'And call me Christina,' said Dr Talamantes.

In a short time, the group was reassembled on the aft deck with their backpacks. George and Miguel helped them into the lifeboat and took them back to the beach. When the boat was empty again, Sam and Remi pushed it off into deeper water.

'We'll miss you,' said Miguel.

'Good,' said Remi. 'Friends should miss one another. But we'll all have stories of adventures we can tell when we meet again.'

As the lifeboat putted out to the yacht, Sam picked up their backpacks, and he and Remi walked off the beach and up the street toward the schoolhouse that was being used for temporary shelter. He said, 'You know we're stranded now, don't you?'

'Stranded in a tropical beach town with the man I love?' Remi said. 'Big deal.'

'A very romantic thing to say for a woman who's been shoveling gravel and asphalt into cracks in a runway. I just hope those adventures you were talking about are as much fun as you implied to Miguel.'

She went up on tiptoes and kissed him. 'This will be fine, and we'll do some small bit of good. If we weren't here, we'd be at home, bugging the electricians and carpenters, so our house would never get finished.'

'You're right,' he said. 'Let's go see if there's room for us to sleep in the school. We'll call Selma so she doesn't get worried, and tomorrow we can ask around to see how to form a relief party to the mountain.'

4

Volcán Tacaná, Mexico

By noon the next day, Sam and Remi were among a dozen volunteers sitting under the hot sun in the back of a flatbed truck, bouncing along the bad road toward Volcán Tacaná. Beside them were their former ship-mates Dr Christina Talamantes and Dr Maria Garza, and, on the other side, were others they had come to know during the past week. There were two brothers in their twenties named Raul and Paul Mendoza, who had been brought up out in the countryside near the vol-cano, and a tall, quiet man named José, who'd had a law office in Tapachula that had been damaged by the earthquake. José Sánchez had a thick mustache that veiled his mouth, so one seldom knew whether he was smiling or frowning.

As they rode away from the city past miles of culti-vated fields on their way into the interior, Remi stared into the distance at the blue triangle of Tacaná. Chris-tina Talamantes pointed out, 'There doesn't seem to be any more smoke. Maybe it'll settle down again for another hundred years or so.'

'And maybe it's saving its strength to spit fire and ash

45

on our heads and bury us in lava,' José said. 'The word "Tacaná" is Mayan for "House of Fire".'

'Let's hope it doesn't live up to its name, for now,' Sam said.

They rode for another hour before they reached the small town of Unión Juárez. There were two small brick buildings along the main street that had partially collapsed and two others that had lost some roof tiles. In the central square, the driver and the Spanish-speaking volunteers got out to talk with the people loitering there. Sam and Remi stuck close to Christina, who obliged them by translating. After talking briefly with an Indian-looking couple, Christina told the Fargos, 'The road ends in about seven kilometers.'

'Then what?' asked Sam.

'Then we walk,' she said. 'The lady says it's a foot trail, and there are lots of smaller trails branching off it that lead to the mountain villages.'

Remi said, 'Did she say anything about conditions up there?'

'She warned me that it will be cold. It's over thirteen thousand feet at the top.'

'We're ready for that,' Remi said. 'In fact, I have some things I can share with you. I brought some shells and fleece linings on the yacht because sometimes the Pacific can be cold at night, especially when the wind blows.'

'Thank you,' said Christina. 'I brought some warm clothes too, and so did Maria, because we thought we'd be sleeping outdoors. But we may take you up on your offer in a day or two.'

'Did the lady say anything else?'

'They've had some avalanches from the shaking, and some of the villages' water supplies may be contaminated. There are a few injuries that Maria and I can treat, and possibly some that we can't. Those people will have to be evacuated.'

Sam said, 'We'll look for places near each of the villages where a helicopter can land.'

'Thank you,' said Christina. 'Right now, I'm going to the church to join Maria and see if we can interview people who have come down from the mountain to find shelter. Want to come?'

When they entered the church, Maria and Christina met with five families from mountain villages. As they talked with the parents, the children came to Remi and sat on her lap. They were fascinated by her long auburn hair and loved to hear her sing little songs in her exotic native language, English. She gave them protein bars with nuts and chocolate as treats.

After a while, the truck driver appeared in front of the church, and everyone climbed into the flatbed truck for the last leg of their ride. Where the road ended, there was a stone to mark the beginning of the foot trail. Each of the volunteers climbed down from the truck and shouldered a heavy pack full of supplies. They all helped one another adjust load straps, and then set off.

47

The walk up the steep mountain trail was hard and slow. The forests had been cut and cleared for most of their journey but had never been cleared on the mountain, so foliage overhung their path. They made camp on a level clearing surrounded by trees with fruit that looked like small avocados the Mendozas called *criollo*, and slept until dawn, when the sun woke them. As they reached higher altitudes, the lowland trees were replaced by pines called *pinabete*.

They followed the same pattern for three days, breaking camp each morning, walking until they reached the next village, and meeting with its inhabitants to find out what kind of help they needed. At each one, Christina and Maria examined patients and treated injuries and illnesses. Remi assisted them, keeping the inventory of medicines and supplies, bathing and bandaging and administering prescribed doses while the doctors moved on to the next patient. Sam worked with a crew of volunteers and local farmers to rebuild and strengthen houses, replace broken pipes and wiring, and fix generators to restore electrical power.

At the end of the fifth day on the mountain, as they lay in a tent at the edge of a village near the twenty-five-hundred-meter level, Sam said, 'I have to admit I'm glad we decided to do this.'

'Me too,' Remi said. 'It's one of the most satisfying times of my life.'

'You have wonderful taste.'

'You have wonderful self-esteem,' she said. 'And I'm going to sleep.'

The following morning, Sam and Remi led the way to the last village. They took the smaller side trail that the mayor had told them led to their final stop and soon they were getting too far ahead of the others. They waited until the rest could see them and then went on. But, before long, they were much farther ahead again.

Sam and Remi reached a slope that had suffered an avalanche during the night and covered a stretch of the trail with dirt and rocks that looked like basalt. They made a detour above it, carefully navigating around the big boulders that had fallen. Then they both stopped.

One of the enormous chunks of basalt that lay in the path was not natural. It was a perfect rectangle with rounded corners at the top. Without speaking, they both stepped closer. They could see the carved profile of a man with the hooked nose and elongated skull of a Mayan aristocrat and an elaborate feathered head-dress. There were columns of complex symbols that they could tell were Mayan writing. They both looked up the side of the mountain, their eyes following the gash in the green foliage upward, tracing the path of the avalanche to its beginning.

Irresistible attraction made them begin to climb at once. They went up the steep hillside to a surface that was perfectly flat like a shelf, about thirty feet long and twenty feet wide. The space was bordered by trees, but there were none within the ring. They could see that a portion of the shelf had broken off and gone down in the avalanche.

Sam dug down a few inches with his knife, and they both heard the blade strike stone and scrape when he moved it.

Remi looked around her. 'A patio?' she said. 'Or an entryway?'

They looked at the sheer face of the mountain. There was one area that had a layer of new dirt on it, which had fallen from higher up on the mountain, and a bit of a recessed spot. 'This looks like it might have slid down when the big block fell,' Sam said. He poked it with his knife, then set down his pack and took out his folding shovel. He used it overhand, scraping down more of the dirt from the rocky wall.

'Careful,' Remi said. 'We don't want to bring down the rest of the mountain.' But she set down her backpack, took out a hatchet they'd used for splitting firewood, and joined him. When the dirt was cleared, they faced a wall of black volcanic rock. Sam stabbed at it with his shovel a few times. It was brittle and porous, like pumice, and chipped off in chunks. He nodded at Remi's hatchet. 'May I?'

'Be my guest.' She handed it to him.

Sam hacked at the layer of volcanic stone, knocking it away. 'It looks as though at some point there was a lava flow, and it must have come down like a curtain.'

'Over the entrance?'

'I didn't dare to put it that way,' he said. 'We don't

know it's an entrance to anything, but that's sure what it looks like.' He hacked harder until a bigger chunk fell inward and a hole appeared.

'You just had to knock hard,' said Remi. 'What do you think? Tomb?'

'Way up here? I'm guessing a sacred place, like a shrine to whatever god was in charge of volcanos.'

Sam enlarged the opening, took his flashlight from his pack, shone its beam into the hole, and then stepped through the opening. 'Come in,' he said. 'It's an ancient building.'

Inside was a room made of cut stone, then plastered in white. All of the walls had been painted with colorful pictures of Mayan men, women and gods in a procession of some sort. A few humans sacrificed to the gods by cutting themselves or pushing thorns through their tongues. But the figure that dominated the pictures on each wall was a skeleton with dangling eyeballs.

But Sam and Remi didn't let their flashlights linger on any of these scenes. They both stepped deeper into the room, drawn by a singular sight. On the white-washed stone floor lay the desiccated body of a man, dark and leathery. He wore a breechcloth, and a pair of sandals of woven plant fiber. In the stretched lobes of his ears were large green jade plugs. There were jade beads around his neck and a carved jade disk. They both ran the beams of their flashlights up and down the withered figure. Beside the man's body was a wide-mouthed, lidded pot.

Remi twisted the neck of her flashlight to make the beam wider. 'I've got to take some pictures before we get any closer.'

'Or before there's another aftershock and the roof falls in.'

Remi handed Sam her flashlight, then took flash pictures with her phone. She circled the dead man, taking every angle. She shot the four walls, the ceiling, the floor, and then the pot by the man. 'He's mummified. He looks a bit like the Inca mountain burials and the Moche and Chimú on the Chilean coast.'

'He does,' said Sam. 'But this isn't a burial.'

'No,' Remi agreed. 'It looks as though he was sheltering here, at least temporarily, and then died. He's got carved-out wooden vessels over here with some seeds in them. Probably the fruit just rotted away. There's another one that could have been a rain catcher.'

'He's got an obsidian knife in his belt, and a few flaked pieces he used for carving over by the wooden trough.'

Remi was photographing the pot, which was painted with Mayan scenes that seemed to be about one man – eating, wielding a shield and a war club, kneeling to a fearsome-looking deity that seemed part feline and part troll.

Sam said, 'I wonder what was inside.'

'Whatever it is, it's probably still there. The lid seems to be stuck on it with some kind of seal – like glue. We'd better not try to open it or we'll damage it. Get out of the frame. I want to send these pictures to Selma before my battery dies.'

'Good idea.' Sam stepped out through the hole in the lava curtain, and used his phone to take pictures of the entryway and the mountainside above and below him. As he shot downward toward the trail and the chunk of worked stone that blocked it, he saw the rest of the volunteers coming along. 'Hey!' he shouted. 'Up here!'

The column of people stopped and looked up, and he waved his arms so they would spot him two hundred feet above them. They hesitated for a moment and then began to climb toward him.

While Sam was waiting for the others to arrive, Remi came out of the shrine's entrance on to the surface where he stood. 'What are you doing?'

He pointed down at the others. 'I asked them to come up to take a look.'

'I suppose we couldn't keep this to ourselves.'

'Not even for a day. Not with that carved doorpost lying on the trail down there. We're going to need their help to keep this place safe until we can turn it over to the authorities.'

'You're right,' she said. 'This could be an important find. I'm not aware of any other mummified Mayans.'

In a few minutes, Christina and Maria, the Mendoza brothers, and José Sánchez joined them. Christina looked around her. 'What is this place?'

'We're not sure,' said Remi. 'It's a Mayan ruin, and it seems to have been buried in a lava flow. We think it's a shrine or holy place, probably dedicated to the mountain. The Mayans also had lots of gods that lived in the sky or the interior of the Earth. On a volcano, I suppose it could be either. I remember one called Bacab who did both.'

Maria looked at the entrance. 'Can we go inside without damaging it?'

'We've been inside,' Sam said. 'It should be okay as long as you don't touch anything. There are the remains of a man in there. He's been mummified – not intentionally but by the conditions. The altitude and the dry air up here probably preserved him the way it preserved the mummies in Peru and Chile. At some point, a lava flow sealed the entrance, and that probably made a big difference.'

The volunteers all took their flashlights and went in one at a time. As each one came out, another entered. When they had all been inside, they stood on the flat entry, hushed and awed.

'What do we do about him?' asked Paul Mendoza.

José Sánchez said, 'We get the news out. Then people will pay to come up here.'

'No,' said Maria. 'We've got to get the authorities up here. The archaeologists –'

'The archaeologists can't do much right now,' said Christina. 'The roads are closed, and, when they're reopened, it would be wrong to evacuate a corpse first when there are people down there waiting to be transported to hospitals.'

'He's not just a corpse,' said Sánchez. 'He's a national treasure.'

'Whether he died yesterday or in 900 AD, the point is that he's dead,' said Maria. 'He's not in danger, like a patient who needs a transplant. If we make sure he's preserved, that's all we can do for him.'

Sam held up a hand. 'Please, everyone. It never came up before, but Remi and I have some experience with this kind of find. We've been on archaeological expeditions in different parts of the world. We don't know when this man came to the shrine yet. But he has an obsidian knife and nothing that's made of iron or steel. The site looks like the classic Mayan period, which means it's probably from between 300 and 900 AD. You saw he has jade jewelry, which places him in the highest social class. He was probably either a priest or nobleman. Scientists can learn from him. We're not aware of any classic Mayan remains that are so well preserved.'

'What do you think we should do?' asked Paul Mendoza.

'Normally, we'd say to seal the entrance up again and call in archaeologists,' said Remi. 'But we're in the middle of a disaster area. It will be a while before they're able to get here. And there's no way to hide the site with that carved pillar on the trail.'

Sam said, 'I think we've got to try to stand watch over the site for the night. Then, we can get the mayor of the last village to understand the importance of this site to the people so he can persuade his neighbors to help. Other parts of Mexico and Central America have benefited economically from archaeological sites. People will want to come and study this one and possibly do some excavating. But if we tell outsiders about it now, advertise it widely before the scientists can study it, then it will be destroyed. Looters and pot hunters will come and dig everything up in all directions before scholars can get here.'

'You're pretty sure of everything, aren't you?' said Sánchez. He was angry.

'Of that much anyway,' said Sam. 'We've seen it happen. Priceless artifacts were taken before they could be indentified, walls undermined and broken, human remains thrown aside and exposed to the elements.'

'And what if it did happen? We own it, not you. Anything from the old days belongs to the people of Mexico. It's ours by law and by moral right. These people were our ancestors.'

'You're absolutely correct,' Sam said. 'Every Mexican citizen owns one hundred thirteen millionth of what we found. We'd like to see those citizens all get their share, and that means turning him over to the Mexican authorities.'

Christina said, 'José, don't be a donkey. This is a piece of Mexican history. Of course we'll preserve it.'

'You're awfully friendly with Sam Fargo, aren't you? That ride on the yacht must have been very pleasant.'

Sam said, 'The doctors came with us because the roads were out and they needed to get here to help the injured. Please don't insult them by implying it was anything else.'

Maria said something very rapidly in Spanish through clenched teeth.

José Sánchez looked shocked and a bit ashamed. 'I'm very sorry I said that. Please accept my apologies, all of you. I'll go along with everyone else and do my part to preserve what's here.'

'Thank you, José,' said Remi. 'What we need to do now is set up a camp for the night. It should be a bit away from this site so nobody sees it and gets curious.'

'I'll look for a spot,' said José. He walked off alone, exploring the plateau. After a minute, he disappeared around the curve of the mountain.

The Mendoza brothers looked after him, seemingly tempted to follow and have a say in choosing the site.

'I'd leave him alone for a while,' said Sam. 'He'll be back when he's gotten over it.'

'All right,' said Raul.

Sam turned to the doctors. 'Christina and Maria, I think Remi and I may have caused a problem by opening the lava seal on the entrance to the shrine. The man who's lying on the floor in there was probably preserved by his airless environment, and now we've changed it. He's exposed to the atmosphere. Do you have any advice?'

'The best thing would be to freeze him, which we can't do,' said Christina.

Maria said, 'I think you were right about the conditions

up here on the mountain preserving him. The dry, cool days and cold nights above ten thousand feet are ideal. So, for the moment, he'll probably be fine. It's taking him down to sea level to a tropical forest that is the risk.'

Sam said, 'Maybe we can improvise a container that's cold and airtight and carry him down.'

'That's our best hope,' said Maria.

'Where's the nearest ice?' asked Christina.

'Above us,' said Sam. 'There seem to be ice fields up above twelve thousand feet. I could see them yesterday. Maybe I can climb up and reach the lowest one.'

'The body bags,' said Christina.

'Body bags?'

Maria said, 'When medical teams go into disaster areas, sometimes there are fatalities that need to be bagged to prevent the spread of disease. So we carry a few bags. We can use three or four at once to keep the body's temperature even. They're airtight and strong. If we put him inside one and then pack ice around him and put a bag or two over that, he should stay fresh.'

'I'm going with you,' Remi said, just beside Sam's ear.

He shook his head. 'Risking both of us doesn't seem like the best idea.'

'Climbing up to an ice field alone is a worse idea.'

'Not necessarily,' he said. 'It could save a valuable specimen.'

'You're a pretty valuable specimen yourself, and two

of us can bring twice as much ice,' she said. 'Argue with that.'

'Do you get the impression I argue with you just to get my own way?'

'Never,' she lied.

'All right, then,' he said. 'We'll both go.'

'At least we'll have those nice body bags if anything goes wrong.'

They emptied their packs of almost everything but a body bag each, a hatchet for Remi, a shovel for Sam, water, and their fleeces and jackets. Then they set off to climb.

It was still midday when they began, but the climb was steep. They were able to accomplish the necessary progress without climbing gear because the irregular surface of the mountain offered footholds. After a time, they reached a windswept slope above the tree line on bare ground; they felt tired and winded.

'I'm glad we spent a few days above ten thousand feet before we tried this,' Remi said.

'Me too. I just hope this works. I'd like to get up there and be well on our way back before dark.'

'If we keep up this pace, we should be able to do it.'

'Sure,' he said. 'Anybody could do it if they could keep up this pace.'

They laughed, and found themselves going even faster. Soon they were climbing in silence, too winded to feel comfortable talking. Once in a while, Sam would turn and say, 'You all right?' and Remi would reply, 'So far.'

In the late afternoon, they reached the snow-covered part of the mountain and stopped to look ahead. There was a big caldera at the top and three smaller ones along a ridge. Sam pointed to the white streaks. 'See? The snow is only on the crests of ridges radiating out from the caldera.'

'The caldera must be hot,' Remi said.

'Well, let's see if we can grab some ice and get down quickly.'

They walked along the rocky badlands between the calderas to reach the streaks of ice. When they got there, they dug down below the snow and found solid ice. They chipped at it with Sam's shovel and Remi's hatchet to free chunks they could break out. They gathered ice until they had as much as they could carry, then placed it in the body bags, wrapped the bags in their fleeces and jackets, put them in their backpacks, and began to walk back toward the top of the trail.

As they were hurrying toward the trail, there was a deep rumbling sound, and the rocky ground below them began to shake. They knew they wouldn't be able to retain their balance. They each bent their knees, sat, and slipped the backpack straps from their shoulders while they waited out the earthquake. The shaking and rumbling continued for a minute, then another minute.

'Are you scared?' Remi asked.

'Of course I'm scared,' said Sam. 'I have no idea

whether this is just an aftershock or we're about to have the mountaintop blow off and hurl us into the stratosphere.'

'Just testing your sanity,' she said.

As the rumbling abated, they became aware of a new sound, a hiss that was almost a whistle. It grew to a rushing sound, and then a roar that reminded them of an airplane's engine. As they looked around for the source, a cloud of steam rose into their line of sight across the snowfield. It was white, spewing out of the mountain at high pressure from somewhere below them.

As soon as they had shouldered their packs again and shifted them to balance the weight of the ice they were carrying, they set off. They walked quickly, sometimes approaching a trot in places where the volcanic rock was clear and solid.

When they reached the beginning of the trail they had taken upward, the sun was low, its rays already horizontal and glaring in their eyes from Mexico on the west side and casting an enormous shadow on the green forests of Guatemala on the east. They moved downward without delay, passing spots they remembered. This time, they had to guard against letting their momentum propel them past a foothold into open air.

Now they could see the source of the noise and the steam cloud. It was a rift in the rocky mountainside where a plume of hot air and water was shooting out under immense pressure. They edged away from the steam, but they couldn't stray too far without losing their way. Once they were below it, they felt a tentative relief. But an hour later, as they were descending a rock formation that looked like a series of frozen waterfalls, the rumbling in the earth began again.

'Better hold on,' said Sam, and they both found handholds and sat, Remi's head on Sam's shoulder. They kept their places while the rumbling increased and the mountain shook. The shaking seemed more violent, and it dislodged two showers of rocks a few dozen feet to their left that rolled down, hit other rocks, and caromed off into the air, then hit far below with audible impact.

The silence returned, and they began to descend again. They had to go more slowly now because, in places, new rockslides had fallen across their path, covering their old footholds and making them tread on untested spots. When darkness came, they used flashlights to choose every step. The shaking returned once more, but they were in an open, unprotected area, where they were extremely vulnerable to falling rocks, so they could only push on.

It was not until about 1 a.m. that Sam and Remi reached their starting point. They walked back above the main trail until they reached the site of the ruined shrine. As they approached the little plateau, they could see the artificial glow of a cell phone. 'Somebody else must have a satellite phone,' Remi said. 'I think José does,' Sam said. She called out, 'Hello, down there. It's us.'

The glow of the phone disappeared and a human shape moved along the patio. 'This way!' It was José's voice. He turned on a flashlight and lit the way for them to reach the shrine. 'You must be tired,' he said. 'I'll show you the way to the camp.'

'First, we've got to get our friend on ice,' Sam said.

Sam, Remi and José went into the shrine. They laid out a fresh body bag and carefully lifted the man into it, then zipped it shut.

'He seems so light,' José said.

'He's mostly skeleton now,' Remi said. 'The bones are only about fifteen per cent of our living weight, which is mostly water.' They packed ice around the bag, slipped another bag over it, and then a third.

They heard footsteps approaching outside. Raul Mendoza called, 'It's my turn to stand guard,' then stuck his head into the entrance. 'Oh, Fargos. It's good to see you. When the mountain was shaking, we all got worried.'

'We're fine,' said Remi. 'After some sleep, we'll be even better.'

The Fargos followed José on what must have been the remnant of an ancient trail on the mountainside to another flat space, where all the tents had been pitched. Sam played his flashlight's beam up the mountain. 'What's above us?'

'No overhangs or big rocks. Nothing came down today during the shaking.'

'Thanks, José. And thanks for your help with the mummy.'

'Good night,' he said, and the Fargos crawled into their tent and closed the flap to ward off the morning sun that would come up too soon.

5

Volcán Tacaná

Sam woke to the buzz of Remi's satellite phone and realized that the sun was up already. He patted the floor of the little tent and found the phone. 'Hello?'

'Sam?' said Selma Wondrash. 'Where are you two?'

'About ten thousand feet up an active volcano called Tacaná. We're coming down today. Is something wrong?'

'I'll let you be the judge,' she said. 'I just sent you an article that appeared this morning in a Mexico City paper.'

'Okay. I'll call you back when we've seen it.'

He terminated the call, went online, and found the e-mail with the attachment. He clicked on the article and was greeted by a color photograph of the interior of the Mayan shrine, the body, and the painted pot. 'Uh-oh,' he said.

Remi opened her eyes and sat up. 'What?'

He turned the little screen toward her and she gasped. 'How did that happen?'

Sam thumbed through the article, looking at the photographs. There was a picture of the whole group in the last mountain village. He showed Remi. 'Remember when this picture was taken?'

'Sure. We all lined up, and then . . .' She paused. 'José handed his cell phone to the mayor's brother.'

'And then he handed the phone back to José. So we know where this came from.'

'José sent it to a reporter, obviously, along with this article. I'm going to get a better translation than I can do.' She took the phone from Sam, ducked out of the tent, and disappeared.

When Sam caught up with her, she was sitting beside Christina, who was translating. 'The discovery was made by Sam and Remi Fargo, members of a volunteer relief expedition bringing aid to the remote villages on Tacaná . . .' She paused. 'He gives you full credit, but he doesn't leave anyone out. The picture has everyone's full name, and the narrative seems accurate.'

'I respect him for his honesty,' Remi said. 'It's just that we thought we had more time before the rest of the world knew.'

'Well, we don't,' said Sam. 'We'd better decide what to do.' He looked around at the camp. 'Where's José?'

Remi stood and looked around. 'He was guarding the shrine when we came in last night.'

Sam began to run. He dashed along the plateau, ascended the narrow path until he reached the place where it widened again near the entrance to the shrine. There was Raul Mendoza. 'Good morning, Sam,' he said. *'Buenos días.'*

'Buenos días,' Sam said. He leaned into the entrance and saw that everything was as it had been. The body was still in its body bags, the pot had not been moved, and the wooden vessels were untouched. He returned to Raul. 'Did you happen to see José go by this morning?'

'No,' said Mendoza. 'Not since he was with you last night.'

'I think we can leave the shrine for a few minutes,' said Sam. 'We all need to have a talk.'

'All right.'

They returned to the camp, where the others were just stowing their tents and gear in their backpacks and putting out cook fires. When Sam and Raul arrived, Remi said, 'Apparently, José took off by himself. His tent and gear are gone.'

'We should talk.'

'We've been talking,' Remi said. 'Everybody agrees that we can't do much to hide the shrine. We can bury the carved stone pillar, but we can't move it. All we can do is make sure we've got the best possible photos of the interior of the shrine and take our friend and his belongings with us.'

'We should also explain to the villagers what they've got here.'

During the morning, they brought the village mayor and his two closest friends to the shrine, then showed them the article in the Mexico City newspaper. Sam warned them that people would be coming. The ones from the government and from universities should be welcomed and the others kept away, for the present.

When they were finished explaining and the mayor said he understood, the volunteers left the shrine. Sam carried the Mayan pot across his chest in a rudimentary sling, and the Mendoza brothers carried the body on a makeshift stretcher: just two poles with the body lashed between them. The doctors sealed the wooden vessels, and the remains of the fruits and vegetables found in them, in sterile, airtight plastic bags.

Every few hours, Sam stopped and drained off some water from the melting ice and made sure the body bags were intact. It took two days of walking to get down the long trail to the village of Unión Juárez, but Maria used Remi's satellite telephone to call ahead to be sure that a truck was waiting to take them to Tapachula.

On the bumpy ride back to Tapachula, Sam protected the pot from shock by keeping it on his lap. The Mendoza brothers protected the mummy by holding the stretcher suspended between their knees, where it couldn't touch the bed of the truck. As they drove to the city, Sam spoke with the others. 'I think that at least until the publicity dies down, we've got to keep our friend's location secret. Maria, Christina, I'm wondering if I can ask you for a favor.'

After some discussion, Sam had the truck take them to the hospital at Tapachula. Dr Talamantes and Dr Garza went inside alone. A while later, they returned with a gurney and wheeled the body in, where they could keep it refrigerated in the morgue. When they came back, they had news. While they had been up on the volcano, the city had made great progress. The electrical power had been restored, the roads to the west and the east were open again, and the airport had resumed commercial flights.

The four shared a cab that wound through recently cleared and half-repaired streets to the airport. While Sam paid the driver, Christina Talamantes said, 'Sam, Remi, we'll miss you both.' She hugged them, and then Maria Garza did the same. 'But it will be good to fly to Acapulco so we can get back to our own work.'

'We'll miss you too,' said Remi. 'In a couple of weeks, some people from our foundation will be in touch.'

Christina looked puzzled. 'Why?'

'This won't be the last disaster,' said Sam. 'But maybe our foundation can help in advance to prepare for the next one. We want you and Maria to tell us what needs to be done and to decide how to spend the money.'

Maria, who was usually the shy one, threw her arms around Sam and kissed his cheek. When she released him, she hurried off toward the terminal. Christina smiled, and said, 'As you can tell, we'll be delighted.' She turned and trotted after Maria to catch up.

Sam and Remi sat down in the airport bar. Sam said to Remi, 'You know what I'd like? To drink something that's ice-cold. It's been a while.' He ordered two bottles of beer, and called Selma.

'Hello, you two,' she said.

'Hi, Selma,' said Sam. 'We're back in Tapachula, at the airport, and it's time for us to go somewhere else. Can you find us a resort on the Pacific Coast that hasn't been affected by the earthquake?'

'I'll do my best. Keep your phone where you can reach it.'

Before they had finished their beer, Sam's satellite phone rang. 'Selma?'

'The very same. You have tickets waiting for an Aero-mexico flight to Huatulco in forty-five minutes. It's close but not damaged at all. Your hotel is Las Brisas, which is a very good one on the beach, and your room has a balcony overlooking the ocean. I've rented a car for you and you pick it up at the airport.'

'Thanks, Selma.'

In Huatulco, Sam and Remi signed for the car and drove to the Las Brisas Hotel. They went to the pool to soak and lie on long deck chairs, drinking margaritas. After about an hour, Remi turned to Sam, lifted her sunglasses, and said, 'If you were to invite me to a great dinner at seven o'clock tonight, I would try to find time in my busy schedule to accept.'

They bought new clothes in the shops at the hotel and went to the restaurant at seven. Sam ordered pheasant in almond red sauce and Remi had seafood posole with snapper, cod and shrimp. They selected an Argentine Malbec and a Chilean Sauvignon Blanc to go with them. They had Mexican *tres leches* cake and *polvorónes de Caulle*, a local type of cinnamon cookies, for dessert.

After dinner, they walked on the beach and then went to the bar on the patio to sip a Cabo Uno Lowland Extra Añejo tequila that had mellow undertones of vanilla. Remi said, 'Thanks, Sam. I like it when I can tell you remember I'm a girl, and not your old army buddy.'

'Not a likely mistake unless I get hit on the head.' He sipped the aromatic, powerful tequila. 'This is a nice change for both of us. Living in a tent and spending your days burying sewer pipes is only fun for so long.'

They finished their tequila, and Remi stood, stepped behind Sam's chair, put her hands on his shoulders and leaned down to kiss his head, letting her auburn hair fall to both sides of him like a silky curtain for a second, then she straightened. 'Shall we?' she said.

They walked, holding hands, to the entrance and went up in the elevator. Sam opened the door of their room but suddenly put his arm out to keep Remi from entering. He turned on the light and stepped in. The room had been ransacked. His pack and Remi's had been poured out on top of the bed. The closet doors were open, and the extra pillows and blankets had been swept off the shelf to the floor. Sam said, 'Luckily, we didn't use the room safe. What's missing from the packs?'

Remi pushed some of her clothing aside, opened a zippered compartment in the pack, then stepped back and looked around the room. 'Not a thing. I don't bring fancy jewelry on boat trips, and our only expensive gear is the satellite phones and dive watches. We had them with us.'

'I'm not missing anything either.'

'Please tell me you still have the receipt from the parking attendant,' she said. 'The pot is in the trunk of the car.'

'Here's the receipt.' He held it up so she could see it.

'Let's check anyway.'

They took the elevator to the parking garage, found their rental car, and opened the trunk. There was the pot and Remi's computer, wrapped in their jackets, and the airtight packages of seeds and husks with the wooden vessels the Mayan had used.

'Everything is here,' Remi said.

'Whoever it was apparently didn't see the car or didn't connect it with us or couldn't get to it.'

'What do you think is going on?'

'I don't think it was a regular hotel room robbery. I think somebody recognized us from the newspaper article, or the viral Internet version, and figured we had something valuable from the shrine.'

'The pot?' she asked.

'It might be valuable, and it's the only thing in our possession, but they couldn't know that, whoever they are.'

'Then the thing to do is get out of here,' she said. 'We need to make sure these people don't follow us.'

Sam said, 'We'll check out right now and move to another hotel.'

'Where?'

'On the other side of the country.'

'Sounds far enough.'

'Wait here. I'll go up and use the express checkout and bring the packs down here by the back stairs.'

'While you're doing that, I'll call Selma and let her know where we're going.' She paused. 'Where *are* we going?'

'Cancún.' He hurried into the hotel.

In a half hour they were on the road in the rental car, beginning the nine-hundred-mile drive from Huatulco to Cancún. It was now late in the evening so there was little traffic. Sam drove hard, watching to be sure they weren't followed. Remi took her turn driving after two hours, and they kept going until four. They pulled over at a closed gas station in Tuxtla Gutiérrez and slept until it opened at eight, filled the tank, and drove on to Centro on the Gulf Coast. All day they kept changing drivers at intervals until they reached Cancún. They checked into the Crown Paradise Club, showered, and slept until morning.

In the morning, they drove to El Centro, the central part of the city, to shop. They found a number of small stores that had been designed, built and stocked with American tourists in mind. They bought a number of souvenirs, all of them cheap replicas of Mayan artifacts – pots, bowls, wall hangings, mats and fabrics that more

73

or less reproduced Mayan art and writing. Everything bore images of Mayan kings, priests and gods, but crudely and garishly painted. At a hobby shop, they bought a water-soluble acrylic paint set that included silver and gold paint and brushes.

At the hotel, Sam went to work on the genuine Mayan pot from the shrine. He painted designs and altered pictures to make the painting on the pot look as cheap and crude as the souvenirs he and Remi had bought. He used sparkly gold paint to cover the pieces of jewelry the Mayan king wore. Parts of his shield and war club Sam highlighted with silver.

When the paint was dry, Sam and Remi asked the concierge at the hotel where they could find a mailing company that would ship their souvenirs home. He replied that the hotel would do this for them. Sam and Remi watched him pad a large packing box, load the pot into it, fill all the spaces around it with the mats, wall hangings, and fabrics, then fill the box the rest of the way with Styrofoam peanuts and seal it up. With the concierge's help, Sam and Remi filled out the customs declaration, saying the contents were 'souvenirs from Mexico,' and declared the price they'd paid to be under a hundred dollars.

They paid the cost of shipping the souvenirs to their house in La Jolla, gave the concierge a large tip, and went off to the beach to do some snorkeling in the shallows after their hot morning in the city.

That night, Sam and Remi called Selma from their room.

'Hi, you two,' Selma said. 'What is it this time, a flood?'

'Not yet,' said Sam. 'We just wanted you to know that we've sent some souvenirs from Yucatán to the house in La Jolla.'

'I'll watch for them. Is this one big box?'

'Yes,' said Remi. 'There's some pottery, which we really don't want broken.'

There was a very slight pause, during which they could tell that Selma had understood what the package was. 'Don't give it another thought. Are you on your way home?'

'As soon as we can get a flight,' Sam said.

'Have you given any thought to where you plan to sleep when you get to San Diego? The fourth floor of the house is still a process, not a product.'

'Until yesterday, we've been sleeping on the side of an active volcano,' Remi said. 'We'll manage.'

'You could stay at the Valencia Hotel. I can reserve a suite or even a villa. Then each day you can walk home across the lawn or down to the beach.'

'Sounds good,' said Remi. 'If we rent a villa, will they let Zoltán stay with us?'

'I'll see if they can arrange it. I can even bring him there to show them what an exemplary animal he is,' Selma said.

'Maybe that's not such a good idea,' Sam said.

'A hundred-and-twenty-pound dog who sits when you say sit is still a little scary.'

'I'll sing his praises, then, and offer to put up a damage deposit.'

'Make sure it's enough to cover any kindergartners he might eat.'

'Sam!' said Remi.

'We'll call before we get on the plane.'

Sam used Remi's computer to buy plane tickets home. Then he researched the names of American archaeology professors specializing in the Mayans. It was a pleasant surprise that one of the most distinguished seemed to be Professor David Caine at the University of California at San Diego. Sam e-mailed Dr Caine and said that he and Remi had made an unusual find at Volcán Tacaná, and attached the Mexican news article about it. He asked Caine if he would meet with them when they returned home. He asked Remi to read the e-mail before he sent it.

She did, and said, 'My advice is, click send.'

'You don't think we ought to include something about ourselves? Maybe list the places we've excavated in other countries and so on?'

'Nobody needs to do that anymore. When he reads this, he'll be sitting in front of a computer. He can Google us and get much more than he wants to know.'

'I suppose.'

Within an hour, Professor Caine answered. He said

he would be happy to meet with them and was eager to learn more about their latest find. Remi pointed at the screen. 'See that? Our "latest find". He Googled us first thing.'

That afternoon, Sam and Remi checked out of the hotel and hired a taxi for the ride to the airport south of the city. The driver put their two backpacks into the trunk. As she was about to get into the cab, Remi hesitated for a second.

'What?' Sam said. 'Something wrong?'

She shook her head. 'Just a guy waiting outside the main entrance. When we came out, he ran.'

'Where to?'

'I don't know. Down the street, I guess.'

'Could he be a parking attendant going to retrieve somebody else's car?'

'Sure. That's probably it,' she said. 'I guess I'm a little jumpy today. Some of the experiences we've had lately . . .'

They got into the backseat, and the driver said in English, 'Which airline?'

'Aeromexico.'

The cab dived off down the long driveway toward the federal highway. The airport was about ten miles away and the traffic was moving steadily, so they made good time. They looked out at the Gulf of Mexico and enjoyed the ride.

Just as they could see the airport ahead to their right,

a black car came speeding up behind them. It pulled up beside them, and a stern-faced man in a dark suit gestured to them to pull over.

Their driver muttered, *'Policía,'* and coasted, looking for the best place to stop. Sam looked out the rear window and saw that as the cab pulled over, the black car pulled up behind them and came to a stop a few feet from their bumper. Two men got out. One walked up beside the window of the cab and held out his hand. The driver handed him his license. The man handed it back and glanced at the Fargos, sitting in the rear seat.

The second man stood behind their cab and to the right, with his hand on the gun in the holster at his belt. Remi whispered, 'The guy back there is the one I saw running before.'

The man beside the driver said, *'Abra el maletero.'*

The driver pressed the button to pop the trunk. The man in back of the car unzipped their backpacks.

'What are you looking for?' asked Sam.

The man beside the driver glanced at him but said nothing. Sam opened the door an inch to step out, but the man threw his hip against it and slammed it shut, drew his gun, and held it on Sam.

Sam sat back in his seat and kept both hands in his lap. The man backed away from the window.

The cab driver said quietly, 'Please, señor. Those men are not policemen. They'll shoot all of us.'

They waited while the men put the two backpacks in

78

the trunk of the black car, got in and drove away. Sam asked, 'Who were they?'

'I don't know,' said the driver. 'Most of the time, we don't have to deal with people like that. Everybody knows they're here – *narcotraficantes* use this as a shipment point – Zetas come to town looking for somebody. Somehow, those two picked you. Maybe you can tell *me* why.'

Sam and Remi looked at each other grimly. 'Just take us to the airport,' Sam said. 'We have a plane to catch.'

When they arrived at the circular drive in front of the terminal, Sam handed the man a large tip. 'Here. You earned this.'

As they entered, Remi said, 'They had to be after the you know what.'

'I know,' said Sam. 'If I ever run into José Sánchez again, I'll be sure to thank him for all the free publicity he gave us. Let's get to our gate before somebody else tries to murder us because of that stupid article.'

The flight home took eight hours, including a stop at Dallas–Fort Worth. As they flew in above San Diego after dark, they looked down at the lights of the city. Remi held Sam's arm. 'I missed this place,' she said. 'I miss my dog. I want to see what they've done to our house.'

'It's good to have a chance to rest up between vacations,' Sam said.

She pulled back and looked at him. 'You're already thinking about leaving again, aren't you?'

'I'm delighted to be home,' said Sam. 'I don't have any specific plans to go anywhere.'

She leaned against him again. 'I guess that'll have to do for now. No specific plans means we won't be leaving tomorrow.'

'True,' he said. 'As of today, we don't even own any luggage.'

6

La Jolla

On their first day back from Mexico, Sam and Remi walked from the Valencia Hotel with Zoltán, their German shepherd, through the ground floor of their house at Goldfish Point, marveling at the newly remodeled building. Nothing revealed to the uninformed eye that a few months ago the house had been attacked by an assault force of more than thirty men armed with automatic weapons. The thousands of bullet holes that had pierced the walls and splintered the hardwood, the dozens of broken windows, the front doors that had been battered open with a pickup truck were all long gone. Everything was new.

Only the upgrades might have hinted to an astute observer that a battle had taken place here. The steel shutters that they'd had in the original design in case of a once-in-a-century Pacific storm were replaced by a set of thick steel plates that were designed to come down by force of gravity and lock at the press of a button. The surveillance system now included cameras mounted on all sides of the house and even in the tall pine trees at the edge of the grounds. As they walked the floor, Selma sounded like a tour guide. 'Please notice that every window is now double-paned safety glass. I'm assured that a man couldn't break them with a sledgehammer.'

Selma walked straight to a bookcase, tugged out a particular book, and the case opened like a door. Sam and Remi followed her into a passage and swung the door shut. 'See?' she said. 'The light goes on when you open the bookcase. The rest is just the way you designed it.' She led them to a stairway that led to a steel door with a combination lock. Selma punched the code in and the door unlocked. She opened it and took them into a concrete chamber. 'We're now under the front lawn.' She pointed at the ceiling. 'You'll notice that the ventilation comes on automatically, and the lights. They laid two hundred feet of concrete culvert, seven feet in diameter, to make the shooting gallery.'

'We prefer the term "firing range",' said Remi.

'That's right,' said Sam. 'If we call it the shooting gallery, we'll have to give people the chance to win Kewpie dolls and teddy bears.'

'Suit yourselves,' said Selma. 'If you'll look behind you, you'll see that I had them install two extra-large gun safes so you can store guns and ammunition here. And, over here, behind the bench rest, is a workbench for cleaning and adjusting weapons.'

Remi said, 'You seem to have taken a lot of interest in this project. You never used to care for guns.'

'Our experience with Mr Bako, Mr Poliakoff and Mr Le Clerc and their friends has caused me to acquire an affection for firearms that I didn't feel before.'

'Well, thank you so much for watching over all this construction,' Remi said. 'What's at the other end?' She pointed at the far end of the range.

'That's a sheet of steel set at a forty-five-degree angle to deflect rounds downward into the sand, so there will never be a ricochet.'

Sam said, 'Did they put in the other exit?'

'Yes. Behind the sheet of steel is a second stairway that leads up into the stand of pines near the street.'

'Great,' said Sam. 'Let's go back upstairs and see how the wiring changes for the new electronics worked out.'

'I think you'll be pleased,' Selma said. 'They've been working on it for months and finally finished last week. Instead of one emergency generator, there are now four, for different circuits supporting various functions. This is now a very difficult house to deprive of electricity for even a second.'

They came up to the short corridor, through the bookcase door, and back into the office. Selma said, 'That's funny, that wasn't here before.'

Sam and Remi looked where she was pointing. It was a large cardboard box. 'It's our souvenirs from Mexico,' said Remi.

Wendy Corden was working at one of the computers in the area across the room. 'That came a few minutes ago. I signed for it.'

'Thanks,' said Sam. He lifted the box up on to a worktable, giving it a gentle shake. 'I don't hear anything broken.'

'Don't even say that,' said Selma. 'I can't believe you shipped it that way – just mailed it home like a . . . a piece of crockery.'

'You had to be there to appreciate our choices. People kept trying to steal it.'

Selma produced a box cutter from a desk drawer and handed it to Sam. 'Can we see it?'

Sam opened the box. He removed some of the packing peanuts, then some of the wall hangings and mats.

Selma unrolled one of them, then two others. 'These are truly dreadful,' she said. 'That king looks a bit like Elvis – who was, come to think of it, The King.' She unwrapped a small pot. 'And look at these – sparkly paint in case this warrior gentleman isn't fancy enough.'

Remi laughed. 'I think those were the inspiration for Sam's improvements to the real pot.'

Sam reached in and gently lifted out the genuine Mayan pot. He set it upright on the table. Selma moaned. 'That is horrifying. Gold and silver paint? That's vandalism.'

'It comes off,' he said. 'I read one time that a lot of great Egyptian art got to Europe disguised as cheap replicas. The trick still works.'

Sam used his cell phone to dial Dr David Caine's office at the university. 'Dr Caine?' he said. 'The delivery I was waiting for has arrived. Would you like to take a look?'

'I'd love the chance,' Caine said. 'When can I come?'

'Anytime from now on. We'll be here until evening.' Sam recited the address.

'I'll be there in an hour.'

Sam terminated the call and then turned to the others. 'He'll be here in an hour. I'd better wipe this sparkly paint off right away or he'll be as horrified as Selma.'

Later, their guest arrived. Dr David Caine was in his mid-forties, very fit and tanned, wearing jeans and a summer-weight sport coat over a black polo shirt. As he stepped through the doorway into the vast office space, he saw the pot on the table across the room and could barely draw his eyes away from it. He stopped and shook Sam's hand. 'You must be Sam. I'm Dave Caine.'

Remi stepped up. 'I'm Remi. Come this way. I can tell you're dying to see the pot.'

He followed her across the open hardwood floor, but when he was still six feet from the pot, he stopped and stared at it for a moment, then walked around it, looking at it from every angle. 'I read the article and looked at the pictures you sent me, but seeing one of these in person is always a moment,' he said. 'I always feel a bit of excitement. The pottery, the paintings, always contain a little bit of the personality of the art-ist. When I see a water pitcher shaped like a fat little dog, it's like going back in time to meet the potter.'

'I know what you mean,' Remi said. 'I love that too, when the actual human being is staring back at you from a thousand years ago.'

Caine came in toward the table and looked closely at the pot. 'But this one is different. It's obviously a prime piece, classic period. A day in the life of the king of Copán.' He straightened and looked at the Fargos. 'You know that discoveries like this have to be reported to the government of Mexico, right?'

'Of course,' said Sam. 'We were in the middle of a natural disaster and there wasn't any reasonable, safe way to do that or any authorities who had time to deal with it. We'll return the pot when we've had a chance to learn what we can about it.'

'It's a relief that you know the rules,' he said.

Remi said, 'Are you sure it's from Copán? We found this at Tacaná, north of Tapachula, Mexico. That's at least four hundred miles from Copán.'

Caine shrugged. 'Native people in the Americas sometimes covered a lot of ground on foot. There's also trade.'

'How old is it?'

Caine cocked his head and looked. 'Wait. Here we go. The king is Yax Pasaj Chan Yopaat, the sixteenth ruler of Copán. It says so here.' He pointed at a group of vertical columns with rounded designs like seals.

Sam said, 'You can read those?'

'Yes. These columns each consist of one to five glyphs and each glyph is a word or phrase or an indication of a position in a sentence. You read from top left to right, but only for the first two columns, then go down a line and read the left one and the right one and so on. There are eight hundred and sixty-one glyphs that we know.'

'There are over twenty Mayan languages,' said Remi. 'Does this form of writing work for all of them?'

'No,' he said. 'The only ones we have were written in Ch'olan, Tzeltalan, and Yucatec.'

Sam stared at the pot. 'So this comes from Copán. I wonder how it got from Honduras all the way across Guatemala to the border of Mexico.'

'And when,' said Remi.

'Exactly what I was wondering,' said Caine. 'We could do a carbon date on any organic material associated with the find and on the man himself. That would do it.'

'I'll call Dr Talamantes and Dr Garza and see if they can arrange to have the man tested,' said Remi. 'He's in a hospital morgue in Tapachula. They signed him in, mostly on the strength of the goodwill they built up with the medical community in the area after the earthquake.'

'Are they also archaeologists?' asked Caine.

'No, just medical doctors,' said Sam.

'Then would you mind if I stepped in and got a couple of Mexican colleagues to go to work on this? They're first-rate scientists and very well respected.'

'We'd be delighted,' said Remi.

'Then I'll call them this afternoon and get them going on it. You've done a good job of keeping his location quiet since the first blast of publicity, so there hasn't been a crush of people trying to get in and see him. But you can be sure that lots of people are waiting and listening – some scholars and scientists, and some crackpots and some charlatans as always.'

Sam said, 'The publicity came from another volunteer who was up there with us. He didn't believe in keeping the find quiet, based on his own principles: the discovery belongs to the people so the people should be told about it. We thought we'd talked him into waiting, but he went public without us. After that, we took steps to give the scientific community a chance to see things before the tourists and souvenir hunters destroyed them.'

'It's a good thing you did. Do we have anything here we can carbon-date?'

Remi said, 'Quite a bit. Our guy made himself a pair of dishes out of hollowed-out pieces of wood. There was some plant residue in one of them.'

'Perfect,' said Caine. 'Anything living begins to lose carbon 14 the minute it dies.'

'I'll get them.' Remi went off to the other end of the room, disappeared through a door, and came back with the two plastic bags containing the wooden vessels, seeds and husks.

Caine returned his attention to the pot. 'This pot has

a lid. The seal looks translucent, a bit like beeswax. Have you opened it?'

'No,' said Sam. 'We realized that the minute we cleared the lava out of the doorway to the shrine, or whatever that building is, we exposed the man and his belongings to air and started the clock ticking. We didn't want to do anything that might harm the pot. We've carried it around quite a bit, so we know the contents aren't liquid and they aren't stone or metal, but it's not empty. Something shifts around a little when you move it.'

'Shall we try to open it now?' asked Caine.

'We have a good place to do it,' Remi said. 'In our remodeling, we've had the builders put in a climate-controlled room – low temperature, low humidity, no sunlight – just like a rare-book room in a library.'

'Wonderful,' said Caine.

'Follow me.' She led them to the door she had just emerged from, opened it, and turned on the light. The room had a long worktable and a few chairs and a wall of glass cabinets, all of them empty for the moment. In the corner of the room was a tall red tool chest on wheels that looked like the ones in car mechanics' shops.

Professor Caine carried the pot into the room and set it on the table. Sam wheeled the chest over and opened the top drawer, which held a collection of tools for working on small, delicate objects – brushes, tweezers, X-Acto knives, dental picks, awls, magnifiers and high-intensity flashlights. There was also a box of sterile surgical gloves.

Caine put on gloves, chose a pick and tweezers to examine the seal and pull some of it off. He looked at it under a magnifier on a stand. 'It seems to be a glue made from some kind of plant resin.' He switched to an X-Acto knife and methodically cut away the translucent substance from around the lid.

'What's in there can't be food. It's glued shut,' said Remi.

'I don't dare guess,' said Caine. 'Archaeology is full of high hopes and pots that turn out to be full of mud.' He gripped the lid and twisted. 'Interesting. I can turn the lid a little but not raise it. What it looks like is that he heated the pot a little, sealed it, and let it cool. That would produce a partial vacuum in it to keep the seal tight.'

'Just like canning,' said Remi. 'Maybe it is food.'

'Now, I wonder how to get it open without breaking it.'

Sam said, 'We could heat it a bit again to get the air inside to expand. Or we could take it up to a high altitude, where the air pressure is lower.'

'How could we warm it a bit without harming it?'

'If we do it evenly, the pot shouldn't break,' said Sam.

'I agree,' Caine said.

'Another modification to the house: we put in a sauna,' said Remi.

They climbed the stairs to the second floor, and Sam

entered the sauna, placed the pot on the wooden bench, then turned on the heat, slowly raising the temperature. At the end of ten minutes, he re-entered the sauna, wrapped the pot in a towel, and brought it out. He held the pot while Caine tried the lid. It came up and the pressure was equalized. Sam put the lid back on, and they all went back downstairs to the climate-controlled room.

'The big moment is coming,' said Remi.

'Don't be disappointed if it's just a mess of organic matter that used to be food,' said Caine. 'Sometimes the best bits of information don't look like much at first.'

Sam set the pot on the table. Caine, still wearing surgical gloves, took a deep breath and reached in. He pulled out a mass of what looked like dried weeds. 'Packing material?'

He picked up a small flashlight and looked inside the pot. 'Oh . . .' He stood up and peered down into the vessel. 'Is it possible?'

'What is it?'

'It looks like a book,' he said. 'A Mayan book.'

'Can you get it out?'

Caine put both hands into the vessel and lifted out a thick brownish rectangle and gently set it on the table. He reached out slowly with only his gloved index finger, lifted the outer layer an inch. His voice was a hoarse whisper. 'Intact. I can't believe it.' For a moment, he stood still, lost in thought. He withdrew his finger and only then seemed to notice the Fargos again.

His whole face brightened. 'It's a Mayan book, a codex. It seems to be undamaged. We have to take our time examining it because we don't know how fragile it is, and there's no way to know how many times a page can be turned or even touched.'

'I know they're very rare,' Remi said.

'The rarest of all Western Hemisphere artifacts and by far the most valuable,' said Caine. 'The Maya were the only people in the Americas who developed a complex system of writing and it's good. They could write anything they could say. If they'd had the urge, they could have written novels, epic poems, histories. Maybe they did. There were once hundreds of thousands of these codices. Today there are only four that have survived and made it into European museums – the Dresden Codex, the Madrid Codex, the Paris . . . and there's also the Grolier Codex, but it's so inferior to the others that many experts think it's a forgery. But the first three are full of Mayan knowledge – mathematics, astronomy, cosmology, calendars. This could be a fifth.'

'You said there were once thousands,' said Remi.

'Hundreds of thousands, is a better estimate,' he said. 'But there were two problems. The codices were painted on a fabric made from the bark of a wild fig tree called *Ficus glabrata*. The fabric was folded into pages and the pages painted with a white mixture like stucco. That gave the Maya white pages they could write on. They were better than papyrus, almost as good as paper.'

'What were the problems?'

'One was the climate. Most of Mayan country was humid jungle. When books get wet, they rot. Some codices were buried in tombs – some at Copán, some at Altun Ha in Belize, some at Uaxactún Guytan. The fig-bark fabric rotted, leaving little piles of painted stucco fragments too small and delicate ever to be pieced together. But the biggest problem arrived in ships.'

'The Spanish conquest,' said Sam.

'Mainly the priests. They made a point of destroying anything to do with native religions. Mayan gods looked like devils to them. They burned every book they found and then searched every hiding place so no book could survive. This went on from the beginning of the Mayan conquest in the 1500s until the 1690s, when they took the last cities. That's why only four are left.'

'And now five,' said Remi.

'It's a spectacular find,' said Caine. 'Do you have a place to put it where it will be safe?'

'We do,' said Sam. 'We'll lock it up tight.'

'Good. I'd like to get started on the dating process and then come back tomorrow to start examining the codex. Is that possible?'

'I'd say it's mandatory,' said Sam. 'We're as curious as you are and we can't satisfy our curiosity without you.'

7

La Jolla

The next afternoon, Sam and Remi were waiting when David Caine arrived. They took him into the climate-controlled room, where Remi put on surgical gloves, opened one of the glass cabinets, and set the codex on the table. Caine sat for a moment, staring at the cover. 'Before we begin,' he said, 'the carbon dating is complete on the seeds and husks that were in the wooden bowls and on the wood itself. The samples all had 94.29 per cent of their carbon 14. The wood and the plants died at about the same time, which is four hundred and seventy-six years ago, in 1537.'

'Isn't that sort of late for a classic Mayan?' asked Remi.

'It's well into the end-time of the civilization. Most major classic cities had been abandoned by around 1000 AD. Others stood until the Spanish got to them, beginning around 1524, when Pedro de Alvarado attacked the Maya with a huge army of native allies from Tlaxcala and Cholula. But there were many Mayan kingdoms that took a long time to be conquered. The last few fell in 1697, more than a hundred and fifty years later.'

Remi said, 'So what we found was a high-ranking man who picked up a pot from somewhere near Copán in Honduras. He put a book inside it and set off on foot. He went four hundred miles or so, then climbed all the way up the side of the Tacaná volcano in Mexico and put it in a shrine.'

'I would say it's almost certain that something of that sort happened. Why he did it, we can only guess at this point.'

'Do you have a guess?' asked Sam.

'I think that he was taking an extremely precious book to a secret and remote place to hide it from the Spaniards. Judging from your photographs of the site, you're probably right that it was a small stone shrine. Inside are pictures of Cizin, god of earthquakes and death, who was the bringer of earthquakes. He's the dancing skeleton with the dangling eyeballs.'

'Then what?'

'I'm just guessing, remember. At some point, the shrine was covered by a lava flow from the volcano. It's even possible that he intentionally placed the book in the shrine, knowing the likelihood that it would be covered by lava, believing that a god was giving him a perfect way to seal the book in a safe place.'

'Do you think he would do that?'

Caine shrugged. 'The Mayans had a strong belief in an afterlife in which they would be rewarded or punished. They also believed that the universe was kept in balance by what they did. Much of the knowledge they accumulated in books about astronomy and mathematics was intended to tell them what they should do to keep the universe from spinning out of control and destroying itself like an unbalanced machine. By 1537, this man's universe had been showing signs of coming apart for hundreds of years. There had been terrible droughts from 750 to 900 AD, a series of wars between cities, disease. And then the Spaniards came. Their arrival in 1524 was like the landing of aliens in a horror movie. They carried weapons nobody could fight against or make for themselves. They were bent on destroying what remained of Mayan civilization and killing or enslaving every Mayan person. It was the final curse after a long series of curses. A Mayan – and this was a person of the royal class – would have taken the long view. These are people whose calendar was divided into cycles 5,125 years long. He might have believed that the book he was saving contained information essential to keeping the world intact or rebuilding it in the future.'

'I suppose, then, he wouldn't hesitate to sacrifice himself to save the book.'

Caine said, 'Imagine that powerful, humanlike creatures arrived here in spaceships, killed or enslaved everyone they could find, and then began the process of finding every computer, every book, and burning it. Oops! There goes the history of art, and, after it, every painting. There goes calculus, algebra, even arithmetic. They're burning the books of every religion – all Bibles, the Koran, the Talmud, everything. Did they forget philosophy? Nope, it's all going into the fire. Every poem, every story, ever written? Up in smoke. Physics, chemistry, biology, medicine; the history of the Romans and Greeks, the Chinese, the Egyptians. All gone.'

'What a terrible, sad idea,' Remi said. 'We'd be back in the stone age with no map for the way back here.'

'It also makes me even more curious about the codex,' said Sam. 'What was it that our friend managed to save from the fires? What's in here?'

Caine shrugged. 'That's what's been keeping me awake for two days.'

There was a knock on the door. 'Come in,' Sam called.

Selma entered. 'Am I too late?'

'No,' said Remi. 'Professor David Caine, this is Selma Wondrash, who is kind enough to work with us as our chief researcher. Whatever the subject is, if Selma doesn't know the answer, she knows where it can be found.'

Caine stood and they shook hands. 'Wondrash. It's not a common name. Are you related to the S. I. Wondrash who helped catalog the Inca *quipu*?'

'I am S. I. Wondrash,' she said. 'But the *quipu* project was a long time ago.'

'And there hasn't been much progress in deciphering them since then,' said Caine. 'The strings and knots the Incas used to keep track of things are still incomprehensible to us.'

'I keep hoping somebody will find an old Spanish

document that records what an Inca informant said when he revealed how to interpret the different kinds and colors and lengths of strands in *quipu*.'

'We all do,' said Caine. 'The Spanish burned thousands of *quipu*. There are only a few hundred left, but, thanks to you, we at least know what exists.'

Selma looked down at the codex on the table. 'Meanwhile, we have this.'

'We do,' Caine said. 'Is everyone ready?'

The others all nodded. Caine put on his gloves and carefully opened the first page to reveal a striking painting. Tiny Mayans moved across the page, carrying baskets. They were accompanied by warriors in full-feathered battle regalia, wearing quilted armor, carrying round shields and wooden clubs with obsidian chunks along the edges. They went through plants that seemed to signify jungles. In one place, they passed over what appeared to be mountains, then arrived at a river valley. There were columns of glyphs covering the top third of the page.

'This is amazing,' Caine said. 'The page is a kind of stylized map, a set of directions. It says it leads from Copán to the Motagua River Valley, which is in Guatemala. See this glyph? It's *ya'ax chich*, the Mayan term for "jade".'

'Are those people with the baskets going to find jade?' asked Remi.

'More likely, to trade for it,' said Caine. 'Yes, it's trade.

They're bringing valuable jungle products – bird feathers, jaguar skins, coca – to trade for jade.'

Selma said, 'Jadeite was the most valuable substance in the Americas. The only known sources are Burma, Russia and the Motagua Valley. This appears to show where that is.'

Caine said, 'After the Spanish came, the Mayans stopped going there and never told the Spanish where the jade came from. The Spanish wanted only gold and silver, so the location was forgotten. It was quite a mystery for a long time. Then, in 1952, a hurricane passed over the Motagua Valley, and chunks of jade the size of cars washed out of the hillsides.'

'Then, until 1952, what we're looking at would have been a secret?' asked Sam.

'Absolutely,' said Caine. 'To the Mayans, a very important secret.'

'And this is only the first page,' said Remi.

As Caine turned the pages carefully, they stared in amazement. There were paintings of gods and heroes engaged in epic stories of creation and the end of eras. There was a factual account of the warfare between Tikal and Calakmul in which Copán backed Tikal. Caine deciphered and translated only enough of each set of glyphs to determine its subject.

After about thirty pages, Caine turned a page to see a partial picture. Since the book was folded like an accordion, he could unfold two pages, lay them flat, and unfold two more to make one four-page display. There were paintings of forests, lakes, mountains. And all over the display were tiny pictures of Mayan buildings.

Sam said, 'It looks like a map.' He pointed at a shape jutting out into water. 'That looks like the Yucatán Peninsula.'

There were some buildings on the page that looked bigger than the others. 'What would that be?' asked Sam.

'The glyphs say that's Chichen Itza,' said Caine. 'This on the coast is Zama, the ancient name of Tulum. Down here is Altun Ha, so this section is Belize. Here in Guatemala is Tikal. There's Palenque in Mexico.'

'Are these all places you know?' asked Remi.

'Quite a few of them are – Bonampak, Xlapak, Copán. But there are many more names here. There are a number that I've never seen before. The current estimate is that about sixty per cent of Mayan cities are known and mapped – over a hundred of them. But this shows – what? At least three hundred of the large buildings that seem to be cities? I can see many I've never heard of. And there are lots of other sites that seem to be smaller cities. I'll have to compare them with the current inventory of sites.'

Caine looked at his watch. 'Oh. I can't believe we've been at this for five hours. I have to get back to my office to pick up some things and then get home to start going over the existing sites to see what's not included. Can we take up where we left off tomorrow?'

'Sure,' said Remi.

'I can get here around noon. My classes are all morning seminars tomorrow.'

'We'll see you then,' said Sam. They walked Dr Caine to the door and watched him drive off.

8

La Jolla

At ten the next morning, Sam and Remi were sitting together on the first floor, working at their computers, to try to learn more about various aspects of Mayan civilization. While he was thinking about something he'd read, Sam's eyes moved off the screen to Remi. She wore a jade green linen-and-silk dress that set off her eyes and her hair, and a pair of Manolo Blahnik sandals in bone leather. Zoltán lay at Remi's feet, looking contented. But suddenly the big dog let out a low growl, got up, walked through the house to the big double doors at the front, and stood, watching them expectantly. Remi stood up and followed him, glancing out the window on the way.

'Sam,' she called, 'we've got visitors.'

'Oh?' he said. 'Did Dave Caine come early?'

'It's some people in a black limo.' Sam stood up and was walking toward the doors when the doorbell rang.

Remi answered the door. 'Hello,' she said. 'Can I help you?'

It was a woman, accompanied by three men in dark suits. The woman was very attractive, with deep blue eyes and golden blond hair pulled back into a perfect bun. She was expensively dressed in a blue suit. As she stepped forward and held out her hand, she spoke. 'I'm Sarah Allersby, Mrs Fargo. Remi, isn't it?' Her British accent was distinctly upper class.

'Well, yes,' Remi said. 'Is there something –?'

'Please, call me Sarah. And these gentlemen are my attorneys – Ronald Fyffe, Carlos Escobedo, and Jaime Salazar. May we come in?' Remi stepped back and shook each attorney's hand as the four filed past her into the first floor of the house.

Sam was waiting just inside. 'And I'm Sam Fargo,' he said. 'May I ask what brings you here?'

'Charmed. I hope you don't mind my taking the unusual step of dropping by like this, but it was unavoidable and urgent. I live in Guatemala City, but I happened to be in Los Angeles last night on another matter when I heard the news, and it was too late to call – long after business hours.'

'We're not in business anymore,' Sam said.

'How lucky you are. I'm an amateur archaeologist and collector specializing in Central America, but I still have to attend to mundane responsibilities.'

'What news have you heard?' asked Remi.

'That your find at Volcán Tacaná in Mexico included a precious jar from Copán.' She paused. 'And also a Mayan codex.'

'Interesting,' Sam said, hiding his shock. 'Where could you have heard that?'

She laughed softly. 'If I told people about my confidential sources, they wouldn't be confidential and they'd stop being my sources. They'd hate me.'

'And their sources would hate them,' said Sam.

'And so on,' she said. 'It's a whole ecosystem we have to protect.'

Remi could feel that an awkward moment was stretching into an ordeal, and something about the woman's tone, or scent, was making Zoltán bristle. Remi petted his head to reassure him, and said to her, 'Please come in and sit down.'

Sarah Allersby looked at her watch as she followed Remi into the large open sitting area on the first floor. Sam led the guests to the leather couches arranged around a large glass coffee table near the ocean-facing windows.

'Drink?'

'Tea for all of us, I should guess,' said Sarah. The three lawyers didn't look eager, but she clearly was enforcing her own rule that she always guessed right. Sam sensed that she wanted to get Remi out of the room and start talking business.

Remi walked off for a minute only. When she returned, she said, 'Selma will bring it in when it's ready.' Zoltán had followed her in. As she sat, Zoltán remained at her feet in a sphinxlike pose, his head erect and his ears straight up, his yellow-and-black eyes unblinking. Remi noticed it and scratched the back of his neck, but he remained as he was, his muscles ready to bring him up and into motion. Remi caught Sam's eye.

Sam nodded slightly. He and Remi both knew that with these visitors, Zoltán was on guard. 'This is Zoltán. Don't let him make you uncomfortable. He's very obedient.' He paused. 'What can we do for you, Miss Allersby?'

'I came because I hope you won't mind letting me see what you found on the volcano.' She smiled. 'I mean the codex, of course.'

'We haven't said there was a codex,' said Remi.

Sarah Allersby's eyes moved to one of her attorneys, and Sam and Remi both caught a hint of irritation so fleeting that most people would have wondered if they'd imagined it. 'I'll be perfectly open,' she said. 'Several different confidential sources have confirmed that what you have is, without question, a genuine codex.' She smiled and looked at Remi.

Remi watched her, saying nothing. So did Zoltán.

Sarah persisted. 'While you're being cagey, Dr Caine has made some calls to other academics here and abroad – linguists, archaeologists, historians, geologists, biologists. He's told them what he's seen and what he thinks will be in the rest of the codex. So I know pretty much what you know. He's as good as verified publicly that the find is not a forgery. It's a genuine fifth codex.'

Remi asked, 'Why would any of those people reveal their conversations with Dr Caine to you?'

'I have no illusion that I'm the only one who's been told. I just move faster than most of the others,' said Sarah Allersby. 'I and my family also control a great deal of money for grants and donations to universities. I sometimes let it be known that I'm interested in owning certain things, if they should ever turn up. And of course no matter who owns certain objects, the objects will be kept in museums and universities. It matters a great deal to some people which ones are chosen.'

'Does Dr Caine know that his colleagues are sharing his conversations with you?' asked Remi.

She laughed. 'I wouldn't know that. I assume he has his own patrons and sources of backing for his research and tells them what he wants them to know.' Her smile was almost a smirk. Her blue eyes were especially cold when she spoke to Remi.

Sam could see that Miss Allersby had assumed that she would come in and dazzle him with her beauty while the mousy wife faded into the background somewhere. She hadn't been able to adjust to being the second-best-looking woman in the room, and she didn't like being double-teamed by two questioners. She seemed to will her ego to deflate a little bit. 'I don't flatter myself that I'm the only nonacademic who knows. That's why I came immediately. And I've come such a long way. Can't I please see it? I've already shown you there's no reason for secrecy. The secret is out. And I am someone who genuinely cares about preserving and protecting these irreplaceable treasures and have spent many millions doing it.'

Sam looked at Remi, who nodded slightly. 'All right,' he said. 'But we've got to be very careful with it. Only the first pages have been opened. We can't open more without risking having two surfaces stick together and damaging them. These couple of pages will have to do.'

'Agreed,' she said. 'Where is it?' She looked around the large space with such eagerness that Sam felt uneasy.

'The pot and the codex are in a climate-controlled room,' said Remi. 'It's right down here.' She and Zoltán walked to the door of the room. She unlocked it. 'I'm afraid there's only space for two of you at a time. We can take turns.'

Sarah Allersby said, 'Don't worry. They're not here for that. They don't need to see it.'

She stepped in, Sam followed, and Remi entered and closed the door. Remi put on gloves, went to the cabinet, and produced the pot.

Miss Allersby's eyes widened. 'Incredible. I can see it's in the classic style of Copán.' She looked up at the rows of shelves behind the glass doors like a spoiled child who had been given a gift and grown tired of it already. 'And the codex?'

Sam and Remi exchanged a glance, a mutual question: *Do we really want to do this?* Sam went to the rows of cabinets, unlocked one, and took down the codex. He carried it to the table, and Sarah Allersby's body turned toward it as though it had a magnetism that pulled her only. As Sam set it down, she leaned very close to it – too close.

'Please be careful not to touch it,' Remi said.

Sarah ignored her. 'Open it.'

Sam took a moment to pull the surgical gloves up his wrists so the fingers would be tighter. 'Open it,' Sarah repeated.

Sam lifted the cover to reveal the page about the jade deposits in the Motagua Valley.

'What is that?' asked Sarah. 'Is that jade?'

'We're pretty sure it's a group from a jungle city going to the Motagua Valley to trade for it.'

As they went to the next page, she showed more and more signs of excitement. 'I think this is part of the Popol Vuh,' she said. 'The creation myth and all that. Here are the three feathered serpents. Here are the three sky gods.'

When Sam reached the end of that section, he stopped, closed the book, and lifted it to its place in the glass cabinet, then locked the cabinet. Sarah Allersby took a moment to collect herself, returning slowly from the world of the codex.

They all went back to the couches in the sitting room, where Selma was serving tea and small pastries to the lawyers. As they returned, Selma served Sarah Allersby and the Fargos. Zoltán followed Remi to the couch and sat, watching the four visitors.

'Well, that was a thrill,' Sarah said. 'It's everything I've heard and more. If the rest of it is blank, it's still amazing.' She sipped her tea. 'I would like to make a preemptive offer before this goes any further. Does five million dollars sound fair?'

'We aren't selling anything,' said Remi.

Sarah Allersby bristled. Sam could tell that she had now used the second of her two best weapons to little effect. Her looks had already failed to impress. On rare occasions when that was the case, her family's money almost always restored the proper awe. Remi had passed over the money without comment.

'Why on earth not?'

'It doesn't belong to us, for starters. It belongs to Mexico.'

'Surely you aren't serious. You've already smuggled it all the way here. It's in your house, in your possession. Why would you go to that trouble, risk arrest and imprisonment, if you don't want it?'

Sam said, 'It was an emergency. We did what we could to preserve the find, which was to remove what was portable away from the site before it got carried off by thieves, or the earthquakes and the volcano destroyed it. We also enlisted the local people to protect the shrine. Once we've given the experts a chance to study and preserve the codex, it has to go back to Mexico.'

Sarah Allersby leaned toward him as though she were about to spit. 'Seven million?'

'May I?' asked Fyffe, the British attorney. 'Virtually nobody knows that you have the codex. All you have to do is sign a sale agreement and a nondisclosure agreement and the money will be wired to a bank, or collection of banks, of your choice in the next few hours.'

'We're not selling anything,' said Remi.

'Careful,' said Sarah. 'When I walk out that door, it will mean that we couldn't agree. Since you've demonstrated that you weren't above smuggling it out of Mexico, I have to assume that the true obstacle was that you want a higher price.'

The Mexican lawyer Escobedo said, 'I assure you, this is the best way to proceed. At some point, the Mexican government will take an interest. We can deal with them far better than you can. You've been in the Mexican newspapers. If you have the codex, you must have stolen it from the shrine on Tacaná. If Miss Allersby has it, she can say it came from anywhere – one of her plantations in Guatemala, perhaps. And Tacaná is on the Guatemalan border. A few yards this way or that and transporting the codex becomes perfectly legal.'

Salazar took his turn. 'If you're worried that the codex will be locked away where it won't be studied by scientists, don't be. The codex will be in a museum and scientists will be able to apply for access to it just as they do all over the world. Miss Allersby simply wants to be the legal owner and is willing to protect you from any litigation or government inquiry.'

'I'm very sorry,' Sam said, 'but we can't sell what we don't own. The codex has to go to the Mexican government. I believe there's information in it that might be used by grave robbers, pot hunters and thieves to locate and destroy important sites before archaeologists could ever hope to reach them. We're not rejecting your offer, we're rejecting all offers.'

Sarah Allersby stood and looked at her watch. 'We've got to be going, I'm afraid.' She sighed. 'I made you such a large offer because I didn't want to wait years to buy it from some Mexican institution at auction. But if waiting is necessary, I can do that. At some point, rationality sets in, and bureaucrats realize that a whole new library is better than one old book. Thank you for the tea.'

She turned and in a moment she was out the door. Her lawyers had to hurry to get out and down the sidewalk in time to open the car door for her.

Remi said, 'I have a feeling about her.'

'So do I.'

Zoltán stared out the window at the limousine and growled.

Sam and Remi walked back to the climate-controlled room, put on surgical gloves again, took the pot and the codex and carried them out. They went through the secret door in the bookcase, down the stairs to the lower level of the new firing range. Sam opened the gun cabinet, put the codex on a shelf with the pot, closed the safe, and spun the dial of the lock.

They went back upstairs, and Remi asked Selma, 'Are all the new security systems up and running yet?'

'Yes.'

'Good. But don't sleep here tonight. Arm all the systems and go to your apartment. We're going to have a break-in.'

It was only quarter to eleven, so Sam and Remi drove to the campus of the University of California, San Diego. They found a car park not far from the Anthropology Department, then walked.

As they approached David Caine's office, they saw the door open and a male student leave his office, looking down at a paper and frowning. Caine said to the student, 'Just get the bibliography and notes in shape before you hand it in.' Then he saw the Fargos. 'Sam! Remi! What's up?' He beckoned them into his office and shut the door, then moved piles of books off chairs for them. 'I thought we were going to meet at your house.'

'We had a visit about an hour ago from a woman named Sarah Allersby', said Sam.

'You didn't.'

'You know her?' asked Remi.

'Only by reputation.'

Sam said, 'She's apparently been fed information by at least one of the colleagues you spoke with. She offered us seven million dollars for the codex. She knew what was in it.'

'Oh, no,' he said. 'I only spoke with people I thought I could trust. I never took into account the sort of temptation a person like that can offer.'

'What do you know about her?' asked Remi.

'More than I want to. She's one of a whole class of people who have been filling gigantic houses in Europe and North America with pilfered artifacts for over a hundred years. They used to travel to undeveloped countries in the nineteenth century and take what they wanted. In the twentieth century, they paid galleries huge prices for objects that grave robbers dug up. By buying some, they created a market for more. They couldn't be bothered to wonder what some object really was, where it came from, or how it was obtained. As things stand today, if I were in a hurry to find the most sacred objects in existence, I wouldn't dig for them and I wouldn't search in museums. I'd look in the homes of people in Europe and America whose families have been wealthy for the last hundred or so years.'

'Is that the Allersbys?' asked Remi.

'They're among the worst,' Caine said. 'They've been at it since the British arrived in India. It wasn't even frowned upon until about thirty years ago. Even now, if an object left its country of origin before the United Nations treaty signed in the 1970s, you can do anything you want with it – keep it, sell it, or put it in your garden as a birdbath. That loophole exists because rich people like the Allersbys exerted influence on their countries' governments.'

'Sarah seemed pretty comfortable with the idea that we'd smuggled the codex out of Mexico for sale,' said Remi.

He shook his head. 'It's ironic. I've heard the British tabloids spend a lot of ink on her bad behavior in the Greek islands and the French Riviera. But what she does in Guatemala is worse and it's serious.'

'Why?'

'Guatemala had a civil war between 1960 and 1996. Two hundred thousand people died in that war. A lot of the old Spanish landowning families sold out and moved to Europe. The ones who bought those huge stretches of land were mostly foreigners. One of them was Sarah Allersby's father. He bought a gigantic place called the Estancia Guerrero from the last heir, who had been living high in Paris and gambling in Monaco. When Sarah turned twenty-one, her father settled a lot of property on her – buildings in several European capitals, businesses, and the Estancia Guerrero.'

'It sounds pretty routine for rich families,' said Remi.

'Well, suddenly this twenty-one-year-old girl just out of school in England became one of the most important people in Guatemala. Some people predicted that she would be a progressive force, someone who would stand up for the poor Mayan peasants. The opposite happened. She visited her holdings in Guatemala and liked the place so much she moved there. That is, she liked Guatemala just the way it was. She became part of the new oligarchy, the foreigners who own about eighty per cent of the land, and an even higher proportion of everything else. They exploit the peasants as much as the old Spanish landowners they replaced.'

'That's disappointing.'

'It was to everyone except the peasants, who can't be surprised anymore: meet the new boss – just like the old boss. She's got a great hunger for Mayan artifacts but no love at all for the living Mayan people who work in her fields and her businesses for practically nothing.'

'Well,' said Sam, 'obviously, we're not selling her anything. Where do you think we should go from here?'

'We should do something about my colleagues. I need to know who is honest and who isn't. I'd like to tell each of the people I've told about the codex a different lie about what's in the rest of it and see which lie Sarah Allersby acts on.'

'I'm afraid it's too late for that,' said Remi. 'When we asked about her sources, she wouldn't answer. I'm sure she'll be expecting us to try to find out.'

'What we've got to do is try to pursue two paths at once,' Caine said.

'What are the two paths?' Sam asked.

'The codex has to be examined, transcribed and translated. We have to know what it says.'

'That's hard to argue with,' said Remi.

'The other line of inquiry is a bit trickier. At some point, we've got to find out whether the codex is fiction or a description of the world as it was in those days. The only way to do that is to go down to Central America and verify that what it says is true and accurate.'

'You mean to visit one of the sites it describes?' asked Sam.

'I'm afraid so,' Caine said. 'I had been hoping to lead a scientific expedition to one of the sites that is mentioned only in this codex. But we're two weeks into the spring quarter, with nine more weeks to go. I can't leave my classes now. And it takes time to get a big expedition together. With Sarah Allersby involved, time is scarce. The longer we wait, the more difficult she'll make it. She's capable of setting people up to follow any expedition we organize, getting us arrested, doing anything to get us to sell the codex or make sure we can't have access to it.'

'We'll be the expedition,' Remi said. 'Sam and me.'

'What?' said Sam. 'I thought you didn't want to travel for a while.'

'You heard him, Sam. There are two things that have to be done. Neither of us knows how to read the eight hundred and sixty-one glyphs in the Mayan writing system, and we don't know the underlying language. What's it called?'

'Ch'olan,' said Caine.

'Right,' she said. 'Ch'olan. How's your Ch'olan?'

'I see what you mean,' Sam said. 'Dave, see if you can find a site that fits the criteria – mentioned only in this codex, never explored, and small enough that we don't need a big group that will attract attention. I'd like to slip in there, find it, and get out.'

9

La Jolla

Early the next morning, Sam, Remi and Zoltán arrived at the house above Goldfish Point before the electricians and carpenters, who were still working on the fourth floor. As they started up the walk, Selma opened the front door and came out to meet them. She put her hands on her hips. 'The police just left.'

Remi said, 'So we had visitors last night?'

'Yes,' said Selma. 'The burglars tried the front doors but couldn't get them to budge. Banging on them and trying to jimmy the latches caused the steel shutters on the first and second floors to come down automatically. The silent alarm from the outdoor surveillance cameras and motion sensors had already alerted the police. The cameras got only the images of two figures dressed in black with ski masks.'

'Were you hoping to see their best work?' Remi asked.

'No,' Sam said. 'But I'm wondering if they might not have suspected in advance that this place wasn't going to be easy.'

'Oh?' said Selma. 'That implies that they'd been here before.'

Sam shrugged. 'If I were to guess, I'd say that you probably served them tea yesterday. I don't mean Sarah Allersby came back with a crowbar. I mean that she just may have read us wrong – thought that if someone showed us that it's dangerous to have a valuable artifact around, then we'd jump at her offer.'

'One more thing,' said Selma. 'Dave Caine left a message on the house phone last night. He wants to meet with you this morning about your next little trip.'

Two hours later, they were in the climate-controlled room with David Caine. They stood around the work-table, comparing the map in the codex with a topographic map on a computer screen. Caine placed a small arrow pointing to a spot in the jungle. 'This site meets our criteria. It's not included in any inventory of known Mayan sites. It isn't large enough to be a major city. It has the advantage of being in an area of the Guatemalan high-lands that's sparsely populated and remote.'

'What do you think it is?' asked Remi.

'The glyphs say it's a sacred pool. I believe it's a cenote – a hole in the underlying limestone bedrock caused by the action of water.'

'Like a sinkhole?'

'Exactly. Water was an extremely precious commodity to the Mayans, and it became more so in the late classic period. You would think water would be plentiful on the floor of a jungle, but it isn't. And after the

Mayans had cut and burned miles of trees to clear fields for agriculture, the climate got hotter and drier. During the late period, many cities depended heavily on cenotes as a water source. We've even found man-made cisterns they dug and plastered at El Mirador that were imitation cenotes, with artificial streams leading to them for catching water.'

Sam said, 'You want us to look for a pool of water?'

'Cenotes were more than that. They were doorways to the underworld. Chac, the god of rain and weather, lived down there, among other places. You have to understand that these were people who believed that what they did kept the universe operating correctly. If you wanted rain, you would throw sacrifices into a cenote where the gods would get them.'

'And this is the best site?'

'There are new cities on this map. Either they're imaginary or lost, we don't know which. But you can't go down there with a huge crew and try to excavate or even map a city without months of preparation. And if you did, it would compromise the site and expose it to looters. A cenote can be hidden or overgrown, but it's something you can verify without attracting too much attention. There. I've just given you all the reasons why it's a good choice.'

Remi said, 'I sense there are reasons why it's not.'

'You're right,' he said. 'It's near a vast piece of land owned by a foreign landlord. It's called the Estancia Guerrero.'

'Sarah Allersby?' said Remi.

'Yes,' he said. 'It's an unfortunate coincidence. But anywhere in Guatemala, we would be on or near one of these big estates. They occupy hundreds of square miles, much of it uncultivated.'

'Maybe not so unfortunate,' said Sam. 'While she's trying to get her hands on the codex, she won't be on her land, causing trouble for us.'

'I doubt that she spends much time on the land, in any case. She leads a very active social, political and business life in Guatemala City.'

'Sounds good,' said Sam. 'While we're gone and you're working on the codex, we'll keep in touch. Selma and her assistants, Pete and Wendy, are ready to offer you as much help as you'd like. Selma you already know. Pete and Wendy are young, but both have plenty of history and archaeology experience.'

Caine looked down at the codex on the table. 'Selma told me about the burglary.'

'It hardly deserves that name,' Sam said.

'I'm wondering if it's safe to keep the codex here while you're out of the country.'

'Do you have any better ideas?' asked Remi.

'I was wondering if you'd let me look into the possibility of keeping the codex on campus.'

'Normally, there wouldn't be a problem with keeping it at our house,' said Remi, 'but there's still remodeling going on upstairs, with workmen coming and going all day, and now Sarah Allersby and her amateur burglars know where the codex is . . .' She paused. 'Would the university be safer?'

'University campuses are full of valuable things – supercomputers, famous works of art, experimental devices of every kind,' said Caine. 'Besides, the university has a few things you don't – like a police force.'

'That sounds like a good idea,' said Sam. 'Look into the possibility of locking it up on campus. If you find it's practical, we'll do it. If not, we can rent a joint safe-deposit box in a bank and you can work there.'

'Good,' said Caine. 'I'll talk to my dean and let you know. When can you leave for Guatemala?'

'Tomorrow,' said Sam. 'We'd like to get there, verify the site, and get back here.'

'If you do, then maybe we can begin to organize a large team to find one of the big cities on the map this summer. I'd like you to consider joining that team. There's nobody I'd rather have with me.'

'We'll consider it,' said Remi, 'after we finish our scouting mission.'

Sam and Remi spent the rest of the day preparing for their trip to Guatemala. They packed, arranged to have the proper scuba gear and wet suits waiting for them, and planned each step of the journey. In the midst of their preparations, Selma came in. 'I've got the licenses you asked for.'

'What licenses?' asked Remi.

'For carrying concealed firearms in Guatemala. These are copies, but the originals will be waiting at your hotel in Guatemala City. It's concealed carry only, by the way. Wearing a gun openly is frowned upon. I guess after their civil war, it's intimidating.'

'Thanks, Selma,' said Remi.

'I've also transferred GPS maps of the Alta Verapaz region of Guatemala to your satellite phones. You should memorize the coordinates of the site because I didn't want to program that in. I did include the numbers of the US Embassy and consulate in Guatemala City and the local police. There has been a lot of crime in the area recently and sometimes Americans look like good people to kidnap for ransom.'

'We'll be careful,' said Remi.

'Please do. Don't take offense, but you two even look rich. I'm glad to see you're packing the clothes you wore doing relief work in Mexico. Keep your equipment invisible.'

'Thanks for the reminder,' said Sam.

'One more thing,' Selma said. 'Dave Caine says the university has assigned him a good place to work on the codex. There's a real, full-scale safe in the library's archival department and a spare room beside it, where he can work. When he's done each day, he can lock the codex in the safe again.'

'That should do fine,' Sam said.

Remi said, 'Now it's our turn to tell *you* to be careful.'

'That's right,' said Sam. 'If either of you is watched or followed, don't go to the university. Drive to the police station.'

'Don't worry,' she said. 'Have a successful trip. Call frequently, and come back soon. I promise, Zoltán will think he's on vacation.'

In twelve hours, Sam and Remi were on a flight heading toward Guatemala City.

10

Guatemala City

Sam and Remi disembarked in Guatemala City and went through customs. They were about to leave the airline terminal when Remi's satellite phone rang. She answered, and said, 'Hi, Selma. You must have tracked our plane.'

'Of course. We've found something amazing and I thought you should know.'

'What is it?'

'Do you remember a sort of lump inside the cover of the codex?'

'I do,' Remi said. 'It's sort of a rectangle shape. I figured it was a patch.'

'It's a sheet of parchment, folded, and then placed under the outer layer and covered with the fig-bark fabric. David and I removed it two hours ago. It's a letter, written in black ink, in Spanish. It says, "To all of my countrymen, blessings. This book and other books of the Mayan people concern their history and their observations about the natural world. They have nothing to do with the devil. They must be preserved as a way to understand our charges, the Mayan people".'

'Who's it from?' asked Remi.

'That's the surprise. It's signed 'Fra Bartolomé de Las Casas, Prior of Rabinal, Alta Verapaz.' '

'Las Casas? *The* Las Casas?'

'Yes – the man who convinced the Pope that Indians were rational beings with souls and had rights. He practically invented the idea of human rights. Dave Caine is beside himself with excitement.'

'Does the paper have a date on it?'

'Yes. January 23, 1537. We may not know everything about the codex yet, but this is the second verification of the year it was hidden. We think Las Casas was trying to give the book safe passage, maybe while the man you found took it to that shrine on the volcano.'

'It's fantastic,' said Remi. 'Be sure to make a copy of it.'

'Well, get on with your trip. I just wanted you to know about this. And by the way, your vehicle is parked in the hotel lot under the name Señor de La Jolla. I bought it online, so you'd better look it over before you leave civilization.'

'We'll do that,' said Sam. 'We'll talk soon.'

Sam and Remi checked into the hotel suite Selma had reserved and collected the documents and the equipment that were waiting for them. Then they went outside to the parking lot behind the building and found the car. It was a ten-year-old Jeep Cherokee with chips and scratches that showed it had originally been red but at some point had been painted over olive drab with a paintbrush. They started it, drove it around the block for a few minutes with the windows closed so Sam's engineer ears could pick up any sounds that might mean trouble, and then opened the hood and checked the belts, hoses, battery and fluid levels. When Sam had crawled under and looked it over, he stood again. 'Not pretty, but not bad either.' The backseat and the floor behind it provided plenty of space for all the equipment they intended to bring. They stopped at a station, filled the tank, bought two metal five-gallon cans, and filled them too.

That evening, they marked their maps to plot a route up 14N toward Cobán, in the north-central part of the Verapaz district, and then on to Xuctzul in the Río Candelária region.

Early in the morning, they loaded their gear, their dive equipment, and the large backpacks that held a small cache of clean clothes and supplies. Each of them also carried a pair of Smith & Wesson M&P nine-millimeter pistols, one in a backpack pocket with six loaded seven-round, single-stack magazines, and the other in a bellyband under a loose shirt.

As the old car moved along the road, it seemed always to be laboring. Alta Verapaz ranged in elevation from one thousand to nine thousand feet. At times, the car seemed to grind upward as though it were dragging itself up by a rope coiled around its axle. At others, the car careened downward while Sam fought for control. They were able to make snack and bathroom breaks in the small towns along the way. Remi, whose Spanish had been getting plenty of practice, used these opportunities to ask about the road ahead. On one of the stops Sam said, 'What do you think of our adventure so far?'

Remi replied, 'I'm glad we just spent weeks climbing a volcano and then walking from town to town, doing heavy labor.'

'Why?'

'Because now my body knows that no matter how hard this ride is, I should enjoy every second of it because, when it ends, life could get a whole lot harder.'

At Cobán, they spent a night at a small hotel, and slept deeply. They were up early to prepare to leave for Xuctzul. The people they met seemed to be a mixture of Mayan farmers and Hispanic visitors. They knew that the farther from big cities they went, the more likely they would reach places where people not only didn't speak English but didn't speak Spanish either. When they were back in the Cherokee, they found the roads got narrower and rougher by the mile.

After another hour, Remi looked at the map and then her watch. 'We should be in Xuctzul soon.'

Five minutes later, they drove through the village. It was only about a hundred yards long.

Sam and Remi stepped out of the car at the edge of the village and stood in the gravel road. They looked at each other. The silence was profound. Off in the distance, a dog barked, and the spell was broken. A few people came out of buildings and looked in their direction as though the arrival of a car was an occasion for curiosity. One by one, they lost interest and went back to their homes.

The gravel road turned into a rutted cart path.

'I hope the Jeep is up to this. At least there seems to be a trail, but we're in for a bumpy ride,' said Sam.

'I hope what trail we have is going in the right direction. I'm not looking forward to blazing one through the jungle,' Remi replied. 'I was hoping the machetes were just for show.' She looked up at the sky, then at Sam. 'It's a long time before we run out of daylight – at least six hours.'

Each took a drink of water from a canteen, took out a machete, put it where it would be easy to reach, and then they began to drive up the trail.

For a time, Sam would periodically check his satellite phone's GPS to be sure they were still heading in the direction they intended. The trail was winding and required steady climbing as it took them into the highlands of Alta Verapaz. Before darkness came they stopped and pitched their tiny tent, with its floor and zippered netting to keep the insects out. They cooked some dehydrated rations on a small fire and then slept. In the morning, they searched for water and found a couple of gallons that had been caught in a half-hollowed log. They filled two plastic containers, put in their military-grade purification tablets, and secured them in the back of the Jeep.

For the next five days they followed the same routine, checking the GPS each day to be sure they were on course. As they drove farther from the populated areas, they were surrounded by squads of chattering monkeys in the trees overhead, flocks of birds flying over at dawn and dusk, and many smaller birds that were invisible in the dense foliage calling out to one another. On the third day, the trail took them down from the crest of a high hill into a valley surrounded by smaller hills, the trail opening up to a surface that had been leveled by human activity.

There were big trees growing in places, and fallen leaves had turned to a thick humus and then become dirt, and then smaller plants had died, rotted, and then been overshadowed by taller neighbors. And even those trees had died, fallen and rotted, several long generations of them. But the strip of land where this had happened was still flat. Remi and Sam looked at the low hills that rose on their right and then the ones on their left. They got out of the Jeep.

Sam put his compass on a level spot, raised its mirror, and used it to sight along the space at the foot of the hills on their right. 'Perfectly straight,' he said.

He paced off the width of the flat space, from one hill to the one opposite. 'Fifty of my paces,' he said. 'Let's try it farther along. I'll grab the pack with the machetes and folding shovels.'

Sam and Remi walked two hundred yards, then set the compass again and sighted along the foot of the next hill, and the one beyond it. Sam paced the width of the flat strip.

'I assume it's fifty,' said Remi.

'Of course.'

'What do you think the hills were?'

'From what I've read, they could have been anything. They used to put up buildings on top of the earlier ones.'

'Which do you prefer?' she said. 'Would you rather dig down below our feet to establish that it's paved, or climb up there and dig to see if the hill is a building that was overgrown by the jungle?'

'If we're way up there, we might be able to see for a distance,' he said.

'That's what I think too,' she said. 'It might be nice to look above the treetops, for a change.'

They left their packs, took their machetes and folding shovels, and climbed. The hill they chose was the center one on the right side. It appeared to be the highest. The hill was steep, rising to a height of about a hundred and twenty-five feet, and its slopes were thick with plants and small trees, which they used as handholds.

When they reached the apex, Sam unfolded the shovel and began to dig. After about four shovelfuls, his blade hit stone. He used his machete to test a few spots nearby and the sound was the same. Remi walked a few yards to get past a thicket of saplings, growing on the top of the building. 'Don't get lost,' Sam said.

'Come here,' she said. 'You've got to see this.'

He took the machete and shovel with him and went through the thicket to find Remi, looking out over the tops of the jungle trees. From here, the canopy looked solid, but there were a few places where it was sparse. She pointed down at the level area they had left. 'It's like a wide road. It starts here and runs between the hills in a straight line. But it runs only a few hundred yards.'

'And over there,' Sam said, 'another flat strip comes in at an angle and meets it.'

'There's another over there,' said Remi. 'Five – no, six – strips, coming in from six directions to meet at one spot.'

'It looks like an asterisk with a high wall circling the center,' Sam said.

'You could fly over this area a hundred times and not really see it,' Remi said. 'The trees make everything seem natural. The shapes are rounded off, but I'll bet this hill we're standing on is a pyramid.'

'It's something big anyway,' Sam said. 'Well, I guess we know where we have to go.'

'Of course,' she said. 'The place where the roads meet.'

When Sam and Remi reached the bottom of the steep hill, Remi said, 'This is creepy.'

'What's creepy?'

'You know they're not hills, they're huge buildings covered with dirt and plants. And these trees around us would be the only things that aren't creepy except that they're growing in the middle of this road. I feel like the people who lived here are watching us.'

'Trust me, they're not.' He looked over his shoulder. 'Nope. Not one ghost. But, just in case, let's leave the Jeep here.'

As they walked, Remi said, 'Look at those trees. The cover was all pretty much the same until we got here. Now look. The trees are all in a straight line.'

Sam stood beside her and sighted along the flat strip, where trees of all sizes and many species ran along the center in a line. He stopped, shrugged off his pack, and began to dig a hole in line with the trees. The dirt was a rich, composted loam that came up easily. Shortly, he had a hole three feet wide and about three feet deep. 'Take a look,' he said, and stepped out of the hole.

Remi jumped in, looked down, and used her machete to probe the surface. 'It's V-shaped and has a stone lining. It looks like an irrigation ditch.'

Sam looked around him, turning his body slowly. 'I think it might be something else.'

'What?'

'Think back. Dave said that whatever else was going on in the Mayan world during the late classic period, it was made worse by droughts – two hundred years of them at least.'

'What do you think this was?'

'I think this flat space wasn't a road. The Mayans had no wheeled carts, or tame animals to pull them, so why make it fifty paces wide? And it doesn't go anywhere. It looks like a plaza, except there are six of them in all directions. I think this place was designed to collect rainwater.'

'Of course,' she said. 'Both sides have a subtle slope down to the groove in the center and the groove would direct the water where they wanted it.'

'And that would explain why there are six strips leading inward from all sides. The place where they meet is the catch basin,' Sam said. 'The six strips aren't roads. They're for catching rain and keeping it from washing away and sinking into the ground.'

'Let's go see if we're right,' said Remi. They hurried along the strip toward the spot where all six converged. At times, the brush and saplings came together to make their progress difficult. Here and there, the surface of the strip was bare even of leaves, cleared by some inundation during the rainy season.

At last, they came to the end. The strip ran to the foot of an ancient stone wall about fifteen feet high. The V-shaped ditch led to an opening in the bottom of the wall, where there was a hole about ten inches wide. They walked around the circular wall and saw that each of the other five strips met the wall in the same way, bringing the water in through small openings at its foot. They found that the wall was not a circle with a gap in it for a door or gate. It was a spiral, so that the circular wall stretched for a full three hundred and sixty degrees, and then continued ten degrees past the beginning spot so it overlapped for about ten feet to form a narrow, curved corridor ending in an entrance. Sam and Remi sidestepped along the corridor and found themselves inside the circular wall. In the center was a pool of water.

They stepped to the edge and looked down. The pool was quite clear, about thirty feet deep. The bottom received no direct sunlight, at least not after the sun was low. The high stone enclosure around the pool included a walkway near the top that could be reached by a flight of steps.

'Why do you suppose they built a wall?' asked Remi.

'I don't know,' said Sam. 'Maybe during the last days of the city they needed to protect their water. Maybe it was the last line of defense if the city was taken. You could do worse than control the water supply in a siege. And, look, this place is only about thirty feet wide. It would be easy to defend. The walls are about six feet thick at the bottom.' He walked along the wall and picked up a loose rock, then looked across the enclosure. 'This rock seems to be a plug. The other holes have fitted stones blocking them too. That would protect the water from poison.'

'I think it's time to let Selma and Dave know that we found it,' said Remi.

'You're right,' said Sam. 'Let's take a few pictures and send them first thing so Dave can tell us what we've found.'

Remi took pictures of the well, the pool, the curved entryway, and then stood on the battlement and took pictures in every direction. She added them to the pictures she had taken from the pyramid and on the strip, and sent them. Then she waited a minute and called Selma.

'Selma here. Fire away.'

'We've found it. We're on the site, and I've just sent you some pictures. Tell Dave Caine that the map is right. There's a pool of water here with a stone margin around it and a high wall above it. It's clear, and it seems to be quite deep – thirty feet or more.'

'What are those flat areas I'm seeing? Roads?'

'We think they're surfaces built to catch the rain and direct it here to the pool. They are all slightly tilted toward the center and they go only a couple of hundred yards.'

Sam stood close to Remi and said, 'We also think the hills along the sides of the strips are buildings – one of them is quite large.'

'So the site could be a city?'

'Let's just say they invested a lot of labor on architecture,' said Sam.

'You've accomplished your mission,' Selma said. 'Congratulations. Well done. Are you coming home?'

'Not just yet,' Remi replied. 'I think we'll dive the pool tomorrow morning and see what's down there. After carrying a scuba rig through a dry jungle, I want to make use of it.'

'I can't blame you,' said Selma. 'I'll forward the pictures to David Caine right away, along with your description.'

'Good,' said Sam. 'We'll talk to you soon.'

As they hung up, Sam said, 'We need to get the rest of the gear here. Do you want to drive the Jeep down or are you still worried about the ghosts?'

'Let's leave the Jeep where it is and bring the gear. It shouldn't take more than a couple of trips with the other pack and the dive equipment.'

They pitched their small tent in the enclosure around the pool, collected firewood in the nearby forest, and built a fire to boil a pot of water for their dehydrated food. After they'd eaten, they used the last hour of light to photograph the site from the nearest hills.

As they were about to go to sleep, Sam's phone buzzed. 'Hello?'

'Sam! It's Dave Caine.'

'Hi, Dave,' Sam said. Then he put the phone on speaker.

'The pictures are fantastic. You've proven the codex is an accurate rendering, not a myth or vague historical rumor. From the looks of the place, it could have been a ceremonial center. The stone around it seems to be limestone, and the crumbling by the pool makes that seem even more likely. A sinkhole gets bigger as the limestone dissolves in the water.'

'We'll get a closer look tomorrow when we dive.'

'Be prepared for a sight,' Caine said. 'The Mayans believed that everything depended on their relationships with a complicated pantheon of gods. They will almost certainly have tossed valuables into the pool as sacrifices to Chac, the rain god.'

'Whatever else went wrong here, it wasn't because of a lack of water.'

'We'll be waiting to hear.'

'Good night.'

11

Guatemala

Sam and Remi woke at dawn, and, as soon as they'd had breakfast, began to prepare for exploring the pool. They put on their dive equipment. Each had an underwater flashlight, a net bag and a dive knife.

'I can't wait to get down there,' Remi said.

'I'm pretty curious myself,' Sam said. 'Don't get carried away. Remember the buddy system. Stay close no matter what's down there.'

'Agreed,' she said. 'I may lose my enthusiasm if it's a pile of skeletons.'

'Ready?'

'Yes.'

They lowered their masks and put their mouthpieces in, then slipped into the water. The water was cold and surprisingly clear. Now that the sun was rising higher, it shone deeper into the pool's depths.

In a short time, they reached the bottom, which was all bare gray limestone. Finding nothing like the objects David Caine had told them to expect, they widened their search, shining their flashlights around them. Sam found a disk, lifted it and brushed the limestone dust off it, and saw that it was made of green jade and was heavily carved. He showed Remi, and bagged it.

Remi caught a glint of something to her left, touched Sam's arm, and moved in that direction. When she did, she could tell that going that way was easier than it should be, as though there was a faint current. She moved beyond the circle of light from above into an area that was dark.

The first object she found was a wide bracelet made of gold. She held it up so Sam could see, and he nodded. They moved along the limestone bed, picking up objects as they went. There were more carved objects of jade and, farther on, more pieces made of gold. There were disks, masks, necklaces, ear plugs, bracelets, flat chest ornaments.

They continued picking up objects for a time, and then Sam touched Remi's arm and pointed. The circle of light that had been directly above them at the start was now about a hundred feet behind them. They had moved along, picking up the objects they'd seen, and now they'd drifted farther than they'd thought.

Together, they swam back toward the opening, bringing their net bags with them. When they reached the light, they slowly floated upward toward it, then broke the silvery surface. They took off their masks and held on to the side of the pool. Sam lifted his net bag to the deck above them, then Remi's. Next, he pulled himself on to the stone and held out his hand to Remi so he could pull her up.

'That was a lot of fun,' she said. 'You just dive down and pick up things where they threw them.'

'It reminds me of an Easter egg hunt.'

'There's a bit of a current down there, though. The jewelry and things had all been moved downstream.'

'If this place was abandoned at the end of the classic period, everything has been down there a while. A bit of a current can make a difference in a thousand years.'

'I'll bet some of the jewelry moved out of sight as it fell,' she said.

'That's possible. When the people looked down and the gifts were gone, I'll bet they thought the gods had accepted them and been pleased.'

They laid out all their finds on the limestone surface and photographed them, then sent the pictures to Selma. They secured the finds in a zippered bag, placing them in Sam's pack.

'We haven't found everything that's down there,' Remi said. 'Don't you want to dive again this afternoon?'

'Whatever this place is – city, fort, ceremonial center – we're not going to find everything or learn everything about it in one trip. The archaeologists will be at it for years. The best we can do is verify what we can and get out.'

'You're right,' said Remi. 'This is about the codex, not about the two of us finding all the treasures in Guatemala.'

'I think we should spend the rest of today and tomorrow mapping, measuring and photographing the complex. The next day, we should get out of here before we run low on supplies.'

'There are tapirs in the jungle. I can make you a nice tapir sandwich.'

'I'm afraid that in another day tapir will start to sound good.'

After changing, they walked the length of each flat strip of land. It was nearly evening when they found a pair of stone pillars at the end of the third strip, placed like gateposts. They were about eight feet tall and carved, one of them a male figure, with the feathered headdress, shield and war club of a king, and the other a female, in a dress, with a basket at her feet and a jug in her hands. There were Mayan glyphs in all the spaces around the two figures. Remi photographed the two from every angle, and sent the photographs to Selma.

She looked up from her phone. 'We're losing the sun. I'll take a couple of flash pictures just to be sure the writing is clear.'

She took two flash photographs of each pillar, and then Sam grabbed her arm and pointed. 'Remi, look!'

Up the hill, on the trail that Sam and Remi had followed to reach this site, they could see a line of men approaching. There seemed to be about fifteen of them, and they were still a quarter mile off but coming down the last gradual slope before the ruins. 'Uh-oh,' she said. 'I guess the flash was a bad idea.'

'I don't know. Certainly not as bad as leaving the Jeep out in the open for anyone to see,' he said. 'I can't tell if they've seen us, and I don't know if they're friendly or not. Maybe we can get back to the cenote and out of sight before they get here. That way, we can avoid finding out.'

They began to trot, moving steadily toward the shelter of a stand of trees that had grown up in the center of the strip. As they did, Remi looked back. One of the men had stopped on the hill and was bringing a rifle up to his shoulder. 'Sam! Run!'

There was the crack of a bullet as it passed over their heads, and, about a second later, the sound of the rifle shot reached their ears. The next sound was the explosion of the Jeep, a gasoline fireball lighting the evening sky. Sam and Remi were running hard now, weaving to keep the trees and brush between themselves and the men. They had the advantage of a level surface and a clear path, where they could sprint without fear of tripping, while the men on the slope had to move along the hillside at an angle to avoid building up too much speed and tumbling down.

Sam glanced over his shoulder as a second man stopped and shouldered his rifle. 'Another one. Take cover!' They both went low and ducked behind a cluster of trees. There was another shot, and the bullet pounded into one of the trees, sending a shower of bark chips in all directions. Sam peered around the trunk and saw the man adjusting his telescopic sight. 'Go!'

Sam and Remi ran, working their way up to a full sprint as they approached the high wall surrounding the cenote. They ran around it to the far side and between the two layers of overlapping wall into the entryway. Sam began to pile loose stones in the narrow way to block it while Remi went to their backpacks and retrieved their four pistols, spare magazines and boxed ammunition. Each of them checked to be sure the guns were loaded.

'I can't believe this,' Remi said. 'Who could they be?'

'Nobody we want to know. They seem to have tracked us, following our trail, then opened fire as soon as they saw us.'

'Who can they think we are?'

'Future dead people.' He put his arm around her and gave her a hug. 'Let's see if we can use this wall to stay alive.'

'I'll go up to the walkway and see what they're up to.'

'Keep your head low,' he said.

She pulled her baseball cap lower on her head. 'Unfortunately, we've been in these situations before.'

'If we live through this one –'

She put her finger on his lips. 'Shh. I know, bubble baths and spa treatments. We've already made each other all the promises we need.' She took a pair of pistols and climbed to the walk along the top of the wall, found her way to a spot where the wall had crumbled a bit and left a small dip, then rose enough to survey the strip of land the men were approaching.

Sam watched her bring her arm up to rest in the chink in the wall and begin to think through aiming her pistol. He had seen her do that before at competitions. Sam had been a respectable shot since the days when a member of a highly secret force had spent a month at a covert base instructing him in close-range shooting and sniper techniques. But Remi was in a different league. She had been shooting competitively since she was twelve, a champion for whom the term 'nail driving' was not a figure of speech.

Sam stood below her and spoke quietly. 'Get down, and stay there until you hear shooting.'

Sam moved to the entryway, climbed over the barrier he'd built, sidestepped along the ten-foot overlap in the walls, and ran to the nearest stand of trees. He moved through the trees beside the level strip, getting closer to the space where the men would pass if they approached the walled pool. As he went, he studied the places he passed, aware that soon he would be running past them in the other direction. He took a position in the thick brush within an arm's length of the strip but outside the causeway, where the plants had grown in fully.

The men came at a run, carrying their rifles across their chests. They ran like they were chasing game, not like men who were about to meet an armed adversary.

Sam crouched and waited. He had estimated fifteen men, but he could see only twelve. They wore khaki pants and short-sleeved civilian shirts and T-shirts. A few of them carried bolt-action hunting rifles with scopes – probably 4 power, because, in these thick jungles, long shots across open space had to be rare. There were two men carrying shotguns, a weapon that probably put food in their bellies. Two had pistols in holsters, and the others carried assault rifles that Sam identified as American AR-15s, probably weapons that had found their way here during the Civil War.

The man closest to Sam carried a hunting rifle. He raised it and took aim at the top of the wall around the pool. Sam was sure the man couldn't see Remi, but he was getting ready for her to stick her head up.

A man who carried only a pistol stood by a tree and shouted in English, 'We know you're in there. Come out now and we'll make it easier for you.'

Sam turned his head away from the men and called into the hills, 'We mean you no harm. Go away.'

Three of the men half turned to see if someone had gotten behind them, and one turned around entirely, his gun ready.

The spokesman said, 'We'll never go away. Come out and we'll let *you* go away.'

Sam could hear the bad news in the man's voice. These men thought they had found very easy prey, an American couple, undoubtedly unarmed and helpless. They were probably already estimating the ransom money. And even if they got it, they'd kill them both.

Sam aimed his pistol at the nearest one, the man pointing his rifle at the top of the wall, waiting for a target to appear. The spokesman waved an arm, and the men moved forward toward the wall. Sam began to move with them to avoid being cut off from the entrance.

The man near him sensed something and swung his rifle toward Sam and Sam shot him in the chest, then dived into the low area beyond the brush. The man fell down, unconscious and gravely wounded. The others had seen him fall, and each fired in the direction he guessed the shot might have come from. Only two of them guessed right, and Sam's thicket was peppered with bullets.

When Sam looked up, he saw that another man had fallen, one of the few carrying AR-15s. Remi must have shot him while the others were firing wildly, having picked him out as a high priority.

The leader trotted over to the man's body, took the rifle and the man's pack. He aimed the rifle at the top of the wall, but Remi kept down, knowing the men all expected her to pop up and fire again.

But Sam had a new problem. A man with a rifle was walking toward his thicket to see if Sam's body was lying there or if he needed to be finished off. Now the man's feet were breaking sticks in the thicket. Sam located the sound and fired three times. The man's rifle went off, and Sam heard him fall. Sam crawled to him, his pistol ready, and found him lying, with an entry wound in his forehead. Sam took the rifle, cycled the bolt, pulled himself to the edge of the thicket, and pushed the brush aside with the barrel.

A man with a shotgun was moving along the foot of the wall. Sam aimed and fired, and the man fell dead. Sam cycled the bolt again and searched for another target. There was a man with a scoped rifle on a sling, climbing a tree so he could get a vantage into the walled enclosure. Sam aimed and fired, and the man went limp and fell ten or twelve feet to the ground. He wasn't moving.

Sam cycled the bolt again and realized that after one more shot he would be out of ammunition. He crawled toward the body of the man he'd taken the rifle from. But, as he did, another man spotted him and cried out to the others. Sam was out of time. He fired, took the rifle with him, and ran into the jungle. He didn't stop, circling toward the walled enclosure around the pool. He couldn't hear any running footsteps behind him. As he ran, he removed the bolt from the rifle and tossed it into an impenetrable patch of low plants. A hundred feet on, he threw the rifle into another patch, and kept moving.

He came around behind the enclosure far from the entryway and carefully stalked around the wall. As he came to the overlap, he saw a man crawling into it with a shotgun slung over his back. Sam fired a pistol round into the back of his head, knelt to take the shotgun, then heard a shot ricochet off the wall inches from his head. He leapt into the entryway just as a burst from an AR-15 turned the space he'd just occupied into exploding stone chips. He clambered over the stones piled in the passage, and inside the wall.

'Honey, I'm home,' he called.

'It's about time,' she said. 'I was worried sick.'

Sam climbed the steps, carrying the pump shotgun. 'I counted them. There were twelve to start with and now there are six.'

'I know,' she said. 'At least we made it cost them something.'

'We did better than that. I'd say at the moment we're winning.'

She slowly shook her head. 'There were more at first. At least two of them ran off into the woods about the time you did. I thought they might be after you, but then I saw them going back up the slope where they'd come from. They must be going for help.'

'Maybe now is our best chance to get out of here,' said Sam. 'Let's pack what we need in our backpacks, leave the rest, and make a run for it.'

'That's all we can do,' she said. 'Let's hope their main camp is far away.'

He set the shotgun down beside her. 'You keep watch. Use this if one comes in range.' He left the scuba gear, the tent and most of the supplies. He packed the extra ammunition, the machetes and the artifacts from the pool in his pack, and left Remi's behind. He climbed up to the wall and picked up the shotgun. 'All right. Slip off into the woods and wait for me. I'll take one last look and see if I can . . .' He paused, looking at the expression on Remi's face. 'What?'

She pointed in the direction of the hillside. In the waning light, they could see a long line of men walking single file down the trail toward them. 'It's not six men anymore. It's thirty-six. They must have heard all the gunshots and started this way to see what was up. Or maybe we're so far from civilization that they can use radios without being overheard.'

'I'm sorry, Remi,' he said. 'I really thought we had a good chance.'

She kissed his cheek. 'You know, there's a lot to be said for bees. When somebody comes to wreck their hive to take their honey, the bees generally lose. But they make it as unpleasant and painful for him as possible. I respect that.'

'It's hard not to.'

'Let's get every magazine loaded while we can still see. And don't forget the shotgun.'

'Right,' said Sam. He went down the steps, crawled to the body of the man he had shot, took the man's day pack, and crawled back with it. There was a box with a dozen shells for the shotgun, but the rest was useless – a canteen, a hat, spare clothes, most of a fifth of whiskey. Sam gathered more stones from the crumbled area at the end of the pool and piled them in the passage, then carefully piled up their supply of firewood in case they needed to start a fire.

He took the powerful flashlights they had brought for diving in the cenote, then climbed to the wall where Remi waited. He checked his pistols and hers to be sure they were fully loaded, then checked the ten spare magazines and reloaded the two they'd emptied. 'See anything yet?'

149

'Nothing I can hit,' she said. 'They're still way back, out of pistol range. I think what they'll do is wait until it's fully dark and then move in close enough to hit us if we show ourselves for a second.'

'That's the time-honored method.'

'What are we planning to counter it?'

'I'm considering another time-honored method.'

There were six, then eight, rifle shots that hit along the top of the wall at intervals of about a yard. 'Too late,' she said. 'They're trying to keep our heads down so they can rush the entrance.'

Sam clutched the shotgun and ran down the steps, then lay against the pile of rocks he'd built. Two men appeared in front of him and he fired, pumped the shotgun, and fired again. Then Sam pumped his shotgun a second time, grasped the barrel of one man's gun, and dragged it inside with him. It was a short sub-machine gun he was familiar with, an Ingram MAC-10. It had been at least ten years since they'd been manufactured, but he had no doubt it would work.

Another man appeared, and Sam fired his shotgun again, pumped it, and retreated back over the rocks. He heard gunfire coming from up on the wall; four rapid shots.

He looked up as Remi ducked down. There were fifteen or twenty shots fired at the place where she had been, but she stayed low and moved over ten feet.

Sam climbed back on the wall, peered over it, and saw four men running toward the entryway. He raised the MAC-10, popped up, and strafed the runners from above. He ducked back, having seen all four fall, but the action of the MAC-10 remained open. He had used up the ammunition. There was a storm of bullets pounding the wall now. He sat still on the walkway, waiting for it to subside. It took a while, but gradually silence returned.

'How many?' Remi called.

'Seven, I think.'

'I only got two,' she said. 'When are you going to try your new strategy? Before or after we're out of ammo?'

'Now might be a good time,' he said. He went down the steps to the entryway, looked around the wall to see if any enemies were in sight but saw none. He restacked the firewood he had piled in the passage, poured some of the whiskey on it, struck a match and lit a fire. As it grew, he kept his shotgun aimed at the opening beyond. When the fire was flaming high and the resin-dripping branches were blazing torches, he took four of them together and ran up to the walkway. He threw one of the flaming brands as far as he could over the wall, then each of the other three so they landed as widely as possible. He sat down on the walkway again and listened while thirty or forty rounds glanced uselessly off the high stone wall.

Remi made use of the concentrated fire. She fired three rounds and then ducked down. 'Make that three,' she said.

'I'll tell the scorekeeper.'

'How's our strategy – Oh, my,' she said, looking over Sam's side of the wall.

Sam looked too. The sky seemed to be lightening. He took the shotgun and stood up to get a better look, then ducked down as the next volley of shots hit.

The torches had started some brush on fire, and the flames were growing, beginning to eat their way into a large thicket where Sam had hidden, crackling and raising sparks. As the gunfire died down, Sam heard men shouting in Spanish. Sam ran downstairs, picked up three still-burning brands, climbed back up, and threw them over the wall on the other side of the enclosure near Remi.

'What are you doing? They're all on that side.'

'I'm giving us light and space,' he said.

'For what?'

'We'll deprive those guys of hiding places and put them in the light of the fire.'

She patted his shoulder and smiled, then pointed at the other side of the enclosure. She and Sam crouched, went to that side, and got ready. Then they popped up at the same time, ready to fire. The men were not visible. In the light of the growing fires, Sam stared but saw nobody.

Remi tugged on the back of his belt. 'Don't give them time to aim at you.'

Sam ducked. 'Listen,' he said. 'We've driven them back.'

'For a while,' she said. 'As soon as the fire burns that brush away, they'll be back.'

Sam shrugged. 'It bought us a little time.'

'Thanks, Sam. I'll still love you for at least two more hours.'

'After that, what?'

'We'll see,' she said. 'It depends on their marksmanship.'

They sat on the walkway, holding hands. Every few minutes, one of them would go along the walk, pick a spot, and pop up to look. The fires flamed along the strip, taking brush and trees but not going any farther because of the pyramids on each side.

As the moon set, Sam looked down the strip. 'I think they'll be coming soon,' he said. 'And it looks as though more of them have arrived. It makes you wonder who they can be.'

'This is starting to get depressing,' she said.

He went through his pockets. 'How much ammo have you got left?'

'Twenty rounds. Eight in each pistol, and one spare magazine with only four in it.'

'I've got fifteen. And five shells in the shotgun.' He hugged her. 'I'm sorry to say, we're about done.' They sat leaning their backs on the wall, silent.

Remi sat up straight. 'Sam!'

'What?'

'The pool. It's not a cenote, like a well.'

'No?'

'It has a current. You could barely feel it, but all the artifacts we found were off to the side, and it moved us in the same direction. It's a sinkhole over an underground river.'

He looked into her eyes. 'Are you saying that's the gamble you'd like to take?'

She nodded. 'If we stay here, we run out of bullets, and we'll be at their mercy. I don't want to go that way. I'd rather drown.'

'All right,' he said. 'We'll give it our best try.'

She glanced out over the wall. 'The fires are about to the end. I can see the men moving down there. We don't have much time.'

Sam and Remi hurried down the steps and got their dive equipment ready and changed into their wet suits. Sam brought the waterproof bag of artifacts out of his pack. 'Put the guns, phones and ammo in here.'

While Remi gathered them into the bag and sealed it, Sam put a pair of shorts, a T-shirt and shoes in the net bag for each of them and lowered their pack into the water.

'That's everything,' he said. 'Maybe they'll think we got out through the fires.'

Remi shook the bag. 'Are you able to carry this?'

'It'll make a good weight.' He removed the lead weights from his belt and attached the bag to it.

Sam and Remi put on the rest of their dive equipment, held their flashlights, and sat on the edge of the pool. He said, 'I'm sorry it comes down to a long shot.'

She leaned over to bump him with her shoulder. 'It's not such a long shot. If there's one sinkhole, there are

154

probably others. We just have to conserve our air to give us more time to find one. We should have about twenty-five minutes.'

He nodded. As he did, there was a ferocious barrage of gunfire that ran along the top of the wall on three sides, knocking chips and mortar into the air. Sam and Remi turned their heads to kiss. Then they put on their masks, inserted their mouthpieces, and slid into the water. They swam downward for ten or twelve feet and then felt the slow current catch them and begin to push them gently away.

12

Guatemala

Sam and Remi swam cautiously in the deepening darkness, just going with the current for about a hundred feet to make sure that no one standing above the cenote could see them turn on their flashlights, and they increased their speed to move along the stone corridor of the underground river. The water rose all the way to the ceiling of the cavern, leaving no airspace above the surface. At first, the walls were about twenty feet apart but thirty or forty feet deep. Each time the space between the walls narrowed, Sam and Remi would feel a growing dread. When the space opened up a little, their relief was intense.

They kicked their fins steadily to keep their speed up, and the current helped them along. They held their flashlights ahead of them, but what they saw was always the same – more curving tunnel. When the tunnel narrowed, Sam would wonder whether it was merely a fissure in the rock opened up by one of the frequent earthquakes in the region. If it was, it could narrow at some point from twenty feet down to six inches, and they would be trapped and drown.

Sam kept checking his watch as they swam. He and Remi had made a dive yesterday morning that had lasted about fifteen minutes. Each of their aluminum tanks still held about twenty-five minutes of air. That meant that for the first twelve minutes, if they reached an obstacle, they might still be able to swim back to the cenote and surface. Maybe if they did, they'd find that the men who had been after them had already stormed the enclosure, seen they were gone, and left to search for them. Sam knew this thought was part fantasy and part nightmare: the possibility that betting their lives on this underground river might be a dead end.

And then it was thirteen minutes, and he knew that if they tried to swim back, they probably wouldn't make it before their air was gone. After five more minutes, they certainly wouldn't.

When twenty minutes had passed, they could count on only five more minutes of air. Even that might be optimistic. They had been swimming steadily, so they had used air at an accelerated rate. He thought about their chances as rationally as he could. There was no reason to believe that they would reach another opening in the ground above them in the next five minutes. Remi was smaller and lighter and used less air than he did. If she had both tanks, she would have twice as much time to find an escape.

Sam shifted his tank to the side so he could turn off the valve, but Remi saw what he was doing. She grasped his wrist with surprising strength and shook her head violently. Sam realized that she must have been thinking the same thoughts, feeling the same fears, and known that Sam would try to give her his tank.

When Remi had grasped Sam's wrist, his flashlight had swept the space above them, and something had looked different. Now he looked back and upward. He had gotten used to the sight of the bubbles they exhaled rising to the ceiling of the cavern, sliding into a depression, and staying there as a single, gelatinous bubble. Now his bubbles disappeared. He swam upward, with Remi still holding his wrist.

They broke the surface together and aimed their flashlights upward. They were in a dome, with the limestone ceiling about ten feet above their heads. Sam removed his mouthpiece and cautiously took a shallow breath. 'The air is good,' he announced.

Remi took out her mouthpiece. They raised their masks and looked around. 'I was afraid it would be carbon monoxide or hydrogen sulfide or something from a volcano,' she said.

'Nope. Just air.'

'It's sweet, clean air,' she said. 'How is it getting in?'

'Let's turn off the flashlights and see if light is coming in.'

They tried the experiment, but there was no light. They waited for their eyes to adjust to the darkness, but they still detected nothing. They switched on their flashlights again. 'At least we can swim on the surface for a bit,' said Sam. They closed the valves on their tanks and began to move.

The space remained above them, and they breathed the air and swam steadily along with the current.

Sam paused. 'I think I know what this is.'

'You do?' she said.

'Rainwater that flows into cenotes or seeps in through cracks feeds the river. The water level must be very high after a rain – maybe even through the rainy season – and then gets lower as time passes.'

'Sounds right,' she said. 'It would explain why the Mayans built those big stone strips like gutters, to catch the rain and direct it to the pool.'

'When there's no rain for a while, much of the underground river probably gets low, and air flows in above it. When the river rises again, air gets trapped in places like this,' Sam said. 'We've got to try to stay on the surface as long as we can to save our air.'

'And by the way,' said Remi, 'don't make any more moves like trying to give me your air tank. I'm already aware that chivalry isn't dead.'

'I was just being rational,' he said. 'You use less air than I do, so you could make it last longer and get farther.'

'All that would accomplish is that we'd both die alone. I plan to die in front of an audience and I picked mine years ago. You're it.'

'Saves you having to send out a lot of invitations,' he said.

'That's right,' she said. 'This is hard enough with you alive. Just stick with me and curb your generosity.'

They swam on along the curving tunnel for an hour until they came to a spot where the wall ahead reached all the way down under the water. They stopped and held on to the wall long enough for an awkward kiss. Then they lowered their masks over their faces and turned on the valves of their tanks. Remi said, 'Remember, it's both of us or neither,' and put her mouthpiece in.

They sank, and found themselves in a long passage that looked exactly like the stretches they had first passed through. As they swam, Remi wished she had looked at her watch before they had submerged. She had timed their arrival at the air pocket at sixteen minutes, but how much time had gone by? And did their tanks actually hold nine more minutes of air? She and Sam had never tested the limits before. Letting their air get this low would have been risky and stupid on any day when they could have simply surfaced and gotten fresh tanks from the dive boat.

There was nothing she could do but swim. As the minutes ticked away, the passage opened into another, wider space. The bottom of the river was oddly uneven, with loose chunks of rock instead of the smooth-worn riverbed they'd seen before. Then she realized she was seeing these things outside the perimeter of their flash-light beams – real light was filtering down from above. They swam upward. As the light grew brighter, Remi laughed and heard herself make a squeaky noise like a dolphin. She saw Sam huff out a big flurry of bubbles in an answering laugh, and they broke the surface smiling.

But Remi's laugh caught in her throat. There was light in this dome, directly above their heads, coming from a circular hole that opened to the starry sky. But the hole was at the center of the dome, beyond their reach, at least six feet above the surface of the river.

'Now, there's a problem,' Sam said.

'What can we do?'

'I'm going down to take a look around. Stay here for a minute.' He lowered his mask again and submerged. Remi waited until he surfaced again.

'Well?' she said.

Sam swam over to the side of the stone riverbed. It seemed to rise in the water, then rose partway out of it, so he was only up to his waist. 'I'm standing on a pile of rock. At some point, a pretty big chunk of wall came down right here. There's also a pile in the center, right below where the roof collapsed.'

'Very dramatic,' she said. 'Does this mean we're not going to the great beyond?'

Sam looked up at the hole in the dome. 'I think it does, but we'll have to work pretty hard to get out. Get ready to move some stones.'

They dived to the bottom, where Sam had been standing, and began to move chunks of stone from the pile along the wall to the spot just below the opening. Sam moved the largest chunks he could, rolling them end over end, to add to the pile in the center. Soon he took off his fins and worked in his booties. It was clear that at some point part of the wall had collapsed to make the pile, and stones gradually falling from the ceiling formed the cenote, with even more stones coming down as it enlarged. Sam and Remi were both free diving and they had to stop occasionally to catch their breaths.

When they had moved the whole pile of stone from the place where it had fallen to the place they wanted it, they stopped at the surface. 'We're running out of stones,' said Remi.

'I think we've got to bet the rest of our air on finding more and building higher.'

'I'm for risking it,' she said. 'This is the only chance we're likely to get.'

They put on their tanks again, swam in a wider radius around the pile they'd built, and brought back chunks of limestone that must have been left by other collapses. They didn't bother to pile the rocks high, just brought them and then went back for more, knowing the air in their tanks must be nearly gone. After a few more minutes, Sam surfaced and took off his tank. Within a short time, Remi surfaced too and took off hers.

'All out?' asked Sam.

She nodded.

'All right. Let me arrange what we've got as well as I can.' Sam ducked under the water and moved a large stone and added it to the pile. Remi went under and did the same. Each time they submerged, they held their breath and moved one stone before they came up for air. It was a slow and exhausting process, and their rest periods grew longer, but, little by little, the pile rose nearly to the surface. Sam even built their empty tanks into the pile to add height.

Finally, after hours of work, Sam sat down for a moment. 'Okay.'

'Okay what?'

'I'll lift you up. You'll stand on my shoulders. You should be able to get your hands up on the rim of the cenote.'

'I'll certainly try.'

Sam bent his knees. Remi took his hands, stepped lightly on his knees, then stepped up to his shoulders. He straightened his legs, and Remi rose. He could feel her clawing and scrabbling with her hands, trying to pull herself upward on the uncertain surface, and failing.

'Step on my hands,' he said. He held them, palms upward, just above his shoulders. Remi looked down, placed a foot on one hand and then a foot on the other.

'Try again,' he said, and she pushed down with her arms while Sam pushed up to straighten his elbows. And then her upper body was on the ground above. She clutched at clumps of plants and dragged herself forward on to the surface.

She looked down at Sam. 'I'm up, Sam. I'm out.'

'That's good news, of course,' Sam said. 'I look

forward to your weekly visits when you come to drop sandwiches down to me.'

'Very funny,' she said. 'What can we use as rope?'

'I'll use my wet suit,' he said. 'I'll cut it into strips while you look for something solid we can tie it to.'

'All right.'

He couldn't hear her anymore and knew she had moved off a few feet. He took off the top of his wet suit, took the dive knife from his belt, and began to cut. When he reached the sleeves, he cut each into several strips and tied them together, then tied these each to the long corkscrew shape he had cut from the torso. He took off the bottom of the wet suit, cut it into strips, and added it to the corkscrew.

Remi looked down over the rim of the cenote. 'Throw me the rope when it's ready,' she said. 'I've got a tree up here.'

'Take this first,' he said. He removed the waterproof pack from his dive belt, held it in both hands, and performed something like a basketball jump shot to sail it up through the opening to the surface. He tied his neoprene rope to his belt with its one remaining weight, then called, 'Ready?'

'Ready,' she said.

He swung the rope back and forth a couple of times, then swung it up toward Remi.

'Got it.' Then she disappeared again, pulling the rope with her. After thirty seconds, she came back to the edge. He could see she had her dive knife in her hand. 'We need some more. This will take a minute.'

Several minutes later, Sam could see Remi's face, looking down at him again. 'It's tied on. Time to do it.'

Sam climbed the rubber rope upward. Initially, it stretched as it took his weight, so the first two or three feet of climbing got him nowhere, but then the stretched rubber remained taut. He climbed it to the cenote, then used it as a handhold to drag himself up on to the ground. He rolled on his back, looked up at the sky, and then at Remi. His eyes widened. 'Nice to see you used your wet suit too.'

'Stop staring, naked boy,' she said. 'At least blink once in a while.' She opened the waterproof bag and tossed a pair of khaki shorts and a T-shirt on his chest, took out her own clothes, stepped into her shorts and pulled her T-shirt over her head. 'Put on some clothes so we can start hunting for civilization.'

He sat up and looked around him. 'I think we're in it.'

She turned, stepped in a little circle, and noticed for the first time the rows and rows of tall, bright green leafy plants that surrounded them and extended in all directions, as far as she could see, under the starlit night.

Sam said, 'I think we're in the middle of the biggest marijuana field in the world.'

13

San Diego

Professor David Caine sat in an archive room in the university library, trying to decipher the Mayan glyphs on the third page of the codex. He had seen nearly all of the glyphs in the first two columns before. They were among the eight hundred and sixty-one that had appeared in other codices, or as carved inscriptions at Mayan archaeological sites, and translated in the context of those inscriptions. He had found two glyphs on the first page that he believed had not been found before. In old languages and writing systems, there were always a few words susceptible to competing interpretations. Even in the surviving texts of Old English, there were a few words appearing only once, and scholars had been arguing about them for centuries.

Caine leaned close to the lighted magnifier on the stand above the painted bark page of the codex. He had photographed all the pages, but when there was doubt about a glyph, it was best to look as closely as possible at the original, examining each brushstroke. The two glyphs could be borrowings from another Mayan language, or possibly be the unique names of historical figures or even two names for one man. They could even be variants of terms he knew but had failed to recognize.

There was a loud rap on the door that startled him and destroyed his concentration. He was tempted to shout 'Go away,' but he reminded himself that he was a guest in this building. He stood up, went to the door, and opened it.

In the doorway stood Albert Strohm, the vice chancellor for Academic Affairs, and behind him were several men in suits. Strohm was a dynamic, effective executive – the academic vice chancellor was the one who actually ran the campus, while the chancellor spent most of his time on public relations and fund-raising – but Strohm looked today like a man who had been thoroughly defeated.

Caine said, 'Hello, Albert,' as kindly as he could. 'Come on in. I was just –'

'Thank you, Professor Caine,' Strohm said, giving Caine a stare that held some message – a warning? Caine was sure it had something to do with the men outside. Strohm said, 'Let me introduce these gentlemen. This is Alfredo Montez, the Minister of Culture for the Republic of Mexico; Mr Juárez, his assistant; Steven Vanderman, Special Agent, FBI; and Milton Welles, US Customs.' As he introduced the agents, they held up their federal identification badges.

'Please come in,' said Caine. He was thinking rapidly. Albert Strohm's formality had been a warning to him to shut up before he said something incriminating. Then he amended it – or, if not incriminating, then something that might weaken the university's position in a legal matter. He had heard of Alfredo Montez, so he held out his hand. 'Señor Montez, it's a pleasure to meet you. I've read your monographs on the Olmec and used them, particularly the ones on blue jadeite, in my own work.'

'Thank you,' said Montez. He was a tall, erect man, with his dark hair combed straight back. He wore an expensive gray suit and highly shined shoes, which made Caine feel a bit grubby in his old sport coat and khaki pants. He noticed that Montez didn't smile.

Montez said, 'We came straight from Mexico City as soon as the Chiapas officials brought this situation to our attention.' He saw that the codex was open on the table where Caine had been working. 'That is the Mayan codex, correct?' He didn't wait for an answer. 'Found in a shrine on Volcán Tacaná?'

'Yes,' said Caine. 'It was hidden in a classic period pot. The finders judged it would be safest to remove what they could from the earthquake zone, and then there were attempts to steal the pot, so they brought it here temporarily. Only when we unsealed the pot did we find the codex. If you have time, I'd love to talk with you about the shrine and the codex itself.'

Minister Montez stepped back and turned toward the FBI and customs agents to answer. 'No, I'm afraid

I'll have to defer that conversation. For the moment, I've heard enough.'

It was as though the legal authorities had been waiting for Caine to say the wrong thing. The FBI man, the customs man, and the assistant stepped to the table. In an instant, Caine knew. As soon as he had admitted the codex had been found in Mexico, anything else he might say became irrelevant. But he had to try to keep them from confiscating it.

'Wait, gentlemen, please. This codex was found, hidden in a classic period jar, with the body of a caretaker, who must have brought it to the shrine to hide. The shrine had been buried by lava in an eruption, then uncovered by last month's earthquakes. There was an emergency, a national disaster. The finders were there on a humanitarian mission, not searching for artifacts. They only acted to preserve what they'd found.'

Special Agent Vanderman said, 'You must be aware that the law and international agreements required them to report the find to the host government and not take it out of the country.'

'Yes, I'm aware. But these people protected the jar and the codex from thieves in Mexico. This isn't a theoretical argument. The codex would have been on the black market that very day.'

'We're here now, and these finders are relieved of the responsibility to protect it further,' said Montez. 'And so are you.'

Caine was frantic. 'Surely you're not going to confiscate the codex now. I've barely had time to examine it.'

'Have you photographed it?' asked Welles, the customs agent.

'That was one of the first things I did,' said Caine. 'It was a precaution, to preserve the information.'

'We'll need those photographs too,' said Welles. 'And all copies. Are they in your briefcase?'

'Well, yes,' Caine said. 'But why?'

'They're evidence in a possible federal prosecution. They prove you were treating the codex as your own and that you were taking your time about reporting it to authorities here or in its country of origin.'

'But that's absurd,' said Caine. 'I've always reported everything I've found in Mexico or anywhere else. There's never been this kind of haste in any case I know of. The codex hasn't been here a month.'

Vanderman, the FBI agent, said, 'Do you want to hand everything over voluntarily or should we begin to search for it?'

Caine lifted his briefcase to the table and produced a thick, nine-by-twelve-inch envelope full of photographs. He turned to Vice Chancellor Strohm, who looked sick. 'Albert –'

'I'm sorry, Professor Caine. The university's legal staff says the law is clear. The codex belongs to the country where it was found. We have no choice but to comply with the official request for immediate repatriation.'

Agent Vanderman glanced at the photographs in the envelope, but then took Caine's briefcase too. He said, 'We'll need your laptop too.' He gestured toward the open computer near the codex.

'Why?' asked Caine. 'You can't say that belongs to the Mexican government.'

Vanderman spoke quietly. 'It will be returned to you as soon as our technicians have looked through the hard drive.' He stared at Caine for a moment, his eyes taking on the flat, emotionless expression that cops use on suspects. 'Just some friendly advice. If there's anything on the drive about selling, hiding or transporting the Mayan codex, then you'll need to hire a good lawyer. I'm sure Vice Chancellor Strohm will tell you that the university's attorneys can't defend you in a criminal trial.'

Strohm didn't meet Caine's gaze.

Caine stood, helplessly watching them pack up the codex, his notes, his photographs, and his computer. He turned to the two Mexican officials. 'Minister Montez, Señor Juárez,' he said. 'Please believe me, this was never a scheme to do anything unethical. The people who found the codex risked their lives to protect it during a time of catastrophe. They alerted the mayor of the nearest village. They called me in and I immediately began consulting with scholars all over the world, including Mexico.'

Montez said, 'You should know that neither I nor the Mexican government can countenance what you've done here. The steps you and your friends took seem to have left out the only legitimate authority, and the legal owner of the artifacts. Saying that the only way to protect the codex was taking it to the United States is presumptuous and paternalistic.' He stepped past Caine and the others, with his assistant, Señor Juárez, following.

After that, the men from the FBI and customs seemed uncomfortable. They took only a minute to finish packing up and walk off, leaving only Strohm and Caine in the room.

'I'm sorry, David,' said Strohm. 'The university had no choice but to cooperate in a situation like this. Of course we'll do everything possible to vouch for you and support you. We'll also vouch for the probity of your conduct. But, you know, you might want to consider what Agent Vanderman said.'

'You mean find a criminal lawyer?'

The vice chancellor shrugged. 'It's a lot easier to get a court to decide in your favor on the first try than to get the next court to reverse the first's decision.'

Outside the building, the officials drove off in a plain coal black Lincoln Town Car. They reached the San Diego Freeway and turned south in the direction of downtown San Diego, but then stayed on the freeway, took the Balboa Park exit, and drove into the vast parking lots of the San Diego Zoo. They went to an area of the largest lot that was far from the pedestrian entrance and where a solitary second black car waited. They pulled up beside it, and both drivers lowered their backseat windows.

From the backseat of the waiting car came a woman's voice with an educated British accent. 'I assume it all went swimmingly?'

'Yes, ma'am,' said Special Agent Vanderman. He got out of his car, carrying a large briefcase, got into the backseat of the other car, and sat beside Sarah Allersby. He placed the case on the seat between them, opened it, and showed her the codex, wrapped in clear plastic.

'Did you get everything? All of his photographs, his notes, and so on?'

'Yes, ma'am,' he said. 'The administrators fell all over themselves to cooperate, and so when we all trooped in, Caine looked like he'd been poleaxed. He gave us everything without much of an argument. I guess he assumed his bosses had already verified who we were.'

'They may have,' said Sarah. 'The names on your identification cards were the names of real officials.' She looked more closely at the briefcase. 'Is this everything?'

'No.' He got out and reached into the backseat of the other car, then handed her a computer. 'Here's his laptop. That's everything.'

'Then it's time for you four to get moving. Here are your itineraries.' She handed him four printed airline itineraries. 'Destroy your fake identification before you reach the airport. You'll each find a rather pleasing bonus in your special bank accounts tomorrow.'

'Thank you,' he said.

'Aren't you going to ask how much?'

'No, ma'am. You said we'd be pleased. I have no reason to doubt that, and, if I'm wrong, haggling won't help.'

She smiled, displaying perfectly straight, professionally whitened teeth. 'You're very wise. Stick with our company and you'll also be rich.'

'I intend to,' he said. He turned and got into the backseat of the other car and nodded to the driver. The car began to move immediately.

Sarah Allersby watched the other black car drive off, then latched the briefcase and set it on the floor. She couldn't keep from smiling as her own car moved off more slowly. She wanted to laugh aloud, to get on the phone and tell a few friends how clever she had been. She had just acquired a Mayan codex, an irreplaceable and priceless artifact, for about the cost of a middle-of-the-lot American car. If she included the price of the false identification cards and badges, the plane tickets and the bonuses, it was, at most, the cost of two cars.

Maybe when she got back to Guatemala City tonight she would get on the secure scrambled phone line to London. Her father would be amused. He didn't much care about the art or cultures of non-European people – he referred to them as 'our brown brothers,' as though he were a colonist out of Kipling – but a good deal on any commodity was what he lived for.

14

Guatemala

The cannabis plants grew in rows, planted like corn, with the stalks as tall as a man. There were irrigation hoses between rows with holes in them to soak the roots.

Remi sat on the ground and put on the sneakers that Sam had placed in the waterproof bag for her. Then she took two of the pistols from the bag, handed one to Sam, and stuck the other in the waistband of her shorts and pulled her shirt down over it. She said, 'I think I know who those men who attacked us were.'

'Me too,' Sam said. 'They must patrol the area to be sure outsiders don't reach the fields.'

'Let's see if we can call home,' Remi said. She tried her phone, then Sam's. 'The batteries are dead. We'll have to walk out of here.'

'If the drug farmers let us,' Sam said. 'They're not going to like us any better than the men at the cenote did.'

They heard the sound of an engine. It was distant at first, but it grew louder. After a moment, they could hear squeaking springs as a stake truck bounced along the dusty road between two fields of crops.

Sam and Remi ran into the forest of tall cannabis stalks and moved away from the sounds. They crouched low and watched. The truck bounced up and coasted to a stop, and a middle-aged man in blue jeans, cowboy boots and a white shirt got out of the passenger side of the cab. He walked one row into the field and selected a marijuana plant. He looked closely at a bud and tested it. He stepped out toward the truck and nodded, and a dozen men jumped from the back of the truck to the ground. They moved along the rows of plants, harvesting the ripe buds.

The harvest proceeded quickly. Sam and Remi had to stay out of sight. When they were sure it was clear, they ran across a gap to the next field. After they had slipped into that field, they heard another engine sound approaching. This time, it was a tractor towing a wagon containing more men, who jumped down and began to harvest the second field.

For hours, Sam and Remi moved from one field of the huge plantation to another, avoiding the harvesters, their trucks and tractors.

The trucks began to pass them again, moving in the other direction. Sam and Remi made their way down a long row of plants in the middle of the field, walking parallel to the roads and maintaining their distance. They came to a forest of bushes, all seven to ten feet tall. 'Interesting,' Remi whispered. 'They look a lot like a blackthorn, don't they?'

'Could be,' said Sam. 'All I know about the blackthorn is that it's what the Irish use to make a shillelagh.

Also that it looks like a coca tree. And this is a coca tree.' He picked a leaf. 'See? You look for two parallel lines on each side of the rib.'

'How do you know about *that*?'

Sam shrugged and gave Remi a sly smile.

When they reached the end of the coca grove, they could see a single-file line of about twenty trucks and tractors waiting to pull up to barnlike buildings. Sam and Remi kept to the fields as they moved to the side and around the buildings.

Sam pointed at the trucks and whispered, 'I think that's our way out.'

Remi said, 'Maybe, but look at all the guards.' Walking the perimeter of the tie-down area were men who carried rifles that looked like AK-47 assault weapons on slings. Sam and Remi could see the curved, thirty-round magazines.

'Interesting,' said Sam. 'They're all facing inward, watching the guys covering the loads of marijuana. They're not protecting the operation, they're making sure the farmhands don't steal any of the product. It's inventory control.'

Remi said, 'Maybe we could just sneak to the road and walk out of here.'

Sam shrugged. 'Would the men who tried to kill us in the forest neglect a road?'

'Probably not,' she said. 'I guess it's got to be a truck.'

'Let's pick one that's already been loaded, covered and parked.'

Sam and Remi made a wide circle around the compound, staying among the tall plants and watching the activities in the center. They avoided the spots where a turning truck might sweep its headlights across them, and they stayed far from the buildings where men were hanging, bailing and loading marijuana.

They stayed under their cover until they were beyond the parked trucks. It looked hopeless. There was a guard standing by the front bumper of the first truck in line, which was fully loaded and tied down. From his tired slouch, he seemed bored. The sling that held his rifle went from his left shoulder across his chest to his right hip, so he would need an extra second or two to bring it around and fire.

Sam and Remi put their heads close, whispered for a few seconds, and then separated and left the woods at the same moment about ten feet apart. They walked silently, but quickly, and converged on the guard from both sides at once with their pistols drawn. The guard turned in Remi's direction, saw her, and began to tug at his sling to lift it over his head to free his rifle, but Sam was beside the man too quickly and pressed his gun to the man's head. Remi stepped closer, grasped the sling, and took the rifle away from him. Without warning, Sam hooked his left arm around the man's neck from behind in a choke hold and held it until he lost consciousness. They each took an ankle and dragged the man into the nearby woods. Sam took the man's pants and put them on, then put on the man's straw hat. Remi held the rifle and watched the trucks while Sam took the man's shirt, tore it, and used it to tie and gag him, then bind him to a tree.

They stepped out of the woods together, Sam holding the AK-47 rifle the way the guards held theirs and wearing the guard's hat and pants. They walked between two of the already loaded trucks, then picked one, quickly letting their silhouettes be engulfed by the silhouette of the truck. They looked in each direction, trying to see where the other guards were, but couldn't see any of them from there.

Then, coming along the front of the trucks, was another guard. 'Guard,' Sam whispered. Remi crouched beside one of the big truck tires. Sam held the AK-47, his left hand on the forestock and his right just behind the trigger guard, pushed the safety off, and stepped a couple of paces in front of the truck in a bored, slouching posture, his eyes turned in their sockets to watch the guard's behavior.

The guard kept coming along for a few steps, stopped, then raised his right hand to wave at Sam.

Sam imitated the gesture as exactly as he could, waving back at the man and assuming it meant that he was alert and all was well. He pretended not to be studying the man for his response, just walked a bit closer to the front of the truck and waited. If he was going to have an automatic-weapons fight, he was going to use the truck's engine as a shield. He took a few breaths and prepared himself. The other guard turned and walked off along the perimeter.

Sam moved back to where Remi waited. They stayed low as they climbed over the gate of the truck to its bed, lifted the rear canvas cover enough to let them crawl under, then pulled it back down to hide. Once under the tarp, they moved some of the marijuana packages to build a cushioning layer beneath them.

Soon they heard footsteps and voices coming to where their truck was parked. Then Sam and Remi felt the truck sink on its springs a little as a man stood on the left step and sat in the driver's seat, then another came from the right side and sat beside him. The doors of the cab slammed, the engine started, they began to move, and very slowly the truck joined a line of trucks on the gravel road.

Sam listened to the engines for a couple of minutes, then put his head near the canvas. He whispered, 'It looks as though five leave at once.' The truck moved up about five lengths and then stopped again.

This time, Remi moved her head close to the bottom of the canvas on the left side. 'We're sitting beside a sign,' she said.

'Can you read it?'

'Estancia Guerrero.'

There was a sudden surge of movement around the truck, on all sides at once. Sam gripped the rifle, and Remi drew her pistol, and they faced away from each other. Men were climbing aboard, sitting on all sides of the canvas behind which Sam and Remi hid. The men laughed and talked, while Sam and Remi, only inches away, held their fire.

The driver shifted into first gear, and the truck moved ahead, gaining rpms, until it was time to shift into second. But, then, they could tell that other trucks were moving too. And by third gear, the workers on both sides had made themselves comfortable, with their legs through the wooden side gates and their backs leaning against the canvas-covered bales of marijuana.

Remi, then Sam, lowered the guns and lay back in uneasy immobility. The trucks kept gaining speed, bouncing along the gravel road, while the men spoke to one another in Spanish, happy that the day had come to an end. After about ten minutes, the truck stopped, and about half the men got off in the center of a small village. The truck drove on again and stopped after another ten minutes, when several others got off near a double row of buildings. Ten minutes later, more workers jumped down to the road.

Sam and Remi listened for another ten minutes or so before they were sure. Remi lifted the canvas slightly and looked out, and Sam lifted the other side. 'Everybody off?' he whispered.

'Yes,' she whispered. 'Thank goodness. I was afraid I was going to sneeze from the dust.'

'I guess the next thing is to get off the truck and make our way to a town,' he whispered.

'I can't wait,' she said. 'Let's hope they don't reach their unloading point before we can bail out.'

They pulled aside the canvas a little and watched the sides of the narrow road while the truck wound its way through heavily forested stretches and up on to plateaus, where, for brief periods, they could see sky above them thick with stars. The distance between trucks had grown greatly during the drive. Now and then, on a curving stretch going up or down a slope, they would see the next truck's headlights a half mile or more behind them.

Finally, they reached a steep incline where the road wound upward for a long distance. The driver downshifted as the engine labored. Remi darted out over the tailgate, stared ahead and said, 'There's a town up ahead, at the top of the hill.'

'Then maybe we'd better bail out before we get there,' Sam said. 'Get ready to jump.' They got on the right side of the truck and looked out. There was the gravel road heading upward, and, by the side of the road, a covering of low plants and bushes that didn't seem in the dark to be woody enough to be dangerous. They moved close to the back of the truck to be ready. The road turned, so the truck slowed, and the driver needed to be looking ahead, and Sam said, 'Now.'

Remi jumped and rolled, and Sam jumped after her. They scrambled off the dusty road into the bushes, and watched the truck bounce and rumble upward away from them. At the top of the hill, they could see a church, with a pair of short, square-sided steeples on the front. When the truck reached that point, it seemed to level and disappear.

Sam and Remi stood up and began to climb. She looked down. 'Your leg – is that blood?' She bent and looked closer.

He looked too. 'I guess it is. I must have scraped it on something when I hit. I'm all right.'

They walked up the last few feet of the hill and around to the other side of the church and sat in the moonlight to look at Sam's leg. The blood streak went from his knee to his ankle, but it was already drying. 'No harm done,' he said.

They kept to the side of the church, sat down in the dark shadows by it, and watched the second truck make its way up to the level of the church, where the town's main street began. The truck traveled along the street without slowing. At the end of the block of closed shops and restaurants, the road curved a little and went downward, and the truck disappeared.

Sam and Remi stayed at the back of the church building and waited while the other trucks climbed the road and passed through the town, one by one. Their small convoy had consisted of five trucks, but the Fargos stayed where they were as long as they could see headlights in the distance. They counted twenty trucks before the road was clear again. It was nearly dawn when they walked out of their hiding place and saw that there were people in some of the shops already.

They passed a baker's shop, where a man was firing up a big wood-burning oven behind the building. There were people in the yards outside their houses, gathering eggs, feeding chickens, starting fires.

Sam said, 'I'm hungry.'

'Me too. Did any of our Guatemalan Quetzales survive our swim?'

'I think so. I'll look in the bag.' He opened the waterproof bag, shuffled around in it, and found his wallet. 'That's good news. My wallet survived.' He looked inside. 'The money too. Let's see if we can buy some breakfast.'

They walked toward the shop where the man was stoking the oven and saw two men heading for the same place. One wore a wrinkled seersucker suit and the other a priest's black coat and collar. They strolled down the center of the street, chatting in a friendly way, as they approached the little restaurant.

They and the host had a quick exchange of greetings, and then the priest turned to the Fargos and said in English, 'Good morning. My name is Father Gomez. And this is Dr Carlos Huerta, our town physician.'

Sam shook their hands. 'Sam Fargo. And this is my wife, Remi.'

'So,' she said, 'the parish priest and the doctor together at dawn. I hope nobody has died during the night.'

'No,' said the priest. 'A baby was born a while ago. The family sent for me to baptize the little boy immediately, so we thought we might as well begin the day here. Miguel Alvarez saw us coming. And to what do we owe the pleasure of your company?'

'We were hiking and camping north of Cobán and we seem to have wandered a bit and gotten lost,' said Sam. 'We had to abandon most of our gear. But we found our way to a road, and here we are, safe and in a town.'

'Yes, you are,' said Dr Huerta. 'Will you join us for breakfast?'

'We would be delighted,' said Remi.

They talked while the restaurateur's wife and two of his sons arrived and began to cook. They produced a feast of thick, handmade tortillas, rice, black beans, fried eggs, papaya, slices of cheese, and sautéed plantains.

After a few remarks about the area, the climate and the people, Father Gomez said, 'You came from that way, beyond the church?'

'Yes,' said Remi.

'Did you stop at the Estancia Guerrero?'

Remi was uncomfortable. 'It didn't look to us like a friendly place.'

The priest and the doctor exchanged a meaningful look. Dr Huerta said, 'Your instincts served you well.'

Sam looked at Remi, then said, 'I'm afraid we got a pretty good look at part of the place. The reason we had to abandon our gear was that some men were trying to shoot us.'

'This isn't the only story like that I've heard,' said Father Gomez. 'It's a disgrace.'

Dr Huerta said, 'Father Gomez and I have been trying to do something about it for a year or more. First, we wrote to the woman who owns the Estancia, an Englishwoman named Sarah Allersby. We thought she would want to know that a part of her huge property was being used as a drug plantation.'

Sam and Remi exchanged a look. 'What did she say?' asked Sam.

'Nothing. The response came from the regional police, who told us we didn't know marijuana from sugarcane and were wasting everyone's time.'

Remi said, 'Do you know Miss Allersby?'

'No, we've never seen her,' said the priest. 'But who can tell what she knows, far away in Guatemala City, or in London, or New York?'

The doctor said, 'Meanwhile, heavily armed men roam the forests, and trucks full of drugs come through town every few nights. Lots of the villages around here have young men who work there. Some come home, others don't. Are they all right? Who knows?'

'I'm sorry,' said Remi. 'Maybe we can talk to the authorities in Guatemala City and pass on the story. Sometimes outsiders can seem more objective to the police.'

'I've been thinking about that,' said Dr Huerta. 'If the drug people saw you and shot at you, they might be searching for you even now. Just to be safe, we ought to get you out of here. I've got a car and I'll be driving to the next town this morning. I'll take you with me and put you on a bus to Guatemala City.'

'Thank you,' Sam said. 'We would appreciate it very much.'

'Yes, we would,' said Remi. 'Doesn't the bus stop here?'

'Not anymore,' said the priest. 'Santa Maria de los Montañas isn't big enough. There are only two hundred souls, and few have any business elsewhere.'

Dr Huerta said, 'Let's give it another half hour, just to be sure the drug trucks have passed, before we get on the road.'

'While you're waiting, I'll show you our church,' said Father Gomez. 'It was made by the first generation of converts in the sixteenth century, under the direction of the Dominicans.'

'We'd love to see it,' Remi said.

They walked to the church with the priest. The front had a pair of low bell towers with a flat façade between them. There was a large pair of wooden doors, opening on a little plaza that ended at the road. It occurred to Remi that the style was similar to some of the smaller California missions. Inside were carved statues of Mary and baby Jesus above the altar, flanked by angels with shields and spears.

'The statues were imported from Spain in the eighteenth century,' said Father Gomez. 'These pews were made by parishioners about that time.' He sat in the front row and the Fargos joined him. 'And now all that history culminates in the town turning into a drug traffickers' paradise.'

'You should try again for help,' said Sam. 'The national police in Guatemala City might be more interested in this. As Remi said, we can tell them what we saw.'

'If you could get a message through to Sarah Allersby, the woman who owns the Estancia Guerrero, it might help even more. The doctor and I have hopes that she's like a lot of absentee landlords. She doesn't pay much attention, but when she learns what's been happening on her land, she'll react.'

Remi sighed. 'We can try.'

'You seem doubtful. Why?'

'We met her recently, and I think she might take a letter or a call from us. But our personal impression, and what we've heard about her, tells us that she won't help anyone unless she gets some personal advantage out of it.'

'You think she's aware of the drug smuggling?'

'We can't say that,' said Remi. 'Just because someone makes a bad impression on us doesn't mean she's a criminal. But she struck us as a very spoiled and selfish young woman who didn't care much about rules.'

'I see,' said Father Gomez. 'Well, please try. Having these bandits patrolling the area is a terrible thing. If the drugs disappeared, so would they.'

'We'll try to talk to her,' said Sam.

'Thank you. We'd better get you to Dr Huerta. He has patients waiting in the next town.' They got up and strolled down the aisle of the church behind Father Gomez. He opened one of the big doors a couple of inches, then said, 'Wait.'

Sam and Remi followed his gaze and saw a small squad of heavily armed policemen had arrived in a personnel carrier. They had stopped Dr Huerta's car on the street, and their sergeant was talking to him. He said little and seemed to be annoyed by the intrusion. Finally, he got out of his car, walked across the street with the sergeant, and opened a storefront door, then stepped aside.

The sergeant and two of his men went inside and looked around and then came out. The doctor locked the door again. Then he walked back to the car with the sergeant, who directed him to open the trunk. He opened it, they looked inside, and he closed it. The sergeant nodded to the doctor, and got into the passenger seat of the personnel carrier. His men climbed aboard, and, at his signal, they drove off in the direction of the Estancia Guerrero.

Huerta walked into the church. 'That was the same squad of police who came after we wrote to Miss Allersby about what's happening on her land.'

Father Gomez said, 'What did they want with you?'

'Today they're looking for two people they say are involved in drug smuggling – two strangers, who may be Americans, a man and a woman. They were seen a few miles from here, and when the police raided their camp, they found a large amount of cocaine in their backpacks.'

Sam looked at Remi. 'That's quite a story.'

'I think we've got to get you out of here,' said Father Gomez.

'Yes,' said Dr Huerta. 'Come, I'll take you now.'

Remi said, 'We don't want to endanger you. If they'll frame us, they'll frame other people too – maybe you.'

'They've given me their message and that will be enough for now. And the sergeant knows even with his friends the drug men, he might be the one who needs a doctor some day. I'm the only one for many miles.'

Remi said, 'Father Gomez, we'll try to let you know how our talk with Sarah Allersby works out.'

'I hope it does. God bless you in your travels.'

They got into the doctor's car, and he drove them in the direction the trucks had traveled in the night. Almost as soon as the car reached the end of the short main street, the pavement gave way to gravel again. The road wound down and away from the town into a forested valley.

Huerta said, 'The town of Santa Maria de los Montañas was a late Mayan settlement. It was built a couple of hundred years after the great cities were abandoned. As you can see, it's high up, approachable only by one steep road on each side. It was probably a place of refuge after the collapse of the larger society.'

'It must have been a tough place for the Spanish to conquer.'

'They couldn't do it,' said Dr Huerta. 'The Indians in the area were very warlike. What happened was that Dominican missionaries, friars led by Las Casas, came and converted the Indians peacefully.'

'Bartolomé de Las Casas?' asked Remi.

'Yes,' said Huerta. 'He's a national hero. He founded a mission at Rabinal, pacified the Indians, and baptized them one by one. That's why this region is called Las Verapaces. It means "Lands of True Peace".'

Sam noticed the doctor's expression as he drove on. 'Is something wrong?'

Dr Huerta shook his head. 'I'm sorry, I was thinking sad thoughts about Las Casas. His dream of a Guatemala where the Mayans had equal rights never came true, even now. The Mayan people have suffered a very long time. And during civil wars in any country, the ones who suffer most are the poorest.'

Remi said, 'Is that why you practice medicine way up here?'

He shrugged. 'Logic would dictate that I work with the people who need me the most. Whenever I want to leave, I think of that.'

'What's that up ahead?' said Remi. 'It looks like one of the marijuana trucks.'

'Get your heads down,' said Dr Huerta. 'I'll try to get rid of them.'

Sam and Remi ducked down in the backseat. Sam lay on his side on the floor; Remi lay on the seat and covered him and herself with a blanket, so it looked as though she were sick and the only passenger.

Dr Huerta drove ahead. The truck was stopped in the middle of the road, and the driver and the guard were out of the cab, waving Huerta's approaching car to a stop. 'It looks like they have engine trouble. They want me to stop,' Dr Huerta said to Sam and Remi.

'You don't have much choice,' said Sam. 'Do it.'

Dr Huerta stopped behind the truck, and the driver walked up to his window. He addressed the doctor in Spanish, and the doctor replied, waving his arm in the direction of Remi lying on the backseat. The man quickly stepped back two steps from the car and gestured to the doctor to keep going. Dr Huerta drove on.

Remi had been listening. 'What is *parótidas*?' she asked.

'It's a common viral illness. In English, it's called mumps. I told him you had a case at its most contagious stage. In adult males, it can cause impotence.'

Remi laughed. 'Very quick thinking.' She pulled the blanket aside so Sam could sit up beside her.

An hour later, Dr Huerta dropped them off in a larger village, and soon they were sitting in the back of a bus heading down toward the city of Cobán. From Cobán to Guatemala City was another hundred and thirty-three miles: a five-hour trip.

When they reached Guatemala City, they checked

into the Real InterContinental Hotel in the center of the Zona Viva, the tenth zone, where the best restaurants and nightlife can be found. When Sam and Remi were up in their room and could plug in their telephones to replenish their charges, Sam called the Guatemala City branch of an American bank where he had an account and arranged to rent a safe-deposit box.

He and Remi walked the three blocks to the bank, rented the box, and placed the gold and jade artifacts they'd found in the underground river in it, where they would be safe.

They walked back to their hotel, stopping in fashionable shops along the way to buy new clothes and a pair of suitcases, and then they called Selma.

'Where have you two been?' she asked. 'We've been trying to call you for two days.'

'Our phone batteries ran down when we took them for a swim,' said Remi. She gave Selma the name of their hotel, their room number, and a brief version of how they had come to be there. She ended with, 'And how is everything at home?'

'Bad,' said Selma. 'I'm almost afraid to tell you.'

'I'm going to put you on speaker so Sam can hear too,' said Remi.

'All right,' said Selma. 'Someone arranged to have four men come to the university and impersonate FBI and US Customs agents and two Mexican cultural officials. They showed credentials, and the university administrators looked up the names to verify these people existed. So –'

'Did they get the codex?'

'Yes,' she said. 'I'm sorry. I hope you won't blame David Caine. The university's lawyers said the codex had to be turned over to legitimate Mexican officials, so the academic vice chancellor led these men right to the archival room where David had the codex under a magnifier. We found out that the administrators even had the campus police standing by in case David had to be restrained.'

'We're not blaming David,' Sam said. 'See if you can find out where Sarah Allersby was at the time. The fact that we had a prowler right after she and her lawyers tried to buy the codex makes her my favorite suspect.'

'Her private plane took off from Los Angeles late the night after the theft,' Selma said. 'She had been scheduled to fly out the evening after she came to the house, but a new flight plan was filed the night she actually left.'

'Where was she headed?' asked Sam.

'The flight plan was for Guatemala City.'

'So she's here?' Remi said. 'She brought the codex here?'

'It would seem so,' said Selma. 'That's an advantage of a private plane. You don't have to hide what you steal in your luggage.'

15

Guatemala City

For over two hundred years, Sarah Allersby's mansion in Guatemala City had been the home of the wealthy Guerrero family. It was a Spanish palace, built with a massive set of stone steps, a carved façade and high double doors in front. The wings of the two-story house continued all the way around to enclose a large courtyard.

When Sam and Remi knocked, a tall, muscular man in his mid-thirties with the face and build of a boxer, and who might have been the butler but was probably the chief of security, opened the door. 'Mr and Mrs Fargo?'

'Yes,' said Sam.

'You're expected. Please come in.' He stepped back to let them pass and then looked up and down the street as he shut the door. 'Miss Allersby will see you in the library.' Dominating the foyer were a pair of eight-foot-high stone slabs with carvings of particularly fierce-looking Mayan deities that seemed to be guarding the house. He led the Fargos past them to a doorway off the foyer that had a high, ornately carved stone lintel that Remi judged was from a Mayan building. Inside was the sort of library that could be found in English country houses, if they were old enough and the owners were rich enough. The man waited until Sam and Remi were seated on a large, old-fashioned leather couch and went out.

The room was designed to convey long tenure and social standing. There was an antique globe, about four feet in diameter, on a stand. Antique lecterns along the side of the room held large, open books – one an old Spanish dictionary and the other a hand-tinted, seventeenth-century atlas. The walls were lined with tall bookshelves that held thousands of leather-bound books. Hung along the inner wall, above the bookcases of nineteenth-century works, were portraits of Spanish ladies, with mantillas over their hair and in lace gowns, and Spanish gentlemen in black coats. It occurred to Remi that this room was not Sarah Allersby's doing. She had simply got the Guerrero house and occupied it. Remi verified the impression by looking at the nearest shelf of books, which had Spanish titles embossed on their spines in gold.

At the far end of the room, a glass case displayed beaten gold and carved jade ornaments from the costume of a classic period Mayan dignitary, a selection of fanciful Mayan clay pots shaped like frogs, dogs and birds, and eight figurines of cast gold.

They heard the pock-pock of high heels striking the polished stone floor as Sarah Allersby crossed the foyer.

She entered the room at a fast walk, smiling. 'Why, it really is Sam and Remi Fargo. I think I can honestly say that I never expected to see either of you again, and certainly not in Guatemala.' She wore a black skirt from a suit but without the jacket, black shoes, and a white silk blouse with a ruffle at the neck, an outfit that conveyed the impression that she had been occupied with business in another part of the house. She looked at her watch as though starting a timer and then back at them.

Sam and Remi stood. 'Hello, Miss Allersby.'

Sarah Allersby stood where she was, making no attempt to shake hands.

'Enjoying your stay in our country?'

'Since we met you in San Diego, we've been exploring in Alta Verapaz,' said Remi. 'I suppose the codex raised our consciousness of Mayan country and we decided to take a closer look.'

'How adventurous of you. It must be wonderful to be able to drop everything and go off to satisfy your curiosity on a whim. I envy you.'

'It comes with retirement,' said Sam. 'You should take more time away from acquiring things.'

'Not just yet,' said Sarah. 'I'm still in the building phase. So you came down here and the first person you decided to visit was me. I'm flattered.'

'Yes,' said Sam. 'The reason we're here is that our trek took us close to an estate that you own – the Estancia Guerrero.'

'How interesting.' Her expression was guarded, alert but emotionless.

'The reason we had to pass that way was that a contingent of heavily armed men were chasing us. They opened fire as soon as they saw us, so we had to run and we took a shortcut through your property. What we saw when we crossed your land was a very large marijuana plantation with about a hundred workers, harvesting the crop, drying, packing and shipping.'

'What a wild day you had,' she said. 'How, pray tell, did you escape from all these armed men?'

'Don't you think what you should be asking is "What are all these criminals doing on my ranch?",' said Remi.

Sarah Allersby smiled indulgently. 'Think about the Everglades National Park in your country. It's about one-point-five million acres. The Estancia Guerrero is more than twice that size. It's just one of several tracts that I own in different regions of Guatemala. There's no way to keep everyone off that land. Parts of it are unreachable except on foot. The peasant people have been in and out of there for thousands of years, no doubt plenty of them up to no good. I do employ a few men in the district to prevent commercial logging of rare woods, poaching of endangered species, and the looting of archaeological sites. But armed combat with drug gangs is the government's job, not mine.'

Sam said, 'We thought we'd let you know about the illegal activity going on inside your property.'

Sarah Allersby leaned forward, an unconscious posture that made her look like a cat about to spring. 'You sound as though you have doubts.'

Remi shrugged. 'All I can be sure of is that you're informed now.' She offered her hand to Sarah, who took it. 'Thank you for giving us a few minutes of your time.' They stepped through the door to the foyer, and Sarah emerged behind them.

'It's not likely to happen again,' she said. As she walked across the old tiles in the other direction, she added, 'I just assumed you were here to say something amusing about my Mayan codex.'

Remi stopped and turned. '*Your* Mayan codex?'

Sarah Allersby laughed. 'Did I say that? How silly of me.' She kept walking. As she disappeared through another doorway, the front door opened behind the Fargos. The servant who had let them in appeared. Now he was accompanied by two other men in suits. They held the heavy door open so the Fargos' exit would not be delayed.

As soon as they were outside, Remi said, 'Well, that wasn't very satisfying.'

'Let's try another way to get some action,' Sam said.

Sam and Remi walked down the steps and out to the street. They turned to the right and walked another hundred yards, and then Sam stopped and waved down a taxi. 'Avenida Reforma. The embassy of the United States.'

At the embassy, the receptionist behind the desk asked them to wait while she tried to get a member of the staff to speak with them. Five minutes later, a woman appeared from a door beyond the desk and walked up to them. 'I'm Amy Costa, State Department. Come to my office.' When they were inside, she said, 'How can I help you today?'

Sam and Remi told her the story of what had happened on and near the Estancia Guerrero. They told her about the men who had tracked and attacked them, the vast plantation of marijuana plants and coca trees, the truck convoys. They described the doctor and the priest who had asked them to submit their pleas to Sarah Allersby, and her response. And, finally, Sam told her about the Mayan codex.

'If the codex is in her possession, or is found to have ever been in her possession, then she got it by getting men to impersonate federal officials at the University of California in San Diego and steal it.'

Amy Costa wrote a report as she listened, only interrupting to ask for dates or approximate location data that had been recorded on their phones. When they had finished their story, she said, 'We will be passing this information on to the Guatemalan government. But don't be too impatient about results.'

'Why not?' asked Remi.

'The government has been doing a valiant job of trying to control the drug traffickers and growers, who are also destroying the forests, particularly in the Petén region, to make giant cattle ranches. But the drug gangs have them outnumbered and outgunned. In the past couple of years, the police have taken back about three hundred thousand acres from the drug lords, but that's a tiny fraction of the total.'

'What about Sarah Allersby?'

'We've been aware of her since she arrived in the country, of course. She's a very visible personality on the European party scene – beautiful, rich, uninhibited, flamboyant. She's almost a celebrity in this city. And I'd not be at all surprised if she is behind the theft of the Mayan codex. She thinks laws are local customs for the unintelligent and unimaginative. But like aristocrats everywhere, she doesn't do the unpleasant things herself. She hires people like the impostors who took the codex. It's highly unlikely that she would ever be charged with a crime here.' She paused. 'Any crime.'

'Really?' said Remi. 'But she's a foreigner just like us.'

'There's a difference.' She paused. 'What I'm about to tell you is off the record. She's been here for years, making herself socially and financially useful to lots of powerful people. She's a huge landowner, and while you can't buy the old owner's social status with the land, obvious wealth is certainly a good way to get invitations. She's always contributed to the political campaigns of potential winners – and, even more important, to the sure losers who are well connected. She can accomplish a lot with a phone call, or even a hint dropped at a party.'

Sam said, 'Can't we at least get the Guatemalan police to take a look at the Estancia? Thousands of acres of plants in the fields and tons of buds in the drying barns are pretty hard to hide. And if they examined her operations, her offices, her houses, they couldn't help but find –'

'The Mayan codex?'

'Well, that's what we'd hope. But certainly evidence that she's been profiting from these drug operations.'

Amy Costa slowly shook her head. 'That would be too vast an undertaking. The authorities know that in the north and the west, the cartels have been operating in the big stretches of wilderness. The police would love to stop them. But what you're describing won't happen. If they found every single thing you saw, they still wouldn't arrest Sarah Allersby. Don't you see? She would be the prime victim. They could arrest a hundred poor Mayan peasants who took jobs tending the crop. All the action – the dirty deals, the money changing hands – took place in somebody's fancy house here in the capital. In Guatemala, if you're rich enough to own millions of acres in the countryside, you're too rich to live there.'

'But you'll pass on the information to the police?'

'Of course,' she said. 'This isn't one crime, it's a war. We just keep on trying. What you've told me may turn out to be helpful, even important, sometime. It may put somebody away.'

Sam said, 'Do you think we should go to the federal police too?'

'You can if you want. But maybe we can do it together. Are you free for an hour or so?'

'Absolutely.'

'Give me a minute to call ahead and then we'll go.' She dialed a number and spoke briefly in rapid Spanish. Then she buzzed the receptionist. 'Please have a car for me. We'll leave as soon as it's ready.' She explained to the Fargos, 'It's in zone four, a bit too far to walk.'

They were driven to the federal police station on Avenida 3-ll. The police officer at the door recognized Amy Costa and let them in. Costa walked up the hall to an elevator, which took them to an office.

The uniformed officer, who stood as they entered, was young and clear-eyed. 'This is Commander Rueda. This is Sam and Remi Fargo. They're two American visitors who saw some things you might wish to know about. Mr Fargo . . . ?'

Sam told the story, and Remi filled in details and supplied the GPS locations of the places described. Whenever the commander looked puzzled, Amy Costa translated the words into Spanish. At the end of the Fargos' recitation, the commander said, 'Thank you very much for bringing this information to our attention. I will file a report, conveying your experiences, to the central command.' He stood to terminate the visit.

Sam remained seated. 'Will anything happen? Will Sarah Allersby's properties be searched or her bank accounts audited?'

The commander looked sympathetic. He sat down again. 'I'm sorry, but those things will not happen. The armed gang was certainly one of the groups who patrol the north to protect the ranches where drugs are grown and shipped. Marijuana is a stable, reliable crop that can be grown in any remote area by anyone. But there's no proof of a connection with Sarah Allersby. Any piece of jungle – including national parkland – can be infiltrated by these criminals. We raid them and they turn up elsewhere. When we go away, they come back. Do they pay a landlord for the privilege? Sometimes, but not always. Your report of seeing coca trees, frankly, disturbs me most. We haven't had coca growing here. Until now, we've only been a stop on the route from South America.'

'If you were to have a reason to search the Allersby houses, banks and businesses for one thing and found another, could you still arrest her?'

'Yes, provided we had a good legal reason to search. This time, we don't have a direct connection to her.' He seemed to make a decision. 'I'm going to tell you something confidential. Like many rich and active businesspeople, she has been investigated from time to time. In fact, it's happened twice that I know of in this office. We found nothing.'

Remi said, 'No money she couldn't explain? No Mayan artifacts? She calls herself a collector, and we saw plenty in her house.'

The commander said, 'If she has money she didn't declare here, it's no mystery. She has interests in many countries, and a wealthy family. If there are Mayan artifacts, she could say they were part of the estate she bought from the Guerrero family, or some things her workers found recently that she would have reported. There's nothing criminal there unless she did something definite and final – sell them or take them out of the country.'

'What would you advise us to do?' asked Remi.

'What Miss Costa undoubtedly told you to do. Go home. If you want to, you could search the online markets for codices or parts of them. Often, things are broken up and sold. If the codex turns up, we'll file charges and confiscate it.'

'Thank you,' said Remi.

Sam shook the commander's hand. 'We appreciate your willingness to listen.'

'Thank you for your evidence. And please don't be discouraged. Justice is sometimes slow.'

Amy Costa had the embassy car drop them off at their hotel. Once they were in the room, they called Selma and asked her to get them a flight back to the United States. While they were waiting to hear from her, they went out to an English-language bookstore to buy books to read on the long flight home.

Their itinerary included a stop in Houston, but the flying time was only seven hours and forty-one minutes. Sam slept through most of the flight to Houston while Remi read a book on the history of Guatemala. On the second flight, Remi slept while Sam read. When the plane lost altitude on its approach to the runway in San Diego, Remi's eyes opened. She said, 'I know what's wrong. We're missing our best ally in this.'

'Who's that?'

'Bartolomé de Las Casas.'

16

San Diego

Sam and Remi stepped out to the curb at the airport and found Selma waiting for them in the Volvo sedan. Zoltán was sitting sedately on the backseat of the car. Remi ducked in and sat beside Zoltán, who licked her face while she hugged and petted him. 'Zoltán. *Hianyoztal.*'

'What did you say?' Selma asked.

'I said I missed him. I missed you too, but you aren't a Hungarian dog.'

'Likewise, I'm sure,' said Selma. 'Hi, Sam.'

'Hi, Selma. Thanks for coming to meet us.'

'It's a pleasure. Zoltán and I have been moping around the house since the robbery at the university. David Caine calls every day, but I told him you'd get in touch when you were home.'

'That reminds me. We won't be here long. We're going to Spain,' said Sam. 'But first we want to meet with you and David. We can bring one another up to date on everything and then get busy on the next step.'

'All right. When we're home, I'll get going on your reservations,' said Selma. 'It's a shame you're leaving.

While you were in Guatemala, the workmen completed the painting and finish work. Your house is, well, your house again.'

'No carpenters, painters or electricians left?' said Remi.

'Not one,' Selma said. 'I even had a cleaning crew in to be sure there's not a dimple of a bullet hole, a microscopic stain from a drop of blood, or a sliver of broken glass anywhere. Everything's new.'

'Thanks, Selma,' said Remi. 'We're grateful.'

Sam said, 'We'll try to keep it nice by not discharging firearms in the living room.'

Remi said, 'Selma, I want you to spend some time with me before we meet with David Caine. I need to know everything you've got about Bartolomé de Las Casas and about the four known Mayan codices.'

'I'll be delighted,' said Selma. 'I've been hoarding information on those topics since you were in Mexico.'

Six hours later, they were on the ground floor of the house, sitting around the conference table. In the center was a photocopy of the letter from Bartolomé de Las Casas.

Sam said to David Caine, who had just arrived, 'I think Remi would like to start.'

'I just want to say thank you to Selma for having photographed the letter before turning it over to me,' David interjected.

Remi began. 'By the time the Dresden Codex's existence became widely known, an Italian scholar had made a tracing of it. Before the Madrid Codex ever got to the Museo América de Madrid, a French abbot made a copy. The Paris Codex was copied by the same Italian scholar who traced the Dresden. Somebody at the Bibliothèque Nationale actually threw the original in a bin in a corner of a room, which damaged it, so it's a good thing there was a copy.'

'An interesting set of coincidences,' said David Caine. 'Where are you going with it?'

Remi said, 'We know that this codex was at one point in the hands of Bartolomé de Las Casas. This letter proves that he touched it, that he knew it was important and thought it must be saved.'

Selma said, 'We know that he was a passionate defender of the native people's rights and a believer in the value of their cultures and that he studied and spoke their languages.'

David Caine slapped his hand to his forehead. 'Of course! You're saying there's a chance that Las Casas might have made a copy.'

'We can't be sure,' said Remi, 'but we think it's worth checking.'

'It's a long shot,' said Caine. 'As far as I know, there's no mention in any of his writings of his making a copy of a Mayan book. He does mention seeing the priests burning them.'

'That would be a good reason not to mention his copy,' said Selma. 'Books weren't the only things getting burned in those days.'

Remi said, 'After Las Casas left the mission at Rabinal, he became bishop of Chiapas, Mexico. From there, he went back to the Spanish court, where he was a very powerful adviser on issues having to do with the Indians in the colonies. And here's the promising part. When he died in 1566, he left a very large library to the College of San Gregorio in Valladolid.'

David Caine considered. 'You know, I think your observation about human nature may be right. Everybody in Europe who saw the importance of the Mayan codices seems to have made a copy. Even I made photographic copies. It was practically the first thing I did. If only I hadn't given them up to those fake officials.'

Selma quickly diverted the conversation back to Las Casas. 'Then we're agreed. We know Las Casas saw it and was somebody who would have wanted a copy. If he made one, then it was almost certainly kept with his own books and papers rather than, say, submitted to the Spanish court. His books and papers are in Valladolid, Spain. If the copy existed, and if it's been in a library in Spain all this time instead of the hot, humid Guatemalan jungle, then it will probably have survived.'

David Caine said, 'That's a lot of ifs. But to bolster the argument a bit, we know he would not have left any susceptible or incriminating papers in the New World, where his enemies, the Franciscans or the *encomiendas*, could find them. He definitely would have taken them with him to Spain.'

Remi said, 'A lot of ifs, all right, but each one has a lot of arguments in its favor and not many against.'

'Let's call it an educated, long-shot guess,' Selma said. 'It really should be checked.'

Sam said, 'Okay, Selma. Please make arrangements to get Remi and me to Valladolid. Make us a copy of the letter so we can recognize his handwriting if we see it.'

Sarah Allersby sat in the giant office of the Empresa Guerrero in the old part of Guatemala City. It had once been the business office in the capital of the powerful and wealthy Guerrero family. They had occupied the building from colonial days, until the modern civil war bled many of its businesses and made the younger generation leave for lives of leisure in Europe. The office was near the Palacio Nacional because the big ranching families, of necessity, had been involved in the government.

Through all of the nineteenth and most of the twentieth centuries, a man in the Guerrero family would push out his chair from the big mahogany desk in the office, take his hat and cane from the rack near the door, light a cigar, and walk up the street to government headquarters to protect and further the interests of the Guerrero family companies. The building had an impressive but low baroque façade, a set of double doors that were so heavy that Sarah Allersby had to have an electric motor installed to help her push them open, and floors of antique tiles made and decorated by the same craftsmen who had done the Iglesia de La Merced. The ceilings were fifteen feet high, and every few feet a big lazy fan still provided the proper subtropical atmosphere even though the air it circulated was air-conditioned to seventy-two degrees.

Sarah used a 1930s-era desk telephone with a scrambled line that was checked by her security people twice each day to detect a change in ohms of resistance that would indicate a listening device. She said, 'Good morning, Russell. This line is safe so you can speak freely.'

The man on the other end had a contract with the Estancia Guerrero, but Sarah's family had used his services many times in the years before they had acquired the Guatemalan holdings. He was the man who had impersonated an FBI agent in San Diego. 'What can I do for you, Miss Allersby?'

'It's more trouble over the item we picked up in San Diego. Sam and Remi Fargo have been here in Guatemala and even managed to find their way on to the Estancia. They've been defaming me and my company to anyone who will listen. They seem to think that the marijuana operation on the Estancia is mine, as though I were some tawdry drug dealer. They wanted the police to search my house and all of my properties, if you can imagine.'

'Is there any chance the police will do that?'

'Of course not,' she said. 'But I can't simply ignore them. They left for the United States yesterday. I know they won't get anywhere with the authorities here, but I have no way of knowing what they can do there. I need to have them watched for a while.'

'Certainly,' he said. 'There are two ways to go about this kind of thing. We can simply hire some local San Diego private detectives. That would mean leaving a record that we had hired them and taking the risk that they might have to reveal who hired them in court sometime. Then there's –'

'The other way, please,' she said. 'What we've already done in San Diego could generate terrible legal problems. And I worry about this Sam Fargo. He's vindictive. He won't be able to let this go. And if he wanted to, his wife wouldn't let him. I think she's developed a jealous fear that I'm a threat to her marriage. She's got nothing going for her but her looks, and as soon as somebody prettier is around, she knows she's in trouble.'

'All right,' Russell said. 'The Fargos haven't seen me. I can do this myself with one good man. We can be in San Diego in a couple of hours.'

'Thank you, Russell. I'll have some money sent to your company to cover the initial expenses.'

'Thank you.'

'Just knowing you're personally paying attention to the problem will make me sleep better. I'm just one person, and I can't be expected to pay attention to everybody everywhere who wants to harm me.'

'Would you like to set a limit on how expensive this gets?'

'No. If they leave the United States, send people wherever they go. I want to know where they are. And I never want them suddenly showing up on my doorstep again. But I don't want to leave a record that I had them followed. I really can't have them ruining my reputation.'

Russell was already preparing for the trip while he listened. He took a suitcase out of his closet and set it on the bed. 'I'll let you know as soon as there's anything to report.'

'Thank you, Russell.'

Next, Russell called the number of Jerry Ruiz, the man who had impersonated the Mexican Minister of Culture when they had confiscated the codex. 'Hi, Jerry. This is Russ. I'd like you with me on a surveillance job.'

'Where?'

'It's back in San Diego, but it could go anywhere from there. We're to keep track of a couple, period. We can split what Sarah gives us, even.'

'It's for her? Okay, I'm in.'

'I'll pick you up in a half hour.'

Russell hung up and returned to his suitcase. He packed the sets of clothes he used for surveillance – black jeans and navy blue nylon windbreaker and black sneakers, baseball caps in several colors, some olive drab hiking pants that unzipped into shorts, a couple of sport coats in navy and gray, some khaki pants. He and Ruiz would fly down and rent a car and after a couple of days he would turn it in and get another one.

He had found over the years that even a minor change in his appearance had a dramatic effect. Just putting on a hat and a different jacket made him a new person. Alternating drivers, getting out of the car and sitting at a restaurant table, made him invisible.

He completed his packing by throwing in some equipment: a shooter's 60-power spotting scope, with a small tripod, and his personal weapons and some ammunition. He knew that Ruiz would come prepared. Ruiz habitually carried a pistol, even in Los Angeles, and had a boot knife, because that was the way he had come up. He had been a collector for a street gang as a teenager and then he became a cop for a while. It was a strange twist that as he'd come into middle age, he had begun to look like a Mexican politician or a judge. His appearance made him a good man for the job. He wasn't automatically a suspect. He was also fluent in Spanish and that helped many times.

When Russell took this kind of job, he liked to have more time to prepare, but he would manage. He threw in his passport, five thousand dollars in cash, and a laptop computer. He closed his suitcase and went out to his car. He locked the house, then stopped for a second to be sure he'd forgotten nothing essential. Then he got into the car and drove toward Ruiz's house, thinking about the job.

Sarah Allersby was on the verge of taking a big step toward learning who she was. That was the way he thought about it. He had worked for many bosses over the years and he had seen the way they learned. They started out with the proposition that they were better than other people and therefore had a responsibility to lead them. In exchange for that brave work, they gained most of the available wealth. Once they had the wealth, it was theirs, and they had a right to protect it and the privileges it bought. If that was true, then they also had a right to get more in the same way – or, really, in any way, including taking it. They got involved in businesses that killed people indirectly, where they didn't have to see it. Diego San Martin, the drug lord who paid Sarah for the security of being able to raise marijuana on the land of a rich, respectable woman, had killed people. He was probably killing people all the time. Little by little, she was getting used to the idea that it didn't matter. Russell had met Sarah's father after Mr Allersby had already reached that point. Russell's first job for the older Allersby was to kill a man – a business rival who was preparing to file a patent infringement suit.

Russell knew, although Sarah hadn't taken the step yet, that she was very nearly ready to buy the deaths of these Fargo people. That could happen at any time. It occurred to him that he had better stop at the office and pick up a couple of additional items. He drove to the back of the building and went up the exterior stairway, unlocked the door and turned on the light.

He went to a locked filing cabinet and opened it. He took a pair of razor-sharp ceramic knives, which wouldn't set off metal detectors, and a diabetic's travel kit, with needles and insulin bottles, in a leather case. The insulin in the bottles had been replaced with Anectine, a drug that surgeons used to stop the heart. They would restart it with Adrenaline, but, of course, restarting hearts wasn't the business Russell was in so he had none of that. He opened the leather case and looked at the prescription date. It was the new one, only a month old. He took the kit with him and put it in his suitcase.

As Russell drove on toward Ruiz's house, he felt better. When Sarah got around to recognizing what she really wanted done, Russell and Ruiz would be able to take care of it without uncertainty or delay. Upper-class customers like her hated uncertainty, and they hated waiting. They wanted to be able to signify their will and have it carried out right away, like gods.

17

San Diego to Spain

Remi and Sam boarded their plane out of San Diego two days later. The flight took them to New York JFK, where they had to wait for their next plane to leave for Madrid in the late evening. The flight brought them into Madrid-Barajas Airport early in the morning.

When they had been hiking in Guatemala, they had tried to look like ecotourists or history buffs so they'd brought only well-worn tropical clothes, which they had rolled up and carried in their backpacks. This time, they were traveling as a pair of rich American tourists who couldn't possibly be doing anything serious.

They had bought new matching luggage that looked as expensive as it was. Each piece had an embossed leather tag sewn on that said 'Fargo,' and one was packed with the Brioni suits Sam had bought a few months ago in Rome, the other with some of Remi's fashionable dresses, shoes and jewelry. Remi brought a Fendi perforated-leather sleeveless dress with a nude silk lining she'd been saving, a Dolce & Gabbana floral-print dress, and a short J. Mendel silk crew-neck dress that had made Sam watch her walk all the way across the room when she'd tried it on.

Also inside their bags were small digital spy cameras, two embedded in watches and two in clear eyeglasses. They knew that if the copy of the codex existed, they would not be able to remove it from the building, and getting permission to photograph it would be at least difficult and maybe impossible. Even worse, just asking permission would announce to the rest of the world that the copy existed and would soon reveal what it contained.

They flew first class on the transatlantic flight, and, when they arrived, they took a taxi to the Chamartin station and boarded the streamlined Alta Velocidad Española bullet train to Valladolid. The train took only an hour and ten minutes to cover a hundred and thirty miles, including passing through a seventeen-mile tunnel. Selma had made a reservation for them at the Zenit Imperial Hotel, a fifteenth-century palace next to the Town Hall and the Plaza Mayor. She also downloaded a digital version of a guidebook to Valladolid on Remi's iPad.

Sam and Remi spent their first day exploring the city, validating their appearance as rich tourists who had time to spare. The modern city of Valladolid is a manufacturing and communications center and a major grain market, but they entertained themselves by seeking out the old city, where the remnants of the Middle Ages still stood.

Remi read from a guidebook as they walked from place to place. 'The Spanish conquered the city from the Moors in the tenth century. Unfortunately, they forgot to ask the Moors what Valladolid meant, so we don't know.'

'Thanks for that,' said Sam. 'Anything else on the list of missing facts?'

'Loads. But we do know Valladolid was the chief residence of the kings of Castile. Ferdinand and Isabella were married here and Columbus died here. Cervantes wrote part of *Don Quixote* here.'

'I'm impressed,' said Sam. 'And I'm serious.'

Their last stop was the Colegio de San Gregorio, where Las Casas lived for several years after he returned from the New World. They walked to the front of the great stone building as Remi checked her guidebook. 'The portal to the chapel – the building in front of us – was built by Alonso de Burgos, confessor to Queen Isabella, in 1488. The chapel itself was finished in 1490.' She looked down at the stones of the pavement. 'So, right now, we're standing where Columbus, Queen Isabella and Ferdinand probably stood.'

'Not to mention Bartolomé de Las Casas,' Sam said quietly. 'It's really an amazing piece of architecture.'

'Las Casas came here to live in 1551. He rented a cell in the college. During this period, he was very influential at Emperor Charles V's court. He died in 1566, in Madrid, but left his extensive library to the college. Our next mission is to see if we can find it.'

On the other side of the street there was a gaggle of German tourists being led by a tall blond woman who was lecturing them on the sights. In the center of the group were the two men who had followed Sam and Remi to Spain, Russell and Ruiz. When Sam and Remi stepped into the entrance, Russell and Ruiz separated themselves from the German tourists and moved down the street to watch the chapel from a distance.

Sam and Remi walked through the entrance and into the chapel. It was a dream of white stone, carved and polished five hundred years ago and still the same in the echoing silence as though time had only passed by outside, not in here.

'The upper tier must be where Las Casas rented his room,' said Sam, 'and where he wrote his last few books.'

They walked through the college while Remi scanned the guidebook. 'Life wasn't all pretty here,' she said. 'In 1559, the Inquisition burned twenty-seven people at the stake in Valladolid. And, at one point, an enemy denounced Las Casas to the Inquisitors too, but the accusation didn't go anywhere. When Las Casas signed over the rights to his *History of the Indies* to the college, he added the condition that it not be published until forty years passed. He said that if God destroyed Spain for its sins, he wanted people in the future to know what exactly they had done wrong – they had treated the Indians with such cruelty.'

'Let's keep looking. If we find his library, maybe we

can make an appointment to get in and take a look at it tomorrow,' said Sam. They continued to search and eventually found their way to a museum of Spanish sculpture. They approached the man at the desk near the entrance. 'Here goes,' Remi whispered.

Remi said to him in Spanish, 'Sir, do you know where we should go to see the library that Bishop Bartolomé de Las Casas donated to the College of San Gregorio?'

'Yes, I do,' replied the man. 'First, you must know that it's all part of the University of Valladolid.'

'I suppose the books had to be moved to a modern university.'

The man smiled. 'The university was founded in 1346. But, yes, it's modern. It's an active institution, with thirty-one thousand students. The College of San Gregorio is a part of it but serves mainly as a museum of art and architecture now. The monks are gone. I believe what you're looking for is quite close by in the History Library.'

'How do we find the History Library?'

'Go down the Calle Gondomar to the main university. Outside is the patio. There are three levels set on octagonal pillars. On the right side is the chapel and on the left is a semicircular porch. Go left. The first level houses the History Library.'

As they walked to the library, Sam noticed that two men were on the same course, walking far behind them on Calle Gondomar. He wondered for a moment if they could be following him and Remi. He and Remi had, after all, put Sarah Allersby on notice that they weren't going to let her rob them and forget it. But they were a long way from Guatemala City, and they'd just arrived in Valladolid. Could these men have followed them here already? They would have had to be watching them in San Diego practically from the time they'd come home from Guatemala, then caught the same plane or the one after it.

They reached the History Library, and Remi asked in Spanish whether they could see the collection of books that Bartolomé de Las Casas had left the College of San Gregorio. They were pleasantly surprised to learn that they could sign in as visiting scholars, and a librarian would admit them, without too many intimidating formalities. They only had to prove their identities and leave Remi's purse and their passports at the desk. When they entered a large reading room, there were already a few graduate students reading old books at tables.

A second history librarian showed them to a rare book room, gave them gloves, and allowed them to examine the volumes in the Las Casas collection for about three hours, going from one volume to the next. All of the volumes were bound or rebound in old leather. Some were hand-copied Latin or Spanish in archaic handwriting, some were incunabula – works printed before 1500 – a few in medieval Gothic script with hand-painted illumination. Most were religious works in Latin. There were commentaries on the Bible, collected sermons, multiple copies of breviaries. There was a copy of the Corpus Aristotelicum. There were also Spanish volumes written or copied in a hand that was clearly the same as the writing on the letter that had been hidden in the Mayan codex. Whenever they saw one, it excited them, but none was what they had come so far to find. The treasure they searched for would consist of Mayan pictures and glyphs, not Spanish text.

At the end of the day, just before it was time for visitors to leave the library, the desk librarian made an announcement that readers should return books. The Fargos gave theirs up immediately, went to the desk to retrieve Remi's bag, and left. As they emerged on to the patio outside the building, Remi whispered, 'Have you seen those two men before?'

Sam stopped, apparently to look around him at the medieval Spanish architecture but took a moment to find the men she meant. They were already walking off in another direction. 'I saw a couple of men earlier on the Calle Gondomar, but I can't tell if those are the same ones. What did they do?'

'I could feel them staring at us.'

Sam smiled. 'You could feel them staring at *you*, more likely. You should be used to that.'

That evening, Sam and Remi began their exploration of the city's nightlife with the Plaza Mayor, right outside their hotel. They sampled the coffee in the Continental, then went for *pinchos*, the favorite local iteration of tapas, at Restaurante Los Zagales. The *pinchos* were made of morcilla sausages, red onion and pork rind, all wrapped into a roll.

Each day, Sam and Remi walked from the Zenit Imperial Hotel and returned to the History Library to examine the next group of five-hundred-year-old books.

After the library closed in the afternoon, Sam and Remi returned to their hotel for a nap, then got up at ten to begin their evening of exploring. That night they tried Taberna Pradera, known for the fresh calamari cracker in its own ink. The following night, they tried Fortuna 25, which served a free-range chicken stuffed with mussels and algae. Another night, it was Taberna del Zurdo. They drank Rueda, Ribera del Duero, and other fine Spanish red wines, moving from place to place as though each evening were a celebration.

They made good progress with the Las Casas collection, making their inventory and, in the process, getting to know a little about the man who had owned these books. Most of them were books like the *Rule of Saint Benedict*, the work that set the tone for the monastic life, the *Moralium Libri* of Pope Gregory I, and others that were appropriate for a monk in the sixteenth century. They found several copies of the works of Thomas Aquinas, and a handwritten volume of commentary on them.

It was on their eighth day in the library that Sam and Remi ran into another trove of volumes in Spanish that had been written on vellum in the hand of Bartolomé de Las Casas. They were tall, in a ledger format, all in a sequence. The first were his attempts, written in Mexico, at collecting a K'iche' language glossary. There were also observations on the other languages of the Mayans, written in 1536. The next volume was a journal recording the daily activities that had gone on at the Dominican missions he had founded at Rabinal, Sacapulas, and Cobán. Records of expenditures and harvests were interspersed with various notes on the building of churches in the region and the names of Mayan converts who had come to live outside Rabinal. Remi read that he was opposed to mass conversions of Indians. He believed in teaching each prospective Catholic and then letting him or her make an informed decision, so the inventory of converts made sense.

The date of the volume after that was October 1536, and it extended through to April 1537. It began with the now-familiar figures and notations on vellum that had been divided into columns by straight lines. It went on for many pages, and then, at a certain point, the quality of the vellum changed.

The first pages were routine quality, made from the skin of an animal, treated by removing the hair, wetting, stretching and drying the skin until it was a thin white surface for writing on both sides. But sewn in after fifty or sixty sheets was a long section of pages of a different quality vellum. These had been rubbed so thoroughly with pumice stone or a similar abrasive to make a perfectly smooth writing surface that they were translucent.

Sam turned the first page in this section and saw a startling sight. It was an exact copy of the letter from Las Casas that had been hidden in the binding of the Mayan codex. He touched Remi's arm, and they both stared at the familiar Spanish words:

'A todos mis compatriotas, bendiciones. Este libro y otros de los maya se refieren a su historia y sus observaciones acerca del mundo natural. No tienen nada que ver con el Diablo. Ellos deben ser preservados como una manera de entender nuestras tareas con los maya.'

'I can make out most of the words and can hardly believe it,' said Sam.

'I can hardly breathe,' said Remi. 'I'm afraid to turn the page.'

Sam reached down and carefully turned the page. What appeared was the opening page of the Mayan codex they had found on the Mexican volcano. They turned page after page, slowly, gently. Each time the vellum turned, there was a familiar display. The four-page map was there in all its complexity. The illustrated story of the creation of the universe was there. The story of the war between the cities was there. Each small glyph was drawn with a fine-cut quill pen, its intricacies reproduced exactly.

Sam stood up. 'Excuse me.' He went to the men's room, made sure it was empty, took out his satellite phone, and called Selma in San Diego. 'Selma?'

'Yes?'

'We've found it. Turn everything on, and prepare to

receive live video starting in fifteen seconds. We won't be able to speak to you until it's over.'

'Got it. Making the connection to all four cameras now.'

'Got to go.'

Sam returned from the men's room and whispered to Remi, 'Your eyes must be getting strained. Don't be vain. Put on your glasses.'

Remi and Sam put on the two cameras disguised as glasses and went back to the first page. As they turned the pages, they were sending digital video with the camera glasses. They could see that the copy Las Casas had made was done with extreme care. He had not made an attempt to reproduce the colors of the original, but everything else was the same. The pages had been scored with a straight edge to divide the space into columns, usually six but sometimes eight, as the original had been. The pages had not been given Arabic folio numbers, but Sam and Remi could tell from memory that at least the beginning thirty pages seemed to be in order. Selma's voice came through the tiny earphones embedded in the stems of their eyeglasses. 'I'm receiving everything clearly. Keep going.'

Sam and Remi kept turning pages and filming until they reached the one hundred and thirty-sixth and final page. Then they started over again at the end of the section and took still photographs of each spread of open pages, using the cameras in their wristwatches.

When they had finished, Sam folded his glasses and

put them into his jacket pocket. 'I'm getting tired. Let's go back to our hotel.'

They returned the volume to the librarian for reshelving and then retrieved Remi's bag and the briefcase Sam had brought. They thanked the librarian and left the building.

As they went down the steps in the late afternoon and turned to walk along the street toward their hotel, Sam reminded Remi, 'No matter what happens in the next few minutes, don't be startled, and hold on to your glasses and wristwatch.'

As they walked along the Calle de las Cadenas de San Gregorio to the Plaza Mayor, they were only two tourists in a large, open space with hundreds of people. When they were about halfway across the plaza, they heard a new sound – the deep, throaty sound of a motorcycle engine. The engine grew louder as the motorcycle came around a corner somewhere behind them. Remi started to turn to look over her shoulder, but Sam put his arm around her and whispered, 'Don't look or you'll scare them off.'

The motorcycle sped up directly behind them, and Sam turned suddenly. On the cycle were a driver and a man riding behind him. Both men were wearing helmets with tinted visors over their faces. As the motorcycle swooped in, the driver made an attempt to snatch Sam's briefcase out of his hand, but Sam held on to it, tugging back, as the driver pulled. The power of the cycle added to the driver's force, but Sam trotted alongside, still holding on. When the second man saw the way Sam held on, he joined the struggle, grasped the briefcase with both hands, and wrenched it away. The driver gunned the engine and accelerated, and the motorcycle roared off around the side of the Plaza, turned, and disappeared up a narrow street between tall buildings.

Sam held up his empty hand so Remi could see it.

'Sam! He stole your new briefcase!'

He smiled. 'A little engineering project.'

'What are you talking about? Those men stole your briefcase! We've got to call the police!'

'No need,' he said. 'Those are the two we noticed about a week ago outside San Gregorio. I saw them watching us a few times since then. They were too interested to be nobody. So I bought the briefcase and began my project.'

'Your briefcase is an engineering project?'

'Didn't I say that?'

'Stop being mysterious and tell me what you've done.'

'You know those booby-trapped bags of money that banks give to bank robbers?'

'The ones that blow up and cover the thief with indelible ink? Oh, no. How did you even get an explosive on the plane?'

'I didn't use explosives. This one works with springs. Undo the latch and the first spring pops the case open wide, and that allows the second to spring upward and push a piston, like a jack-in-the-box. The cylinder is full of ink. I bought the briefcase, the springs and the ink here.'

'What would have happened if the librarian had inspected it?'

'He didn't open anything for the first two days, so why do it later?'

'What would have happened to him?'

'He would have a bright blue face. *"Azul"*, as they say here.'

'You couldn't just watch these men and not play some dumb prank?'

'I did watch them. I noticed they spoke English to each other, and one of them spoke Spanish to everybody else – rapid, fluent Spanish that didn't leave anybody looking confused. I thought about who would spend several days watching us like that without doing anything. The only answer is that Sarah Allersby must have sent them.'

'Why would she do that? She has the codex. She doesn't need a copy.'

'To find out what we're doing and what we've accomplished.'

'And?'

'And now she knows. Once her men followed us to Valladolid, I'm sure she could figure out what else might be here. All I could do is make sure we know them if we see them again in the next few days.'

They walked quickly to their hotel, downloaded the

photographs from the digital cameras to Remi's laptop computer, and then sent two versions to Selma's computer in San Diego as a backup. While Remi waited for the transfers to be completed, she made a reservation to fly to San Diego on the red-eye leaving in four hours.

As she and Sam finished packing, Remi's phone rang. She said, 'Hi, Selma. Are the pictures all clear? Good. We're coming home.' There was a pause. Then she said, 'Because a couple of men stole Sam's briefcase. When they open it, they're going to want to kill us. If they don't succeed, we'll see you tomorrow night.'

18

Valladolid, Spain

Russell was in the bathroom of the hotel suite in Valladolid, dabbing at his blue face with a cotton ball soaked in acetone. The thick nail-polish-remover smell stung his sinuses. Added to the smell of the isopropyl alcohol and the turpentine he had tried first, it made the small, enclosed space unbearable. He looked in the mirror above the sink. 'This isn't working either. And it stinks.'

'Maybe if you rub a little harder,' said Ruiz. He could see through the blue dye on Russell's face that his chin was getting blotchy and irritated, but Ruiz didn't feel like going out again searching Valladolid for more chemicals and solvents.

Russell handed him the bottle and then used soap and water to wash the acetone off his face. 'Get something else.'

Ruiz said, 'This stuff almost always works. We used it to wash checks years ago. It would take off the ink in a couple of minutes.'

'We're not washing checks now,' said Russell. 'This is my face. But you gave me an idea. Remember, there was a secret to washing checks. If the dye in the ink was polar, the best thing to get it off was a polar solvent, like alcohol and acetone. Well, we've tried those. So let's try a nonpolar solvent like toluene.'

'Toluene?' said Ruiz. 'What's another name for it?'

'Methylbenzene.'

'Where do I go for that?'

'A paint store, the kind for artists, might have it. You go in and ask for paint thinners. Get every kind they have. Try that first. If you pass by a dry cleaner, try them too. Say you spilled ink on a couch and you'll pay for some of the stuff they use for ink stains.'

'I'm getting hungry,' said Ruiz.

'Buy something to eat on the way, then. I can't go out like this and shop for thinners, and the smells are making me sick, so I couldn't eat anyway. Just get me something that will take the ink off. We've got to fix this now.'

Ruiz picked up his jacket off the chair and went down the hall to the narrow, cagelike elevator. When Russell heard the elevator's grating slide to the side to admit Ruiz, he rinsed his face again and looked in the mirror. His face felt so hot that, if the blue were removed, it would be glowing.

The trap had sprung when he had unlatched the briefcase. One spring mechanism had snapped the briefcase open, and the other had pushed the circular bottom of an ink-filled cylinder upward like a piston. It had been sealed at the top with only a layer of wax paper. Ink had shot out on to his face and chest.

Fiendish. What kind of person thought that way?

The trap had required that Fargo figure out in advance that somebody was going to take his briefcase. Russell was sure he hadn't been spotted. Had Ruiz made some stupid mistake? Or did Fargo always walk around in foreign cities carrying a booby trap?

Russell rubbed some cold cream all over his face and neck, desperate to soothe his burning skin. He dialed his satellite phone.

'Hello,' said Sarah Allersby.

'It's me,' he said. 'We went to San Diego and then followed them to the airport. They flew to Spain. That's where I'm calling from – Valladolid.'

'What are they doing there?'

'We've been watching them for a few days. At first, all they did was go sightseeing in the daytime and out to expensive restaurants every night.'

'By now, they must have hit nearly all of them,' Sarah Allersby said.

'Pretty near. For eight days, they've been going to the University of Valladolid every day. They seem to be really interested in all the old buildings in town. But they've been doing some sort of research.'

'I'm starting to feel uncomfortable. Reassure me. What are they researching?'

'They go to the History Library and look at old books. Everywhere she goes, she has a big leather bag. After a couple of days, he started carrying a briefcase. They had to leave them with the librarian when they got there and pick them up when they left.'

'What was in the cases?'

'I figured they might be pulling a scam. The people who go to these old libraries to steal things like valuable prints or maps or illuminated pages all do it pretty much the same way. They go into a rare book room and read the books. They bring in a razor blade, hide it in one hand, and, when nobody's looking, run it down a page to cut it loose. Then they slip the page under their clothes. I couldn't watch them much, so I never saw them do anything.'

'You're getting me very nervous about this. Did you find out what books they looked at?'

'Ruiz went in once right after they left and took a look. The binding on the book said *Las Casas*. That means "the Houses", right?'

She sighed deeply, trying to use up a few seconds to avoid calling him an imbecile. She said calmly, 'It's the name of the Dominican friar who colonized the Alta Verapaz area of Guatemala. He was active around the time when the Mayan codex was buried by the landslide. I'm not sure what they could have thought they were accomplishing by reading about him.'

'I decided today that I was going to find out exactly what they'd been up to. Ruiz and I got on a motorcycle, and while they were walking in the plaza, we went by them fast. I snatched the briefcase out of Fargo's hand. It's a kind of robbery that happens all the time in Spain and Italy. Before the mark knows what happened, the bike is gone.'

'Were there pages inside the briefcase?'

'No.'

'What do the notes say? I'm sure you read his notes.'

'There were none. The briefcase was a booby trap. As soon as I clicked the clasp, a spring mechanism popped the case wide open, and another spring pushed a piston up a cylinder full of blue ink. It's all over my face.'

'Oh, my gosh!' she said. 'So he saw you watching them.'

'I don't think that's a fair assumption,' Russell said. 'The briefcase might have been only a precaution.'

'Then he knows about you now, doesn't he?'

'He only knows that he got robbed. He can't know why. They've been walking around here at night for over a week, wearing expensive clothes, staying in a fancy hotel, eating in exclusive restaurants. That attracts thieves.'

'I can't believe this,' Sarah muttered. It sounded to Russell as though she was talking to herself. 'These people will not go away and leave me alone. They keep pushing and pushing me. Did I tell you they denounced me to the Guatemala federal police? Well, they did. They're absolutely relentless, like ants. If you block one way in, they'll find another. They're persecuting me. I offered them a fair price. They're the ones who turned me down.'

'I'm sorry we didn't stop them in San Diego. Or here, at least.'

Sarah was feeling more and more sorry for herself. 'Have you gotten cleaned up from the ink yet?'

'Not yet,' he said. 'We've tried several solvents, but, so far, no luck. I just sent Ruiz out for more.'

'Russell, I need somebody to rid me of these people. They've become vicious now, and dangerous – not only to my reputation and my business, but even to you. That ink trap could just as easily have been acid, or an explosive.'

'I'm sure he meant me to understand that. Any non-fatal attack is a warning.'

'We can't go on this way,' she said. 'If someone threatens your life, you're justified in using any force to save yourself.'

'I'm not sure the authorities here would see it that way,' he said. She was assuming he'd just kill the Fargos for free. He had been planning to offer that option for a high price.

She said, 'It doesn't matter what the authorities want. There's such a thing as natural rights.'

'I'm afraid that if you decided on an aggressive defense, I would have to charge an additional fee,' he said. 'I have to pay Ruiz, and so on.' He waited for an answer.

When it came, she sounded distracted, distant. 'Oh. Yes. I was thinking of you as an equal. But, of course, I had no right to do that. You're someone who works for me and has to think about money. How does an extra five thousand sound?'

'I was thinking it would have to be ten,' he said.

'Oh, Russell. I'd hate to think you called to get me all upset about what they'd done to you so you could take advantage of my sympathy to raise your prices.'

'No, Miss Allersby,' he said. 'I'd never do that. The figure is the minimum I'd actually need. I'll have to get my color back so I don't stand out, buy weapons for one-time use in a European country where they're heavily controlled, pay to dispose of the bodies, find a quiet way out of Spain and back to the US, and compensate Ruiz.'

'All right, then. Ten.'

'Thank you,' he said.

'But you have to do it, not just promise it and take the money in advance.'

'We're getting ahead of ourselves. I haven't gotten rid of my blue face yet.'

'You may not know this, but cosmetic companies sell opaque makeup that's designed to cover scars, birthmarks and discolorations. If the blue doesn't wash off, you can cover it up until your skin recovers on its own.'

'Thanks. I'll keep that in mind.'

'Do. When those horrible Fargo people disappear from my life, I'll make you glad they did.' He heard the click as she hung up.

Sarah sat in the big office in the old quarter of Guatemala City. Why was her patience being so sorely tested? These little people, these nothings, were making her life unbearable. Since they had left Guatemala,

Diego San Martin had come to her home to tell her that the Fargos had killed several members of one of his security patrols before they had slipped away into the jungle.

An enraged drug lord was not a pleasant guest. He had labor issues too. If men who worked for him were killed, he had to send big payments to their wives. If he didn't, the others would become timid and reluctant to do their jobs. If Diego San Martin couldn't keep people off the small corner of her land where he was raising and shipping marijuana, he couldn't make a profit and he would stop the commission he was paying her. In the current international economy, having a large stream of passive income was what kept her business profitable.

Sarah opened her computer and tapped in "Bartolomé de Las Casas". She read the entry quickly, and then came to the end. Las Casas had left his whole personal library to the Colegio de San Gregorio in Valladolid. What could a monk's personal library have been in 1566? The man had been the first colonizer of the north of Guatemala, a friend and teacher of Mayan kings. Could he have left a set of directions to find an abandoned Mayan city? A tomb with a fabulous treasure? All this time, Sarah had been thinking that the way to the next big discovery was going to be a Mayan codex, but it could just as easily be a Spanish priest's journal. She had never before considered such a thing, but if the Mayans were going to tell anyone a secret, it would have been Las Casas. He was their confessor, their protector.

The bloody Fargos might have discerned the one way to confound her. Of course, just the fact that they had beaten her to an idea didn't mean the idea was worth anything. The whole idea depended on something that might not have happened at all. Had Las Casas learned any secrets from the Mayans? Probably. Had he written them down and left them in his library of hymnals and catechisms and tracts? Who knew?

She had to get going now, to choose her destination and begin assembling the components of her first expedition. The idea of being beaten to a major discovery by a pair of inquisitive, jealous and resentful upstarts was maddening.

Sarah picked up her telephone and called the vice president in charge of the financial arm of her company.

'Yes, Miss Allersby?' he said. The Spanish-speaking employees of her companies had been instructed never to address her as *Señorita* because it sounded disrespectful to her English-trained ears.

'Ricardo, I need a favor.'

'Certainly, Miss Allersby,' he said. 'If you ask me, it's not a favor. It's my job.'

'I would like you to run credit checks on an American couple. The names are Samuel and Remi Fargo. They live on Goldfish Point in La Jolla, California, which is a section of San Diego. I want to know exactly what charges they're making on their credit cards and where.'

'Do you have any identifiers? Social Security numbers, dates of birth? Anything like that?'

'No. But you can buy them from their banks, can't you?'

'Of course, Miss Allersby, or from middlemen.'

'Then go ahead. They were here in Guatemala a couple of weeks ago. Their hotel will probably have made copies of their passports and will certainly have their credit card numbers.'

'Yes, Miss Allersby,' he said. 'I'll find out where they are and what they're doing and call you.'

'Good. Wait a few hours after that and run their credit again once each day so we can pick up any changes.'

'Certainly, Miss Allersby.'

She hung up and turned her attention to planning her expedition. She made long lists of things that needed to be done and, under them, the people she would order to do them. After about two hours, her cell phone rang again.

'Hello.'

'Miss Allersby, it's Ricardo Escorial. Samuel and Remi Fargo charged some airline tickets a few hours ago. They flew from Madrid to New York. In the afternoon, they'll arrive and take a flight from New York to San Diego.'

'Are you sure they got on the flight at Madrid?'

'Quite sure,' he said. 'Otherwise, by now there would be a refund or an additional charge for a change in reservations.'

'All right. Call me with an update tomorrow.' She hung up, then dialed another number.

'Hello?' It was Russell's voice again. He sounded as though he had been asleep.

'Hello, Russell. It's me. After the Fargos painted you blue, they took a plane to New York. They're booked on a second flight to San Diego in the late afternoon. So don't waste your time searching the tapas bars, looking for revenge. Go home and take care of this problem.'

19

La Jolla

It was early morning, and Remi and Sam sat at an outdoor table overlooking the Pacific at the Valencia Hotel,
where they often ate breakfast with Zoltán, only a few
hundred yards from their house. They'd already finished a morning run along the beach and now they were
having cups of espresso and a breakfast of smoked salmon on bagels with capers and onions. Zoltán had eaten
his breakfast at home before they'd gone out and was
content at this hour with a bowl of water and a few of
the biscuits that Remi carried in her pocket for treats.
When they'd finished, they paid their bill and started
walking across the vast green lawn toward their house.

Zoltán, always alert, stopped and stared in the direction of the beach, then moved forward again to lead the
way home. Remi said, 'What is it, Zoltán? Did you see
somebody that Sam painted blue? The one I wish you'd
paint blue is Sarah Allersby,' she added. She looked at her
watch, then at the stretch of lawn ahead. 'We'd better
move a little faster. David Caine will be there in a few
minutes.'

'Selma will let him in,' he said. 'Before he gets here,

we should talk about what we're willing to do on this project and what we're not willing to do.'

'Have we given adequate consideration to painting Sarah Allersby blue? I, for one, don't think so,' she said.

'The idea is growing on me. But, seriously, we're reaching the point where we may decide something is the next logical move but not want to do it. If a person takes enough risks, the time could come when he loses.'

'Who are you and what have you done with my husband?'

Sam smiled. 'I know I'm usually the one who wants to do something rash. But I can't forget what it felt like that day when our only way out was to dive into an underground river.'

'I haven't forgotten,' she said. 'By the way, that was pretty romantic when you tried to give me your air tank. I don't know if I've ever given you adequate credit for that. Who knew that the way to a girl's heart is through her lungs?'

'Let's talk things over with David, hear what he thinks but make a decision about what we do only after we've taken some time to think it through.'

'Okay.' She looked up at Sam as they walked, then suddenly stood on tiptoe and kissed his cheek.

'What was that for?'

'You know.'

They let Zoltán lead them home and arrived just as David Caine's car pulled up in front of their house. He got out carrying a big, string-tied accordion envelope under his arm. He shook Sam's hand, hugged Remi, and patted Zoltán.

When they were inside, he said, 'What you've done – deducing that a copy might have existed and then going to find it – was brilliant. And I've always been an admirer of Bartolomé de Las Casas, but even he has risen in my estimation. The copy he made seems to me to be nearly perfect. Tracing and copying a hundred and thirty-six pages of pictures and symbols that he couldn't have understood must have taken months. But as far as I can tell, he missed nothing.'

They went to a long table in the first-floor office area, and Caine laid out a series of digital images from Sam and Remi's library transmission. He had enlarged the images so it was possible to see each pen stroke and every mark on the vellum, including pores on the outer side of the hide.

Sam and Remi recognized the four-page map of the Mayan sites, with its text of Mayan glyphs and its stylized pictures.

Remi pointed at the first spot they had explored. 'There's our swimming pool, the cenote, where we had the shootout.'

Next, Caine laid out a series of enlarged satellite photographs of the same territory, placing each one under its Mayan representation. 'Here's the way these places look from above.'

Then he set out one more. 'And here's what I'm excited about – excited and worried.'

'What is it?' asked Remi.

'You remember I said at the beginning that it looked like there were a few major sets of buildings on these maps?'

'Yes,' she said.

'Well, I used aerial photographs and satellite images to see if there was anything in those locations to correspond to the drawings. Here are some of the results.'

'There are certainly buildings,' said Sam. He pointed at the photograph. 'These hills, here and here, are too tall and steep to be anything but large pyramids.'

Caine laid out three more pairs of photographs. 'Here are codex entries for four large complexes that modern scholars don't know exist.'

'How big is the city?' Sam asked.

'It's impossible to tell from photographs,' said Caine. 'There are possible stone ruins within a mile or two in each direction. Does that mean we've discovered a city that was three to five miles across? Probably not. But, then, what have we discovered? There's only one way to find out.'

Remi looked at the aerial photographs and satellite images. 'These things are so deeply hidden by the trees and vines and bushes. You can hardly see them even when you're standing on them.'

'That's why so many sites are still undisturbed,' Caine

said. 'Buildings look like hills covered with vegetation. But the codex tells us which hills aren't hills. You two have made a huge contribution.'

'I'm just glad it wasn't wasted effort,' said Sam.

'Hardly,' said Caine. 'Using the codex you found in Mexico and the copy you found in Spain, we've managed to discover at least five important sites – the complex around the cenote you explored and four ancient cities. The past fifteen years has already been the most productive period of Mayan studies ever. Your find is going to trigger a lot of excavations in short order. I can tell already that just studying the copy of the codex will teach us more about the written languages too. Even that will take years, of course. Linguistic studies require a number of people working to understand one specific grammatical quirk or unfamiliar vocabulary term and then others using that breakthrough to understand other texts. And proper excavation of a city is a job that has to be done with brushes and sifting screens, not bulldozers. We won't live long enough to see all of the important discoveries you've made possible.'

'You don't look happy about all of this progress,' said Remi.

'I'm worried. We have a copy of the codex, but Sarah Allersby has the original. If she pays the right person, she can get it translated, and I assume that's what she's doing. As soon as she can read it, she'll see everything I've just shown you.'

'You mean she'll find out where these cities are?' said Sam.

'And all of the other sites,' said Caine. 'While you were in Spain, I asked a colleague' – Caine saw the alarmed look on Remi's face – 'not the one I mistakenly trusted before. This one is a friend I've known for a number of years. His name is Ron Bingham. He's a professor at the University of Pennsylvania who specializes in Mayan technology. He's one of the world's best lithicists. He can examine a piece of obsidian and tell you where it came from and how it was used, or look at a structure and tell you how and when it was built, where the quarry was, and even how many times it was rebuilt.'

'Interesting specialty,' said Sam.

'The point is, his reputation is spotless. Integrity isn't negotiable and doesn't depend on the situation. But Ron can get invited to join any expedition in Central America, and a fair number anywhere else. He can't be tempted by Sarah Allersby.'

'If you trust him, we do too,' said Sam. 'What did he say?'

'Well, I told him I was planning to visit some of the sites this summer. He said that Sarah Allersby had approached him and several other people he knows to inform them she's mounting a major expedition that will begin soon. She implied that she knows exactly where she wants to go and what she expects to find there. She's already hiring people.'

'What sort of people?' Remi asked.

'Nobody like Ron. People like him run their own fieldwork. But this, she was promising, was something special. She's hiring experienced guides, Guatemalan workers who have been trained on archaeological digs in the past, cooks, drivers and so on. You can be sure there won't be anybody who could put up resistance to whatever she wants to do or question her methods or how she treats structures and artifacts. It's her show.'

'I guess this is the downside of finding the codex,' said Sam. 'Even if she hadn't stolen it, before long everything would have become public.'

'It didn't have to be this way,' said Caine. 'What we've done is hand the worst person in the field of Mayan history a virtual monopoly of the biggest finds over the next twenty-five years. Because of her personal fortune, she can be in the field while legitimate scholars are still writing grant proposals. We've also given her enough of a head start to loot at least four great Mayan cities and innumerable other sites. We'll probably never know how much she quietly sells off in Europe, Asia and the US that never becomes part of the historial record.'

'We can't let that happen,' Remi said. 'We've got to stop her.'

Sam put his arm around her shoulders. 'Wait a minute,' he said. He spoke to Caine as well as to Remi. 'When we were in Guatemala, we barely got out with our lives. I've seldom been so glad to get out of anywhere. When we ducked into that cenote, I thought we were going to die. If that unlikely way out hadn't been there, we would be dead.'

'I know that,' she said. 'I'd try to forget, but I know I can't. But bringing home that pot with the codex inside brought with it some responsibility. You heard David. Between our finding that codex and the university administration handing it over to impostors, we've given a whole field of study over to one nasty, spoiled, lying, thieving woman.'

David Caine said, 'This is really my responsibility. I've been planning my expedition for summer, but I'm afraid summer is going to be too late to head her off entirely. I think once I'm on the scene with a group of reputable colleagues, I can prevent the worst excesses. She's trying to buy a name for herself as an archaeologist. If eight or ten well-known archaeologists are present, she can hardly dismantle features or loot the tombs.'

'And she's already working as fast as she can.' Remi turned to Sam. 'I'll never forgive myself if we don't even try to stop her. About the only thing the Mayans have left is their history. If Sarah Allersby ends up stealing that too, it would be our fault. How are we going to feel in a year when she's publishing false accounts of her "discoveries" and misleading people about everything she finds?'

Sam sighed but said nothing.

'That's the one thing we actually know for sure,' said

Remi. 'All we have to do is look at the four major sites in the codex that David came to show us. We know the way she thinks. She's greedy. She'll start with the biggest one.'

Sam looked at Remi, then at Caine. 'I have to admit, that seems to be the way Sarah Allersby thinks. Which one is the biggest?'

'I'll go start packing,' said Remi. 'And, this time, I'd like to include a lot more ammunition.'

20

La Jolla

Russell stood beside Ruiz at the edge of the paved walkway above the beach at Goldfish Point. They could see the big house where Sam and Remi Fargo lived. So far, he and Ruiz had not agreed on a plan that would accomplish their goal or allow them to venture much closer than a quarter mile.

The problem was that Russell still didn't look right. His face was plastered with opaque makeup that served to cover the indelible blue ink, but the color wasn't right. It was the color of a plastic doll. And when he sweated, as he did on this San Diego beach, a very faint tinge of blue began to show through like tinted gesso behind a painting. He looked profoundly strange.

It seemed to Ruiz that every time he went to a new store to try for the right shade of makeup, he forgot the exact hue of Russell's skin and got a shade that was wrong. The one before last was a match for Ruiz's own skin, which made Russell's face look like a brown mask put on above a pink neck, and it made his ears seem to glow. But the new one, this pink, made Russell look like he wasn't quite human. Since the habitual expression on Russell's face since the accident was suppressed rage, he was scary even to Ruiz.

Even though they were sure the Fargos had never seen their faces, except, perhaps, for a blur on the passing motorcycle in Spain, the blue, or even the cover-up, would draw their attention and the attention of everyone else.

They waited above the beach, facing in the direction of the water whenever people were near, until the sun went down beyond the ocean. Now that it was fully dark, Russell felt better about moving closer to the Fargos' house. He had brought a small backpack, like a man who had spent a day at the beach, but it held a 5.56mm Steyr AUG rifle with a forty-two-round magazine and a stubby bullpup stock. Right now, it was broken down into three pieces that could be assembled in seconds without tools. The fourth piece was a factory-made suppressor that permitted it to fire without much more than a clacking from the moving parts and a spitting sound as the projectile left the muzzle.

Russell and Ruiz walked toward the street where private houses began. The first one on the point was the Fargos' massive four-story cube with balconies and large windows on three sides. The windows on the ocean side were bigger than the others and gave the impression from a distance that the whole place was a glass box. But as Russell and Ruiz came closer, they could see that each window had steel shutters that could be opened or closed.

They reached the Fargo property and stepped off the road into the grove of pine trees, sat down in the deep shadows, and watched the windows. On the first floor there was a middle-aged woman with short hair, wearing a vintage tie-dyed T-shirt and Japanese gardening pants, working in front of a desktop computer with an unusually large screen. Not far from her, at two other workstations, were a small blond woman in her twenties and a tall, thin man about the same age with close-cut brown hair.

And then there was the dog. Miss Allersby had mentioned him while they were planning how to get their hands on the Mayan codex. The German shepherd was what had made her decide she wanted only a half-hearted burglary to give these amateurs an idea of how much trouble it could be to keep artifacts worth millions lying around the house. When Russell had arrived for the break-in, he had been relieved that the dog was not on the premises.

Russell knew the house had been equipped with a number of security systems, sensors, cameras and alarms, so he didn't dare move in too close and certainly wouldn't try to get in. All he wanted was a clear shot at each of the Fargos.

As Russell watched, the dog appeared across the big room on the first floor, walked all the way to the middle-aged woman, and lay down at her feet. Miss Allersby had not exaggerated. He was a fine specimen, with all of the standard German shepherd characteristics.

Shepherds had a reputation for a keen sense of smell and fierce loyalty. This one was also a big fellow. And she'd said he was trained for the work. There would be no fooling him with a piece of prime rib and a pat on the head. If this dog got free, he would have to be killed before he got close enough to leap.

Russell watched the middle-aged woman go to a filing cabinet across the room, and the dog followed her there too. He looked as though he had been given an order to protect her. He leaned close to Ruiz. 'I don't see the Fargos.'

'Neither do I,' said Ruiz.

'We'll give it a little while longer. If she shows signs of letting the dog out, we'd better go.' He was distressed. Where were the Fargos? He had come so far, covered with greasy makeup, hoping to kill them. They had to be here. They had to.

The dog stood up suddenly in a single motion, his strong legs simply straightening under him. He walked to the front window and stared down into the darkness. He must have heard or seen them. Now he was making some kind of racket, probably growling.

The woman came to the window and looked in the direction she thought the dog was looking. Then she went away from the window, and Russell and Ruiz slipped out of the grove of pines to the street. The two men kept moving, trying to run quickly, as Russell pulled the nineteen-inch barrel out of the stock of the

Steyr AUG and shoved both pieces into his pack, then slung it over his shoulder.

They reached the ocean end of the street before the grove of pines lit up behind them. There seemed to be floodlights on every tree, aimed downward at the very spots that a man might mistake for a safe, sheltered vantage.

After another minute of running, they reached the concrete walkway above the beach. Ruiz looked at Russell, and his face took on a look of distaste. 'You've got to get out of the lights, man. You look like a blue vampire.'

Russell glanced down and saw that the sweat soaking the front of his shirt was mixed with the pink makeup. First Russell and then Ruiz vaulted over the railing and walked on the sand.

'How can they be gone?' said Russell. 'Where would they even go?' But he knew they were gone. He knew it as well as he knew anything. If they'd come here from Spain, home had only been a pit stop. They had eluded him again. They were where they could cause the most trouble, in Guatemala.

He waited until he and Ruiz reached his car. He had parked in a lot far down the beach. When he got there, he found a ticket on the windshield under the wiper. The check mark indicated he was parking after hours. He looked around him and saw the sign, unobstructed and bright under the streetlight: 'Lot closes at 8:00 p.m.' He hadn't noticed the sign when he had driven in.

He supposed that he should be relieved that he hadn't found the Fargos, taken a shot at one of them, and left, a parking ticket on record to show he'd been here. But he wasn't capable of being relieved about anything. This was another gratuitous annoyance, an infuriating obstacle laid in his path, in case being blue hadn't been enough.

He looked out each of the car windows, checked the mirrors, and saw no police cars, but he decided to drive with extreme care. He knew it was a bad idea to rely on luck, or even probability, when things were going badly. If he lingered or sped off in a rage, a cop would surely come by, pull him over, shine a flashlight on his blue face, and start asking questions he and Ruiz couldn't answer. He drove out of the lot and turned toward the freeway.

He speed-dialed the number on his satellite phone. He knew she would have hers with her at all times, even when she was asleep, so when she said, 'Yes?' he was neither surprised nor relieved.

'Hello. I'm on the road going away from the Fargo house. There's the older woman you met when you were there, the big dog, and two young people who seem to be employees too. No Fargos.'

'No Fargos?'

'No. I called to warn you. I'm afraid they might've gone back to Guatemala.'

'What do you think they're doing?'

'I don't really know. But now I'm wondering if they

really did find something in the library in Spain. Maybe they had it in the wife's bag, and he was just using the briefcase to keep us from going after it.'

'That sounds possible,' she said.

'Well, I just wanted you to know that you'd better be ready for them to show up down there.'

'I want you to come here. Can you get a late flight tonight or early tomorrow?'

'Uh, I'm a little uncomfortable talking about this. My face is still blue.'

'You haven't gotten rid of that yet?'

'No. I've used every solvent I know of and every kind of wash. I'm still blue. The makeup helps, kind of.'

'I'm going to get one of my doctors to call you. He's very good and will know your problem, so don't hang up on him. He'll have a colleague in Los Angeles who will see you.'

'What can a doctor do about this?'

'If I were to guess, I'd say a chemical peel to remove the outer layer of skin that's been dyed and leave nice new skin uncovered. But I'm not a doctor. He is. His name is Leighton. Whatever happens, I want you in Guatemala City by Thursday. And I want your friend Ruiz so you understand what people say to you.'

'All right,' he said. 'We'll be there. Thanks for your help.'

'It's not a favor, Russell. I need somebody reliable to be here to keep the Fargos from ruining this opportunity for me. This is going to be the most important project of my life, and these people are malicious. No matter how graciously I've treated them, both at their house and my own, or how generous my offer, they've decided to be my enemies. I need you to make them aware of what a bad idea that was.'

21

Belize

Sam and Remi could not tell how much influence Sarah Allersby might have with the authorities in Guatemala, but they decided she was unlikely to have anyone watching Belize for their arrival. They flew into Punta Gorda on a private jet and took a bus down the coast to Livingston, then paid a fisherman to take them upstream on the Río Dulce to Lago de Izabal, across the border in Guatemala. A visitor could enter any of the four countries of the region and deal with customs officials only once, then pass freely to the others.

They hired a second boat to take them the length of the lake. It was a vast expanse of blue-gray under a layer of clouds, and in the distance, beyond the shore, there was a wall of blue mountains. The trip was beautiful, and standing on the deck of the boat was a relief after so many miles on the road.

Sam and Remi were better prepared for their trip into the high country of central Guatemala. They had enlisted in advance the cooperation of like-minded officials: Amy Costa at the US Embassy in Guatemala City, and Commander Rueda of the Guatemalan national police. If the Fargos were to find any evidence that Sarah Allersby was violating the laws of the country regarding the transporting of antiquities, or had possession of the codex from the Mexican volcano, Rueda would arrest her. If necessary, he would fly in a squad of rangers to a remote area to do it.

Sam had spoken to Amy Costa on a conference call. 'He agreed to that? What caused the change of heart?'

'It's always hard to know,' said Amy Costa. 'We ask for cooperation and we always hope to get it. This time we will.'

After Sam and Remi hung up, Remi rolled her eyes. 'You really didn't notice?'

'Apparently not. Notice what?'

'She walked us past about thirty offices full of old married cops and went right into the office of this handsome guy about her age who couldn't keep his big brown eyes off her.'

'You're saying our State Department official is fraternizing with a Guatemalan cop?'

'No, I'm saying she's every bit as smart as she looks.'

Now they were back in Guatemala, and both of their satellite phones were programmed with the embassy number and the office of Commander Rueda. The lake was thirty-one miles long and sixteen miles wide, and as they reached the end at El Estor, Sam and Remi both felt good. Sometimes covering thirty miles in the highlands could take several days of hard climbing.

At El Estor, they hired a small boat to take them up

the Polochic River, which fed the lake from the west side. It was one hundred and fifty miles long, a winding, narrow stream bordered by jungle that came all the way down to the water like a green wall. It was navigable upstream as far as the town of Panzós, with an unpaved road to take them on from there.

As they moved up into the heart of the region, the forest was deeper and thicker, and the few settlements they saw seemed random, like places where people's gasoline or enthusiasm had run out and they had decided to build shelters and stay.

Once again, Sam and Remi had come armed. They still had their Guatemalan carry permits, and Selma had arranged to have four semi-automatic pistols purchased and waiting for them in Punta Gorda. As they had on their first trip, they carried one each in their packs and the others in bellybands under their shirts. They brought considerably more nine-millimeter ammunition, including ten loaded magazines each.

Now that they were in central Guatemala, whatever they had brought in their packs would have to do. There was no going back to pick up one more item. The closest place where Selma could have anything delivered was far away in Guatemala City. When Sam and Remi reached the end of the navigable section of the river at Panzós, they saw a loaded coffee truck parked along the dirt road above the river and pointed west. They asked their boatman to serve as interpreter to ask the driver for a ride, and learned that he was the boatman's friend.

They arranged to pay him a few Quetzales in exchange for a ride to the end of the road.

The ride lasted for two days. Their host had an iPod, with all of his favorite songs on it, and a cable that connected the iPod to the truck's radio speakers. His playlist began with songs in Spanish and then a few in English, and soon the three of them were singing loudly in whichever language came up as they bounced along the rough, rutted road westward through the forest.

At midday on the second day, they pulled into a depot where their dirt road met a larger dirt road. Trucks from other parts of the region were there unloading their coffee sacks on to a conveyor to be weighed, counted, and reloaded on to tractor-trailer trucks that drove on along the larger road. They bid an affectionate good-bye to the driver, who would soon get his turn at the scale, get paid, and go home.

When they walked off to the west, they checked their position on the GPS screens on their satellite phones. They were within twenty miles of their first-choice destination. They walked the rest of the day, heading straight for it. In the late afternoon, they crossed a game trail, and that made walking easier, although the trail angled a bit north of their destination. The vegetation was thick, and the tops of the trees stood over the trail like a line of umbrellas. There was little breeze, but the shade kept them from suffering under the sun.

They checked their position frequently and continued on the game trail. As they moved farther from the road and closer to the place they were looking for, they walked in near silence. When they needed to talk, they would stop to rest on a fallen log or a low, twisted limb, put their heads close, and whisper. They listened to the calls of birds and the screeches of the troops of howler monkeys passing overhead, trying to discern whether they'd been disturbed by human beings somewhere up ahead.

Sam and Remi had trekked through wilderness together many times, so they were comfortable moving through the Guatemalan highlands. The rhythms of the forest immediately became their rhythms. They got up as the sun was beginning to restore colors to the world, but it would not be above the horizon for another hour. They ate simply and broke camp so they could get in three or four hours of hiking before the day grew hot. They stopped when the sun was beginning to sink so they could select a site and set up their camp while they could still see. They used each opportunity to replenish their water supply by boiling and treating springwater or the water from streams. Their fires were small, made in shallow pits that Sam dug. If the wood was damp enough to smoke, they would go without the fire and eat preserved food from packets.

On the morning of the third day, the Global Positioning System on their satellite phones showed that they were close to the ruined city. They used Remi's phone to call Selma in San Diego.

'Good morning,' said Selma. 'How is it going so far?'

'We're getting very close, so we're calling now and then expect to be texting for a while to maintain silence,' Remi said.

'Have you seen anyone yet?'

'Not since we left the road three days ago,' said Remi. 'Even then, we were the only truck on the road. Are you tracking our phones' GPS signals?'

'Yes,' Selma said. 'Very clearly. I know right where you are.'

'Then we'll text you if we learn anything.'

'Please do,' Selma said. 'I'm getting a huge e-book bill and a ghostly pallor because I don't want to leave the office to go to a bookstore and miss your calls.'

'Sorry,' said Remi. 'Kiss Zoltán for me.'

'I will.'

'Bye.'

They hung up, and the next sound they heard was so shocking in the silence that they both swiveled their heads to locate its source. There was the faint thrum of a helicopter in the distance. They tried to spot the helicopter, but they were in a low dale beneath a thick canopy of leaves that obscured the sky. The engine grew louder until its roar overwhelmed all of the natural sounds of the forest.

They knew better than to stand and climb up to see it. After a minute, the helicopter passed overhead, and Sam and Remi looked up at it, seeing the wind from its rotors whipping the leaves of the upper tree branches around wildly before it swept on to the north and out of sight. They could hear the engine at about the same decibel level for another two minutes, and then the sound stopped entirely.

'I think it landed,' said Remi.

'So do I,' said Sam. 'Ready to take a closer look?'

'Going to find them is probably better than letting them find us.'

Sam and Remi put their packs in order. They loaded their spare pistols and moved them to a zippered outer compartment of their backpacks and hid Sam's phone in another compartment. They took with them only one pistol each, under their shirts, and Remi's phone. They hid their backpacks under thick foliage, marked the nearest tree, then moved off up the game trail.

As they walked, they did not speak, just directed each other's attention with a nod or a simple hand gesture. They would stop every twenty yards to listen but heard only the sounds of the forest. On the fourth stop, they heard human voices. Several men were talking loudly in Spanish, their voices overlapping and interrupting in cascades of words too fast for the rudimentary Spanish Sam had begun to learn.

And then the forest ahead of them brightened. Beyond the rank of trees was a large clearing. A group of men unloaded equipment from the helicopter and carried it to a place where a sun awning had been erected. There were several aluminum cases, a couple of video cameras, tripods, and unidentifiable accessories.

They could see the pilot, standing beside the open

door of his helicopter, with earphones on and a wire connecting him to the instrument panel. He spoke to someone on the radio.

Sam and Remi moved cautiously inside the forest, venturing closer to the edge. Suddenly Remi raised her eyes and pointed. At the right side of the large open area of low weeds and grasses, a high wooded hill that had been only partially visible looked different from this angle. From this side, Sam and Remi could see a stone stairway, straight and uninterrupted, running from the ground to the apex. The partial excavation of the steep hill revealed that what had seemed to be natural irregularities were layers of the pyramid. They were flat, with trees and brush growing on them, but in places the roots had dislodged stones from the structure and collapsed a corner from one level to the level below, making the profile more like a hill than a building.

This was unquestionably the step pyramid that had been depicted on the codex map and had appeared in the aerial photograph. A crew of about a hundred workmen were attacking the structure with axes, picks, mattocks, shovels and buckets to clear the pyramid of about a thousand years of accumulated leaves, humus, dirt and living plants. They moved quickly and swung hard, more like a demolition crew than archaeologists. Other workers were cutting and burning brush in different parts of the complex. Their labor was baring stone structures in all directions. Sam reached to Remi's hand, took her phone, and began to take pictures.

Remi whispered, 'If David Caine could see the way this place is being pounded and abused, it would kill him.' After a minute, she noticed a platoon of armed men moving single file out of the jungle, on the far side of the complex. There were about twenty of them, all carrying rifles on slings. There were a few other armed men stationed on the upper levels of the buildings. A couple of them waved to the men just arriving.

Sam was busy taking photographs with Remi's phone. He reviewed the shots, then sent them to Selma. He put away the phone and tapped Remi on the shoulder. They stayed low and slowly edged away from the cleared area. When they could, they stood and walked back up the game trail until they judged they were out of earshot. Sam pressed a number on Remi's phone and then the call button.

'Policía federales.'

'Hello. This is Sam Fargo.'

'And this is Commander Rueda,' said the voice. 'I've been keeping this line clear for your call.'

'Thank you, Commander. We're at the coordinates we gave you before we left home. As the Mayan codex indicated, what's here is a large city with a temple complex. We've been watching a crew of around a hundred men clearing away dirt and vegetation as fast as they can. There are also armed guards. A little while ago, a helicopter landed with what looks like a film crew.'

'Are they doing anything criminal?'

'They're uncovering the buildings with picks, mattocks

and shovels without much regard to the damage they do to what's beneath. But I'd say that the main problem so far is the one we've told you about. The only way that Sarah Allersby could have found this place is if she has the stolen Mayan codex from the University of California, San Diego.'

'If I send a squad of men to that location, will they find anything to charge her with?'

'I think they'll find notes that indicate where she learned the location, or even a photocopy of the codex page, which would prove it's been in her possession,' Sam said. 'Either way, maybe police can get the workers to excavate properly and not destroy what they're uncovering.'

'All right. I'll send a helicopter with soldiers to check on the excavation. That's all I can promise.'

'That's good enough for me. Thank you.' He handed Remi her phone.

Remi called Selma. 'Hi, Selma. We've been to the site. Have you seen the pictures? You can tell David it's as big as he thought. Sam just called the cops to come and take a look at the terrible job they're doing on this dig. We're hoping they'll also find evidence that she used the map in the codex.'

'Don't let the police forget that it could be in a computer or her phone, or it could be disguised as something else.'

'Don't worry. It's a fishing expedition, and we know fish don't all look the same.'

'Good luck.'

'Thanks. We're on our way back to the site.'

Sam and Remi moved up the trail again to the clearing. As they crouched in the brush, looking at what must have been the great plaza of the ancient Mayan city, they heard the distant chop of another helicopter. This one came from the south like the other, but its engine sounded different. The helicopter came straight in over the jungle, hovered above the center of the plaza, and then came down not far from the first helicopter.

The four-man camera crew that had been loitering under the sun awning snatched up their equipment and trotted to the helicopter, where the rotors were just slowing down, and began to film. Among them were a soundman, carrying a microphone on a long pole, a cinematographer with a video camera on his shoulder, a lighting man with battery-operated lights and a white umbrella on a tripod, and a fourth man with a large pack who paid out a length of insulated cord that led to a box under the awning.

The helicopter's engine stopped, and a door on the side opened. The first one out was Sarah Allersby's security guard, who looked like a cage fighter. He was broad and muscular, wore olive drab pants and a khaki shirt, and carried a small weapon on a sling that looked like a machine pistol. He stood by with the open door at his back while the main occupant of the helicopter stepped down.

271

Sarah Allersby's golden blond hair was tied straight back in a ponytail that shone on the back of her hand-made, light blue cotton work shirt. She wore a pair of slacks of tropical khaki, but they were tailor-fitted. She wore tie boots designed like combat boots but made of a soft brown, polished leather. Her costume looked perfect for an adventure but would not have stood up to a strenuous hour in this jungle.

As Sarah Allersby stepped away from the helicopter, the cameraman and his assistant sidestepped along beside her, recording her arrival as if she were General MacArthur stepping off the landing craft on to the beach at Leyte. As she walked, men in jungle gear, who had been waiting for her, approached and spoke to her with exaggerated respect, bowing, and then joined her entourage as she advanced, pointing out parts of the pyramid that towered above them.

The group walked all the way to the bottom of the great stairway and climbed a few steps upward. The cameraman said something, and Sarah Allersby stopped. She conferred with the man. Then they all walked back to the helicopter.

Once again, the crew filmed Sarah Allersby, swinging her legs and hopping out of the helicopter, then chatting knowledgeably with the overseers of her excavation crew, as she walked with heroic determination to the foot of the pyramid. The cameraman stopped the action, talked to Sarah Allersby, played back some of the tape for her, and pointed out various aspects of it. They all returned to the helicopter, and the drama was repeated once more.

After the first scene, in which she took symbolic ownership of the pyramid, had been perfected, there were a few other scenes. Sarah Allersby sat at a table under the awning. She and her supposed colleagues had a large paper, unfolded and spread on the table, with stones from the nearby temple holding down the corners. She pointed at various spots on the map, or diagram, as though she were explaining her plan of attack to a group of lieutenants.

Sam and Remi could not hear what was being said, and they assumed it was beyond their Spanish comprehension, but they watched, fascinated, as Sarah Allersby documented her discovery of the ancient Mayan city.

The filming took a couple of hours. Between takes, a woman Sam and Remi had assumed to be an archaeologist when she'd followed Sarah Allersby from her helicopter, would open a large black chest and redo Sarah Allersby's makeup and hair. At one point, the two of them entered a tent and returned a half hour later. Sarah had changed into a different outfit, a pair of designer jeans and a silk blouse. The cameraman filmed her pretending to excavate a shallow hole that had been dug before she arrived and divided into squares with strings on stakes. There were close-ups of her using a brush to clean dirt off a set of obsidian tools that had been planted in the hole for her to find.

During this process, Sam and Remi took their own brief movies of the action. But as Sam was aiming Remi's telephone in the direction of the false dig, he saw in the viewfinder the head of one of the guards across the plaza suddenly turn toward him. The guard pointed and shouted something to his companions. Sam covered the phone. 'I'm afraid that guy caught a reflection off the phone,' he whispered.

Sam took Remi's arm and began to back away into the jungle. They could easily outrun the men, who were hundreds of yards away, but others on the pyramid repeated the alarm, and men who were only a few yards from Sam and Remi heard and dashed toward them.

'Ditch your gun,' said Sam, and they both dropped their guns in the brush and covered them with a thick layer of leaves.

'Now what?' asked Remi.

'Now we can arrive for a peaceful surprise visit with our pal Sarah instead of a shootout with thirty guards.'

Sam and Remi walked out of the jungle and on to the ground that was once the great plaza. They walked toward the pyramid with open, smiling faces, pointing up at various features and commenting to each other. Remi said, 'So what do we say to them?'

'Whatever comes to mind. We're taking up time until the cavalry arrives.' He pointed up the long staircase, and said, 'That temple really is incredible, though, isn't it?'

'Maybe we can arrange to be sacrificed instead of shot and improve next year's harvest.'

Just as they were approaching the shallow dig, Sarah Allersby glanced up at the commotion and saw them. She threw down her brush, bobbed to her feet, and stood with her hands on her hips, her face contorted with rage. She stepped up out of the dig just as the armed men arrived to surround Sam and Remi.

The Fargos simply stopped and waited for Sarah Allersby to push through the ring of men from the other side.

'You two!' she said. 'What does it take to make you leave me alone?'

Sam shrugged. 'You could give back the codex or we could surrender it to the Mexican government with your good wishes. That would probably do.' He turned to Remi. 'How about you? Would you be satisfied if she gave the codex back?'

'I think I would,' Remi said. 'Of course I don't agree that we've been bothering you, Miss Allersby. How could we possibly know in advance that you would be here today?'

The armed men who were standing by were exchanging dark looks. It wasn't possible to be sure which ones understood English, but they seemed to see that whatever Remi had said had enraged their employer.

Sam said, 'Since we're all here, would you like to show us around the site? We'd be interested in seeing what your men have uncovered so far. Since you're busy filming, maybe we could just walk along behind the crew.'

Sarah Allersby was so angry that her jaw muscles seemed to be flexing over and over. She stared down at the ground for a second, raised her head, and shouted, 'Russell!'

From somewhere behind her, among the film people, came a voice. 'Yes, Miss Allersby?'

The man who appeared had a bright red face. From the roots of his hair to the neck of his shirt, his outer layer of skin had been removed. It seemed so tender and inflamed that it hurt to look at it. Over the red skin was a thick, shiny layer of Vaseline. He wore a hat with a wide brim to keep any hint of direct sunlight off his face.

Sarah Allersby said, 'These visitors want to be taken on a tour. Can you please oblige?'

'I'll be happy to, Miss Allersby.'

The man turned and gave Sam a hard push on the back to send him stumbling toward the jungle across the plaza. As a second man took a step toward Remi, she turned and caught up with Sam. The second man called out something in Spanish, and about ten of the armed men came along too.

The man with the red face wore a .45 pistol in a holster and he kept his right hand beside it as he walked, occasionally brushing the handgrip with his thumb as though to reassure himself that it was always in reach.

One of the armed escorts spoke in Spanish to the red-faced man's companion. The man called to his friend, 'Hey, Russ? He said they're bored. If you don't want to do it, they will.'

'Thanks, Ruiz. Tell them they can go back now. I'd like to finish this ourselves.'

'What for?'

'There are some things I like to do myself. If you don't feel up to this, why don't you go back with them?'

'No, I'll stick with you.' Ruiz turned and dismissed the others in Spanish. One of the men handed him an entrenching tool, a short handle with a shovel blade. He took it, and said, *'Gracias.'* The group went back toward the pyramid while Sam, Remi and their two captors continued walking.

'Maybe you should have let those guys do it,' said Sam. 'It's a lot easier to rat out two men than ten.'

'What are you talking about?' said Russell.

'You just got Sarah's permission to kill us,' said Remi. 'Once you do, then anybody who knows about it owns you. That includes all of those men who just left.'

'No,' said Russell. 'They own you if they *see* you do it.'

'Oh come now,' said Sam. 'You march us off, they hear gunshots, and only you come back. Not exactly the perfect crime.'

'Keep walking,' said Ruiz.

Remi said, 'We're a bit too well prepared to be the sort of people you can just kill and nobody asks questions. The United States Embassy knows the exact GPS position of where we were going to be today.'

'Don't worry about us,' said Russell. 'We'll manage.'

'By the way, what happened to your face?'

'You did.'

'Really?' said Sam. 'How did I do that?'

'Your little booby trap in Spain. The blue ink didn't come off, so I had a chemical peel.'

'Does it hurt?' asked Remi.

'Of course it hurts. But it's feeling better every second. Pain is easier to take when other people feel it with you.'

He led them into the jungle, and they walked on a path that took them through thick stands of trees and across a couple of ditches that must have been streams during the rainy season. When they were a mile or more from the archaeological site, they reached a secluded valley with a dry streambed at the center of it. Russell said to Ruiz, 'Give him the shovel.'

Ruiz kept his distance and tossed the small olive drab tool at Sam's feet.

'Dig,' said Russell.

Sam looked at Russell and Ruiz, never at Remi. He was beginning the process of getting them to forget about her. Sam and Remi had, for some years, known that when they were in dangerous places, they were always possible targets of kidnapping, robbery, or other violence. They had discussed and practiced a number of different tactics to use in tight situations and many of them involved getting opponents to underestimate Remi.

She was a slim, delicately beautiful woman. She was also very smart. Now Remi was waiting for the proper moment to do what she had always done in athletic competitions: match her superior reflexes, speed, balance, flexibility and coordination against an opponent who didn't dream that her advantages even existed and who was – only for the moment – living under the mistaken impression that all the advantages were his.

Sam dug. He was right-handed, and he pushed the shovel's blade in with his right boot, lifted the dirt and tossed it to his left, the side where their captors stood. He didn't look directly at them or at Remi, but he could see that she had already picked out the right kind of stone. It was at her feet, and she had worked it free as she'd sat there, looking weak and weepy.

As he dug, Sam thought he heard the faint sound of a helicopter. *No,* he thought. *It's more than one this time.* The sound was deeper and throatier, and, as they approached, he became sure they weren't Sarah Allersby's helicopters.

Ruiz looked up in the air, but the tall trees formed a roof above them. Ruiz observed, 'That noise could help cover a gunshot.'

As Sam and Remi both instantly knew he would, Russell reflexively turned to look in their direction while he considered Ruiz's suggestion.

Sam moved his shovel in exactly the same arc as he had fifty times before, except faster and higher, and propelled a few pounds of fine, sandy dirt toward

Russell's raw, wounded face. Then he charged out of the shallow hole, swinging the shovel toward Ruiz's legs.

Russell raised both hands and forearms to fend off the dirt flying toward him. That kept his hands up and far from the pistol in its holster at his belt, and it kept his eyes closed as Remi hurled the stone at him and leapt.

The stone hit the side of Russell's head and knocked him off balance. Remi lunged forward and, as Russell toppled, she was already plucking the pistol out of his holster.

Sam completed his swing, slicing the shovel in hard at Ruiz's right leg. The fear made Ruiz jump to avoid it, and the impact brought him to the ground. As Ruiz reached for the pistol stuck in the front of his belt, Sam jabbed that hand with the shovel blade, dropped his knees on Ruiz's chest, snatched the pistol and stepped backward, aiming at Ruiz.

The helicopter rotors beat harder and louder as Sam and Remi stood over their two injured opponents.

'Now that we've got them, what do we do with them?' asked Remi.

'Hold this.' Sam handed her his pistol so she now had one pistol aimed at each fallen enemy. Sam knelt, tugged off the two men's boots, then pulled the long leather laces out and used them to hog-tie the two. He stood. 'I guess that's the best we can do for the moment,' he said. 'We've got to get back to the site while they search. We're the only ones who've seen the codex.'

Sam walked up the jungle path, carrying the two pairs of boots. Remi looked back once at the two incapacitated men, then hurried after him.

22

The Ruined City

Sam and Remi approached the forested edge of the open plaza and stopped for a moment to exchange a brief embrace. Remi said, 'Remind me never to get a chemical peel.'

'I doubt that you'll forget, but I think his was worse than most,' Sam said.

'Yes. It's amazing what some men will do for a little extra beauty.'

Sam chuckled. They returned to the great plaza and saw it was dominated by two big CH-47 Chinook troop carrier helicopters that had set down on both ends of the cleared space. Soldiers in battle dress had taken positions in various parts of the ruin, and there was a squad surrounding the sun awning, where Sarah Allersby and her group stood uneasily while Commander Rueda spoke with her.

Sarah Allersby raised her eyes and seemed stricken when she saw Sam and Remi arrive, looking a bit disheveled, sweaty and dirty.

'Hello, Sarah,' said Remi.

'How dare you come back here?' Sarah Allersby

turned toward Commander Rueda. 'I just had some men escort these interlopers away from this vulnerable site.'

Sam said, 'What she means is that she gave two of her thugs her blessing to murder us in the jungle.'

'That's absurd! Me? That's laughable.' As though to prove it, Sarah managed an unconvincing laugh.

Commander Rueda said, 'Everyone save this conversation for headquarters.' He turned to the lieutenant in charge of the squad. 'You and your men search everything – tents, helicopters, every bag, box or case.'

'You have no right to do that,' Sarah Allersby protested.

'You'll have your chance to argue with our methods in court.'

'I'll remember you said that,' she said coldly.

Sam said, 'Commander, we left the two men who were supposed to kill us tied up in the jungle. We shouldn't really leave them like that.'

'Of course,' said Commander Rueda. He turned to the lieutenant again. 'Assign three men to go with the Fargos and take the suspects into custody.'

Remi took a step, but Sam held her back. 'You've earned a rest.' He moved his eyes in the direction of the men searching Sarah Allersby's campsite.

Remi nodded in agreement, and Sam kissed her cheek. 'Nice work back there. See you in a little while.'

Sam walked across the plaza with the three soldiers. As he walked, he noticed that Rueda's soldiers had lined up the armed guards in a shaded area by the pyramid. Their rifles were stacked in a pile a hundred feet away.

Sam led the men along the path. The distance Ruiz and Russell had taken them came as a bit of a surprise to Sam. On the first trip, he had been trying to make the walk as slowly as possible to give the federal police time to get here. On the way back, he and Remi had been running. This time, the mile of jungle path seemed to take forever. But at last he reached the little valley where Ruiz and Russell had taken them.

Russell and Ruiz were gone. Sam was silent for a moment while the three soldiers looked at him. He pointed at the spot. 'This is where we left them tied up. I guess I did a bad job of tying.'

The sergeant said, 'Are you sure this is the place?'

Sam pointed. 'There's the grave they had me dig.'

One of the soldiers squatted nearby. 'I found something,' he said. 'One of them rolled from there to here, where the other one was.' He picked up a strip of leather from the ground and examined it closely. 'He chewed through the other one's leather cord.'

'I should have thought of that and tied them to trees,' Sam said. 'Maybe we can pick up their trail.'

The soldier who seemed to be a tracker walked around the perimeter of the clearing, staring at the ground, then touching the foliage. He started into the jungle, then came back, tried another place and came back. 'I can't find any footprints. I don't know which way to go.'

'They're barefoot,' said Sam. 'We took their boots, so there won't be any boot prints.'

The sergeant shrugged. 'They won't get far barefoot. They'll have to go back to the camp or die out here.'

Sam stared at the ground for a few seconds, reluctant to give up. The three soldiers began to move off up the path, and Sam turned to follow. He stopped, walked through the bushes around the clearing but found nothing. Finally, he sighed, then trotted off after the soldiers.

When Sam and his companions returned to the plaza, the army helicopters' doors were open and people were climbing aboard. Soldiers loaded the two civilian copters with the camera equipment, folded tents and supplies. The camera crew, Sarah Allersby's assistants and the dig supervisors got in.

What caught Sam's eye was Sarah Allersby in handcuffs, being escorted by Commander Rueda to one of the two big military helicopters.

Remi stood, waiting for Sam, at the field. She ran to meet him. 'Where are they?'

'One of them rolled over to where the other one was and chewed through his leather shoelace. They got away.'

'I'll bet it was Ruiz,' Remi said. 'He has beautiful teeth.'

'The sergeant says they'll never get anywhere on foot. On the other hand, I keep remembering that lots of people in this part of the world don't have shoes. What's going on?'

'Rueda said that Sarah had photocopies of the four pages of the codex that made up the map in her suitcase, with this site marked. She also had aerial photos of the same four sites we picked out, and a few more. It's not the codex, but it's proof that she at least had the original codex long enough to photograph it.'

'She's under arrest?'

Remi nodded. 'She's on her way to be booked in Guatemala City for possession of stolen property and for damaging this site. I think Rueda wants to arrange something public, to discourage the other people who do this kind of thing.'

'If we want a ride to civilization, we'd better go retrieve our backpacks,' said Sam.

'I did that while you were gone,' she whispered. 'I also went back to retrieve our pistols in the woods. I broke them down and put the pieces in the packs. I've already put them aboard.'

'Good thinking. Thanks.' Sam looked around him as the soldiers climbed into the helicopters. A half dozen of them remained near the pyramid, setting up a camp of their own, to guard the site. 'We'd better get seats in the chopper before they run out of room.'

Remi climbed in, and Sam followed. There were seats of crisscross nylon netting along both walls. They selected a pair, strapped themselves in, and a minute later the engine growled to life and then lifted the big chopper into the air.

*

Jerry Ruiz looked up at the sky. First one, then another, then the last two helicopters soared overhead. He judged that they were moving southward toward Guatemala City.

'It's safe to head back to the pyramid now,' Russell said. 'Two of those were definitely the big troop carriers.'

'Okay. Let's go,' said Ruiz. 'Keep your eyes open to see where Fargo threw our boots.'

Russell walked for a few feet, then stepped on a sharp stone, hopped on one foot, and landed on a pointed stick in the path. 'Ow! Ah!' he said, sat on the path, and stared at the soles of both feet, then got up again and moved ahead gingerly. Russell's already red and painful face now looked worse. Much of the sandy gravel that Sam Fargo had thrown in it had been stuck to his raw skin and was held there by the Vaseline, and when he'd been hog-tied on the ground, his face had also picked up more dirt, grass and small sticks.

Ruiz wisely said nothing. There was no need to remind Russell of his face or to warn him that the path was treacherous and studded with sharp stones or that the low brush on both sides had thorns. Russell had already sworn about it six or seven times in the last ten minutes.

Ruiz had trouble walking too. The shovel had left a shallow cut and a large bruise on his leg just above the knee, his right hand hurt, and his breathing was labored because of some damage to a rib or two. Nevertheless, he had managed to roll over to where Russell lay and chew his way through Russell's leather bonds. It had not been easy, but he'd known that they had to get free or they'd be dragged into the Guatemala City jail and charged with attempted murder. And even if the soldiers didn't find them, they could easily die out here.

Ruiz had been raised in a remote village in Mexico. He knew that two bleeding, helpless men could hardly go unnoticed by the jaguars that patrolled the jungles at night. He also knew that the worst dangers didn't always look the worst. Fatal malaria, Chagas' disease or dengue fever could come from the bite of a tiny insect. So he had done what was necessary to free them. They'd lain still in the jungle, covered with fallen leaves, while the soldiers came and went. Maybe now all would be well. But he was concerned about Russell, who had gotten a little crazy since he'd been painted blue. He was in a constant state of rage, goaded on by the pain in his face and the pain of his anger.

Ruiz was worried. Poor judgment was a vulnerability. Mistakes one could shrug off in a city would kill a man out in the jungle. Ruiz hobbled off the path and selected two five-foot saplings from a stand of little trees growing where a big one had fallen, and broke off the branches to make two walking sticks. 'Here. This will help.'

Using their sticks, they moved on in silence for a time. Leaning on the sticks kept them from stepping down too hard on sharp stones and gave them enough balance to avoid some of the worst spots. It took them about an hour to reach the ancient city. While they were still on the edge of the jungle, they could see that the whole site had been evacuated except for a half dozen soldiers, who loitered by the great pyramid's steps. They had built a small fire and pitched three two-man tents.

Russell stepped toward the open area, but Ruiz held him back. 'Wait,' said Ruiz. 'They're soldiers.'

'I can see that.'

'What if they've been left here to wait for us?' asked Ruiz.

Russell stopped and thought, but he didn't seem to be getting anywhere.

Ruiz prompted him. 'The Fargos must have told the soldiers we tried to kill them.'

Russell said, 'All this is beside the point. We're a hundred miles from anywhere. We don't have shoes, water or food. They do.'

'They also have guns. Assault rifles, full auto,' said Ruiz.

'We can wait until they're asleep, crawl up and cut their throats.'

'There are six – two in each tent. Even if each of us could kill two men in a tent with a knife we don't have, the one would yell while the other was being killed. There would still be two in another tent who would hear it and open fire on us.'

'We can't walk out of here barefoot,' said Russell. 'It's too far to civilization.'

'Wait,' said Ruiz. 'Look over there. They left the sun awning up. We can wrap our feet in the canvas and walk out.'

Russell's expression made him look like a wounded animal, but when he saw what Ruiz was talking about, he seemed to calm down. 'Okay. Let's try it. I don't want to get into a fight with six men any more than you do.'

Ruiz was relieved. 'I'll go get the canvas.' Without waiting for an answer, he started off in the jungle outside the open space. The rough, unpredictable ground tortured his feet, but he got there. He looked in the direction of the pyramid to be sure the soldiers by the steps couldn't see him. Then he used the sharp end of one of the aluminum poles to cut a hole in the canvas, tore a large swatch of the fabric off, rolled it up, and carried it with him.

When he reached Russell, they tore four squares, put a foot in the center of each, and used the remnants of their leather shoelaces to tie the canvas around their ankles. They looked at the late-afternoon shadows of the buildings on the plaza to judge the compass points, took up their walking sticks, and began to hobble off into the jungle toward the south.

'Next time, I won't fool around with neatness,' Russell said. 'No grave digging, no taking them off somewhere else so nobody ever knows. If I see them, I'll open fire. If there are witnesses, I'll shoot them too.'

As Ruiz and Russell made their way along the jungle

paths, Ruiz had to listen to a constant, unending litany of complaints. Each time Russell started up again, he promised to kill Sam and Remi Fargo in more elaborate and time-consuming ways. Ruiz walked in silence. Some might have advised that talking would have eased the pain in Ruiz's feet, ribs and hand. But the pain served to take his attention away from Russell's complaints, and that was enough for now. Later on, if he and Russell ever made it through this green prison and Ruiz kept the use of his limbs, he would be happy to talk about the killing.

23

Guatemala City

The arraignment was held a few days later in the central court building in Guatemala City. Sam and Remi arrived with Amy Costa from the embassy. As soon as they were seated, Costa said, 'Uh-oh. I don't like the look of this.'

'What is it?' asked Remi.

'I'm not sure yet,' said Amy. 'But it looks as though this isn't going to go the way we thought. Take a look at the row of men sitting behind the defense table.'

Remi held up a compact, ostensibly to check her makeup, and used the mirror to study each man. There were six of them, in expensive tailored suits. About half the people in Guatemala were of Mayan descent, and most of the rest were mestizos. But these men all looked about as Spanish as the people Sam and Remi had met in Valladolid while they were looking for the Las Casas papers. 'Who are they?'

'The Minister of the Interior, the chief judge of the courts, two important commerce officials, two senior political advisers to the president.'

'What does it mean?'

'It's like the bride's side and the groom's side at a wedding. They're sitting on the defendant's side.'

'Are you surprised?' asked Remi.

'I suppose I shouldn't be, but I am. In 2008, the country set up the International Commission Against Impunity. It was formed to clean up the court system and rid the country of illegal security forces just like the one you faced in Alta Verapaz. At least three of these men are members. I guess they're not against impunity for their friends.'

A moment later, a side door of the courtroom opened, and Sarah Allersby was escorted in by two police officers, who were followed by the Allersby attorneys. Remi nudged Sam. 'Look familiar?'

Sam whispered to Amy, 'The first three are the team who came to our house to make the offer for the codex.' The Mexican, American and Guatemalan attorneys who had been at that meeting were joined by three others.

'The other three are partners in a respected local law firm,' Amy said.

Sarah Allersby and the lawyers all remained standing. After a moment, the bailiff called the court to order, and the judge came in, climbed the steps to the bench, and sat. He hammered the gavel a couple of times and called for order. Everyone sat down.

Just as the cloth of the judge's robe touched his chair, attorneys from both the defense and the prosecution hurried to the bench. They conferred with the judge for several minutes. Sam whispered, 'I don't see any arguing.'

'Neither do I,' Amy whispered. 'I think the case has been settled.'

'How could it be?' asked Sam.

'And if it is, what are all the important men doing here?' asked Remi.

'I'm guessing they're lending the weight of their support to the winning side, so even if justice is blind, it won't be foolish enough to cause trouble.'

The judge made an impatient gesture at the attorneys, who all scurried away like a flock of chickens and dispersed to their places behind the tables.

'The court has received the following settlement proposed by Miss Allersby's counsel and seconded by the people of Guatemala.'

'Why would the prosecution settle?' said Sam. Several people nearby turned to look at him with disapproval.

The judge consulted his notes, then began again. Amy translated. 'The charge of possession of a Mayan codex should be dismissed for lack of evidence. No such book was found. The charge of threatening people with violence should be dismissed. The two supposed suspects were never found.'

'That's ridiculous,' Sam said. 'Don't the police get to produce evidence?' There was a murmuring, and people turned to stare a second time.

The judge rapped his gavel and glared at Sam. Amy Costa whispered, 'He's considering clearing the courtroom. Please stay calm or he'll throw everyone out, and we might have to wait weeks for transcripts.'

The judge set aside the paper he had been reading and picked up another. He began to read again in Spanish.

'I'm not catching that,' said Sam. 'What's he saying?'

'Miss Allersby is claiming to be the uncontested discoverer of the ruined city. She's asked for a ninety-nine-year lease on the land in exchange for a sum of money to be used by the Interior Ministry to protect wildlife in the Alta Verapaz district.'

'Unbelievable.'

Amy Costa whispered, 'He's describing the negotiated settlement. That doesn't mean he'll accept it. Nothing you say will change the terms.'

Sam sat still, watching in silence.

Amy whispered, 'Now it's Commander Rueda. She has asked that he be reassigned so he can't retaliate against her.'

Sam winced and looked down at his shoes but said nothing.

Amy Costa listened for a moment while the judge said something in a loud, stern voice. Amy translated. 'I approve the terms of the settlement and declare this case closed.' He rapped his gavel.

Amy Costa stood up, as a number of other spectators were doing, so they could clear out before the next case began. 'Come on,' she whispered to Sam and Remi.

Sam said, 'What? It's over? We can't testify or present any evidence?' He stood.

Remi watched while half the courtroom turned to stare at Sam again. One of the people who turned to look at Sam was Sarah Allersby. A barely detectable smile of delighted amusement played on her lips for a second, and she turned to face forward again.

'No,' said Amy Costa. 'It was settled out of court ahead of time. It happens everywhere.'

'This time, it's a fraud. The richest person doesn't just win, she never even gets charged.'

Sam didn't need any translation when the judge pounded his gavel and ordered, 'Remove that man from the court.' He stood and stepped to the aisle. 'Don't bother. I'll remove myself.'

It was too late – the order had been given. Two large police officers seized him. One twisted his arm behind his back and the other placed him in a headlock, as they hustled him down the aisle, pushed the double doors open with his head, and kept going down the hall. When they reached the larger doors at the entrance to the building, they pushed them open with their free hands and then released Sam with a little push toward the steps.

When Sam found himself outside the imposing building, where the rush of people and traffic surrounded him, he was relieved. He had already been mentally preparing himself for a booking session and a night in the Guatemala City jail. He stopped and waited for Remi and Amy, who appeared a moment later.

As they walked down the steps, Remi said, 'I know he's a friend of yours. I'm so sorry that we got him in trouble. The evidence against Sarah Allersby really was conclusive. You can't take a picture of something that isn't in your possession.'

'Don't worry,' Amy said. 'Commander Rueda knew what he was doing and he'll be fine. He has allies too, and in a week, after this is forgotten, they'll go to work on his behalf. This is how countries go from corrupt little backwaters to modern nations. People have to push them every step of the way – people like Commander Rueda and people like you.' She gave Sam and Remi a sharp look. 'Don't let up on Sarah.' She turned and walked off toward the American Embassy, leaving Sam and Remi standing in front of the courthouse.

'Come on, let's go,' said Remi. 'I don't want to be standing here when Sarah Allersby comes out, gloating over her great victory.'

Remi and Sam walked along the street in the direction of their hotel. 'So, what do you want to do?' she asked.

Sam shrugged. 'I don't think we can let her go on doing this kind of thing, do you?'

'No, but what can we do about it?'

'We use the Las Casas copy of the Mayan codex to figure out where she's going and beat her to it.' He smiled. 'Then we do it again. And again. And again.'

24

Alta Verapaz, Guatemala

Sam and Remi sat in the passenger seats of the Bell 206B3 Jet Ranger helicopter with their earphones on to cut the noise while Tim Carmichael, president and chief pilot of Cormorant 1 Air Charter, guided the craft above the endless miles of green treetops. Carmichael spoke over the radio in his Australian accent. 'We should be at your next set of coordinates in a few minutes.'

'Great,' said Sam. 'We spend one day at each site. At the end of each day, we climb aboard the helicopter and get out of the jungle for the night. The following morning, we fly to a new site.'

'It's the perfect job for a charter,' said Carmichael. 'Fly in, take a nap, fly out.'

'The sites have all been pretty remote,' said Remi. 'And all of them are in heavily forested parts of the highlands.'

Carmichael smiled. 'No worries. We've been in this business since the 1960s and we haven't lost anyone this week.'

'Good enough for me,' said Sam. 'Here's the aerial

shot.' He handed Carmichael an enlarged photograph with the coordinates marked on it in the white border.

Carmichael stared at it, checked the coordinates on his GPS, and handed the photograph back. 'We should be there in under five minutes.'

They looked out at the treetops. There were ranges of low bluish mountains in the distance, a deep blue sky, and puffs of unthreatening white clouds. Earlier, they had seen a few roads and small towns, but it had been a long time since they had seen any signs of human inhabitants. Carmichael looked at the GPS.

'There.' Remi pointed at a place in the jungle canopy where gray stone protruded between trees. 'It's right over there.'

Carmichael brought the Jet Ranger around, tipped at an angle so they could look at the site as he circled it. 'I definitely see something the color of limestone,' he said. 'It comes right up through the trees.'

'That's it,' said Sam. 'Let's find a place to land.'

Carmichael widened the circles, spiraling outward from the ruins. After a few minutes, he said, 'I don't see anything that looks like clear ground.'

'No,' Remi said. 'It's all thickly forested.'

Carmichael went farther out until he found a spot that was empty of trees. It was a patch of jungle that had burned to the ground. Carmichael said, 'Finally. That'll have to do.'

'It looks like there must have been a fire,' said Sam. 'Everything's charred.'

'Yeah,' said Carmichael. 'Way out here, it was probably a lightning strike the last time it rained. I'm afraid you'll have a long walk to the ruins, though.'

'I have an idea,' Remi said. 'Is that rescue gear working?' She pointed at the side door in the bay, where there was an electric winch and a cable with a harness.

'Sure,' Carmichael said.

'Can you operate the winch while you're flying?'

'I've got a second set of controls right here. I can set down here, rig you up, and lower you over the site, if you're up to it. But I have to warn you, that's a scary ride.'

Remi said, 'I know, but we don't mind.'

Carmichael looked at Sam for a reaction. Sam said, 'We can rig ourselves up. Do you think you can set us down on the upper part of that gray stone? It seems to be the top of a building.'

'There's not much wind today. I'm willing to give it a try if you are.'

'Remi, want me to go first?' asked Sam.

'Nope,' she said. 'Help me get rigged.'

Sam and Remi unbuckled their seat belts, climbed over the seats to the back, and then got Remi into the harness. 'Okay, Tim, let's see where we can lower her.' They flew in lower and hovered over the spot where they had seen the gray limestone structure jutting through the treetops. 'Ready?' asked Carmichael.

Sam opened the side door. Remi sat on the edge with her legs dangling out, waved good-bye to Sam, and slid out the door, the rotor wash blowing her ponytail around wildly. 'Now,' said Sam. The winch lowered Remi as Sam watched her progress. 'Lower, lower, lower. Hold there, Tim. Just hover.' Remi reached the gray stone surface, then freed herself of the rescue gear. 'She's removing the harness. Okay, she's clear. Raise the cable.'

When the empty harness came up, Sam slipped into it and picked up his and Remi's day packs by the straps. He sat on the floor of the open doorway. 'Okay, Tim, come back for us at five.'

'I'll be here.'

Sam slid out and watched the top of the pyramid coming closer and closer as the winch lowered him to its top tier. There was a small temple on top, and he had to use his feet to keep from swinging into it, but then he was on the platform and the cable went slack. He slipped it off, then waved to Tim to raise it.

Tim's helicopter rose straight up, and he activated the winch to bring the harness up as he flew off to the west toward the burned clearing. Sam and Remi began to look through their packs. Remi said, 'Pretty quiet all of a sudden, isn't it?'

He put his arms around her and kissed her. 'It's kind of nice to be alone.'

'It is,' she said. 'But if we don't get this place photographed, we'll have to come back tomorrow.'

'Let's get it done.' Each of them opened a day pack, took out a pistol, stuck it in the bellyband they both wore under their shirts, and then took out a digital camera.

They worked systematically, taking shots from each side of the pyramid, so that in all four directions they photographed a quarter of the surrounding city complex, which looked like an arrangement of steep hills covered by trees. They went into the house-sized temple atop the pyramid and took photographs of its walls, floor and ceiling. The temple had two rooms plastered with stucco and then painted with murals that were in fairly good shape. They depicted a procession of Mayan people bringing bowls and plates to a hideous figure who must have been a god.

They slowly descended the pyramid, taking photographs of it, of the steps, of the monumental buildings in every direction. Much of the time, each of them included the other person in the photograph to establish scale and to prove that they had been there.

When they reached the ground level, they walked a quarter of a mile in each of the four directions from the pyramid, still photographing everything they could see. At the end of the afternoon, they returned to the foot of the pyramid and stopped on the east side. Sam took a foot-length section of PVC pipe, capped and sealed on both ends, from his pack. Inside were rolled papers, printed statements in English and Spanish. They said that Remi and Sam Fargo had been at this GPS position on this date to explore and map these Mayan ruins. There were also telephone numbers, e-mail addresses, and street addresses for contacting the Society for American Archaeology, the World Archaeological Congress, and the Society for Historical Archaeology, all of which had been notified of the discovery, as had the Guatemalan government. Sam dug a hole and buried the pipe in front of the eastern steps and then marked the spot with a small red plastic flag, like the ones that gas companies use to mark gas lines.

'So much for that,' said Remi. 'I feel a little like the old-time explorers who used to plant flags on other people's property and say they owned it.'

'Let's just settle on the idea that we were here and registered it with the people who are qualified to study it and learn more about it,' he said. 'That's enough for me.'

'And this is our fifth city,' Remi said. 'Four major cities in ten days.'

'We must be the world's greatest tourists.'

Remi looked at her watch. 'It's after four. Let's climb up on our perch and get a phone connection with Selma's computer so we can send her our photographs.'

As they moved up the enormous work of earth and stone, they could see trees nearly as tall on all sides. At the top, Remi turned on her satellite phone, connected it to her camera, and sent her cache of photographs to Selma's computer in San Diego. They had arranged at their first site that Selma would save all of the material and then forward it to David Caine at the university. He, in turn, would notify all of the international organizations that another previously unknown Mayan city had been found, partially mapped, and photographed.

When Remi had transferred her photographs, she took Sam's camera and transferred his. She looked at her watch again, and said, 'It's almost five. Didn't Tim say he was coming at five?'

'Yes.' Sam took his satellite phone and called Tim Carmichael. He heard the sound of ringing for a minute, then hung up. 'He's not answering.'

'He's probably flying, and he can't hear the phone with the earphones on.'

They waited about ten more minutes, listening for the sound of a helicopter, and then Remi said, 'Nothing.'

Sam called again, then hung up. He called the office of Cormorant 1 Air Charter in Belize and put on the speaker so Remi could hear.

'Cormorant, Art Bowen.'

'Mr Bowen, we haven't met. This is Sam Fargo. Tim Carmichael took us to a spot in the highlands of Guatemala. He was supposed to pick us up at five, but he hasn't. He's not answering his satellite phone. I wondered if you could please get him on the radio and check to be sure he's all right.'

'I'll try,' said Bowen. 'Hold on.'

Bowen went away from the phone for a minute. More time passed, and Sam and Remi could hear low voices in the background. Bowen might have been on the radio or he might have been talking to someone in his office. After a few more minutes, he was back. 'He's not answering his radio either,' said Bowen. 'We're going to send another helicopter out there and see what's up. Can you give me your exact position?'

'Hold on.' Sam handed the phone to Remi, who had their notes in her day pack. She read the coordinates to Bowen, then repeated them. She gave him her satellite phone number and Sam's. 'Tim was going to wait for us about five miles due west of our current position, on a flat space that looked as though it had been recently burned.'

'And can you be seen from the air?'

'We're standing on top of a Mayan pyramid. Tim lowered us on a rescue cable, and he was going to pick us up the same way.'

'I'm going to come get you myself. But I don't have a chopper here with that kind of equipment on it right now. Is there a place I can land and get you?'

'We'll have to walk to the place where Tim landed. Everywhere else in any direction seems to be covered with vegetation.'

'If that's the only option, okay. But do it carefully. Don't count on the idea that anybody you meet out there is okay. There are a lot of criminals in the wild country, where the police and the army can't find them. I'm bringing two men with me and we'll be armed.'

'Thanks for the warning. We'll do our best not to make contact with anybody. We're heading for the landing site right now.'

'We'll probably get there about the same time. See you there.'

As Sam and Remi scrambled down the side of the pyramid, they oriented themselves to the west, where Tim Carmichael had gone to land.

Remi said, 'I hope Tim didn't catch a rotor on a tree branch or something and crash.'

'I hope he didn't either,' said Sam. 'I couldn't see any smoke from up on the pyramid, but there's no guarantee there would be a fire. Anything could have happened.'

'I hate to get all worried when we're too far away to even know what to worry about.'

'I'm withholding my anxiety,' Sam said. 'But only to the extent that I'm leaving the first aid kit in my pack and the safety on my pistol.'

As Sam and Remi began to be sure of their footing, leaving the base of the pyramid, they sped up. They trotted when the path was clear and walked at a strong, steady pace when the vegetation was thick. They navigated by walking toward the glare of the late-afternoon sun on the tree leaves. They estimated that, over a long period, their walking and trotting probably averaged three miles an hour, and so they kept at it for a half hour before they stopped to check their GPS position.

They sat on a stone outcropping, drank water, and caught their breath while they reoriented themselves. They had come about halfway, and they agreed that this time they would go for fifteen minutes before they stopped again to check their position.

They ran steadily in single file, still using the reflected sun to navigate. They concentrated on making progress, but, as time went on, they began to pay more attention to making as little noise as possible. They knew that Tim Carmichael wasn't the type to simply show up late or to take them into the wilderness in an aircraft that wasn't well maintained and fueled to capacity. He had a radio in the helicopter as well as a satellite phone. There was no way to know what had gone wrong until they got to the landing spot, but neither imagined the story would be a happy one. Their thoughts centered on the hope that Tim wasn't dead.

At the end of their third leg of silent jogging, they were very close to the patch where Tim Carmichael had said he'd land. There was no helicopter sound in the air, which meant that Art Bowen was not yet close with a second helicopter. The silence was thick and ominous.

Sam and Remi stood cheek to cheek so that they could whisper in each other's ears to keep their conference silent. They agreed on a plan of approach, drank more water, and moved on.

They walked, staying low and alert, until they reached the burned land. They peered out of the thick foliage that had been spared by the fire and saw Carmichael's Jet Ranger. It had landed in the cleared field, far from any trees that could have interfered with its rotors. The land was quite level, and the helicopter sat evenly. There was nothing out of place and there were no bullet holes. But there was also no sign of Tim.

Slowly, Sam and Remi moved along the perimeter of the cleared area. When they had gone about a hundred yards, they stopped suddenly and listened. There were voices. At first, they wondered if they were hearing the helicopter's radio. These were male voices speaking Spanish. The voices came from behind them.

Sam and Remi turned to face the sounds coming from the forest. They were between the grounded helicopter and a group of men. They could see a path that had been trampled in the brush recently. The bent and broken plants still had green leaves.

Remi gestured to Sam that she would go around the men to the right. Sam nodded and began to make his way to the left so he and Remi would be positioned on both sides of the group. They both stayed well back from the group, where they could not easily be seen and where any noises they made might be lost in the men's conversation.

Sam made a ninety-degree arc around the sounds, then stopped and waited. He knew Remi would already be in position. Her sure-footed fencer's body could move through vegetation better than his. And he knew that when he moved in, he could initiate the most frightening close-in attack while Remi, the pistol champion, could do much more damage from a moderate distance. He took the pistol from his belly and began to crawl toward the voices. It sounded to him like six men and they seemed to be close, arranged in a circle. Maybe they were sitting around a fire – no, he would have smelled a fire. Around a circle anyway. What were they doing way out here?

And then he saw them. There were actually five men in their twenties, unshaven and wearing jeans, khakis, bits of old military uniforms, T-shirts. On the ground in the center of their circle they had laid out an olive drab plastic tarp. Spread on it were Tim Carmichael's belongings – his satellite phone, all three sets of earphones, the maps from the helicopter, his wallet, his keys, pocketknife, sunglasses.

Set on the ground beside each of the five men was a Belgian FN FAL 7.62mm military rifle. Sam moved closer, searching for some sign of what had happened to Tim Carmichael, and then he saw him. Tim was a few feet off, at the edge of the thicker vegetation.

Carmichael was standing, his hands tied behind his back, his ankles tied. He had a noose around his neck, the rope thrown over a thick limb of the tree above him and then securely tied to the trunk. If he got tired, he still had to stand. If he leaned, the noose tightened around his neck. His left eye was black and swollen, he had scrapes on his face and grass stains on his clothes, and his hair was stuck together on top of his head from drying blood from a blow to the skull.

Sam worked his way around the clearing at a distance, trying hard to avoid discovery. When he was directly behind Carmichael, he slowly crawled to him through the thick jungle vegetation. Staying hidden by the trees and Carmichael's body, Sam reached out with his knife and sawed through the rope at Carmichael's wrists, then his ankles. He took out his second pistol, switched off the safety, and placed it in Carmichael's right hand. Then he crawled a few feet farther and cut the rope from Tim's noose where it was secured to the tree trunk. He tucked an inch of the rope end into the remaining loop of rope behind the tree so it would look the same.

Sam crawled backward, retreating deeper into the brush. He took his time, selecting a spot where he, Remi and Tim would have the men in a perfect cross fire. Now and then, one of the men around the tarp would turn and glance at Carmichael and see that he was still standing with his hands behind his back and the noose around his neck.

When Sam judged that he, Remi and Carmichael were each a hundred and twenty degrees apart on the circle, he raised his pistol, stepped close to the circle, placed his body behind the trunk of a tree, and showed only his right eye and his gun hand. 'You!' he shouted in Spanish. 'Leave those guns on the ground and step away from them!'

The men were startled and jerked their heads toward Sam's voice. One started to raise his rifle, but Sam fired, and the man collapsed backward.

Carmichael shouted, 'Drop the guns!'

Some of the men looked and saw he was suddenly free, aiming a gun at them. They set their rifles back down. One man saw this as unacceptable, pivoted with his rifle to aim at Carmichael, but Carmichael was no longer visible. He had slipped into the bushes. The man raised his weapon to aim, but a shot was fired from Remi's side of the circle. It hit his arm and made him drop the rifle on the ground.

The remaining men moved back from their rifles and put their hands on their heads. Sam came out from behind his tree, knowing Remi and Carmichael were covering him. He kept his gun on the men as he took each rifle and tossed it to his side of the clearing so they formed a pile.

When Sam had the rifles, Tim Carmichael showed himself, holding Sam's second pistol on his captors. Sam said, 'Are you hurt?'

'Just a little. None of these clowns shot me anyway.'

'Do you know who they are?'

'They're as talkative as a bunch of crows, but they never said anything to reveal that. I guess they're just a bunch of guys who saw the helicopter, knew it was valuable, and tried to take it.'

'Is your helicopter all right?'

'It's fine. I thought I'd get out of it and take a nap in the shade. When I woke up, I had already lost a fistfight.'

The sound of a helicopter in the distance drew their attention. The roar grew louder, the leaves on trees began to whip back and forth in the wind, and the helicopter hovered. Looking up, Sam and Remi could see through the treetops that there was a man in an open doorway holding an M16 rifle.

'Maybe you'd better let them see you, Tim,' said Sam.

Carmichael stepped into the area by his helicopter and waved both arms while Sam and Remi kept their guns on their prisoners. The radio in Tim's helicopter squealed. 'We see you, Tim. You all right?' It was the voice of Art Bowen.

Tim snatched the microphone. 'Yes. The Fargos are here with me. We've got five prisoners, two of them wounded.'

'Sit tight. We're coming in.'

The helicopter landed, and three men came running, carrying M16 rifles. The middle-aged, stocky man piloting the helicopter came more slowly, but he was also armed with an M16.

As Sam and Remi walked with Tim Carmichael to watch Art Bowen and his men load the five prisoners into the helicopters, Remi said, 'I'll bet Tim would like to take a few days off after this.'

Carmichael climbed into the pilot's seat and put on his just-recovered sunglasses. 'You know, I just might. When I was listening to those five talk, I realized that the only reason I'm alive is that, without me, they couldn't move the helicopter.'

25

The burned patch in Alta Verapaz,
three weeks later

Sarah Allersby walked from the pair of parked helicopters into the thick Guatemalan forest. The brush had grown over this trail a thousand years ago, so it would be difficult to demonstrate to her guests that this was a Mayan trail, although she was sure it was. She hacked her way along with a machete, watching her feet to find a spot that would be clear enough for the revelation.

She glanced back along the trail. There were fifteen journalists, all of them carrying complicated camera equipment and recorders and satellite phones. But they were all chattering away with one another about God knows what. They weren't paying attention to the special place where she had brought them.

Sarah looked down and stopped, then called for their attention. 'Look, everyone. We're on a Mayan thoroughfare. It's a paved foot road.' She stepped aside to let the journalists come forward to take pictures of the pavement. A few listlessly snapped the ground, with its layer of whitish cobbles, but more were inclined to take photographs of Sarah hacking through the overgrowth. That, she reflected, was all right too.

She pushed ahead, then looked back beyond the photographers at the longer line of armed men she had brought into the jungle, carrying their Belgian rifles. It was costing her a great deal of money, but this time she was going to be sure she had the manpower to keep everything under control. After the disappearance of the five men Russell had sent to clear the helicopter landing spot, she had left little to chance. She knew the ruin was only a short distance away now, so she kept moving, hacking at the vines and brush in her way. She finally burst through the bush and stepped on to the great plaza. 'There,' she shouted. 'There is the city, the lost city I've found.'

She stepped boldly forward on the plaza. Ahead of her, on both sides of the wide-open space, were huge pyramids, and to her side was the biggest one so far. And while the reporters were ignorant about the structure, she had already seen the beautiful paintings on stucco inside the temple at its top. The architecture and art revealed a society that had been rich and complicated, colorful and full of life. And the place had been abandoned before the Normans invaded England.

There were sure to be hoards of priceless artifacts hidden deep in the royal tombs of a place this size. It was spectacular. She had already found a few things and they had stimulated her appetite. But even more, she wanted these newspeople to see her doing some excavating. A couple of photographs and some actual footage that could be shown on television in Europe and the United States would further the process of her transformation. Right now, she was dismissed as just one more heiress with exotic tastes. When her discoveries were all revealed, she would be a major power in the world of archaeology. Nobody would know her discoveries had all come from her Mayan codex, so she could still stage a 'discovery' of it years from now and get full credit for that too.

She was perfectly dressed in a tailored explorer's outfit, a tan shirt with epaulets and the sleeves rolled up, tailored pants in the same fabric, and polished boots, and she strode ahead with a kind of heroic energy, moving toward the huge pyramid that dominated the end of the plaza as though it were a beast she was conquering, when she heard a sudden wave of chatter behind her. She stopped and looked over her shoulder.

The journalists had come about thirty yards into the great plaza. They all seemed to be awed by the enormous size and imposing character of the city's buildings, all of them partially sheathed in vegetation. Unlike most of the lost cities Sarah had visited, the tallest buildings were not totally obscured by the plants and dirt. Their outlines were fairly clear.

But something was wrong. They weren't all rushing after her, elbowing one another to get close and congratulate her, to pepper her with questions about the city. They were all standing in a tight knot, looking down at their telephones and reading text or facing away from the others with their phones held to their ears. Others were facing one another, talking rapidly in their various languages, as though they were discussing some piece of astonishing news.

The only ones not in the gaggle of chattering writers were the photographers, who stood in a loose circle, filming not the miracle of human accomplishment that towered over them but the reporters and their exclamations and questions and gestures of what seemed to be shock or outrage.

One of the journalists in particular caught Sarah's attention. He was Justin Fraker from *The Times* (London), a classmate of her brother, Teddy, at Eton. He had come because Teddy had promised him something – she suspected it was an invitation to a future reception at No. 10 Downing Street.

She had high hopes that Justin would make the case for her at home. She stared at him now because he was the nearest of the English speakers and it was easiest for her to read lips in English. He seemed to be saying, 'This is insane. She must be joking. She can't be serious.' She wondered who he could be talking about. She sighed. It would be just her luck if some American actress did something so outrageous that it took their attention away from her.

She turned and walked back toward the crowd of newspeople. Michelle Fauret, a stringer for *Paris Match*, had agreed to come because of Sarah Allersby's reputation as a partygoer in Europe. She hurried toward Sarah, calling out, 'Sarah! Sarah!' She was holding a small video camera.

Sarah Allersby was reassured. The idea that she was about to become an even bigger celebrity was titillating. She had always liked being the very rich girl, with mysterious holdings in Central America, who would sometimes appear at parties in southern France or the islands of the Mediterranean. She sensed that she was about to go from 'interesting' to 'fascinating.' She smiled, and said, 'What is it, Michelle?'

'They're saying that you're a fraud. They say this site is already registered with all the archaeological organizations – that you didn't find it. Someone else did.'

Sarah was not pleased that while Michelle was saying all this, the red light in the front of her video camera was on. She feigned an amused smile. 'That's silly,' she said. 'Why would I do such a thing?'

'Look at this,' said Emil Bausch, the German columnist. He held up an iPad tablet with a photograph of the large pyramid that dominated the plaza. 'This is a picture that's on the website of the Society for American Archaeology. This whole site has already been photographed and charted.'

Jim Hargrove, an American from *National Geographic*, said, 'How could this happen? Don't you consult any of the organizations in the field?'

'Of course I do.' Sarah hadn't done it lately. She had been so busy.

'Apparently, not often enough. This set of ruins is on the lists of existing finds.'

'I don't know what you're talking about,' said Sarah Allersby. 'Is this some kind of joke? I invited very few reporters here to share in an extremely rare experience. Are you now accusing me of faking something?' She waved her arm in the direction of the ancient buildings around them. 'Did I build all this to fool you? These buildings are masterpieces, and the last people here left a thousand years ago.'

'The people here left three weeks ago,' said Justin Fraker. 'It's listed in the British catalogs of discovery too.' He pointed at the image on his satellite phone. 'They've got a complete description. The map coordinates are identical. And they marked it with a pipe with a red flag that pokes out of the ground below the stairs.'

'Who are these people who supposedly left three weeks ago?' said Sarah Allersby.

'The names listed are Samuel and Remi –'

'Fargo!' she interrupted. 'They're criminals, people who have no qualifications or academic intent whatever. They're treasure hunters. This is a trick.'

'The find is listed as a joint project with the University of California,' said Van Muckerjee, the *New York Times* correspondent. 'The University of California would seem to have academic qualifications and academic intent.'

'I have no more to say about these people,' she said. 'I'll be leaving here in a half hour. I would advise you all to make your way to the helicopter landing area as soon as possible. The pilots will not be flying anyone out after dark.' She turned and began to walk along the path.

Sarah held her shining blond head high and walked in silence. The chosen group of journalists trotted after her, the photographers racing ahead so they could get a picture of her face with a snarl or a tear. Both sold a lot of papers.

Guatemala City

The next afternoon, Sarah Allersby sat in her bedroom and looked at her computer. Posted on YouTube was a video of Sarah Allersby. She looked beautiful and triumphant as she hacked her way through the brush and stepped on to the great plaza of the old city. Then, almost immediately, things changed. The newspeople were already preparing to surround her, saying in several languages that she was a fraud. It didn't matter whether the viewer could speak all of those languages because the reporters yelling in his language would tell him the simple version of it: 'This site has already been discovered by someone else.' 'This city is known.' 'It's already registered with the international organizations.' 'You're trying to fool everyone.'

As the accusations were repeated and amplified, Sarah walked quietly away from the mob of angry reporters. The reporters ran after her, then ahead of her, taking her picture and accusing her of worse and worse impostures. It went on and on. As Sarah watched on her computer, it made her want to cry for the poor, tormented woman in the video. Then the video faded out, and she saw the title: 'British heiress caught in fraud.' Views: 330,129. As she sat motionless, staring at the picture that was as motionless as she was, the number changed to 339,727. She clicked on the X at the corner of the screen to banish the sight, then stood up and walked away from the computer.

She picked up the telephone and dialed a number she had called only a few times. This time, she was nervous.

'Hello?' It was the voice of a young woman, probably one of the women who kept appearing on Diego San Martin's arm at parties and charity events, and then being replaced by another, and another.

'Hello.' Sarah's voice was honeyed, and her Spanish was sure and fluid. 'This is Sarah Allersby. Is Señor San Martin available?'

'I'll see,' the woman said carelessly. She dropped the phone on a hard surface.

Sarah imagined her from her voice. His women were always models or actresses or beauty contest winners from Mexico or various South American countries. It was astounding how many of them there seemed to be, passing through a capital like Guatemala City – an endless supply.

'Sarah.' San Martin's voice was gruff but friendly.

'Good afternoon, Diego. I wondered if you and I could have a talk tomorrow.'

'Do you want to come here?'

'If you don't mind coming to my house, I would consider it a favor. Just now I've been having some bad publicity. I don't know who might be waiting to follow me around. I'm keeping myself out of sight for now.'

'All right.'

'Come for lunch at twelve.'

The next day, by eleven-thirty, she was prepared. The table that had been set in Sarah Allersby's garden was superb. She'd had the servants lay out thick white linen, crystal glasses, and the heaviest antique silver, all part of the Guerrero house furnishings. The china was a subdued Wedgwood, cream white, with a pattern of lavender leaves and a gold rim. It was an eighteenth-century pattern she'd learned was in a warehouse in Mumbai that belonged to her family. She had been fond of rescuing things of that sort when she was a teenager – old china and pottery from shipments passing through India that an ancestor had picked up, old paintings and books from English and French houses the family had bought during times of economic disaster. Many of these things had been moved to company warehouses on the London docks, others left in place while the company leased the homes out for various purposes or converted them to hotels.

The flowers in the vases were from beds not a hundred feet from the table. The old, Spanish-style

Guerrero house was the perfect place for private conversations, a two-story brick structure with a courtyard in the center. The tree-shaded court was protected on all sides. No remote sensing device or telephoto lens would be of much use here.

Sarah looked at everything critically and with a cold eye. The food, the setting, the location of the table, even the likely path of the sun, had to be right. Men like Diego San Martin had little tolerance for inconvenience.

At exactly noon, her front-door man, Victor, ushered San Martin through the foyer and the French doors into the courtyard, where Sarah awaited him. He was about fifty-five, but he was vain about his appearance and kept himself in fighting condition. He carried a panama hat with a black band and wore a beige linen suit with a pale yellow shirt and blue tie. He looked cool and sweet, Sarah thought, like an Italian ice. He was followed in by two bodyguards.

She admired the easy, casual way San Martin traveled about with bodyguards. He was never hampered or hemmed in by their presence. When he arrived at a building, one of them would step in first, look around, and open the door for him. When San Martin entered a room, one man stayed at the door to keep it securely under his control and the other stationed himself at a second strategic spot – beside a window or by a staircase – away from the civilians. San Martin always behaved as though the two ice-eyed killers were invisible.

He took Sarah's hand and leaned in to kiss her cheek.

'It's wonderful to see a beautiful and noble lady at any time, but to be invited to her home for lunch is a great privilege. And the light here is made for you.'

Sarah Allersby would never say it, but it *had* been made for her. She'd had the long table removed today and replaced with a round one because she didn't want to set off any thoughts of precedence. A man like San Martin would expect to sit at the head of any table, but letting him do it here would be dangerous. He instinctively took charge of things, and she could not let him begin to think of her as an underling in his empire or of her house as territory.

'Please sit here,' she said, and pulled a chair out. She moved to the chair beside that one, knowing that it would make the place she'd chosen for him desirable.

Once they were comfortably seated side by side, she nodded, and the waiter poured some wine for both of them. She tasted it, then said, 'Leave us. I'll ring.' The waiter moved off toward the kitchen. She said, 'I've invited a trusted associate, who's waiting in the library. His name is Mr Russell. May I bring him in?'

'All right.' San Martin turned toward his two body-guards to be sure they'd heard. They said nothing but headed into the house and across the foyer. After about a minute, they returned with Russell and resumed their posts.

Sarah said, 'This is Mr Russell, and this is Mr San Martin. Diego, Mr Russell has helped me and members of my family a number of times and his discretion is absolute. I wouldn't invite him today if I didn't trust him with my life.'

Diego San Martin took the wine bottle out of the ice bucket and looked hard at Russell. Sarah looked hard at Russell too, imagining what San Martin was thinking. Was she imagining just a faint tinge of blue remained on his face?

Russell picked up his wineglass and held it out so San Martin could fill it. Both men's faces were empty and serious, each staring into the other's eyes. Neither man's hand shook. 'Thank you,' said Russell.

'Well, gentlemen,' said Sarah. 'While we're having a chilled drink together, let me bring up my problem, and then I'll ring to have the food served.'

'Excellent idea,' said San Martin. 'Right to the point.'

'A few weeks ago, an American couple named Sam and Remi Fargo began to spy on me. They went into the country around the Estancia Guerrero and then on to the Estancia itself. They were the ones your security people saw near the sacred cenote in the ruins of the ceremonial center. I believe they wounded or killed about a dozen of your employees.'

'Yes,' San Martin said. 'Their visit was an expensive one for me.'

'They also visited the Estancia itself and saw your marijuana crop and the coca trees. They came to this house to complain about them to me.'

'Interesting.'

'They have also gone to some trouble to get me

arrested on the charge of stealing a Mayan codex from them and for attempting to have them killed by Mr Russell. I had the charges dropped, but only after days of humiliation and a public court appearance.'

San Martin sipped his wine. 'That must have been unpleasant.'

'Yes. They're a potential threat to me, so I'm afraid to let them go on this way. But they're even more of a threat to you. They've already found your operation on the Estancia. I know you feel people should solve their own problems instead of bringing them to you, but I think these people are a problem we share.'

He laughed. 'You've learned to know me so well,' he said. 'You're a perceptive woman. You may actually be the perfect woman.'

She laughed too. 'Of course I am. Being a woman is all I do.' She refilled the glasses.

'All right. Tell me how I can be a good friend to you. And then we'll have lunch. I promise to give you my answer when we've finished.'

'Mr Russell? Can you help me explain?'

Russell was filled with appreciation of her cunning. She knew that San Martin would be most comfortable with her as the ultra-feminine woman who appeared not to know the violent details. He also knew that San Martin had no interest in knowing him, so he had to be brief. 'Miss Allersby has a list of Mayan sites that she planned to visit. At one of these sites we had a group of five men clear and guard a helicopter landing area so

Miss Allersby could bring journalists with her to see the ruins. The men were heavily armed. Yet they had disappeared by the time Miss Allersby arrived. And we now know that the Fargos visited the site before she did.'

'Thank you,' said San Martin. He turned to Sarah. 'And now let's do justice to your beautiful table and have the lunch you've planned.'

Sarah rang the little silver bell by her, and the lunch was served. There was poached salmon with a caper sauce and asparagus. The wine that was poured with it was a 1998 Veuve Clicquot La Grande Dame. There was sorbet to cleanse the palate before the salad was served, in the French manner, after the entrée, and then small, delicate pastries with strong espresso.

As Señor San Martin finished his coffee, he sat back in his chair. Sarah Allersby looked at the servants, gave a little flip of her hand, and they dissolved into the doorways along the side of the house that led to the kitchen and pantry. Then she poured another cup of espresso for San Martin.

San Martin looked at Russell with eyes so cold and devoid of feeling that they looked dead. 'I'll try to find out what happened to your five men. The forest is a dangerous place, and not everybody with a gun works for me. If the Fargos are responsible, the five might be in jail somewhere.' He handed Russell his calling card. 'Here, Mr Russell. Come and see me tomorrow afternoon. I'll supply you with a small army of professionals who won't be troubled by a couple of American tourists.'

26

Alta Verapaz, Guatemala

Sam and Remi loaded their backpacks into a Jeep. This time, it was a rental car and a few years newer. They drove the narrow, winding road toward Santa Maria de los Montañas, the town where they had jumped off the marijuana truck and been helped by the priest and the doctor.

As they drove, Remi said, 'Do you think we're having an effect on her?'

'Sarah Allersby?' Sam said. 'I'm sure we are. We've visited the six biggest, and probably most important, undiscovered sites mentioned in the codex and registered them. That burns them for her. She can't claim to discover them if we did.' Sam drove on for a minute. 'The police in Belize say the five men who attacked Tim's helicopter haven't talked yet, but I wouldn't be surprised if she hired them to control access to that Mayan site.'

Remi said, 'I know she's angry. In fact, if nothing else had happened, seeing herself ridiculed in the European magazines would have been plenty. People envy the rich bad-girl celebrities who are always in the tabloids, but envy isn't the same as admiration. There's a complicated mixture of feelings involved. Whenever one of these women gets embarrassed or hurt, a lot of the people who were busy fawning on them are delighted to see it happen.'

'She's pretty sophisticated. The fickleness of crowds can't be a surprise to someone like her.'

'I know,' said Remi. 'I've just been thinking about her and feel this isn't going right. We're locked in a competition with her, and I'd like to be able to foresee a happy ending, but I don't.'

Sam said, 'The ideal end would be if she would stop pretending to be an archaeologist and send the codex she stole to the Mexican government.'

'Of course. But do you honestly think we'll wear her down enough for that?'

'Not likely,' he said.

'So maybe what we ought to be doing is thinking of ways to steal the codex back and return it ourselves,' said Remi.

'I have been.'

'Really? What have you thought of?'

'I'm stuck on phase one – finding out where she keeps it.'

In the afternoon, Sam and Remi approached Santa Maria de los Montañas in the only way possible, from the road that rose drastically upward from the valley below. The Jeep climbed back and forth up the hairpin curves, unprotected by guardrails, followed by a long, straight rise through thick forest to the crest. The trees on the forested upper altitudes kept drivers from seeing much of the road ahead.

When they were nearly to the last stretch of road before the rise, Remi pointed at a spot that was bare except for bushes and brush. 'I think that was the place where you landed when we jumped off the marijuana truck. Want to do it again in daylight so I can get a picture for my scrapbook?'

'Thanks for offering, but I think I won't have trouble remembering.'

'Suit yourself,' said Remi. 'Can we stop at the church and see Father Gomez?'

'I think we have to,' Sam said. 'We said we'd let him know how our meeting with Sarah Allersby went.'

When they reached the top of the hill, they parked on the plaza near the old church, then walked to the small house behind it that served as the priest's home and office and knocked.

In a moment, Father Gomez appeared at the door. He smiled. 'Señor and Señora Fargo. I'm delighted to see you again.'

'Thank you, Father,' said Sam. 'We thought we'd stop by for a talk.'

Father Gomez said, 'I can tell from your serious expression that the news will not bring me joy. But we must talk. Do you have time to have tea with me?'

'Of course,' said Remi. 'We'd be delighted.'

'Come in, come in,' he said, and ushered them into

his simple office with its dark wooden furniture. If it weren't for the open laptop computer, the room could have been from the sixteenth century. He led them into a small, old-fashioned dining room, with a long table in the same dark, heavy wood. An elderly lady, with brown skin, pronounced Mayan features and her gray hair tied in a tight bun, entered the room.

Father Gomez said, 'Señora Velasquez, this is Señor Fargo and Señora Fargo. They'll be joining us for tea.'

Señora Velasquez brought out plain white china and utensils, which Father Gomez and the Fargos arranged on the table. After Señora Velasquez brought the tea and cookies, she returned to the kitchen.

'Won't Señora Velasquez join us?' asked Remi.

'It's not her custom,' Father Gomez said. 'In a small town parish, when people meet with the priest, they like privacy. Please, Señora Fargo, will you pour for us?'

'I'm happy to,' Remi said. She took over the ceremonial role, pouring the tea and distributing the cups on saucers.

'Now,' said Father Gomez, 'are you ready to tell me what happened when you went to visit Miss Allersby?'

Remi and Sam told him the whole story, beginning with Sarah Allersby's visit to their house to buy the Mayan codex and ending with the ambush that awaited them at the burned landing patch outside the ancient Mayan city. 'We've learned a lot about Sarah Allersby. She intends to use the map in the Mayan codex to locate and pretend to discover all of the most promising sites.

We're using the same information from Father Las Casas's copy to get to each of the sites first. A professor at the University of California in San Diego uses our photographs and GPS data to register them with the international archaeological organizations before she can reach them.'

Father Gomez looked troubled. 'I'm sorry that she has turned out to be such a selfish, misguided woman. Do you think the authorities will force her to stop letting narcotics traffickers use her land?'

Sam sighed. 'I'm told by responsible people in Guatemala City that things will get better in time. The existence of the Mayan site near the fields is known now. And the fields themselves have been drawn to the attention of the national police. But improvements happen slowly, and Miss Allersby has some powerful friends who can make it even slower.'

'It was good of you to come all the way back here to report this to me,' said Father Gomez.

Sam held up both hands. 'No, please. That wasn't the only reason we're here.'

Remi said, 'We told you that we were rushing to verify, photograph and register the Mayan sites in the codex. That's the other reason we're here.'

'Here?' Father Gomez looked shocked. 'Not in Santa Maria de los Montañas?'

'Not in the town,' said Sam. 'We think it's above the town, on a plateau. The map shows it as something that looks like a tower or a fort.'

'Very interesting,' said Father Gomez. He looked uneasy. 'Would you please allow me to hire a guide for you? I'd hate to have you get lost up in these hills.'

'No thank you, Father. We have the precise location on GPS and also aerial photographs,' said Remi. 'We're getting good at finding these places. What would be helpful is if you could tell us where we can store our car safely.'

'Yes, of course,' he said. 'There's Pepe Rubio's garage. He's the town's mechanic and keeps cars overnight quite often.'

'That sounds perfect,' said Sam. 'He can give us an oil change at the same time.'

Remi stood and began clearing the plates from the dining table while Sam and Father Gomez chatted. As she entered the kitchen, she caught Señora Velasquez stepping back from the door as though she had been eavesdropping. Remi smiled and handed her the plates, but Señora Velasquez didn't return the smile.

They set out from the priest's house, and Remi told Sam about Señora Velasquez. 'I'm sure she was listening,' said Remi.

'No harm done. We would have been happy to have her join in the conversation.'

'I know. But I'll bet a lot of people around here wonder how their secrets get out.'

Soon they found Pepe's garage. They could see they had the right place from the cars parked all over the block and in front of the house. They found Pepe putting on a set of tires. Sam hired him to service their car and keep it safe.

Pepe referred them to the nearby house of the Pérez family, who were willing to rent them a guest room for the night. In the evening, they ate at the small restaurant where they'd had breakfast with Father Gomez and Dr Huerta on their first visit.

The following morning, as the sun grew bright, they set out on foot to find the structure they'd seen on the map in the Mayan codex. It was a beautiful day as they crossed the fields, cleared for planting corn and beans, and then entered the forest. After some searching, they found a path that led up the side of the plateau, above and beyond the town.

After climbing about a hundred feet on the path, Remi stopped. 'Look at this.'

She stood at a place where the path turned upward and to the left. There was a steep incline to the next level, but they could see that it had been reinforced with slabs of rock laid horizontally like giant steps.

'I guess this means we've found the right trail,' Sam said. He joined her in climbing toward the turn ahead.

'That's right,' she said. 'But in all the other sites we've visited, the stone was all overgrown. This is exposed.'

They walked along the path, climbing steadily. Sam said, 'This is closer to a place where people live than the other sites were. And it does make sense to use a perfectly good path when you find one instead of blazing a new trail.'

They climbed for a while, unimpeded by thick brush or centuries of fallen earth. Remi said, 'The part I haven't figured out yet is why.'

'I know,' Sam said. 'Maybe there's something else up there – good fields or something.'

'I'd hate to carry the harvest down this path,' Remi said.

'Then what do you think it could be?'

'I'm hoping it's a shortcut to another village that has an air-conditioned spa and restaurant.'

'A good working theory,' he said. 'I'll accept it until we find something better. That's the way we scientists operate.'

In ten more minutes, they reached the head of the path. They climbed up on to the level top of the plateau and looked around. There were several large mounds of earth that might be buildings, but they were not on the scale of the buildings in the cities they had found. They weren't high or steep, and the plateau wasn't large enough for monumental architecture. It was only about three hundred feet across.

They both noticed something else. The perimeter of the plateau had a low ridge around it like the rim of a bowl. They walked along the ridge, taking pictures, and then Sam stopped at a section that had fallen down. It revealed the ridge to actually be a pile of stones and earth.

'It's a wall. It's like the old Roman forts you find in Europe – low walls of stone piled up to stop an enemy attack. This was built for a battle.'

'It's not like any of the other ruins we visited,' Remi said. 'It feels different – not empty, somehow.'

They walked the rest of the way around the plateau. In the middle of the flat space, there were more low mounds of earth and stone, all of them overgrown with small plants. The only sounds on the plateau were the movements of the leaves in a soft wind and the calls of birds. At times, it was so quiet that Sam's and Remi's footsteps were the loudest sounds.

Remi said, 'This isn't a place where people would live. It reminds me of the cenote a few miles from here. The wall around it seemed to be made for a last stand too.'

'I know what you mean,' said Sam. 'This and the cenote must be relics of a war between cities.'

They came across a trench about three feet deep and only wide enough for a man to stand in it and dig. It ran from the stone wall at the rim of the plateau for about a hundred feet and directly into one of the mounds. 'Uh-oh,' said Remi.

'Do you know what that is?'

'I think it's the kind of trench that pot hunters and grave robbers dig to find underground chambers and caches.'

Sam raised his satellite phone and took a few pictures of it, then sent them to Selma. He and Remi walked along the trench, looking into it. 'If that's what it was, it seems to have failed. It doesn't lead to a bigger hole, where they might have found something and dug it up.'

The trench stopped at the base of the mound. When they reached the spot, Remi said, 'It doesn't seem to have stopped here. The rocks that are piled on the side of the mound are different. I think somebody dug into the mound and then covered the hole after they were done.'

'It's puzzling,' said Sam.

'The word is "creepy",' Remi said.

'Creepy, then.' He bent and began to lift the stones that had been placed in the opening and toss them to one side.

'You're going to dig into it? That's not why we came here. We were just locating sites, photographing them, and describing what's in them so David Caine can register them.'

'I can't very well describe what's here unless I know,' said Sam. 'This could be anything.'

'It could be a tomb. Judging from the trench, that's what whoever beat us here thought.'

'Or it could be a pile of the right-sized rocks for throwing down at invaders. Or a big pile of potsherds, which, as you know, is the most common find at any archaeological site.'

Remi sighed, knelt beside Sam, and began lifting stones from the mound and tossing them aside. They worked until the stones revealed the straight, even sides of an entrance. 'A doorway,' she said. 'So much for the rock-pile theory and the broken-pot theory.'

'Still have a bad feeling?'

'More and more,' said Remi. 'I'm just going along with this to show you what a great sport I am.'

'We're almost in,' Sam said.

Remi stepped back from the opening and let Sam haul the last few rocks away. Then he said, 'We're in.' He stood, took the flashlight from his pack, aimed it into the opening, and crawled inside.

There was silence. Remi sat still for a minute, listening. Finally, her curiosity overpowered her caution. She took her own flashlight out and entered.

As soon as she was inside, she realized that the space was large and hollow. Her flashlight beam caught white stucco walls covered with realistic murals of old Mayans. There were many glyphs, and between them were pictures of dozens of men in feathered head-dresses and wearing jaguar skins. Some carried short spears, round shields, clubs with sharp obsidian teeth. They were going into battle.

When her flashlight reached the floor, Remi jumped and gave a small cry. Lying on the other side of the chamber was a corpse. The body was in a state similar to the mummified man she and Sam had found on Volcán Tacaná in Mexico. His skin was brown and leathery, his body skeletal. He was lying near a second doorway. There were strips of cloth, a tanned belt, and boots on him, and beside him was a broad-brimmed felt hat.

Sam appeared in the second doorway. 'I'm sorry, I should have warned you.'

'Every day is Halloween lately,' she said. She knelt by

the dead man and gave him a closer look. 'What do you suppose got him – a jaguar? His clothes are torn, and he has big wounds.'

'Take a look at his revolver.'

Remi saw the old-fashioned, long-barreled revolver by his right hand. She bent low to look into the front of the cylinder and then rotated it. 'He fired all six.'

'Right. And I don't see any jaguar bones.'

'Do you recognize the gun?'

'It looks like a Colt Single Action Army, which would date it – and him – at 1873 or later.'

She said, 'His skull is crushed on the left side.'

'That was one of the details I was going to mention after we were outside in the daylight.'

'This man was clubbed to death,' she said. 'He was murdered.' She got up, and they both walked into the inner chamber. Inside was a low bier made of cut stone. On it lay a skeleton adorned with a gold breastplate, a strip of gold with carved jade stones for a headpiece, jade ear plugs. There was an obsidian knife, a club, and a large number of carved-jade and beaten-gold objects.

'The tomb is intact,' said Remi. 'How can it possibly be intact? Whoever killed that guy out there must have known there was gold in here.'

Sam and Remi both heard a shuffling sound and then another. They stepped to the doorway. Gathered in the outer chamber were a half dozen people from the nearby town – Señora Velasquez; Pepe, the mechanic; Señor Alvarez, the restaurant owner, his son, and two others they didn't know. Three of them were holding guns of some description, the others knives, and all of them looked furious.

Sam said, 'Hello, ladies and gentlemen.'

Señora Velasquez said, 'Come out of there very slowly and carefully.'

'We meant no harm,' Remi said. 'We just saw that –'

'Quiet or you'll be as dead as he is.'

Sam and Remi walked past the armed townspeople into the sunlight. Waiting in a large circle around them were about fifty other residents of Santa Maria de los Montañas. Some of them held machetes, others axes or hatchets. There were a couple of baseball bats. A few people held hunting rifles or shotguns, and there were pistols nearly as old as the one beside the man in the tomb.

The menace was palpable. The rifles and shotguns were aimed at Sam and Remi. There were two men with ropes, which seemed even more ominous than the weapons.

A man they had not seen before stepped out of the crowd. He had the sun-darkened face and sinewy arms of a farmer. He looked at Sam and Remi with eyes as hard as obsidian. 'I'll volunteer to dig graves. We can throw the bodies down from here and bury them where they fall. Who will help me?'

27

Santa Maria de los Montañas

'I'll help dig graves.' A second man stepped forward and joined the first on the outside of the circle. After that, a couple of others just waved hands and joined the burial crew.

Pepe the mechanic stepped into the circle. 'Remember, we have no reason to make these people suffer. Someone shoot them in the head with a hunting rifle and make it fast.'

Sam spoke loudly. 'We would like to know why you would want to harm us at all.' He whispered to Remi, 'Help me with the language.'

Remi called out, 'We came to your town twice. Both times, we told whoever would listen what we were doing here. Yesterday we told Father Gomez what we were going to do today. We came with the most peaceful of intentions.'

Señor Alvarez, the restaurant owner, said, 'I'm sorry that you have to die. Nobody here hates you. But you've found this place. It's a sacred place to us. We're not rich people, but we have a rich past. Our town was founded as part of this complex nearly two thousand years ago. This was a refuge where the people of the city twenty miles to the east came after they were defeated in war. This mesa is one of the highest places in Alta Verapaz. The king and a few loyal survivors came here, turned and fought. Then, hundreds of years later, a period of war came again. Then again. Each time a king of the city was defeated, he and his faction fell back to this place and held out. Up here there are the remains of five great kings. When the Spanish soldiers came the first time, the king prepared the place one last time. But they defeated the Spanish again and again and never needed to come here. Instead, they made peace with the priests. The watchtower on the hill was torn down and made into a church. Nobody from this town has ever betrayed its secrets.'

Sam said, 'This place can't be a secret forever. It's marked on a map in a Mayan codex we found on a volcano in Mexico. It's shown up on satellite photographs and been noticed by university professors.'

'We don't have to let you dig up our ancestors and steal their belongings,' said Señora Velasquez. 'You're like Columbus and the Spanish. You think knowing about them makes them yours.'

Remi said, 'You don't have to let us study your special place. If you didn't want us to climb up here, you could have told us while we were with Father Gomez. We thought we were finding a place nobody knew about.'

There was a roar of derisive laughter as the towns-people looked at one another with grim amusement. One of the men was angry. 'You see graves on a satellite photo and think it's all right to dig them up? It never seems to occur to you people that we know anything about the places where we've always lived. It was our ancestors who built these tombs, who made the mesa into a fortress. We've all been coming here since we were small children. Do you think we can't see walls and burial mounds? You think that if we don't dig up our ancestors and sell their treasures, we must be ignorant.' He turned away from Sam and Remi and took a rifle from one of the men near him. He cycled the bolt to load a round.

'Stop!' The voice was powerful but strained. As everyone turned to look, Father Gomez's head rose above the rim of the plateau by the trailhead, and he took the last step up on to the plateau. He was panting and wheezing from the long, steep climb. He held up his arms. 'Stop! Don't do this. Arturo, put down that rifle. What you're about to do is just murder. It has no higher meaning.'

The angry man looked at his feet, then opened the bolt of the rifle and handed it back to its owner.

Father Gomez seemed to be relieved, but his expression showed he knew this was not over.

Pepe, the mechanic, spoke. 'You're not from this town, Father. You're not one of us. You don't know.'

A man who seemed to be a relative of Señora Velasquez said, 'Since the days of the kings, we've had nothing except this place. The walls are where brave men and women fought to their deaths, and great leaders lie inside each of these mounds. Nobody has been allowed to desecrate this place or take away what's buried here. The second king who led his people up here respected the remains of the first, and the one after that respected him.'

He paused and pointed at the mound Sam and Remi had reopened. 'Only once before did a stranger make it up to this spot. He's lying in there now, although it's been more than a hundred years and nobody now alive has seen him before today. Everyone knows that he was killed by townspeople with hoes and hatchets. The secret was safe again.'

'No! No! No!' said Father Gomez. 'I may not have been born in Santa Maria, but I've lived here longer than many who were and I'm responsible for the state of your souls. Do you think the men who committed that murder a hundred years ago aren't suffering for it in hell?'

A few people looked down at the ground and others crossed themselves. A couple spat.

Pepe said, 'We've lived for centuries at the mercy of men in Madrid or Guatemala City, signing pieces of paper to make others rulers over us and control what we have – men who never even saw us. This is more of the same. All we're doing is trying to protect the bodies of our ancestors from the men far away who own everything.'

343

Father Gomez took a breath to speak, but Sam said, 'Hold it, Father.' He turned to the people in the circle. 'My wife and I had no plans to take anything away from here. The people we work with are university professors who are only interested in gaining more knowledge about the Mayan people. We're here for that reason alone. There are other people who already have maps with this spot marked. One of them is Sarah Allersby, who owns the Estancia Guerrero. Even if you kill us, she and people she hires will come to find this place. She'll dig up whatever there is and leave things looking like this.' He turned and nodded toward the open trench.

People were disturbed, in doubt, murmuring among themselves, while others seemed to be angrier. Small arguments began.

A new voice came across the plateau. 'Señor Fargo is right. Listen to him.'

People turned their heads to see Dr Huerta come around the mound near the trailhead.

'What are you doing here?' asked Señor Lopez, the storekeeper.

Dr Huerta shrugged. 'I noticed people were gone, so I asked some of your children. And, over the years, I've found that whenever there were a lot of people out, carrying sharp objects and firearms, there has been plenty of work for a doctor.'

'What are these people – friends of yours?' asked Señor Lopez.

'This is only the second time I've seen them,' Dr Huerta said, 'but I find I like them more and more. I'll show you why.'

He stepped up to Sam and Remi, lifted Sam's shirt, and pulled his semi-automatic pistol from its hiding place and held it up. There was a murmur from the crowd. He released the magazine, looked at it, pushed it back, then stuck the pistol back under Sam's shirt. He lifted Remi's shirt slightly to reveal her gun. 'After all these years as a doctor, I'm good at seeing things on people that aren't part of their bodies.' He stared at the circle of townspeople. 'Some of you are eager to kill them. If they'd wanted to, they could have killed plenty of you. But they didn't want to. They were here on a friendly mission and didn't let your threats change that.'

He put a hand on Sam's shoulder and the other on Remi's and began to walk them toward the trail to town.

'Stop.' They stopped and slowly turned. It was Señor Lopez again. 'Maybe you're right and these people should be freed. But we need time to decide what to do.'

The townspeople responded with a roar composed equally of approval and relief that they didn't have to make such a momentous decision right then. The people swarmed around Dr Huerta and the Fargos and swept them along the trail, down from the stronghold, and into the town.

When they reached the main street, the crowd ushered Sam and Remi into an old adobe building. There was an outer room, with a table and chairs and a big, heavy wooden door. On the other side of the door was a row of three cells with thick iron bars and padlocks. The crowd pushed Sam and Remi into one of the cells, and someone locked the door and took the key. Then the people trickled back outside.

After a minute, Father Gomez entered the cellblock. 'Sam, Remi, I'm terribly embarrassed by this. I apologize for them. They're good people, and they'll come to their senses very soon.'

'I hope so,' said Sam. 'Could you make sure our backpacks don't disappear?'

'They're already in the outer office. If you need anything from them, Señora Velasquez will be here to get it out for you.'

'Thank you,' said Remi.

'And one more thing,' said Father Gomez. He held out both hands, pushing them through the bars.

Sam and Remi took their guns out from under their shirts and handed them to the priest. He put them into his coat pockets. As he left, he said, 'Thank you. I'll keep them safe for you in the church.'

A minute later, Señora Velasquez opened the big wooden door, propped it open, and returned with a tray with soft drinks and glasses on it. She slid it through the feeding slot at the bottom of the bars.

'*Gracias, Señora Velasquez,*' said Remi.

'I'll bring your dinner in an hour, and I'll be outside the door all night,' said Señora Velasquez. 'Just shout if you need anything.'

'You don't need to stay,' said Sam.

'Yes I do,' she said. She reached into her apron and held up an old but well-oiled long-barreled .38 revolver that could have been from the 1930s. 'If you try to escape, someone has to be here to shoot you.' She put it back in her apron, took her tray, and disappeared through the doorway. After a second, the heavy wooden door swung shut.

28

Santa Maria de los Montañas

At dawn, the sun shone into the jail through a ventilation shaft, impeded only by the motionless blades of a fan. At some point in the night, Sam and Remi had fallen asleep on the two bunks, which each consisted of a shelf like a door on hinges folded against the wall during the day and lowered at night on a pair of chains that held it horizontal.

Sam woke to find Remi sitting on her bunk and swinging her legs. 'Good morning,' he said. 'Why are you looking at me like that?'

'I was thinking how cute you are when you're lying there in your bunk,' she said. 'Too bad I don't have my phone to take your picture. You could be Cellmate of the Month in women's prison.'

Sam sat up and pulled on his shirt, then began to button it. 'I'm flattered, I think.'

'It's just an observation, and I don't have much to look at,' she said. 'It doesn't look as though they use this jail much. No graffiti, not much wear and tear, since the last paint job.'

'Have you seen anybody yet?'

'No, but I've heard the front door close a couple of times, so we're still under guard.'

A moment later, there was a loud knock on the wooden plank door at the end of the cellblock. Remi smiled, and called, 'Come in.'

Señora Velasquez opened the door and came in, bearing a tray with two covered plates, some glasses of orange juice, and other good things.

'It was nice of you to knock,' said Remi.

'Nobody said you can't have any privacy,' said Señora Velasquez. 'You just can't leave yet.'

'Yet?'

'People have been listening to what Father Gomez and Dr Huerta say about you. I think we'll all meet in the afternoon, and you can be on your way after that.'

'That's a relief,' said Sam. 'But I'm glad they didn't let us out before breakfast. That food smells so good.'

'Yes it does,' said Remi. 'You're very kind to us.'

Señora Velasquez slid the tray under the bars, and Sam picked it up and set it on the shelf that served as his bunk. 'I wish we had chairs and things,' said Señora Velasquez. 'We weren't expecting anyone like you.'

'Thank you for what you've done.'

As Señora Velasquez went out the door, there was no mistaking the sound of a big bolt being slid into place.

Just as they finished their breakfast, they heard the morning silence of the little town broken by the sound of a truck laboring up the long hill to the main street.

They could hear the transmission whining, the engine's revolutions speeding up on the last hundred yards, and then the engine idling in the street in front of the church. After a moment, there was a man shouting, and then other men jumping from the truck to the pavement, and then running footsteps.

Sam and Remi looked at each other. Sam stepped to the space below the tiny, high window in the wall, bent his knees, and knitted together the fingers of both his hands to make a step for Remi. She put her foot in his hands and he lifted her up. She grasped the bars of the little window and looked out.

Men in a mixture of camouflaged fatigues, T-shirts, khakis and blue jeans ran from the truck and entered buildings along the main street. They kicked in doors and shouted at people to come out to the street. 'They're rounding up the townspeople,' she said.

Men, women and children came outside, looking confused and worried. They joined their friends and neighbors, adding to the growing crowd. Groups of armed men ran up the side streets and brought back more people. 'They're gathering the whole town.'

The cab of the truck opened and two men got out. 'It's the two men!' Remi whispered.

'What two men?'

'The ones who tried to kill us for Sarah Allersby. The ones from Spain. The one you painted blue.'

'How does he look?'

'He looks sunburned but still has a trace of a blue tinge, like a dead man.'

'I can't wait to see him.'

Outside, Russell and Ruiz stepped to the bed of the truck, climbed up, and used it for a stage. Russell took out a thick sheaf of legal documents and handed it to Ruiz, picked up a bullhorn, and spoke. 'Testing.' The word was loud, echoing from the hills. He held it for Ruiz, who read the Spanish text.

'Citizens of Santa Maria de los Montañas,' he said. 'Your town is situated in the middle of a tract of land that has been set aside as an archaeological preserve. In five days, you will be removed and taken to a new town a few miles from here. You will be provided with a place to live and given employment in exchange for your cooperation.'

An old man stepped out of the crowd. He wore an ill-fitting blue sport coat and an old pair of khaki pants. He stood near the truck and spoke in a loud voice. 'I am Carlos Padilla, mayor of Santa Maria.' He turned to his people. 'These men want to move us to the Estancia Guerrero. The work they offer is growing marijuana, and we would live in the barracks they built years ago when the gangsters moved in. They'll charge us more for rent than they pay us for the work, so we will always owe them money and can never leave. The land we're on has been ours for twenty centuries. Don't give it up to be slaves.'

Ruiz read on into the bullhorn. 'You will all sign

a paper, accepting the offer of relocation, housing and a job. Doing so will end any claim you might have to land in or around the town of Santa Maria de los Montañas.'

Russell jumped down from the truck, holding a paper. He went to old Carlos Padilla, pulled a pen from his pocket, and held it out to the old man. 'Here. You can be the first to sign.'

'He's trying to get the mayor to sign,' Remi whispered.

The answer was loud. 'I would rather die than sign that.'

One of the men from the truck waved his arm, and four men rushed the mayor. They slipped a loop of rope over him and tightened it under his arms, threw the end of the rope over a large limb of a tree beside the road, hoisted him up, and tied it so he hung there.

'No!' Remi whispered. 'No!'

Sam said, 'What are they doing?'

The man who had waved his arm took out a pistol and fired a round through the mayor's head. All of the witnesses, including Remi, groaned in horror.

Sam said, 'What was that shot?'

'They killed the mayor.'

Ruiz spoke into the bullhorn. 'Let no one move his body from this spot. We will come back in five days. If he's not here then, we'll hang five others up there in his place. If this paper is not signed by every one of you, we will put ten who have not signed up there and ask again.'

'Did you understand that?' Remi whispered to Sam.

'I'm afraid I did.'

Russell stepped to the nearest building, which was the church. He nailed the papers to the front door. Then he and the other men climbed back into the truck. They turned around in the space in front of the church and drove back to the crest of the hill and began to coast down the long road in the direction of the Estancia.

The wails of women began immediately and soon reached the window of Sam and Remi's cell. Remi said, 'They're gone,' and jumped to the floor.

A half hour later, they heard footsteps in the outer office. The plank door opened and several people filed in – Señora Velasquez; Father Gomez; Dr Huerta; Pepe, the mechanic; Señor Alvarez, the restaurant owner; and the two farmers who had volunteered to dig their graves. Father Gomez said, 'Do you know what happened?'

'Yes,' said Remi.

Señora Velasquez unlocked their cell, and they all walked through the office, where Sam's and Remi's backpacks sat. Dr Huerta went to his office two doors down the street and returned with a wheeled stretcher. He wheeled it across the street to a spot below the hanging body of the mayor. He and Sam held the rope taut while one of the farmers produced a knife and cut the rope so they could lower the mayor on to the stretcher. They lifted the stretcher to straighten the legs, covered the mayor with the blanket, and pushed him to Dr Huerta's infirmary. Many of the townspeople followed them in and others stood outside.

Inside the office, Remi said, 'Is there a regional government to handle this?'

'Not one with troops,' said Father Gomez.

'The police?'

'You saw them,' said Dr Huerta. 'They were the ones trying to arrest you for smuggling drugs after you fought the killers who attacked you on your last visit.'

'Then it has to be the national police in Guatemala City,' Sam said.

Dr Huerta said, 'I just spoke with them on my satellite phone. They said they would send an inspector to take our statements next month, two months at the latest.'

'One inspector?' Sam said.

'Yes.'

'Oh, by the way,' said Father Gomez, 'I brought you these.' He took the two pistols and two spare magazines out of his coat pockets and handed them to Sam and Remi.

'Thank you,' said Remi.

'Your car is ready too,' said Pepe. 'No charge. I'm sorry for what we did to you. Maybe when you're back in the big world, you'll tell people we weren't so bad.'

The door opened, and the crowd parted to let a small

group of townspeople enter the clinic. Sam and Remi recognized many of them. Señor Alvarez, the restaurateur, seemed to have been chosen as a spokesman. 'Señor and Señora Fargo,' he said. 'What just happened was exactly what you said would happen. Those men came from the Estancia Guerrero. Instead of asking to look at the old stronghold peacefully, they made us watch them murder the mayor. They're going to take our town and the stronghold and even our homes and families. We won't ever be able to complain, because they'll keep us deep in the Estancia. If we try to get help, they can kill all of us, and there will be nobody left to say what happened. We were wondering – I know it's more than anyone has a right to ask – if you would stay and help us fight.'

Remi said, 'After what just happened? Of course we'll stay.'

'I have to warn you that we're not soldiers,' said Sam. 'But we'll do everything we can to help.'

Dr Huerta said, 'You fought the men who were guarding the marijuana fields and won – just the two of you.'

'They attacked us, we defended ourselves for a while, and then we got away. That's not winning.'

'You killed a dozen of them and you're just fine,' Huerta said. 'I call that a victory – a big one.'

Sam said, 'I don't think we'd have much chance against these people in a fight. They're heavily armed with modern weapons, they're trained and organized, and they've clearly fought before. Our best chance is to keep trying to get the authorities to protect the town.'

'I agree,' said Dr Huerta. 'I hope we can, and we will keep trying. But we should also be ready to fight.'

'Yes,' said Señor Alvarez. 'We're all willing to fight, but all we have is five days before they come back. We need to start preparing.'

'I'll get started by making a few phone calls,' said Sam. He put an arm around Remi's waist, and they stepped toward the door.

'But you're going to stay?' said Dr Huerta.

Remi said, 'You bet we are. When he's all gruff like that, it means he's digging in.'

'Thanks,' Sam said.

'Just don't get in any more trouble for now,' replied Selma.

'No, we've got enough to last us.'

Sam hung up and called the number of the US Embassy in Guatemala City. He identified himself and asked for Amy Costa.

In a surprisingly short time, he heard Amy's voice. 'Sam!' she said. 'Good to hear from you. Is everything all right?'

'I'm afraid not,' Sam said. 'We're in the town of Santa Maria de los Montañas, maybe twenty miles west of the Estancia Guerrero.' He told her about the truckload of armed men arriving, the demands, and the murder.

'Oh, Sam,' she said. 'I can hardly believe this. You said they gave the town a deadline. What is it?'

'They said they'd be back in five days to get the signed agreements and presumably to move the townspeople to barracks on the Estancia. But it doesn't seem to matter much to these guys how the town gets vacated. They drilled the mayor in front of two hundred witnesses.'

'Five days,' Amy Costa said. 'It's the worst possible timing. Commander Rueda is the only one we can count on to react the way we want and he's suspended for the next thirty days.'

'I'm sure that isn't a coincidence.'

'Sarah Allersby makes her own coincidences,' said Amy.

'Can you get us any help?'

'I'll try. But the high-ranking officers all know what happened when Rueda agreed to go after Sarah Allersby. It will take time to get somebody else to stick his neck out.'

Sam said, 'Do you know of any way we can get some weapons to defend the town?'

Amy said, 'Weapons? I'm sorry, but involvement in unauthorized firearms transactions would get the embassy expelled from the country. And it would require going all the way up the chain of command to get permission at the highest levels. Some of my superiors don't see Sarah Allersby as our business. They think the locals should take care of her.'

'Let's just hope the townspeople are still alive when that happens.'

29

The Estancia Guerrero

Sarah Allersby was waiting in the old countinghouse, a relic from the days of the Guerreros. She sat at the biggest of the old desks, directly under a ceiling fan operated by a belt attached to a long shaft along the ceiling and turned from outside the building, originally by hand but now by electric motor. She sat back, closed her eyes, and took a couple of deep breaths to relax. Russell had telephoned her a half hour ago, so she guessed they were almost here by now. Soon she heard the sound of the truck gearing down on the highway, then making the turn on to the drive. It still amazed her how quiet the Estancia could be. There was noise whenever there was a flurry of work – harvest, planting, or shipping – but for weeks on end there was almost no sound out here. She stood, stepped up to a window that faced the forest, and looked at her reflection in the glass.

She wore a loose white silk blouse, a pair of fitted black slacks with black knee-high riding boots, and a black flat-brimmed hat that hung down her back from its stampede string. She adjusted the black leather belt on her hips so the gun hung lower on the right, as though she were about to engage in a quick-draw gun-fight. She stepped outside on to the wooden porch, her leather boot heels making a hard clicking noise on the boards.

The truck grumbled up the gravel drive and stopped in front of her. Men jumped down from the truck bed. They looked impressive to her, all carrying AK-47 knockoffs, most of them armed with fighting knives in sheaths. They stood in a wavering line beside their truck and looked at her expectantly. Russell and Ruiz jumped down from the cab and approached her.

She said, 'You sounded on the phone as though it went well.'

'I guess it did,' said Russell. 'We herded them outside and gave them the message.'

'Good.'

He spoke more quietly. 'An old guy who claimed to be the mayor tried to make a speech about not signing. We shot him and hung his body from a tree. We said if anybody moved him before we came back in five days, we'd shoot some more.'

Sarah clapped her hands. 'I never would have thought of that. Brilliant. I'll bet they were utterly terrified.'

'It's hard to tell. They were all sort of stony-faced.'

'Well, watching the mayor rot for a few days should soften them up.' She turned to the men who had been with Russell. She said in Spanish, 'You can all go along now, gentlemen. Mr Ruiz will pay you while I talk with

Mr Russell. Mr Ruiz, the money is in the black briefcase on the desk.'

She and Russell walked toward her car, a black Maybach, which was parked a distance away. 'Without you, my efforts and a considerable sum of money would have been wasted. I'm acutely aware of the hardships you've endured because of your work. You'll be paid very well for everything. The trust you've earned will pay dividends.'

'I hope the risk pays off for you.'

'It's essential that we succeed. These Indian peasants are sitting on a major Mayan site, and we'll need a free hand to exploit it. They have to be removed quickly, before the word gets out and they become "a cause".'

'What I'm worried about is what happens after we've brought them here. Will San Martin let you keep what you find? His mercenaries make him stronger than we are.'

'Trust me,' she said, 'Diego needs me more than I need him. Being on land that belongs to me keeps him untouchable. And as long as you give me your loyalty, I promise you'll be safe.' She stopped walking. 'My driver is new, and I don't know if I can trust him yet. If you have anything else to say, say it now.'

In that moment of her immobility, frozen for two seconds, Russell saw many things – her beauty, which was something she possessed, just like her cars and land and bank accounts. And he knew that this chance to speak and change things was one he would never have after this moment. If he wanted out, the doorway was closing. When the two seconds had passed without his speaking, she turned and walked to the black car. She opened the door herself, sat in the backseat, and closed the door. Her face, even her silhouette, became invisible behind the tinted glass. The driver swung her car wide and brought it back along the gravel drive to the main road.

Santa Maria de los Montañas

The whole town attended the funeral of the mayor, partly because of his heroic death. And Carlos Padilla had been a popular mayor because he did little except to fill out and sign the papers that had to be filed in Guatemala City each year. He was such a comfortable mayor, in fact, that there was some question as to whether he was still legally in office. There had not been an election in some years, and it was possible that he had not wanted to bother anyone with voting again.

Father Gomez said the proper things about him during the mass and then led the villagers to the large churchyard, where their people had been buried for centuries, and placed him in the row created for this year's dead. There, Father Gomez said the rest of the customary pronouncements and prayed that Carlos's goodness, bravery and unselfishness would make his soul rise quickly to heaven.

While old Andreas, the mayor's brother, took his turn filling the grave, Father Gomez asked the townspeople to return to the church for a meeting.

When the people were all sitting in the church, or standing immediately outside where they could hear, he introduced Dr Huerta.

Dr Huerta spoke simply and frankly. 'We have spoken to the authorities in the government offices and embassies, and the earliest that help can come here is thirty days.'

'But we have only five days,' a woman shouted. 'What can we do?'

'You can sign the paper and be taken to the Estancia to work in the fields or you can stay and fight. The choice is yours. But we saw those men shoot Carlos to death. I don't know of any reason to trust them. Once they have you on the Estancia, with no place to hide and no means of fighting back, will they let you live?'

There were cries of 'We have to fight!' and 'We have no choice!'

'There's a third way,' said Father Gomez. 'We can pack everyone up and run away to another town. We can try to hold out there for a month or two and hope the government will act by then.'

'All that will do is get two towns killed,' said Pepe. 'And once we leave, they'll take over everything, dig up the tombs, burn our houses and fields. We'll never be able to come back.'

Within minutes, the discussion was only a series of

speakers who all said the same thing – running was futile and was more dangerous than staying. Signing away the town was unthinkable, and the only way to survive was to fight. At last, Dr Huerta said, 'It's time to hear from Sam and Remi Fargo.'

Sam and Remi had remained silent through the discussion, but now they stood. Sam said, 'If you want to fight, we'll do what we can to help. Tomorrow morning at seven, meet us in front of the church. If you have any guns and ammunition, bring them with you. We'll begin to work out a strategy.'

At 7 a.m., Sam and Remi sat on the church steps and waited. The first to arrive were a few of the hotheads who had helped capture them up on the plateau. Then came people who considered themselves to be part of the gentry – the business owners, independent farmers, and their wives, sons and daughters. After them were others, people who worked for wages or helped on the farms for a share of the crops.

By seven-thirty, the street was full of more people than it had been during the mercenaries' roundup. Sam stood up and called the group to order. 'Beginning with the people on this end of the street, form a line and come talk with us. After you have, then go wait in the church.'

As people came to the steps to talk, Sam and Remi would interview them, always speaking Spanish now. 'Do you have a gun? Let me look it over. Are you a hunter? What do you hunt? Are you a good shot?' When there was no gun, they would ask, 'Are you healthy? Can you run a mile without stopping? Do you want to fight? If you needed a weapon to fight a jaguar, what would you reach for?'

Women seemed to prefer to talk to Remi, possibly out of local standards of propriety. Her questions varied little. 'How old are you? Are you married? Do you have any children? Are you willing to fight to protect them? Are you very strong and healthy? Have you ever fired a gun?'

The older children, the teenagers, were the hardest to interview, but Sam and Remi persisted. All the armies of the past had relied on boys from fifteen to twenty to fill the ranks.

By ten, they were alone on the steps. The town's firepower amounted to seven rifles with about one hundred rounds each, eight shotguns with about one box of twenty-five shells each, mostly bird shot. There were seven handguns, including four .38 K Frame revolvers that looked like old police sidearms, Señora Velasquez's old .38 Colt, and two .32 caliber pistols made for concealed carry.

Sam and Remi stood, staring at the villagers, whose faces were tinged with hopelessness. 'Thank you all,' said Sam. 'Now we have a better idea of where to start. Your ancestors could not fight soldiers trained in modern tactics or go up against new technical weapons and neither can you. You, your wives and children would die within minutes of the first attack.'

Remi could easily see a deep sadness in the villagers' eyes, as mothers pulled their children closer and the men looked around at their friends and neighbors in frustration.

Sam steeled himself against the impossible odds. He nodded at Dr Huerta and Father Gomez. 'Can I talk to you in the vestry?'

They entered and sat down in the hand-carved chairs around the large Spanish-style table. Father Gomez spoke directly to Sam.

'Do you have a strategy?' he asked.

Sam shook his head. 'Nothing I can guarantee.'

'You have no plan, no strategy, to help save my people?' said Father Gomez coldly.

'Nothing I can talk about,' asserted Sam.

'What do you want us to do?' Dr Huerta demanded.

'Take your people up the mountain to the fortress and tombs.'

Father Gomez glared at Sam. 'I believe the villagers would just as soon die in their beds as be dragged down the hill to trucks that will carry them to the Estancia fields, where they would work themselves to death. And then there are the children. It will be like a concentration camp.'

Remi, who had been standing in the doorway unnoticed, stared at Sam with stunned incomprehension.

'You don't know what you're saying. Sending the villagers up to the old fortress is like giving them a one-way ticket to a slow death.'

'The trucks can't navigate the narrow trail up the mountain,' said Sam.

'But a hundred men with deadly arms can't be stopped with a few old shotguns,' Remi argued.

Sam shrugged. 'I see no other way out.'

Remi stepped over to Sam and stared with anguish into his eyes. 'Who are you?' she gasped. 'You're not the man I've known and loved.'

He gave her a look of indifference she'd never seen before.

As Remi turned to speak, Sam had walked from the vestry without looking back at his lovely wife.

30

Santa Maria de los Montañas

The next day, the mothers, children and the elderly were led by Remi to the ruined stronghold on the plateau. There they would gather hundreds of stones to throw down at the attackers if they tried to climb the narrow path up. Remi determined where the best locations were behind a rock-stack barrier to fire at any attacker who reached the top.

Remi kept her mind off Sam's strange behavior and directed her squad of women and children to make effigies of townspeople, stuffing clothing with leaves and brush. 'If your son is firing a rifle, you want the enemy to waste ammunition shooting at the five or six dummies you made and placed around to protect him.'

She had other people bringing empty bottles, cans of gasoline and rags to the plateau and making Molotov cocktails. 'If men are coming up the path, these will stop them for a time. And if it's night, they'll light them up so anyone with a gun can hit them.'

At dusk, Sam stood on the crest of the hill beside the ancient fortress, surveying the preparations the townspeople had made. He knew there were hundreds of human effigies, beginning on the trail to the ancient stronghold. There were pits from building the old rock barrier. Within the walls of the ancient fortress were enough food and water for the whole town for a couple of weeks, and there were shelters for the children. The whole perimeter had dummies at the ramparts, and the supply of rocks and Molotov cocktails was impressive.

Sam was suddenly aware that Remi was standing next to him.

'I can't live without you,' she said softly. 'Please don't stay in the village and die there alone.'

Sam shook his head and looked down. 'I've never asked you to blindly follow my direction. I have to ask you now. Trust me.'

She turned to him and looked for something in his eyes. 'We've never had any secrets between us.'

'I'm sorry, Remi. But I swore an oath many years ago that I have to stand by. And now I have to see this through.'

'I know you have something up your sleeve. But will it work?'

He ran his hand through her hair. 'The final throw of the dice and I can't even tell you what I hope is going to happen.'

Sam looked up at the last of the sun-painted mountain peaks. 'It's time for me to go.'

Sam put his arm about his beloved wife and escorted her to the head of the trail that led down the mountain.

She buried her face in his shoulder.

'You just can't do this. I may never see you again.'

His kiss was as gentle as a soft whisper. 'I've made luncheon reservations at our favorite restaurant here in town.'

After walking twenty feet through the fortress, Remi stopped to get a final look at her husband. But Sam was not to be seen. It was as if he had vanished.

Santa Maria de los Montañas

At dawn, Sam walked across the road to the church and climbed the ladder to the top of the bell tower. His timing was on the money.

He removed a pair of German Steiner 20×80 military binoculars and peered through the lenses at a dust cloud on the road about five miles away.

Almost casually, he sat on a niche in the wall and watched the sunrise. Later, he stared at the approaching military convoy.

Sam was not primed to fight. His job was to observe. He took a small old-fashioned handheld radio he'd borrowed from Dr Huerta, adjusted the frequency, and pressed the call button.

'Viper One. This is Cobra One. Over.'

A voice, clear and sharp, came back almost immediately.

'Cobra One. This is Viper One. I haven't heard your voice in a long time. Over.'

'Six years and seven months, to be exact.'

'We've all missed you, Cobra One.'

'Is that Viper Two?'

'Two hundred meters on your left in an open space in the forest.'

'You have been away a long time,' laughed Viper Two. 'I remember you as the new kid on the block in the old days.'

'You must know,' said Viper One, 'the firm is stepping on important toes to fit this little tea party in the schedule.'

'I'm well aware of it,' replied Sam. 'And, I might add, I'm the only one on this side who knows the score.'

'Okay,' said Viper One, 'why don't you tell *us* the score. Over.'

'Roger,' said Sam. 'A small army of men who work for a local drug lord are planning to come here to take possession of the town and ship the people to a plantation about twenty miles away and put them to work.'

'That sounds like slavery.'

'It is slavery,' said Sam. 'And extortion and theft and kidnapping and murder. Once they have these people in their marijuana fields, nobody will ever see or hear from them again. Over.'

'Nice to know we're the good guys,' Viper Two cut in. 'Hold on. I read a convoy of seven vehicles approaching up the road.'

Sam added what he could see from his perch in the bell tower.

'Each of the canvas-covered trucks is carrying

twenty-five men, all armed with AK-47s. They're escorted by two armored cars. One at the head of the column, the other bringing up the rear.'

'We also see the convoy is escorted by two Mi-8 Russian-built gunships.'

'How can you know everything in my sight when you're behind a forested mountain?'

'We've had many upgrades in our sensors since you were part of the gang.'

Sam aimed his binoculars at the final turn in the road leading up to the village.

'Viper One. They've reached the edge of the town and have stopped.'

'Not surprised. There are no people in sight, living or dead. That must make them wonder.'

'My wife and I herded all the villagers up the mountain to an ancient fortress.'

The pilots and gunners in the Apaches adjusted their helmets with the monocle over the right eye. It was a revolutionary sighting system. The pilot or gunner could slave the chain gun to his helmet, allowing him to achieve accurate sighting on a target by making the chain gun track with his head movements, aiming wherever he looked.

'Viper Two. This is Viper One. We are clear to engage.'

'Time to give them hell for breakfast.'

Viper One turned the Apache in a sharp bank and then entered the main village square, hovering twenty meters off the cobblestones.

31

Santa Maria de los Montañas

Amando Gervais and his copilot and gunner, Rico Sabas, sat side by side in the spacious cockpit of their Mi-8 Hip gunship, one of San Martin's fleet of five helicopters.

The Mi-8 was Russian built and was an oldie but goodie. Production had continued despite the fifty-one years since the first one took to the skies. Utilized by half the military forces in the world, the Mi-8 was considered the most successful design worldwide.

Gervais lightly touched the collective control stick to raise the Mi-8 until it was five meters off the ground. At the same time, he eased the cyclic stick forward, slowly moving the Mi-8 up the rise and around the church and into the village square. Suddenly Gervais and Sabas froze, in a state of shock. Instead of a crowd of villagers with pitchforks and shotguns firing bird shot, Gervais and Sabas found themselves staring at an array of rocket launchers hung on the most malevolent, atrocious and evil attack helicopter in the United States arsenal.

To Sam Fargo in the bell tower, there was no more terrifying apparition than the AH-64E Apache

Longbow helicopter, especially when viewed head-on. It looked like a giant, grotesque bug that could never fly.

'Santa Maria,' muttered Sabas. 'Where did that come from?'

'It's black with no markings,' said Gervais, barely above a whisper.

'What's it doing here?'

The answer never came.

They turned white and speechless when, in the blink of an eye, they saw a flash beneath the Apache an instant before they were blown to shreds.

'Target removed, Viper Two.'

'So I heard. Hold on. My target is locked and I'm firing.'

Down the hill a few miles away, another explosion sent fire and a dense cloud of smoke into the air.

'Viper One, second aerial target eliminated.'

'So much for their air force, Viper Two. Now let's hit their infantry.'

'Cobra One here,' Sam Fargo cut in. 'The trucks and armored cars are continuing toward the village.'

'How can they think they still have air cover?'

'They didn't see your destructive nature. You were out of sight in the village, and Viper Two was hidden in the trees.'

'Thanks, Cobra,' said Viper One's pilot. 'Keep active as our spotter.'

'Will do,' said Sam. 'Glad to be back in the saddle again.'

'Okay, Viper Two. We'll start from opposite ends with the armored cars and work toward the middle of the trucks.'

'Engage before they recover. What do you want to lay on them?'

'Begin with the Hydra missiles to knock out the armored cars and then switch to the M230 cannon against the trucks and infantry. Viper Two, you take on the front armored car. I'll engage tail-end Charlie.'

'Just watch our line of fire so we don't kill each other.'

'Roger, Viper Two. We'll be as careful as ladies at a tea.'

'Roger that, Viper One.'

With a touch of a button, he sent a Hydra missile across the village square into the armored car as it reached the top of the hill. Flames enveloped the disintegrating vehicle as it vanished in a vast fireball.

Sam laughed to himself. 'I'll ring the church bell every time you guys take out a truck.'

'I've never forgotten your sense of humor.'

'Nothing's changed,' said Sam.

'Ready to squeeze the pumpkin, Viper One?'

'Let's ride the dragon,' came the answer.

The Apaches showed their stuff by flying barrel rolls over the hill and turning loops through the village, passing a few feet from Sam's observation post.

'Where are our Mi-8 copters?' asked Russell. He pulled himself back inside the armored car. 'I don't like the looks of this. There's no sign of them, only two plumes of black smoke.'

'Could they have collided?'

Russell shook his head. 'They came at the village from opposite directions. The smoke must be from targets they destroyed in the village.'

'Then why don't they answer our transmissions?'

'That I don't –' Before Russell could finish, the vicious AH-64E Longbow helicopter appeared thirty meters above, the pilot smiling and waving. The Longbow suddenly rolled upward and turned to a firing position. It not only looked deadly, it was deadly.

'Get out!' shouted Russell. 'Jump!'

Ruiz didn't have to be told twice. They burst from the armored car, leaving the gun crew inside. They dropped to the ground and rolled into a ditch on the side of the road.

Less than three seconds later, Russell heard the short scream of the Hydra 70 rocket as it impacted the armored car and blew its turret to pieces. In the black killing machine, the gunner had turned the muzzle of the M230 automatic cannon, mounted under the bow of the fuselage, toward the first truck in the convoy. Called a chain gun, it could spurt six hundred and fifty thirty-millimeter rounds a minute. The blast of shells tore through the first and second trucks' canvas-covered benches, carrying the twenty-five armed killers hired by San Martin, that quickly became fiery charnel houses.

There was no time for a warning. The third truck

drove off the road, spilling out the men as soon as it rolled into the ditch. One man on the fourth truck threw back the canvas cover and began to shoot a mounted gun at the Apache.

'I'm taking fire, Viper Two. I could use help to take him out.'

'I'll send him to dreamland. Just stay on your side of the convoy.'

Viper One could hear shells thumping into the rotor blades and fuselage, which was protected by twenty-six hundred pounds of shielding.

Viper Two dipped under Viper One and unleashed a torrent of fire that smashed the man in the truck bed and his heavy machine gun to a pile of morbid junk.

'Obliged to you, Viper Two.'

'You still in one piece?'

'Roger. Engaging truck five on my goal line.'

'Let's finish the game.'

The flames from one truck, and the explosion and concussion from another, were still tearing the air when the last truck tried to escape across the field. It was quickly smashed to a halt. The survivors spilled to the ground, followed by a hail of shells pouring from the Apache like water from a fireman's hose.

Both Apaches obliterated the rest of the convoy and circled the area, picking off any survivors who did not throw down their weapons or hold their hands up in surrender.

*

As Russell and Ruiz watched from the cover of the ditch along the side of the road, the heat from their flaming armored car was like torture to them. They lay there, staring in fascinated horror at the total destruction of the convoy by the phantom black helicopters.

'It makes no sense,' Russell muttered. 'Who are they and where did they come from?'

'They are not Guatemalan military,' said Ruiz.

'Let's not wait to find out,' Russell grunted, crawling away from the burning vehicle toward the nearest forest undergrowth.

'We have to find a place to lay low 'til it's dark.'

'Sound thinking, my friend,' Russell said. 'Follow me and keep low.'

'Where to?'

'Estancia Guerrero,' answered Russell. 'We've got to get to Miss Allersby with a story to save our hides before another survivor makes it back.'

Remi's heart sank when she heard the explosions and saw the black billowing clouds expanding in the sky above the village. She was helping the mothers with young children, distracting them from the turbulence below.

The silence that followed was even worse. The fear and anxiety finally got the best of her and she ran desperately out of the fortress and down the trail until she reached the village square. She stood there, dazed, after seeing the smoldering wreckage of a helicopter.

Remi saw no sign of Sam and closed her eyes to keep from crying in grief. She could not but think the worst.

She sensed a presence behind her. Then Sam's voice. 'How could our love affair not have a happy ending?'

Remi turned, her eyes flashing in excitement as they locked with Sam's, and he kissed her lovingly on the lips. With his arms wrapped about her, Remi's fear melted.

'Oh, Sam,' she murmured in his ear as she looked over his shoulder at what was left of the Mi-8.

At that moment, Viper One, followed by Viper Two, hovered over the square and gently touched down. The engines hummed, and the four-bladed main rotors slowed and crept to a stop. Sam grinned as four men in flight suits climbed out of the cockpits and approached.

The first reached out his hand and shook Sam's. 'I've missed you, old partner.'

'I'm amazed an old geezer like you is still flying the globe and getting into trouble.'

The pilot from Viper Two laughed. 'We wouldn't be here if it wasn't for your talent for wheeling and dealing.'

Remi stood by as the five men hugged one another and started telling war stories and catching up on old times. Remi thought it odd that none of them called one another by name. Finally, she looked at Sam and interrupted, 'Aren't you going to introduce me?'

They all looked at one another, surprised, and then broke into laughter.

Sam took a confused Remi in his arms, and said,

'This is a very, very unusual group. It's on call around the world for operations such as the Estancia Guerrero. It's also the finest and least-known secret operations force in the US.'

'That's why our names and backgrounds are known only to ourselves,' said the pilot of Viper Two.

'And we all swear an oath of secrecy when we join the force.'

The gunner of Viper One looked at Remi and said, 'So is this beautiful woman the reason you left the force?'

Sam smiled with a twinkle in his eye. 'That goes without saying.' He gave her an affectionate squeeze around the waist. 'Sorry, I can't give you her name.'

The villagers were cautiously returning to the village. They had an expression of disbelief at seeing the Apache Longbows, the wreckage of the Mi-8 Hip, and their village completely intact. Father Gomez and Dr Huerta stood in awe.

Viper Two's gunner nodded at the growing crowd, and said, 'I think it's time for us to fold our tents and silently steal off into the sunset.'

'Thank you,' said Sam as he shook their hands. 'You saved the lives of over two hundred men, women and children, and shut down one of Central America's biggest drug operations.'

'Don't wait so long for the next tournament,' said Viper One with a salute.

'Don't change your phone number,' Sam said, holding Remi's hand and giving her a kiss on the cheek. She looked squarely into his eyes, and said, 'You told me you were with the CIA when we met.'

Sam merely shrugged. 'It seemed like a good idea at the time.'

32

The road to the Estancia Guerrero

Ruiz sat in the cab of a truck beside Russell. 'I feel like I fell out of an airplane,' he said. 'My shoulder hurts from firing full auto at nothing. My knee feels like it's broken from falling in that ditch. I can't believe this.'

Russell kept his eyes on the road ahead. 'Consider yourself lucky we snatched a pickup truck from a tobacco farmer. This is really a setback. And we lost ninety men or more who belonged to Diego San Martin. I'll tell you something else. We've got to fix it before San Martin knows or get out of the country fast.'

Ruiz stared at him. 'We're done, man. It's suicide to go in that town.'

A half hour later, they reached the Estancia Guerrero. As they pulled up the long gravel drive to the space by the countinghouse, Russell saw Sarah Allersby, sitting behind a lighted window. She saw their truck and ran out to meet them.

'Where are they?' she asked. 'The helicopters never returned, nor any of the trucks.'

Russell looked down at her through his cab window. 'As it turned out, we couldn't just drive up there and load them on the trucks. When we got there, we were ambushed. We lost most of the men, and what few survived were captured.'

'Lost? You *lost* a hundred men to a bunch of ignorant peasants,' she said. 'How could you do this to me?'

Russell and Ruiz looked at each other and climbed stiffly out of the truck. Ruiz leaned against it while Russell stood in front of Sarah Allersby. 'Miss Allersby, I apologize. We were defeated. Not by the villagers but by two mysterious black, unmarked helicopters that blew apart our helicopters, the armored cars, and all the trucks.'

Sarah Allersby felt the heat of Russell's rage building. It frightened her a little. She was too intelligent not to foresee what could happen next.

Russell said, 'I think we've come to the end of our usefulness here. We'll be leaving in a few minutes. I wish you luck.' He turned away.

'Wait,' she said. 'I'm sorry, Russell, I didn't mean to be sharp with you. Please don't be upset. I know I was being insensitive, and I know things seem bad right now, but we can save this.'

Russell and Ruiz stared at her.

She said, 'Those are men we borrowed from Diego San Martin. If you both leave and that's all I have to tell him, he'll kill me. And then he'll have people find you and kill you. Don't you know he's a drug smuggler? He has connections and buyers in the United States and Europe. We don't have much choice but to salvage this situation so we can give him some good news along with the bad. We can't give up now.'

'We can't save a disaster.'

'I'll double your pay. I'll also give you a percentage of the money I make on the artifacts from that place. The codex makes it look like a fortress and says that refugees from a city retreated there for a last stand. If they did that, they wouldn't have left their treasures behind to their enemies. It's going to be a huge find.'

'Miss Allersby,' said Russell, 'people died today. If the police are brought in, anybody involved could be charged with murder. Not only were we the leaders but we're foreigners.'

'We also don't know where our attackers came from,' added Ruiz.

33

The road to Guatemala City

Two days later, Russell and Ruiz were apprehended and shackled to the bench seat of the army truck as it rattled along the road toward Guatemala City. Russell kept up a low monologue in Ruiz's right ear. 'It's good that they're taking us right to the capital. I don't want to rot in some provincial jail for six months while the prosecutors take their time getting there and arranging for a trial. If we're in Guatemala City, Sarah can bail us out before we've spent a night – or two nights anyway. And then she'll make the charges go away. That's what has to happen now. If we go to trial as the masterminds of this fiasco she dreamed up, we're going to need a miracle to see the light of day again.'

'Diego San Martin is hiding out. That's a plus.'

'True, but he isn't about to let us off the hook. They resent us. And we're the only Americans. I am anyway. You look like a native and you speak Spanish. I'll bet they think you are Guatemalan.'

'If you're up for huge crimes, it's better to be foreign. They'll think you must be working for a government and they might not execute you.'

'She'd just better have all the lawyers out, waiting for us, when we get there,' said Russell. 'She swore she would.'

'She said we'd never get arrested too, but, here we are, captured and chained.'

Russell was silent for a few seconds, then said, 'She'd better come through after we managed to get his private army wiped out.'

'I know,' said Ruiz. 'We're going to have to take turns sleeping so none of these guys finds a way to kill us.'

They sat in the truck and watched the miles rolling behind the truck into the distance. Russell tried to dismiss from his mind the sight of the few survivors sitting around him in the truck, the hollow look of their dirty, unshaven faces, the sweaty smell of their camouflage battle-dress uniforms, the anger and resentment in their eyes.

He turned his mind to Sarah Allersby. He imagined her in one of those immaculate white silk blouses she wore and a black skirt and high heels. She would be standing by the heavy wooden desk in the two-hundred-year-old building with the thick wooden beams and the big ceiling fans. She would have her golden hair in a tight ponytail, with every strand in place, so it looked like something rarer than hair. She would be holding one diamond earring in her free hand while she clamped the phone to her ear with the other. She would be bringing every bit of her wealth, influence and reputation to bear on the problem of freeing him and Ruiz.

She would say something ridiculous that the government official she was speaking to would want to believe. Russell and Ruiz were just innocent American employees of hers who had gone to the Estancia Guerrero and gotten lost. She would ensure that there were no unpleasant repercussions following their release by flying them out of the country immediately in her private jet. And she would be very grateful to send them away.

Guatemala City

At that moment, Sarah Allersby was in the master bedroom of the big Guerrero house. She was wearing a white silk blouse, a pair of black slacks and a tailored black jacket. She chose a pair of pearl earrings and a pearl choker because she'd be dealing with British Customs. Anyone whose job it was to assess the value of jewelry at a glance would recognize a strand like this – round, silvery white, sixteen-millimeter natural pearls with exceptional luster. They had been found by divers in the Arabian Sea in the fourteenth century. And, for once, the source of a priceless piece wasn't the fruit of her father's ancestors' looting of India. The pearls had belonged to her mother's family. Her father had bought the earrings in Paris forty years ago.

British officials were the biggest snobs. Even if her name didn't spring to their minds, they would recognize her as belonging to the class of people who were not to be harassed with petty rules.

She didn't pack much this trip. Most of her clothes and belongings were still in the closets and the safe. She took only the few things she could gather quickly – the wide, flat jewelry box with the best pieces, a bundle of money in various currencies, and, sealed in its fitted plastic box, the Mayan codex. They all fitted in one suitcase. She locked the suitcase, tipped it up on its wheels, and began to roll it toward the staircase.

Her doorman heard the sound, bounded up the stairs, and took it for her. She wondered – did he know? The case held tens of millions of dollars' worth of jewelry, artifacts, and just plain money. It was worth more than all his ancestors had earned from Adam and Eve until now. She smiled at her thought. It was much better that servants – even loyal ones – not suspect these little moments of vulnerability. She was sure he would have killed her for much less than he was carrying now.

She got into her car, watched him put her suitcase in the trunk, and close it. She said to her driver, 'The airport.'

He drove expertly, maneuvering the black Maybach 62 S through the streets of Guatemala City. He never betrayed any stress and seldom even applied the brakes. The ride was smooth and quiet, the way he knew she liked it. As she watched the city slipping past the windows of the car, she felt a small twinge of heartache.

She had succeeded in obtaining the Mayan codex – almost certainly the last undiscovered one in existence. By now, she should have been famous. She should have had a warehouse full of gold and priceless pottery.

She would have to persuade Diego San Martin that she had not been the cause of his lost manpower. She would explain that the problem had begun with the man he had met at lunch. Russell had assured her that it would all be easy and safe. There would be no risk of disappointing Diego San Martin because Russell had everything under control. What could she, a young woman, have done differently? How could she have known Russell was so wrong?

She listened to her own silent rehearsal and pronounced herself satisfied. San Martin was like everyone else. He would vent his wrath on someone, but it would not be Sarah Allersby. She remained a very useful ally who would cost him money and be trouble to lose. San Martin just needed an excuse to do what was obviously in his own interest.

The Maybach arrived at the airport and floated past the terminals along the chain-link fences to the special entrance to the private jet hangars. The guard opened the gate as soon as her car was in sight. Some crazy revolutionary wasn't going to drive up in a car worth nearly half a million dollars and blow up a plane. Her driver took her to her hangar, and she saw the plane had already been towed out. The pilot, Phil Jameson, was going through his preflight check. The fuel truck was driving off down the line toward its next customer. Sarah Allersby's steward, Morgan, was visible through the lighted windows, refilling the refrigerator and stocking the bar.

The Maybach stopped, and she said to the driver, 'I'll be away for at least a month. You'll get thirty days' pay and then you'll be called when I need you again.'

'Yes, ma'am.' He popped the trunk, took out her suitcase, and rolled it to the plane. Morgan came to take it for her.

He carried it up the steps, placed it in the closet, closed the door, then placed a strap across the opening so even if the door opened, it couldn't move. 'Can I take your coat?'

'Yes,' she said, and shrugged it off. It took only a few more minutes before the cabin door was closed and the pilot began to taxi out toward the end of the runway.

A few minutes more and the plane turned into the wind, sped along the runway, and lifted into the air. As Sarah looked out the window and down, she saw the little country receding below her, keeping with it all the recent strife and disappointment and the unpleasant little people who had thwarted her efforts. As her plane rose above the puffy layer of white clouds into the dark sky, she felt lighter, cleaner, and without unpleasant encumbrances. She was flying home to London. It would be comforting to visit her father and to shelter in his big, powerful presence. And London was still London. Maybe this trip would be fun.

Fraijanes, Guatemala

The truck carrying Russell and Ruiz reached the large, forbidding Pavón prison at the edge of the suburban town of Fraijanes. As they joined the men being herded out of the army trucks, Ruiz said, 'I don't see any lawyers.'

Russell said, 'They'll be here. She wouldn't let us rot in a place like this.'

The soldiers herded them in through a high gate made of iron bars with razor wire at the top. Ruiz whispered, 'I don't even see any civilian guards. I think this is one of those places where the prisoners run things.'

'Don't worry,' said Russell. 'She'd have to be crazy to abandon us.'

'Let's hope she's not,' said Ruiz. 'Either way, we'd better get ready to make our own way out.'

London

It was morning when Sarah Allersby's plane descended over London and then reached Biggin Hill Airport southeast of the city.

The plane landed smoothly on the suburban airport's main runway and taxied to the flight line, where its only passenger would disembark. The plane stopped, and the ground crew chocked its wheels and attached the grounding wire to the electrical ground. Then the steps were lowered.

Sarah could breathe in the cool, damp British air that came in through the open hatch. She stood up just as the British Customs men arrived. They collected the customs declaration that Morgan the steward had filled out and initialed for her. She had brought, as always, fifty Cuban cigars for her father that had been miraculously marked down to less than three hundred pounds. The fully stocked bar in the plane was said to be less than two liters.

The head customs man said, 'Is that your suitcase, miss?'

'Yes it is,' said Sarah Allersby.

'May I look inside?'

She hesitated, her eyes suddenly unblinking and her lips parted. Usually the customs people didn't bother looking so closely. She was a person of importance from an ancient family. She wasn't going to be bringing in explosives or a bag of cocaine. She wasted a tenth of a second wanting to say, 'You never asked before.' And she sensed that her instant of hesitation might be enough to doom her.

The head customs man opened her suitcase on the built-in table. He flipped the jewel box open, apparently just confirming that she'd be carrying more jewels than a Spanish treasure ship. He saw the banded stacks of money and set them aside. Of course she'd have money. No matter. But what's this?

The customs man popped the plastic cover and examined the folded strip of ancient fig bark, caught sight of the paintings inside, and closed it. 'Miss Allersby, this appears to be a genuine Mayan artifact. A codex.'

She looked at the man closely and saw that he was an educated man. She was not going to talk him out of his appraisal of the codex by saying it was a copy or a decoration or something. He was right and he knew it.

Three hours later, a gang of her father's solicitors and barristers, men famous for keeping every kind of inconvenient question unanswered, had rescued her. She was not going to be allowed to leave the country. Her passport was being held for ransom. But most irritating of all was the fact that the codex, her precious Mayan codex, had been confiscated as evidence that she had broken the international law against transporting historical treasures.

It was the most important of the lawyers, Anthony Brent Greaves, who sat beside her in his limousine to spirit her away from the authorities. While they were driving into the city, she said, 'Anthony, I'm too exhausted to jump right into setting up a household. Take me to my father's house in Knightsbridge.'

'I'm sorry,' said Greaves, 'he asked me to tell you it wouldn't be possible right now. He's got a dinner party, and there will be several people there who attract the press.'

'Oh,' she said. 'So he won't see me.'

'I wouldn't put it that way,' Greaves said. 'You may

be the one in the family who knows the habits and taboos of faraway places. But he's the old hand in the jungles of London. He's going to work the powerful in your interest, but quietly.'

'I understand.'

Greaves had won his point. He spoke to his driver. 'We'll take Lady Sarah to her house in Brompton.'

34

Santa Maria de los Montañas

The Guatemalan army arrived in the town of Santa Maria de los Montañas on a Monday. On Tuesday, a helicopter landed in a cornfield a mile from the town. Out of it stepped Commander Rueda.

When Rueda and his lieutenants arrived in the town square, Sam and Remi were among the people waiting to greet him. Sam said, 'It's good to see you again, Commander. What brings you here?'

Rueda shrugged, but he couldn't hide a smile. 'It seems that Sarah Allersby has been arrested in London for bringing a Mayan codex into the United Kingdom. So some powerful people have had to change their positions on these matters quickly. I've been appointed acting commander of the government forces in the region.'

'Congratulations,' said Remi. 'Is it proper to ask what you're going to do?'

'Certainly. I want to be very open about everything we do. Right now, I have troops in the Estancia Guerrero searching for drugs. There are others in Guatemala City searching Sarah Allersby's home, office, and a few business properties for signs that she's been plundering archaeological sites.'

'Hooray for you,' said Remi.

'I hope you'll still feel that way if we ask you to testify,' said Rueda.

'We'll be delighted,' said Sam. 'It will give us an excuse to come back here. We've made some good friends.' He noticed some faces nearby. 'Here are two of them that you should know. Father Gomez and Dr Huerta. This is Commander Rueda, my friends. He is honest, completely aware of the problems in the area, and, fortunately for everyone, the officer in charge from now on.'

Rueda gave a slight military bow. 'I've heard of you both. We know you've been trying to stop the movement of drugs, and, if I may say so, the people of Guatemala thank you for your courage.'

Remi was distracted. She pointed down the long road. Far away, a low black cloud had stretched across the horizon. 'Look!' she said. 'A fire.'

Rueda gave it a glance. 'My men are conducting a controlled burn of the marijuana fields at Estancia Guerrero. I understand they've confirmed your identification of coca trees too. Everything beyond what they've kept for evidence is being destroyed.' He looked at his two aides. 'I guess we'd better be going. There's much to do.'

Sam and Remi drove Rueda and his aides to the helicopter. Just as Rueda was about to board, he took Sam and Remi aside. 'This probably isn't going to mean anything, but I have to tell you that the two men who tried to kill you a few weeks ago were among the men captured. After two days in a prison near the capital, they killed two men who were about to leave on a work release assignment and took their places. We think they've left the country, but we're not sure.'

'We'll keep our eyes open,' said Sam. As the rotors began to turn, he and Remi stepped back to avoid the wash of air and watched them depart. Sam reached for his cell phone and called Selma.

'Sam and Remi, I was worried about you,' she said. 'Did you get everything resolved?'

'I did,' said Sam.

'Has David Caine arrived yet?'

'David Caine? Is he coming?'

Selma said, 'He was always planning to come. Final examinations ended on Friday. It's June, Sam. You're studying the Mayans and nobody has a calendar?'

'Oh,' he said. 'I guess we should have remembered.'

David Caine arrived at the head of a convoy of Land Rovers, which made their way up the hill with relative ease and then pulled up in a row on the street just beyond the church. Caine jumped down and threw his arms around Sam and Remi. 'I've heard what you two did. You're amazing.'

'Thanks,' said Remi quietly. 'What you and your colleagues will find here is more amazing. But you'd better let us smooth the way before you do any exploring. In the meantime, smile at everybody, talk to them about anything except archaeology, and be patient. We've already cleared the way for a public meeting where we can introduce you.'

35

London

Sarah Allersby was bored in London. In Guatemala City, she had been the center of attention. In parts of Europe, she had been invited to everything – Rome, Athens, Berlin, Prague. Even in Paris she had been to the best places with sought-after young people.

But now because of the ridiculous court order, she was not permitted to leave rainy, cold, damp London. Worse, the social climate in London had not been warm. She'd had such bad press for the past couple of months, with the accusations that she'd looted Mayan tombs, claimed to discover sites that had already been registered, and used a Mayan codex she wasn't supposed to have.

Beginning a day ago, rumors about her had begun to circulate, and she was being associated with some huge drug bust in Central America. People had already canceled their RSVPs, so the welcome-home dinner party she was throwing for herself was dissolving. She could hear the fear in their voices. They had been scared their precious reputations would be tarnished if they shared hors d'oeuvres with mad, bad Sarah Allersby.

A year ago, any of them would have come to her party even if they'd had to crawl to her house on their knees.

She stood in front of the big mirror by the door and inspected herself as she buttoned her navy blue coat. The buttons were gold, and the coat looked like a piece of an eighteenth-century naval officer's uniform. She half turned to present her profile to the mirror, stepped to the door, and opened it. The .308 caliber bullet pierced her forehead and passed through the back of her skull, destroying her brain so fast that she never heard the report of the rifle, if there was one.

Through the rifle scope, Russell could see that she had fallen backward, and the heavy front door had begun to swing closed. It had been stopped by one of her feet, so it looked as though it had been partially opened by someone about to leave who had gone back in to get something.

Russell put down the rifle while Ruiz closed and locked the window and then drew the curtain. Russell quickly dismantled the rifle and placed it in his suitcase. He and Ruiz hurried down the back staircase, then into the kitchen and out the back door to the garden. It was midmorning, so there were cars and people on nearby streets, but nobody seemed to have noticed anything.

The house they had been in was for sale. It was only one number down and across the street from Sarah's and it was the same kind of place. Four million pounds was what they'd been asking. Russell and Ruiz had spent only about an hour in the house and had worn rubber gloves.

As Russell rushed through the back garden – such a British thing in itself – he felt satisfied. Sarah had broken her promise and let him and Ruiz go to a Guatemalan jail. So now she had received her payment. Russell got into the car that they'd left waiting at the curb, and Ruiz drove. Ruiz seemed to be better at driving on the wrong side of the road. He stopped the car on the way so Russell could drop the pieces of the rifle in a series of trash cans.

At Waterloo station, they stopped in a men's room to change clothes and wash their hands. They took the big yellow-and-white Eurostar train to Paris. It would take them three hours to get there, but they had premium first-class tickets, and the ride promised to be restful. And anything was better than the prison they'd escaped from in Guatemala.

The train chugged slowly through London and its inner suburbs and then gained speed. After about an hour, it entered the tunnel under the English Channel, and the windows went dark.

Santiago Obregón looked from the passageway of the train at the two Americans in their premium seats. They appeared to be sleeping. It was astounding to Obregón that these two imagined that Diego San Martin would let them waste nearly a hundred of his men and go off

400

to Europe in safety. He was grateful to them for killing Sarah Allersby because otherwise he'd have had to do it.

Obregón sat across from the Americans in their compartment as though he belonged there. He reached into his briefcase and took out his tool, a CZ P-07 Duty pistol with a factory-threaded muzzle and special high sights to provide a view over the sound suppressor. He shot the two Americans in the chest quickly to preclude resistance.

He stood and shot the first American in the head to be sure he died and then aimed the gun at the head of the second. The man addressed him in Spanish. 'Who are you? Why kill us?'

'Why do *you* kill?' said Obregón. 'For money.' He pulled the trigger. He pressed his pistol into the right hand of the dead man. Then he went out and moved to another car. Before too long, they would be arriving in the Gare du Nord.

36

Santa Maria de los Montañas

The town meeting was held in the church, with Father
Gomez presiding. At the end, he said, 'You have all
heard the arguments for allowing the archaeologists to
excavate the stronghold and all the reasons not to per-
mit it. You will each take a piece of paper and write *Sí*
or *No* and put it in the collection box.'

The people lined up and voted. When they had finished, Father Gomez, Dr Huerta and Andreas, the new
mayor, counted the votes. The town had voted over-
whelmingly to allow Dr Caine's team to dig.

In the morning, at seven, the members of the expedition were joined by Father Gomez at the head of a
delegation from the town. As they started the long
climb up the narrow path, Father Gomez said,
'Dr Caine, there are things you need to know and this is
my first chance to tell you. You know this place is sacred
to the local people. The ones buried up there are not
strangers, they're ancestors. They were the rulers of the
city of Kixch'ent and the survivors of a great war
against a city about thirty miles to the east in about
790 AD. When it became apparent that they were terribly

outnumbered and losing, they gathered a group of loyal warriors, along with the most valuable things they owned. They carried them here.'

'You mean this was to be their last stand?'

'Exactly. They built a fortified watchtower where the church is now. Then they brought their people up on the plateau and built a stronghold there. When the enemy came, the stronghold held. But people died and were buried up there, and precious objects were buried with them – weapons, ornaments, everything that was of great value to them.'

'So what's up there is all from a war of the classic period?'

'Not all of it. Two hundred years later, in the 950s AD, the people of the city had to retreat to the stronghold again. Events played out roughly the same. The place was too steep, too high, and too well defended to fall. Eventually, the people returned to their city. Later, when Spanish soldiers came near, the people of Alta Verapaz fought them savagely and held them off. But, as a precaution, the people brought what was most precious to them and their culture up to the stronghold.'

'And nobody has ever dug here?'

'No. A few have tried. The people of the town killed them. Time passed. The people accepted Christianity. The watchtower was torn down and the stones used to build the church. The world forgot the little it ever knew about this place. But the people never forgot any of it.'

Caine said, 'I can see they're very protective.'

'Be aware that they've decided to trust you because they love Sam and Remi Fargo and would do anything that they asked. Don't ever let the people think you aren't living up to what you promised and respecting their ancient kings. You would not last a day.'

The group reached the top of the plateau, where they could see the fortifications along the rim and the burial mounds of the kings.

Caine's attention was drawn to the mound that had been opened a hundred years ago and reopened by the Fargos. There were rows of large pots with lids that appeared to have been sealed. Caine knelt beside one, but Father Gomez touched his shoulder. 'Wait.'

Caine stood up, looking at him inquisitively.

Father Gomez said, 'I haven't gotten to the end, what I had promised the people I would prepare you for. Each time the people of the city fled up here, they brought all of their greatest treasures with them. Obsidian weapons, jade and gold ornaments, precious pottery, it's all here. But what was most valuable and important to them were their books.'

'Books?'

'Old Mayan books, like the one you and Sam and Remi had.'

Caine contained himself, although to Sam and Remi he looked as though he might faint. 'Do you know if any might have survived?'

'I've only seen a few that were opened by the man

executed in the tomb and they survived very well, probably because of the altitude. But the number is certainly in the hundreds. When the old Mayans brought their books here, they carried them sealed in these pots. There are a hundred forty-three pots in this tomb alone. Some of the other tombs might contain more books, all sealed in pots to protect them. So whatever Sarah Allersby took, it was nothing compared to what she was not permitted to take.'

Father Gomez moved past the dead man and the jars and led Caine into the burial chamber, where the bones of the king, adorned with gold and jade, lay on the slab of limestone. 'There's one more thing you should see,' he said. 'Help me move this man and his stone.' When Caine hesitated, he said, 'It won't disturb the remains. We've done it before.'

Father Gomez, Caine and Sam Fargo pushed aside the heavy stone where the king's bones rested to reveal a chamber beneath. Caine shone his flashlight into the dark space. The light that reflected back was the familiar gleam of gold – molded statues of gods and men and animals, beaten gold breastplates and headpieces, bracelets, anklets, earrings, nose ornaments. It was a room full of gold. And with it were jade axes and plates, ear plugs, beads, ceremonial spearheads in a variety of colors from dark green to blue to white, all carved and polished expertly by artists long dead. Caine said, 'This is astounding. Nothing like this has been found anywhere in the Mayan world.'

'It will be again,' said Father Gomez. 'I'm told that each of the mounds was the tomb of a great king and each king felt he had to bring his city's treasures here to preserve them from enemies. And each of the tombs has a secret room dug beneath it, guarded by the king's body. You'll see them all.'

'The people of the town have decided to let us excavate and study the whole complex?'

'Yes they have,' said Father Gomez. 'Part of it is their gratitude to the Fargos for saving their lives and their home and part of it is the Fargos' promise.'

'What promise?' Caine turned to look at Sam and Remi.

Remi said, 'We said we'd help them build a museum in Santa Maria de los Montañas to display, preserve and protect what's found here.'

Sam said, 'That way, the world will learn about this place, but the remains of the kings and their treasures won't have to be permanently removed. Pieces can go out on long-term loans to museums and universities all over the world, but they will always belong here with the descendants of the people who carried them here.'

He just wanted a decent book to read ...

Not too much to ask, is it? It was in 1935 when Allen Lane, Managing Director of Bodley Head Publishers, stood on a platform at Exeter railway station looking for something good to read on his journey back to London. His choice was limited to popular magazines and poor-quality paperbacks – the same choice faced every day by the vast majority of readers, few of whom could afford hardbacks. Lane's disappointment and subsequent anger at the range of books generally available led him to found a company – and change the world.

'We believed in the existence in this country of a vast reading public for intelligent books at a low price, and staked everything on it'
Sir Allen Lane, 1902–1970, founder of Penguin Books

The quality paperback had arrived – and not just in bookshops. Lane was adamant that his Penguins should appear in chain stores and tobacconists, and should cost no more than a packet of cigarettes.

Reading habits (and cigarette prices) have changed since 1935, but Penguin still believes in publishing the best books for everybody to enjoy. We still believe that good design costs no more than bad design, and we still believe that quality books published passionately and responsibly make the world a better place.

So wherever you see the little bird – whether it's on a piece of prize-winning literary fiction or a celebrity autobiography, political tour de force or historical masterpiece, a serial-killer thriller, reference book, world classic or a piece of pure escapism – you can bet that it represents the very best that the genre has to offer.

Whatever you like to read – trust Penguin.